YOU COULD BE IMMORTALIZED AS A CHARACTER IN THE NEXT BEING THERE NOVEL

Imagine being able to point to a character in a major best-selling book series, and tell your friends and family . . .

"That's ME!"

Well, now's your chance.

As part of the "fan interactive" aspect of the trend-setting **Being There series,** you get to send in your idea for a new character or story situation. Then, if your idea is chosen, R.C. Henningsen will write a whole chapter around it for the next book in the series – with YOUR NAME as the new character!

How cool is that?!

You'll also get a copy of the book autographed to you by R.C. himself.

And that's not all – because even if your idea isn't selected, you still have a chance to influence the direction the next story (and the series) takes from start-to-finish. Here's how it works: Each book ends with a "cliff-hanger" that could go any one of several different ways.

All you need to do is read this story, then visit the **Being There: Awakenings** website, and cast your vote for the direction you'd like to see the story go.

Our team will add up the votes, and the "crowd favourite" wins! (You might even be able to get all your friends to vote the same way.)

And finally, even if your idea isn't chosen, and the voting goes against your favourite, you STILL have a chance to pick up a free gift!

You see, everyone who casts their vote to help choose the direction of the next novel is automatically considered an "insider", and gets a free subscription to the **Being There Insiders Newsletter.** And you ALSO have a chance of being one of three random readers who will get their choice of one of three GREAT gifts.

To see the gifts we're giving away – as well as submit your character or situation idea, and cast your vote, once you've finished reading – just visit our website at:

http://rchenningsenauthor.com

. . . and click the "Fan Interactive" tab.

Endorsements
What Readers are Saying

"Awesome! I couldn't put it down—RC.'s descriptive writing brings you deeper into the storyline as if you were there with the characters. An exciting adventure filled with twists and turns. I can't wait for the next in what promises to be the next great series of novels."

Linda Parry, CEO, Product Launchers, Haverstraw

"This imaginative work brings forward the thought of what if? What if you were in Christian's shoes and had his abilities? Would you change the world? Brilliant!"

Lindsay A., Seattle, WA

"Wow! A thrilling journey for Christian and friends as he explores his newly found abilities. This debut book opens the world of possibility for a series of exciting action and emotionally charged adventures."

Debra O., ICU/CCU Nurse, NY

"The perfect combination of excitement and adventure, destined to be a cinematic thriller. This is by far the best book I've read in a while. The author's addictive writing style proves that he is a talent to be watched."

Douglas H., E. Northport, NY

"This is a fast pace novel for a reader looking for entertainment. Be prepared to fall in love with the characters and feel joy, suspense,

sadness and excitement all in one sitting. I shall also warn you, from personal experience, of the attachment and bond you may form with Christian, Amy, CB and of course, Mr. and Mrs. Asher. I eagerly await the next novel of the series and look forward to witnessing the greatness that will surely come from this one."

Peggy M., NY Times Best Selling Author

"While reading this book you feel as if you've become part of the story, experiencing the sense of thrill and excitement, love and loss, adventure and tragedy. It is entertaining and fun to read."

Anna V., Buenos Aries, Argentina

"This creative story flows well as a young Christian Asher discovers his ability to draw on the experience and knowledge spanning multiple lifetimes. It is an entertaining must-read for seekers of action and adventure coupled with an emotionally charged sub plot."

Kristin A., Educator, Baltimore, MD

"This is a gripping story packed with discovery, action and adventure that will draw you into the adventure. It is filled with excitement, intrigue and little of the supernatural. A definite must-read with great potential to make cinematic history . . . I can't wait for the movie!"

Jim Z., AV Engineer, Stuart Manor

Being There

AWAKENINGS

R. C. Henningsen

Published by
Hasmark Publishing
1-888-402-0027

Second Edition, 2016

Disclaimer

Editor: Nita Robinson
Nita Helping Hand?

www.NitaHelpingHand.com

Cover Design: By Jessica
A dear friend

Layout: Ginger Marks
DocUmeant Designs

www.DocUmeantDesigns.com

ISBN-13: 978-1-988071-23-7

ISBN-10: 1988071232

his book is dedicated to all who dare to act upon their dreams and especially to my loving wife without whose love, support and verve for life, I would not be . . .

NOTE FROM THE AUTHOR

I'd like to personally Thank You and Welcome You to the *Being There* Family . . . It is my only desire to provide you with the best in Thrilling Sci-fi, Action Adventure novels that draw you into the storyline. You will share the emotion and excitement of each character and situation as if you were actually there, so . . . Grab a snack and a seat and Enjoy–*Being There Awakenings*!

Please remember, in order to continue to bring you exciting new adventures in the Being There Series, we need your opinion and suggestions, so please Visit Amazon.com and share your experience with the world.

Five Star reviews are best, but please be honest in your rating.

To post your suggestions on Facebook please go to www.facebook.com/BeingThereAwakenings or send your comments to rc@rchenningsen.com.

Life is best when we participate; live it with passion!

R.C.

Contents

ACKNOWLEDGEMENTS

I would be remiss if I did not express my most sincere appreciation to the following individuals, each of whom are outstanding in their fields. They have been teachers, mentors and friends to countless people throughout the world and I am honored that they have shared their extensive knowledge with me in the latest part of my life's journey.

A Special Thanks: My most Grateful Appreciation and thanks to Peggy McColl. A new friend, mentor and a perpetually positive spirit. The motivational source for the completion of the first in a series of exciting adventures. Visit the Acknowledgements tab at www.BeingThereAwakenings.com and learn more about Peggy and how to become a Best Selling Author.

My Sincere Appreciation to Natalie Ledwell who played a starting role in this, the latest part of the journey. Our existence is guided by universal laws. My first realization of this was when I unknowingly manifested a communication from Natalie and acted upon it. I studied with her the laws of attraction. Since that fateful day just about a year ago when I acknowledged the first of many gifts, I have manifested a multitude of people, places and things that were absent to me, even in professional life, that have guided me to new heights in all aspects of life. Visit the Acknowledgements tab at www.BeingThereAwakenings.com and learn how these universal laws affect us and the lives we live.

My Sincerest Thanks to Anik Singal, a rising star in the Fortune 500 world of entrepreneurs and whose dynamic coaching and celebrity-filled programs enable all who act to reach new heights.

Visit the Acknowledgements tab at www.BeingThereAwakenings.com to learn more on how Anik is helping of thousands upon thousands of people achieve their goals.

My Gratitude and Appreciation to Andy Shaw. Self-made a few times over, Andy has the key to success. His direct approach to wiping the viruses from the thought process that plague over 99.9% of the population as it relates to the attainment of one's "goals and desires" . . . Thank you for helping to clear the road-blocks. Go to Give! Visit the Acknowledgements tab at www.BeingThereAwakenings.com to learn what successful forward thinkers have that 99.9% of the population are missing . . .

And to You, and the multitude of friends and fans of the Being There series. My Heartfelt Appreciation for sharing your interest in this exciting new series with your friends and family. Keep an eye out for the next book in the series Being There Discovery. Feel free to Like us on Facebook and share your review on Amazon.com, BarnesAndNoble.com or both.

Become part of the writing process . . . Go to the Contests tab at www.BeingThereAwakenings.com and vote for your favorite ending. What did Dr. Ed Asher see in the elevator? Your vote will help determine the beginning and end of the newest addition to the series, and you will have access to the "BeingThere" newsletter, keeping you up-to-date on the newest developments in the series.

Live life to the max!

R.C.

FOREWORD BY PEGGY MCCOLL

With excitement I accepted the opportunity to write the Foreword for this novel. I met Richard, the author, when he enrolled in a book writing and marketing program that I deliver. From the first time we met, Richard was filled with a positive spirit and creative energy. Reading this book has truly helped me see the power of his amazing creativity.

Before you read this, may I suggest you sit down with a big bowl of buttery popcorn to complement the entertainment? This book will take you on an amazing journey. To be honest, even though I am an author, I have never been much of a reader. That may sound strange coming from the author of 10 books, but it is true. Reading this book wasn't like that of any other novel I have read.

Reading this book was almost as if I was watching a movie. Richard's writing style and character development is three-dimensional and I found myself visualizing the entirety of the events taking place. Richard describes every sight, smell, touch and taste of the characters and their experiences, leading you to feel as if you are right there with them.

Christian seems to lead a perfect life with plenty of friends and family to share in his joy of heading off to school in California. His parents cherished him and raise him with love; he has supportive friends and a quirky cousin, Hailey who he confides in. Christian seems to make friends easily, and effortlessly catches the eye of a gorgeous third year student, Amy. Amy and Christian quickly develop a friendship so strong that the reader cannot help but to feel their true connection.

Throughout the novel Christian (and you) are taken on the journey of a lifetime as he discovers his supernatural abilities. The reader goes through the possibility of a connection between past, present and future.

Living a life on the run, trying to hide his new abilities from his parents and developing new-found relationships is a lot to take on for the protagonist. This is a fast pace novel for a reader looking for entertainment. Be prepared to fall in love with the characters and feel joy, suspense, sadness and excitement all in one sitting.

I shall also warn you, from personal experience, of the attachment and bond you may form with Christian, Amy, CB and of course, Mr. and Mrs. Asher. I eagerly await the next novel of the series and look forward to witnessing the greatness that will surely come from this one.

Kudos to the author on a truly amazing, thrilling and inventive world created. It was a pleasure to read. To all whom are holding this book right now, I will not keep you any longer from immersing yourself in this masterpiece. Enjoy.

INTRODUCTION

Christian Asher had all the promise of any soon-to-be college junior. Handsome, athletic and bright, he prepared to embark on his future, a future filled with events far beyond his wildest dreams; or maybe not? Christian has a secret, a secret hidden deep within the recesses of his mind.

This is Christian's story . . . Travel with Christian as this secret awakens, unleashing a series of new and exciting events bringing discovery, adventure and good fortune. His excitement, however, is short lived when he learns that news of his gift has stimulated unwanted interest and concern, rapidly testing his ability to trust those closest to him.

- One -
Farewell Christian

It was a beautiful eighty degree day in the Hamptons. The sky was clear and the humidity was unusually low. The sun was dipping behind a small bank of light, wispy clouds emitting a rainbow of vibrant colors that filled the sky. The sound of waves curling up to the beach resonated across the neighborhood as a light breeze carried the unmistakable fragrance of summer at the beach across the yard.

This was the best time of the day. The excitement of beach goers had faded slowly as the afternoon progressed. The crickets were chirping and song birds were singing the last song of the day from their perches in the arborvitaes lining the perimeter of the property. The occasional call of seagulls strafing the beach echoed in the yard.

Christian hurried to finish with some last minute set up details. He stacked a multitude of wrapped gifts on a table in the corner of the pool deck. The caterers were hanging a big sign over the pool with *Farewell Christian—Good Luck at Cal Poly* printed on it as the flickering flames from the Tiki torches danced over the still pool.

Christian's parents, Edward and Katheryn, moments before had headed inside to dress for their soon-to-be arriving party guests. They couldn't be prouder, but as with any parents there was underlying concern with his being so far from home, more so from Edward as he was charged with safeguarding this very special young man.

Christian was headed to California in the morning to begin his fifth term in architectural studies at California Polytechnic. He had possessed a fascination with building and heavy equipment since his early childhood. In fact, he had a fascination with just about anything he saw. But designing and building, well, let's just say he loved it. He had an uncanny knack to create, build and fix just about anything.

Edward was a cardiologist. He earned his medical degree after serving four years with the armed services, along with the help of veteran's administration loans. He completed his residency and set up practice on Long Island twenty-five years earlier. Edward is active with the Army Reserves, holds the rank of Major, and is an active administrative board member for regional VA hospitals.

His mother, Katheryn, is a real estate attorney with a penchant for collecting. She and Edward had met when she was attending her pre-law curriculum at Hofstra University. They lost touch with each other for a time following graduation and fatefully reconnected after bumping into each other in the Hamptons.

Katheryn's hobby is collecting Coca-Cola® memorabilia. Her collection rivals that of any private collector. The only thing missing is an actual delivery truck, which I am sure she would have if she could park it in the yard.

They had planned Christian's farewell party months earlier. Katheryn wanted it to be the event of the summer at the Asher household. As the excitement for the upcoming party grew, so did their concerns about him being nearly three thousand miles away, making for a setting of uneasy jubilation during the affair.

As Christian finished some last minute details he heard cars pulling into the gravel driveway. He peered at the gate to see who had arrived so early. The first arrivals entered through the gate and onto the pool deck, "Whew, thank god it's you guys," said Christian, looking at three of his closest school friends, Maddy, Chris and Connor. "I still have to jump in the shower. Would you mind lighting the rest of the Tikis and citronellas for me while I clean up?"

"No problem," said Maddy, giving Christian a quick peck on the cheek before he headed inside.

Maddy was short for Madison, an attractive, longtime friend. She quickly began lighting the candles and the remaining unlit torches as Chris and Connor, also longtime friends, sluggishly followed with their noses buried in their iPhones, listening as Madison barked out orders at them to bring their gift to Christian into the yard before he returned. They had all chipped in to buy Christian a signed jersey from Derek Jeter encased in a large frame. Jeter was Christian's favorite player.

Chris, who everyone called 'Tweet' although Maddy sometimes called him Twit because he was constantly on Twitter reporting his every action which Maddy found disturbing, and Conner struggled with the oversized frame containing the signed jersey as they clumsily made their way past the shrubs partially blocking the entranceway to the yard.

"Hurry up, before he comes out again. Don't ruin the surprise!" squawked Maddy. "Put it over there," she ordered them, pointing at a table snuggled in the corner of the deck behind the bar. "That's the best place, away from all the action," Maddy said.

"Where?" Connor asked, paying more attention to text alarms from his phone than the task at hand. Maddy grimaced and again pointed to a small, shadowy niche behind the bar that was set up in the corner of the deck.

"Over there!" Maddie said.

Christian had made his way into the house and up the back stairs towards his room. As he turned down the hallway he noticed the door to the study was shut, light on, and overheard what he was all too familiar with lately. His mom and dad were "talking". It wasn't an argument, but it wasn't comfortable conversation either. It was more a strong expression of concern by his father, Edward. "What if something happens while he's away?" he heard his father ask.

His mother, Katheryn followed up with a reassuring, "I wouldn't worry about it. That's why we had him stay home for the first two years and look, nothing happened, did it? Besides, now is not the time. This is his party."

Christian had seen this scenario play out many times over with increasing frequency as Christian's departure for college grew nearer. Christian had an uneasy feeling in his stomach. He was unsure if these "heavy" discussions were only about their concerns for him specifically or if his parents were having other troubles and his leaving was a common ground for their conversational engagements. All he knew was that there was an uneasiness in the house that seemed to be getting worse with time.

As Christian opened the door to his bedroom, the creaking noise alerted his parents of his presence. He heard his mother in a somewhat startled voice, "Honey, is that you?"

"Yeah Mom, it's just me," he replied quickly. "I need to jump into the shower," he said deep in thought, then continued asking, "Are . . . are you guys alright in there?" Christian asked.

In an attempt to distract from the situation, Christian's mom opened the study door and replied as she began her way down the long hallway, looking at Christian standing in the doorway to his room, "Of course honey! We were just putting some final touches on something that is, none . . . of . . . your . . . business!" she said with a big smile on her face, giving him a kiss on the cheek and then quickly heading downstairs to join the increasing number of guests that were beginning to arrive.

Christian looked briefly toward the study as Edward slowly closed the door. Seeing the concerned look upon his face while trying to force a smile only served to increase the uneasy feelings Christian had in his gut. He heard Edward sigh deeply as he closed the door to his study, then the unmistakable sound of a cork being pulled from a bottle of Johnny Walker Gold.

Edward wasn't a drinker. He enjoyed the occasional drink now and then so that's why this seemed so unusual. Christian wondered what was going on and continued to dwell on the situation as he got ready for the party, his thoughts eventually yielding to the increasingly noisy activity he heard outside in the yard.

Christian jumped out of the shower, dressed and headed down to the party, grabbing his allergy prescription on the way. Reaching the kitchen he glanced out the sliding glass doors leading to the pool deck holding what appeared to him to be well over a hundred people, mostly familiar and some unfamiliar. The deck was alive with activity. There were people talking everywhere. Some were singing, others were dancing to the variety of tunes the DJ was mixing. There were guests in a room off to the side of the kitchen, noisily admiring the hundreds of Coca-Cola collectibles his mother had gathered over the years.

Mrs. Asher was a definite enthusiast, collecting original posters, wall placards, vending machines, ice chests, serving glasses from Jacob's pharmacy, which was the first place Coke was served, figurines, race car replicas, and an entire original collection of Hutchinson bottles from when Coca-Cola was first bottled in the mid 1890s through the most recent bottles, cans and gadgets. There were also framed papers and notes with Dr. Pemberton's name or signature, the inventor of Coca-Cola. She had just about everything they made, outside of the factory itself and the famous Clydesdales; however, she had plenty of pictures and posters of both, including period sketches and paintings.

Maddy was talking with his mother and father on the deck, accompanied by his Aunt Janice and Uncle Mac who looked in at Christian with a big smile on his face and a thumbs up.

Chris and Connor had separated in pursuit of their own interests. Connor's interest lay with a tall, attractive, blue eyed brunette named Jamie. He stood before her with a smug look as if his advances were well received when in fact, Jamie had her eyes on Tweet who had headed over to another group of partygoers loitering around the car Christian and his father had slowly restored over the past few years.

-Two-
The 302

Christian and his dad had been doing a ground up restoration of a 1970 Ford Mustang Boss 302, one of the classics favored by Dr. Asher and equally by Christian. Having spent hundreds of hours restoring this classic from the ground up, meticulously cleaning, painting and reassembling the smallest of parts, the now mint, Boss 302 was nearly complete inside and out. It sported a fresh dark aqua metallic paint matching the color pantones available in 1970, all done to meticulous perfection, a trait both father and son shared equally. The only remaining task was completing the connection of the power train and a few small esthetic details.

Christian and his dad had planned to complete the car before the end of summer, but schedules and unusually wet weather delayed its completion.

A group of admirers crowding the car grew larger and larger and Tweet found himself repeating his version of the rebuild story over and over to admirers both familiar and unfamiliar.

Tweet was very familiar with the rebuild since that's all Christian liked to talk about over the past few years. Tweet's lecture 'Rebuild 101' covered how they found the car, the extensive amount of time in the restoration including the most difficult parts to find from original Boss 302s.

After the fourth or fifth telling, his rendition was becoming less and less enthusiastic. He was looking forward to his escape when he got his wish He faintly heard Maddy call to him from across the yard. "Chris, hurry up! Christian's coming, get over here!" she shouted.

She focused her gaze towards Connor who was still talking to Jamie with a smile plastered on his face. "Connor! Connor!" Maddy called loudly over the loud ramblings of multiple party guests. "Get over hear, he's coming," she waved frantically. Connor darted over to where she was standing by the sliding glass doors with Dr. and Mrs. Asher, ready to welcome Christian to his party.

As the sliding glass doors opened, the DJ loudly announced Christian's arrival to the guests. He heard a roar and then applause from over 150 people now gathered on the pool deck and around the yard.

Blushing, he walked onto the deck waving timidly at the crowd as he began greeting his friends and family with hugs and kisses. Hugging his mom and dad first, then Maddy, who sensed right off that something was bothering him. Call it women's intuition, she stepped back so he could continue to greet his guests.

Tweet and Connor high fived him, giving him the one sided hug. Tweet whispered something in his ear about leaving town and new beginnings, most of which was inaudible and lost due to background noise. The greetings seemed to go on forever, every step bringing new well-wishers.

Christian continued to move about the crowd, greeting friends and family alike. Eventually he found himself back on the pool deck talking to Connor when he heard a familiar cliché in a voice he had been longing to hear coming from behind him, "Hey good looking, where can a girl get a drink around here?" Christian's eyes gleamed as he excitedly turned to see Hailey, his resplendent cousin smiling radiantly in his direction.

Hailey was the one person in the world Christian had confided in since early childhood. She wasn't an actual cousin, she was the daughter of close family friends, Mac and Janice McDowell that Christian had addressed as aunt and uncle for as long as he could remember.

Christian leaped forward to hug Hailey who responded in kind. "Oh My god, Hailey! What are you doing here? I thought you were away on business!" he asked.

"You don't think for a second I could let you go off to Cal Poly without saying goodbye did you?" Hailey exclaimed.

I can't believe you're here, it's . . . it's so great to see you! I want to catch up with you, there's so many . . . ." and before he could finish, Hailey was beckoned from across the deck by Mrs. Asher.

"Hailey, how . . . when did you get here?" Mrs. Asher asked enthusiastically as she rapidly approached, giving Hailey a hug equal to Christian's. "I thought you couldn't make it!" said Mrs. Asher as she whisked Hailey away, headed towards her husband who was camped out by one of the tables next to the pool.

Hailey looked over her shoulder at Christian, and it was obvious she'd prefer to stay with him as she was pulled away through a crowd of happy party goers. Christian was slightly bothered that he would have to wait to talk with her. He hadn't seen her in months with her busy schedule, and talking and texting weren't cutting it as far as he was concerned. You'd understand if you met her. There was so much he wanted to talk with her about but figured he could catch up with her later on in the evening.

The party continued late into the evening. It was past two in the morning when the last of the guests left for home. The catering staff had cleaned up the majority of the yard before leaving. Christian, exhausted, replayed the events of the evening. He reflected on how happy he was to sit and talk with Hailey for a while, which brought the final smile of the night to his face.

He hugged his mother and father, thanking them for a wonderful party. "Goodnight Mom, goodnight Dad," he said tiredly. "Love you!"

"We love you too honey! Get some sleep, you have a long trip tomorrow," Mrs. Asher said, looking lovingly at her son.

Simultaneously Dr. Asher said, "Good night buddy." Christian headed towards his room for the night.

Morning came quickly that day, but Christian hopped out of bed and started gathering some final personal articles he wanted to bring with him, tossing them into his, Nike® duffle bag with his name on the side. He had an 11:05 a.m. flight to San Luis Obispo, California, home of California Polytechnic State University.

Christian made his way down to the kitchen where his parents were quietly sitting and sipping their morning coffee and tea. There was a tray of croissants on the table with fruits, jams and spreads. This was one of Christian's favorite morning treats that was usually reserved for holidays or when guests were over. "Good morning Mom," Christian said leaning over to give his mom a peck on the cheek. "Morning Dad," he said smiling with anticipation of his trip. "Sleep well?" he inquired with a yawn.

Dr. Asher responded first saying, "Not bad."

Mrs. Asher followed by responding, "Snug as a bug, and how about you honey? I would expect you would be too excited to get any sleep," she smiled anxiously.

"I slept okay," he replied glancing over to his father who looked exhausted from the night before. He actually looked less rested and more stressed than he appeared early last night before the party.

Christian joined his parents at the table, enjoying his croissant with a glass of juice while reviewing his upcoming travel plans. Before he knew it, the doorbell rang. "Oh my god! Is that your ride already?" questioned Mrs. Asher as her eyes began to well up with tears. "I thought . . . I thought we'd have a little more time before you left!" she sobbed, now with a single tear running down her face.

Christian hugged her, whispering in her ear, "I love you Mom, everything is going to be fine," as she hugged him tighter and tighter not wanting to let go.

"Alright, alright, let the boy breathe honey, he'll be fine," said Dr. Asher with a forced smile on his face, hugging him as well. "Have a safe trip buddy."

"Call me when you get there . . . as soon as you get there!" barked Mrs. Asher as Christian opened the door and started walking towards the airport taxi with his bag slung over his shoulder. Don't forget, as soon as you get there!"

"Okay, okay, I won't forget" he responded saying, "Love you" just before jumping into the taxi.

-Three-
Cal Poly

Christian arrived at Cal Poly a little tired but very excited. He didn't get as much sleep during the flight as he had hoped as he was sitting next to a chatty passenger who talked incessantly through the entire flight to LAX and he was way too polite to ask for silence from her.

By the time the plane landed he thought he knew just about everything he wanted to know about Ms. Lombardi, a divorced mother of three, one natural and two C-sections, who was taking her first vacation to Hawaii with some friends.

She was meeting up with them in California so they could all travel together to the Big Island because she heard the other islands were nice to visit but the Big Island had more to offer and you could book excursions from there. She was wonderful enough to share most every detail of each member of the party she was meeting, including childhood stories about two of them. She talked for seven hours, non-stop just like the flight, until his ears were actually numb from listening. Even after landing she continued, and so on and so on and so on . . .

Grabbing his carry-on and checking his ears for blood, he disembarked the plane, laughing on the way up the gangplank because he could still hear Ms. Lombardi talking in the doorway of the plane.

He pulled out his phone to call his mom to report his safe arrival, otherwise his mom would be frantic wondering why he didn't call. "Hi Mom," he said, "I'm at LAX and everything is fine."

Mrs. Asher answered with a rapid-fire set of questions asking everything from, "How was your flight? Do you have everything you need? Did you get any rest? You didn't forget anything, did you? I can send it out tomorrow if you did. . . . Do you have enough money?"

Christian, with a loving smirk on his face responded, "All's good Mom, I've got everything I need."

Mrs. Asher continued for a few more minutes, confirming his responses before Christian interrupted her, "Mom, I gotta go, the connection is boarding, call you tomorrow. . . . Promise." Finishing the call, he made his way through the terminal to the gate. He boarded the connecting flight headed for San Luis Obispo, dosing off quickly after reaching his seat only to be wakened by the screech of the tires upon landing at SLO airport. The sun was gleaming; it was a typical California day. He jumped into a cab for the short ride over to the campus.

Christian reported to Administration which was open late to accommodate arriving first year students and new transfers. There he was introduced to his student advisor, Dylan McAfree. Tall and slender, Dylan was enthusiastic yet relatively soft spoken.

It was his responsibility to show Christian the grounds, classrooms, dorms, transportation schedules, and eateries among the other interesting gathering places around the campus. After receiving his Welcome Packet, ID and WOW schedule (Week of Welcome), explaining all the orientations for the week for the newbies, they began their tour of the campus.

The first words out of Dylan's mouth were "Congrats! You got in the Architect program! That's tough to do. We get something like 1500+ applicants for that and only about 120 spots available."

Christian smiled, "Thanks," as they continued on.

Christian appreciated the tour, realizing that learning the campus grounds on his own would have taken much longer. Dylan quickly showed him the best routes to classrooms and available shuttle locations as well as pointing out all the popular hangouts and eateries, finishing up with the dorm rooms. "Here ya go, this is where you're staying," Dylan said. "Any more questions before I go? I gotta finish up some work before tomorrow."

"No, I think I'm good, thanks," responded Christian, reaching out to shake Dylan's hand.

Dylan shook Christian's hand saying, "No problem, glad to help man." As he began walking away, Dylan turned to remind him, "Your room number is posted on the board inside where you check in, and in your Welcome Packet as well as with your key. You've got my number. Take care!" as he hurried off.

Christian double checked his room number on the board and then checked in with housing staff provided for new arrivals. Before heading upstairs to his assigned room, he sent a text to his mom informing her of his arrival. Mrs. Asher's final words during the LAX conversation were, "Text me when you get to the college, I don't care what time it is here!"

When he reached his room, the door was open; one of his two roommates was mostly set up. Christian stepped into the doorway, knocking gently on the door as to not startle his new roommate who was busy setting up the printer for his laptop. Before Christian could say a word, the chair spun around and up jumped Matthew Henderson with a welcoming smile on his face as he reached out to shake Christian's hand. Matt was a clean cut All-American type from a small town in Iowa. His family owned a small hardware store and most of his family were involved in construction of one kind or another. "Hi, I'm Matt! You must be Christian, nice to meet you."

"Good to meet you too," Christian replied as he looked over the room quickly then back at Matt. "Where can I put my stuff? he asked.

"Just put it over there on the bed for now. We can straighten it all up after we get your boxes from storage," replied Matt enthusiastically.

"Storage?" questioned Christian.

"Yeah, you don't think they deliver your boxes to the room do you?" Matt laughingly asked. "C'mon, let's get your stuff up here then we can grab something to eat. I'm hungry, you must be starving."

"Yeah, I'm kind of hungry too, thanks." Christian replied yawning as they headed out the door to collect the boxes he shipped the week before.

"So how did you end up at Cal Poly?" Matt asked, heading down the stairs.

"I liked the program they offered and thought it would be good to transfer over. I figure I'd finish the last of my undergrad work here then head over to MIT for the graduate program."

"Man, that's got to be tough," responded Matt looking at Christian with interest. "You've got your work cut out for you."

They continued getting acquainted with each other until they reached the student aid at the desk. Matt greeted the SAA, (Student Administrative Assistant), "Hi Amy, we're here to pick up Christian's stuff. Would you mind?"

"Not at all," Amy said glancing up at Christian admiringly.

Amy Kendall was an attractive Oregon farm girl also in her third year. Her long, light brown hair, sparkling green eyes and perfect smile did not go unnoticed by Christian.

She grabbed the keys to the storage room and clumsily stood up, still looking at Christian. She quickly regained her composure and blushingly asked, "What are you in for Christian?" as they walked toward the storeroom.

"Architecture," Christian answered. "How about you?"

"Animal science," she replied. "I worked with animals growing up and want to keep working with them. I'm just not sure which direction I want to go yet. You know . . . vet, tech, or zookeeper."

"That's cool! I like animals . . ." Christian awkwardly replied in an attempt to make small talk. Amy coyly snickered at his stumble.

Christian, a little shy and still feeling awkward, continued quietly down the hall to the storage room door, glancing at Amy off and on until they reached the door. It was apparent to Matt walking just behind them there was a connection. Amy opened the door and pointed out Christian's boxes. Her blush increased as Christian squeezed by going through the tight doorway toward the boxes.

Matt and Christian grabbed the two boxes, thanked Amy and started back toward the room. Matt made eye contact with an obviously smitten Amy on the way out and gave her a little wink. She responded by placing her finger over her lips to hush Matt before he said anything that may embarrass her further.

Back at the room Christian asked, "Where should I put this?"

"Throw them over here," Matt said, pointing to a third bunk.

"Who's that for?" asked Christian as he dropped his box on the unmade bed and flopped down beside it.

"Oh, that was for some guy from Indiana. I hear something came up and he can't make first semester," replied Matt. "That's gotta suck, big time," he continued.

"What could've happened to cause that? "Christian asked curiously.

"Don't know," Matt said raising his eyes and shrugging his shoulders as if he was in the dark about the whole thing. The best part is, we have extra room this semester."

Christian and Matt continued to get acquainted while setting up their respective places within the room. Christian brought up Amy often, probing for as much information about her as Matt could provide. Matt playfully spilled all that he knew about her.

WOW commenced the following day. Christian and Matt, taking the same curriculum, went to the same orientation functions, getting to know each other a little better along the way, Matt curiously inquired about Christian's childhood, where he grew up, what his mom and dad did, etc. They shared stories of favorite activities past and present, including the occasional funny story about some poor judgment calls they had made and some sillier things they did as well, Matt leading most of the conversations. It was all going well; Christian and Matt connected with a few other students in the program that shared the same curriculum.

Daniel Teague was a tall, lanky guy with thinning hair making him look older than he was. He came from Colchester in Essex County, UK. His family had moved there after his dad was posted at the Colchester barracks. He shared a room with Hunter Newman who was from Hamburg, Germany. Hunter was a wall of a man, six foot three inches and two hundred and thirty-five pounds of rock. He was following in his father's footsteps and planned to join the family firm upon graduation.

A third joined later in the day, Anton Orlov from Brooklyn, NY. His parents immigrated just a few months before he was born. His dad was in construction, the labor end of it. Anton had plans to work in the corporate building design area as well as design multi-unit homes for the construction business his dad and brothers ran.

-Four-
Taco Tuesday

Christian and Matt headed over for Taco Tuesday at one of the local eateries. When they arrived, Christian was happy to see Amy sitting with a group of her girlfriends. It was a packed house with everyone trying to talk over everyone else. He glanced over to the table where she was sitting with her friends with a smile on his face when one of Amy's friends, Tina, noticed them coming in. She looked back at Amy and commented, "Look at these two . . . they're cute." Amy looked up and realized she was talking about Christian and Matt.

Her face lit up and without hesitation she jumped up calling, "Christian, Matt, come and sit over here." They worked their way over to the table while the girls inquired how Amy knew them and when they met. After making their way through the crowd they finally reached the table where Amy started making introductions.

It was apparent to all that Christian was happy—elated you might say—that Amy was there. Besides the opportunity to get better acquainted with Amy and her friends, it would give him a break from the incessant getting acquainted with Matt conversations. He didn't mind getting acquainted, but the questions seemed never-ending, making him feel more like he was being interrogated than getting to know someone.

A few minutes later, Daniel strolled in, worked his way to the table and pulled up a chair. Shortly after that Hunter arrived, squeezing Amy and Christian closer and closer together, a welcome inconvenience for both.

The festivities continued in the crowded corner. Multiple conversations were flying back and forth across the table as time flew by. Before they knew it, they were there for better than three hours. Realizing the time, they packed up and headed for the dorms.

Christian enjoyed this time most of all. Trailing behind Matt, Hunter and Daniel he had the opportunity to talk one-on-one with Amy without having to talk above everyone else. It was a fairly short walk, about ten or fifteen minutes depending on how fast you walk, but they each found out more about one another during this short conversation than they did the entire night.

Reaching Amy's dorm, Christian said, "Good night." He watched her until she reached the door.

Amy turned flirtatiously, "See you tomorrow, right?" she asked as she walked through the doorway. Christian, with a smile from ear to ear, hurried to catch up with Matt, Daniel and Hunter. Upon reaching them he received a ribbing from the guys for the smitten look on his face.

"See you tomorrow, right?" Matt joked in a girly-like voice, causing the others to laugh.

WOW came and went and the work began. The course work was tougher than anticipated, keeping Christian in the books, so to speak. Studying and drawing left him little time for socializing. Happily, Christian was able to meet up with Amy off and on as the days passed, an activity that did not go unnoticed.

After skipping a few Taco Tuesdays, Christian and Amy decided to go and hang out for a while. They met up about seven-ish, both arriving at the same time. They had just sat down at a table when Amy noticed RJ Wellington walking in their direction.

"Oh no," Amy thought as RJ, the arrogant son of a controlling local businessman approached. RJ was short for Randolph Jameson. He was named after a person he utterly loathed, his grandfather. A man he never knew who lived a meager existence on the outskirts of town up until his mysterious passing.

His grandfather had built the family empire and was known to be a kind and generous member of the community, traits which were noticeably absent from his obsessively greedy son's persona, as well as his grandson's. Early on in young RJ's training, his father George took control of the family business in a ruthless takeover and dispossessed the entire family, including his own father. They never spoke to one another again and George rarely spoke of his father, but when he did, it was only to ridicule and mock him in front of his impressionable son.

George Wellington was, in a word, a bully. He was about six foot two inches tall and stocky like a linebacker. The kind of build more associated with mob muscle than a businessman, along with a similar mindset. He was a shrewd and ruthless businessman. RJ's limited knowledge of his grandfather came from the stories his father told him. I'm sure it was no accident that RJ had no additional recollection of him other than his name and the disdain he held for him.

RJ had unrelentingly pursued Amy a year and a half earlier. She finally gave in and dated him off and on during her first year. RJ was a pompous, athletic type and being from a well-to-do family that was somehow involved in technology, he thought he was better than everyone else.

Amy saw him for what he was and ended it as quickly as it began. Unfortunately, he didn't like to take no for an answer and continued his pursuit whenever the opportunity arose.

"Hey Amy, what's going on?" RJ inquired without acknowledging that Christian was sitting there.

"Not much," replied Amy avoiding direct eye contact.

"Who's this?" questioned RJ looking snidely at Christian.

"I'm Christian," Christian answered, standing up to shake RJ's hand, more out of habit than desire.

RJ blew him off. "Hey I was thinking we could go to—" but before he could finish, Amy interrupted him.

"RJ, we tried this and it didn't work. Why don't you just let it go, and go back to your friends."

"I just thought you might want an upgrade from your usual diet," RJ sleazily suggested while sneering at Christian.

Christian started to respond, "Hey, RJ, she just—" when Amy jumped in again.

"RJ, knock it off, NOW! It's not going to happen, EVER!" staring angrily at him. RJ, now annoyed and somewhat embarrassed about being shut down so loudly, looked at them both and headed back towards his friends.

"Who was that guy?" asked Christian.

"We had a couple of dates before I realized that he was a spoiled jerk. He keeps trying, and I keep shutting him down. If you don't mind, I'd really rather not talk about it. Can we get out of here?" she asked with suppressed urgency. Christian could feel eyes on the back of his head as they were talking.

"Sure, no problem," he said, feeling uncomfortable himself. "I'll ask the waitress to pack our stuff to go."

Christian made his way over to the server who was just feet away from RJ and his friends. "Would you mind packing our food to go?" he asked.

"No problem," she responded. "Is there a problem?" she hesitantly inquired, glancing at RJ and his friends.

"No, no problem. It's just a little crowded in here," he replied.

"Okay, I'll get it packed up now," she said, putting the check down on the counter.

While Christian was counting out the money for the check, he started hearing taunts from RJ and his friends. They were talking just loud enough for Christian to hear and not draw the attention of anyone else. "Where you going pretty boy? I wonder what number you are." Their comments were getting progressively raunchier as they went on.

"Finally," thought Christian, as the waitress brought his food over, still trying to ignore the taunts. He thanked the waitress with an uncomfortable smile and grabbed the bag as he turned to leave.

He tried to walk past RJ and his friends who had closed off his path back to Amy. As he crossed through them they began pushing and poking him, taunting him more and more. Christian clenched the bag with anger, knowing well this was no place for trouble, especially when it was him against three.

As he tried to move forward, one of them tripped him and RJ assisted with a push to the floor. Christian hit the floor, his bag split open and the contents spilled out and onto the floor.

The whole room was startled by the noise and looked over curiously. RJ and his friends burst out laughing, adding insult to injury as they 'accidentally on purpose' spilled portions of their drinks on him. Others around the action joined in with the laughter, not realizing what had happened. "He must be drunk," RJ shouted laughingly.

Christian was boiling and before he could respond, Amy arrived on the scene and pushed back hard on RJ and his friends, "Back off, jerks," bending down to help pick their wrapped tacos off the floor. "Let's just walk away Christian, just walk away. Okay? This is exactly what he wants," she pleaded.

"Oohh, looks like your little slut has come to the rescue." That was it . . . Christian jumped to his feet and slammed RJ right in the face, knocking him back against the counter. RJ was stunned for a moment. He had never had anyone come at him before. Most were afraid of him because of his father, not to mention his want-to-be thug friends.

RJ wiped his face with the back of his hand. He noticed blood on his sleeve from a cut on his lip and went ballistic, swinging and connecting with Christian's face. RJ's friends joined in, pummeling Christian. Amy was screaming "STOP IT, KNOCK IT OFF!" as she tried to break it up. A few patrons joined in, separating the group, allowing Amy to help Christian up and make it out the door. This wasn't new to anyone who lived in the area. They'd all seen it before and had learned to just avoid RJ and his friends.

"I'm sorry," Christian grimaced. "I couldn't let him get away with that." Blood was dripping down his face from a cut above his eye, and he was holding his side where he was repeatedly kicked. Amy hurried him out the door, heading toward the parking area, straining to support his off balance weight as he staggered further into the lot. "I . . . I . . . just wanted to kick his ass so bad. I really hate guys like that," he struggled.

"I know, I know, me too," Amy said helping him along. "I'm really sorry that happened, but it was nice that you tried." In an attempt to lighten the mood she continued. “But don’t you think you should learn how to fight first?” Christian paused for a moment, glancing up at Amy’s soft empathetic smile and started to laugh a little.

“Ouch, that hurts,” he said, clutching his ribs as they stumbled their way back toward his dorm.

-Five-
Road Trip

Weeks had passed before Christian and the guys had a break from their course work, and with a long weekend coming up because of some type of teacher's conference, they decided to plan a trip to visit the Anasazi Indian ruins in Mule Canyon, Utah.

Matt was interested in designing Passive Housing built into the landscape, utilizing natural resources, and thought that inspecting the architecture at the Anasazi site would add some insight in this area. After all, this was how the Anasazi lived, as part of the land, not on it. Building dwellings into rock faces provided both warmth and cooling that had lasted for centuries.

Christian was psyched about the trip as well. He knew there were areas he could still explore where Indian artifacts might be found. Exploring was something he and his dad shared on trips to upstate NY and the shores of the LI sound.

Long Island is rich with Indian heritage and on one of these trips he had found a couple of arrowheads and two small stones a little bigger than a silver dollar with a depression in the center containing remnants of colored dyes. One of these was reddish in color that, when rubbed with a wet finger, caused the dye to leach out onto his finger. Having the opportunity to explore an Anasazi site excited him. He could only hope that he would find an artifact.

He wrote notes in large letters reminding him to pick up extra batteries, a memory stick and SD card. He was hoping to get some great pictures and thought he might even see some petroglyphs or pictographs that he could photograph.

Matt and Christian excitedly planned the trip calculating distance, drive time, campsite locations and timetables for eating, sleeping and, of course, exploration of the site. It was a long ride to Mule Canyon, about fourteen hours, but they figured they could leave Wednesday after classes and ride through the night, taking turns sleeping on the way. They planned to pack food and drinks for the trip and stop at regular intervals for fuel and bathroom breaks. Their goal was to arrive early Thursday and start exploring.

It was the Sunday before the trip and Christian had borrowed Matt's truck to go for some supplies and equipment. Walking quickly toward the truck he saw Amy who greeted him with a big smile asking, "Hey, what's up?" as she flirtatiously bumped into him, slowing Christian's fast pace to a stroll.

"I'm on my way to pick up some things I need for the trip," he said enthusiastically.

"Trip?" Amy inquired curiously. "Where ya goin'?"

Amy had seen Christian just about every day last week and this was the first she heard of a trip. "It was a last minute thing," Christian explained, "Matt and I were talking about the long weekend and we didn't want to sit around doing nothing, so we decided to go to Mule Canyon to check out the Indian ruins."

"That sounds amazing," Amy said excitedly. "When are you going?" she asked.

"We're gonna take off Wednesday after classes . . . Hey, wanna take a ride to the mall with me?" Christian asked. He was hoping she would come along for the ride. He enjoyed her company and he enjoyed talking with her almost as much as his conversations with his not really cousin, Hailey.

"Perfect," she replied. "I need to get a couple of things myself if you don't mind making another stop," she said clutching his arm and increasing the pace to the truck.

"No problem," he smiled.

Shopping completed, they decided to grab something to eat. Amy was showing real interest in the trip as Christian explained his plans with the excitement of a young schoolboy. She enjoyed that about him, how excited relatively simple things made him.

Somewhere during their conversation it occurred to Christian that Amy would enjoy the trip as well. She also liked exploration and camping, and didn't mind getting her hands dirty, being the natural country type she was . . .

They finished eating and headed back to Cal Poly. Their conversation drifted toward an invitation; however, Christian knew he would need to clear it with Matt first before agreeing. Christian suggested, "Hey, do you think you'd want to come along? I . . . I mean it's . . ." he stumbled.

Amy jumped in. "Yeah! That would be great," looking just as excited as Christian felt.

"Really? Great! I'll clear it with Matt and—"

Amy quickly jumped in again, spinning in her seat to look at Christian while she asked, "You know, my friend Tina is going to be around this weekend too. You remember Tina, you met her during WOW. Maybe she can come along too?"

There was a pause as Christian thought this out. "Really, do you think she'd want to go?" asked Christian. Having Tina along would eliminate the awkward third person situation and he'd get to spend more time with Amy. He felt sure that Matt wouldn't mind.

"That would be great. I'll ask Matt and then you can ask her f she is interested and let me know."

"On it!" said Amy with her phone in her hand as she called Tina's cell. "Hi Tina, it's me," she said. "Listen, Christian and Matt are going on a road trip for the weekend, wanna go?" Listening to Tina's questions, Amy responded, "Utah to check out some ruins." Listening again, she responded, "No, were gonna camp out! Tents, campfires, lakes, the whole thing. It'll be great! Really?"

Amy said in an OMG kind of voice, "What? Say that again . . . Get out of here! That'll work," Amy smiled happily. "I'll call you later. Bye!"

Amy turned to Christian, still smiling, "She's in . . . and guess what. She thinks Matt's cute." Christian paused for a second thinking about what he was getting into.

"Excellent," he responded, hoping Matt would be as happy as he was to have them along.

Back at Cal Poly, Amy exited the truck as Christian firmed up the plan. "I'll talk to Matt and text you. See you later."

"Great!" replied Amy as she made a B-line to her dormitory, fingers crossed.

Christian reached the room just as Matt was headed out the door, "Hey, what's up?" Matt asked. "How'd you make out . . . did you get everything?"

"Yeah, got it all. Thanks for letting me use the truck," he said while tossing the keys to Matt. "Where you headed?" he asked

Matt paused, thinking for a moment, "I'm just gonna grab something quick to eat, want something?"

"No thanks, just ate," Christian responded. "Hold up, I'll walk down with you." As they headed down the hall, Christian started telling him all that transpired while he was gone and the girls' interest in tagging along.

They discussed inviting the girls to join them for the weekend and after some trepidation Matt agreed that it was a good idea for the girls to come along for the ride.

It really never struck Christian why Matt had second thoughts about the girls joining them; he thought it was a no brainer. What guy wouldn't want the company of a couple of pretty girls? "Great!" said Christian, "I'll let Amy know and tell them to meet us Wednesday after classes."

"Sounds good," Matt replied. "I'll see you later." Matt went on his way and Christian turned back toward the room, texting Amy on the way.

"We're on!!!" he texted. It took all of about 30 seconds for Amy to respond, "Awesome, I'll tell Tina! Smiley face, smiley face, smiley face Talk 2 U later."

Classes moved quickly that week for Christian. He wasn't sure if it was just the anticipation of the trip or that Amy and Tina were joining them or both, but before he knew it, his last class for the day on Wednesday had arrived. It was a third year drafting class; however, this day Professor Leone was doing an analysis of Architectural Writings which was the last thing on Christian's mind.

Unlike the classes during the beginning of the week, this class dragged on and on. Christian thought he could hear the seconds straining to move forward on the wall clock, each one seemed an eternity. Click, C-L-I-C-K . . . C-L-I-C-K . . . C-L-I-C-K . . . C-L-I-C-K . . . taking longer and longer for each to pass.

Half of the class was in a stupor from the content, the other half looked as though they were sleeping with their eyes open. Dr. Leone appeared to be trying to stay awake himself, knowing how boring the content of this information was to present. Every once in awhile it seemed he would come to, snapping to attention and changing his tone as well as raising his voice just to ensure no one was actually sleeping; a tactic that had little effect on the comatose class.

Christian was reviewing the checklist of everything he had already packed over and over in his mind. He didn't want to leave anything behind knowing that, once on site at Mule Canyon, there would be no easy place to get supplies.

Finally, after reviewing his checklist about a thousand times, Professor Leone released the class bidding them to enjoy the long weekend. The class began to exit the room lazily, like a bear leaving its den after a long hibernation—but not Christian. He leaped from his chair like a Thoroughbred leaving the gate at The Belmont, bursting with nervous energy as he rapidly maneuvered through the crowd of recovering students and headed out the door. He sent texts to Amy and Matt, letting them know he was on his way. "I'm out!! Heading to pick up my stuff, meet you at the truck."

Making his way toward his room, he crossed paths with RJ and one of his friends who never missed an opportunity to remind Christian of the beating they gave him. "Hey pretty boy, when you coming back for more?" RJ smirked, taunting in his usual arrogant manner, beginning to laugh along with his friend. Christian ignored him as usual and continued on, although slowing his pace a bit. He didn't want to give RJ the satisfaction of thinking he was running away from him.

He reached his room and grabbed his stuff. Matt had already packed the cooler and brought it down to the truck along with his bags. Christian threw his knapsack over his shoulder, grabbed his Nike duffel and headed out the door, turning back to make sure it was locked.

Christian moved quickly out of the housing units toward the truck. As he got closer he could see Matt organizing Amy and Tina's bags in the back while the girls were talking off to the side. "Hey guys, this is gonna be great!" he said with excitement as he approached the truck. He tossed his bags into the back with a smile on his face. Amy and Tina greeted him enthusiastically. They checked the supplies one last time, jumped into the truck and were on their way.

The drive to Mule Canyon seemed to pass quickly even though it was about 900 miles of driving. Matt and Christian shared the driving as planned, taking naps in between shifts. Christian's driving was relaxed and unhurried. Amy likened it to how a little old lady would drive and offered to drive for a while. She took the wheel for a few hours on I-40, the longest leg of the trip at 350 plus miles.

Christian nervously rode shotgun as Amy drove in a fashion that can only be described as completely opposite of his driving. At times he felt like he was in a high speed pursuit. Amy constantly took her eyes off the road while checking texts or digging in her bag for something as the car crossed over into the other lanes. She'd look up and correct her direction with a sharp jerk on the steering wheel, then look at Christian and snicker at the nervous look on his face.

"Hey don't worry, nothing's going to happen other than we'll get there quicker," she smiled. "That's what these roads are for . . . Speed! And there's not another soul on the road," she smiled.

Conversations flew back and forth during the trip. Tina and Matt seemed to be hitting it off well enough, which made Amy especially happy. She could focus more on Christian and used the time to get more acquainted with him.

Dawn was breaking as they arrived at Blandings. The reddish orange glow of the landscape was beautiful. They stopped to freshen up and get a bite to eat before heading out to the site. The food couldn't come quick enough for Christian who scoffed it down as if it was his last meal. He was ready to start his exploration and as far as he was concerned, he would be there already.

Their meal completed, Amy and Tina went to the ladies room one last time before they took off for the canyon. They chatted in the dingy setting of the bathroom while they were freshening up. It was nothing fancy for sure, but they knew it would seem like the loo at Buckingham Palace after two days in the desert. "What do you think of Matt?" Amy asked.

"He's really nice," Tina replied. "I hope to get to know him a little better over the next couple of days though."

"I hear that!" Amy replied smiling and continuing, "I'm going to grab another coffee for the road, want one?"

"No thanks, I'll meet you at the truck," Tina replied as she finished freshening up.

Leaving the bathroom, Amy headed back to the table then noticed Matt and Christian were gone. Thinking nothing of it she grabbed coffee for the road and went outside. When she didn't see the truck she started to panic a little. "Where are they?" she wondered out loud, nervously walking back and forth across the parking spot where they had parked the truck.

Tina showed up moments later noticing Amy looking a little nervous. “What’s up?” Tina asked, then she realized that there was no Matt, Christian or truck. ”Holy Sh*t! Where the hell are they?” she asked loudly.

“I don’t know,” Amy said nervously, still pacing. “You don’t think they—” and before she could finish, Matt and Christian came around the corner in the truck and pulled up next to them.

“Where the hell were you two?“ Tina asked in a high pitch nervous tone. Amy was sporting a nervous smile, rolling her eyes, shrugging her shoulders and raising her arms in disbelief as she looked at Christian. Matt started to laugh and Christian smirked, quickly smacking him on the arm.

“I told you so . . . they’re freaking out,” he said under his breath.

“Very funny,” Amy said as she noticed the smirk on Matt’s face.

“Yeah, what the hell?” Tina said climbing into the backseat.

“We . . . we . . . we just went to fill the truck up,“ Matt stuttered, trying not to laugh while his face turned red from suppressing the laughter. “Wha . . . what’d you think, we drove you to Blandings to leave you here?” Matt asked.

Just as he was finishing the question he got a friendly smack in the back of the head from Tina, causing Matt and Christian both to break out in laughter. “We’re s . . . so . . . sorry,” stuttered Matt, straining to get the words out through the laughter.

“Well, you could’ve told us you were going for gas you idiots! You scared the crap out of us! We didn’t know if you were abducted by some ‘Texas Chain Saw Massacre’ freaks or what,” spewed Tina.

Amy, listening to Tina's hysterics, began to laugh along with Christian and Matt. Tina looked at Amy and was a little surprised that she was laughing as well. It only took another minute or two before Tina came to see the humor in it as well and joined in, laughing with the others, although halfheartedly, as she was still a bit shaken. They drove off the parking lot, Christian and Matt holding their sides from laughing so hard.

-Six-
Trails End Mule Canyon

In no time at all they reached the restored ruins about twenty miles southwest of Blandings on Route 95. Closest to the roadway, it was a good place to start. It was a little chilly still, so the girls put on their light jackets. Matt was taking pictures of the restored dwelling along with a few photo ops with Christian, Amy and Tina.

After fifteen minutes or so Matt herded everyone back to the truck for the short trip to Trails Head just north of 95 on Route 263 by Arch Canyon. On the drive over, Matt explained that Trails Head was where the real exploration would begin. He explained the planned hike into the canyon and what they could expect to see including cave art, petroglyphs and some dwellings.

Matt continued laying out his plans. "The initial hike in is about a mile and a quarter to the first set of ruins with other ruin sites over the next couple of miles leading up to the planned campsite." Matt suggested hiking to the site, setting up and returning to explore the ruins. Everyone was in agreement. It would give them the opportunity to scout the areas they really wanted to explore more closely.

Upon arrival at Trails Head, Matt jumped out the car and put some money into an envelope for the permit fee, grabbed a map he saw next to the envelope, and jumped back in the truck. They headed to the parking lot about a half mile further in. After parking the truck, Christian and Matt got out first, walking to the rear of the truck to get the packs and supplies organized for the hike.

Matt plugged in the coordinates for Trails End, 37.537432, -109.731971 into his Garmin® handheld.

Grabbing the gear, they started for the big pond. Matt was clicking and storing waypoints along the way even though it was a fairly easy trail to follow. Christian had his eyes more on the ground looking for artifacts than on the trail. He stumbled a few times on his way up, once almost taking a header into the girls who were walking close in front of him at the time.

The hike up to the campsite was about 3.5 miles. Matt had researched the area, and besides the incredible scenery, there was reportedly good camping grounds surrounded by a grove of pines with good water nearby for bathing and swimming, called the 'Big Pond' atop Cedar Mesa.

The sights were amazing, which was no surprise to Matt. Hiking up the trail they were entranced with majestic pines that appeared to be growing with twisted, curling trunks and roots rising up from solid rock. Some of the larger trees appeared to be standing as lonely sentinels guarding the trail up the canyon. Reddish and blonde boulders, some the size of buses, lay at the base of the canyon wall.

They saw little wildlife other than birds, maybe because they were fairly noisy hiking in. Matt, in the lead, loudly warned the others of cracks, slippery surfaces and other perceived hazards he came across.

The group slowed passing the first set of ruins, taking them in for a moment before moving on, further spiking the interest to explore. Christian and Matt were discussing how amazing it was that these dwellings were built into the side of the canyon wall. Matt started making jokes about getting out on the wrong side of the bed . . . and watch that first step! You'd understand if you were there; some of them were elevated high above the canyon floor.

Reaching the campsite, they set up quickly. Amy and Tina sorted the supplies and organized the sleeping bags. Matt looked over at Tina, "You're going to want to hang anything you don't want the critters to get off that tree branch over there," he said pointing to a couple of ropes conveniently hanging from a nearby tree from previous campers.

"Really? What kind of critters are we talking about?" Tina asked with curiosity.

"Well, there are all kinds of stuff here. Chipmunks, squirrels, rabbits, other guinea pig looking varmints . . . Oh yeah! We can't forget the deer, long horn sheep and the mountain lions, of course," touted Matt.

"MOUNTAIN LIONS!" Tina yelped. "You mean the only thing between me and a freaking *mountain lion"*, Tina making the quotation mark hand gesture, "is that thin ass tent? Are you out of your freaking mind?" she asked. Matt and Christian started to laugh and reassured Tina that there was little or no chance of even coming across one.

Amy was organizing the supplies during Tina's outburst. She just looked up at Christian and Matt with a smirk on her face, shaking her head. "You guys are bad! Tina, I wouldn't listen to them, they're just messing around with you." Tina playfully jumped towards Matt, smacking him on the butt.

"Knock it off! You must like scaring the crap out of me," Tina said. Matt just smiled.

Christian and Matt finished setting up the tents adjacent to an existing fire pit that was in slight disrepair. They spiked one side of the tents into the shallow soil and used rocks on the other side by placing the stake through the loop, lying it flat on the hard canyon floor and placing heavy stones on top of the stakes. "This should hold," Matt said.

"Hope so," Christian replied.

They grabbed their packs and started out for the ruins. Initially, Matt wanted to head back down to the first ruins they had passed, but changed his plan of thought. "Christian, what do you think if we head further up the canyon and over to the north side to check out that area today, and tomorrow we can check out this side on the way down as we're packing out?"

"Sounds good to me," Christian responded automatically not thinking of what Matt had just said. "What do you girls think? Is that alright with you?" Christian asked.

"Sounds like a plan," Amy said. Tina nodded in approval.

Christian's thought process caught up with the moment. "Wait, what do you mean, packing out?" Christian curiously asked.

Matt responded, "Oh, did I forget to tell you? I booked us a couple of rooms in Vegas!" Matt explained.

"What?" a surprised Christian asked. Amy and Tina looked on with expressions of approval.

"C'mon, think about it—VEGAS!" Matt exclaimed. "Vegas is half-way between here and school, we can head back tomorrow night or Saturday morning, stay over in Vegas and go back on Sunday! It doesn't cost a thing, my uncle got the rooms for us. He has a diamond card or something, and as long as he plays, they comp him," explained Matt.

"Great Idea, don't ya think?" Tina asked.

"I've never been," said Amy,

"We should do it! Yeah. . . . Definitely," said Tina, the wheels turning in the back of her head.

"Well, I guess we're all in," Christian added, joining in the excitement.

The group started to explore the ruins, taking in the sights. They eventually split off into pairs, with Matt and Tina exploring the dwellings and structures. Matt made sure he was always in sight of Christian and Amy who were searching the ruins for petroglyphs and pictographs.

The time flew by for Christian, who focused on taking pictures of the site. He found some petroglyphs climbing in and out of dwellings, and Amy was always close behind. They helped each other across the most difficult parts of the terrain. A couple of hours into the exploration, Amy was looking for a place to relieve herself, and as she turned a corner she came face to face with the petroglyphs Christian was looking for.

"Christian!" Amy called. "I think you'll want to see this."

"What is it? Did you find something?" he asked and started moving quickly toward her.

Amy intentionally responded as casually as was possible, holding back her own excitement, "Yep!" Christian moved even faster, as fast as the terrain would allow.

Reaching Amy, he looked at her asking, "What'd you find?" Amy looked back at him, amazed he didn't even see them. "What is it?" he asked again. Amy, packing a big smile, slowly turned to the canyon wall and looked slightly upwards. Christian followed suit and looked up, seeing Amy's discovery.

"That's amazing!" he said excitedly, moving closer to touch the images engraved on the canyon wall possibly centuries ago.

He continued, "This is incredible! This petroglyph is hundreds of years old and still intact," showing his geeky side which Amy found adorable.

Christian continued to ramble on about the glyphs and started climbing onto surrounding rocks to take pictures from different angles in an attempt to get the glyphs and nearby ruins in one shot.

Completing an exhausting exploration of the ruins, the group headed back to the campsite to rest for a while. Amy was sporting a slight limp from a slip on some loose gravel. Matt and Christian, sitting under the pines on soft piles of pine needles, were sharing pictures from their exploration. Matt was discussing his ideas for incorporating some design aspects of the ruins in the eco-friendly designs he wanted to build.

The girls had retired to their tent for a while they emerged with towels in hand, wearing their bathing suits. "Who's up for a swim?" Tina asked, directing her question to the guys still engrossed in their picture sharing. She looked back at Amy and they headed off toward the Big Pond, giggling along the way. Christian and Matt looked at each other and darted to their tent. They were banging into each other and falling over as they tried to quickly change into their shorts.

They finished changing at just about the same time and headed toward the tent flap leading outside, stumbling as they hurried to exit and almost knocking each other down, taking the tent with them. They moved quickly toward the pond, glancing back at their partially collapsed tent and started laughing.

The girls were already swimming by the time they arrived. Throwing their towels down they both leapt into the pond, submerging simultaneously, their eyes widening as the cold water enveloped their bodies. Pushing upward to break through to the surface as quickly as possible, they both yelped, "Whoa, is that cold!" as they shook the excess water from their heads like wet dogs.

Amy and Tina started to laugh. "C'mon, what are you a couple of wusses?" Tina asked. Her question provoked Matt to jump toward her and give her a dunking that initiated a playful water fight amongst the group.

Finished with their flirtatious play, the girls exited first, followed by the guys. They dried off and enjoyed the remaining sun for a while before heading back to camp to build their campfire.

Christian and Matt got the fire started as Amy and Tina grabbed some food from the cooler pack. They cozily positioned themselves around the campfire to eat as the sun slowly set. "The colors are amazing," Amy said softly while looking at the brilliant bands of color crossing the sky. She looked at Christian affectionately, putting her arm around his and resting her head on his shoulder contentedly.

They sat by the fire for what seemed to be hours, listening as the sounds of the day faded. The songbirds' songs slowly gave way to the chirping of crickets, frogs and the occasional flutter of bat wings swooping toward the fire for the bugs it attracted.

Tina, playing coy with Matt, pulled herself in closer with each swooping bat. The cool night air rushing in prompted Tina to snuggle even closer to Matt for warmth as the day turned into a pristinely clear night.

Exhausted from their travels and exploration, they all moved to settle in for the night. Christian tossed extra wood on the fire from the pile they gathered earlier. Tina walked over to the tent she and Amy were to share, reached in and grabbed her sleeping bag.

Turning toward Matt's tent she looked at Christian and Amy to say "Goodnight." She headed to Matt's tent, making her intentions very clear to Christian by handing him his sleeping bag.

Christian took the bag from Tina and began to lay it down next to the fire he just stoked. Amy looked at him smiling, appreciating his unassuming personality. "What are you doing?" she asked.

"I thought I'd sleep out here by the fire," Christian replied.

"That's ridiculous," Amy responded, grabbing his sleeping bag and bringing it to her tent. She placed the sleeping bag next to hers and motioned for Christian to come in, patting the top of his sleeping bag. Christian and Amy sat talking for a while before sleep caught up with them. Snuggled together, they drifted into sleep for the night.

-Seven-
The Awakening

It was about two a.m. and Christian got up to check the fire. Quietly unzipping the flap and stepping out of the tent so as to not disturb Amy, he headed to the wood pile. It was cool and crisp, and the night had become eerily quiet. He stoked the fire with a few more long branches while glancing around the campsite. Turning back to the tent he noticed flashing lights in the sky just over the ridge above the campsite, accompanied by a low rumbling, reminiscent of a far-away lightning storm. Looking up and seeing the sky above was still very clear and brightly moonlit, he decided to head up to the flat atop the ridge to see the show.

He opened the tent flap and began stirring around in the dark looking for his flashlight, waking Amy who sleepily asked, "What's going on, is everything okay?"

"Sorry, I didn't mean to wake you. I'm going to head up to the mesa to watch the storm that's rolling in," he softly replied as he closed the tent flap and headed for the ridge up to the mesa, flashlight in hand.

Christian followed the path up the ridge. As he climbed the trail, he reached a large boulder that blocked a portion of the path and partially obscured the view of the top of the mesa. Maneuvering around the boulder he took the last few steps to reach the top. He gazed up at the night sky, taking notice of a large cloud formation off in the distance. It appeared to be about two or three miles across and emitted a multicolor light show that resembled heat lightning above the cloudbank.

Finding a comfortable place to sit, he watched the light show for a few minutes, not realizing how quickly the storm cloud was moving in his direction. He continued to watch, fixated on the bright flashing lights above the cloud as it drew nearer and nearer. The colors were different than he'd ever seen before with heat lightning, which he attributed to the desert climate. Bright flashes of silver, blue-green and orange-like colors above the cloud grew brighter as it approached. He watched the light show intently, having no concerns with the increasing proximity of the cloud bank since he hadn't noticed any ground strikes.

Below at the campsite, Amy was becoming concerned that Christian had been gone a good while and had not returned. Noticing the fire he had stoked just before heading up to the mesa was nearly burned out, she decided to go and look for him. She gathered herself, grabbing a soft flannel shirt and flashlight and started up the path to the mesa. It was eerily quiet except for the muffled rumbling from the storm. Passing the half-way point to the top, her concern was coupled with curiosity, as she too began to see the colorful display of flashing lights of the now not-so-distant storm cloud.

Before Christian knew it, the cloud was directly overhead. The flashing multi-color lights were less visible with the cloud cover directly above. He noticed the once faint rumbling of thunder was becoming louder and louder, the sound was becoming so loud it felt as if his ears were going to explode. He could sense stronger and stronger vibrations, like pressure waves, moving through his entire body and he suddenly felt nauseated.

His gaze of wonderment began turning into a sense of fear. Knowing something wasn't right, he struggled to get to his feet, but it felt like something was holding him to the ground. He finally got to his feet and started to turn toward the path heading back down to the campsite.

He developed strong stomach cramps and cold sweats, the ones you get when you're extremely nauseous. He attempted to move toward the path only to realize he was hardly moving at all. He put every ounce of strength he had into taking each step forward, straining to gain each and every inch. In a last attempt to move, he bent over, supporting his weight with one arm and grabbing his pant legs one at a time with the other. He gripped each with all his strength and tugged sharply to move his foot off the ground and slightly forward. He was making little to no progress in this struggle to move to the path. Whatever was holding him back had an unbreakable grip on him. His fear was now full blown panic.

The air that had remained relatively still to this point suddenly whipped into a frenzied whirlwind between him and the path, blocking his exit from the mesa. He spun around awkwardly, seeing other whirlwinds were forming while surrounding his position atop the mesa. Shielding his eyes from the stinging sand whipping around him, he gathered all of his strength and continued his struggle, stumbling to make his way toward the path.

Looking down through the whipping sand he noticed a lone flashlight on the path headed up to the ridge. Squinting through the sandstorm that enveloped him, he tried to see who it was without success. "Stay there, I'm headed down," he yelled, not realizing it was Amy heading up. His words, muffled by the deafening sound from the storm, prevented her from hearing his warnings.

Amy was on the top third of the path when the whirlwinds whipped up on the mesa. Startled by the sight of the sudden onset of whirlwinds she yelled up to Christian, "Oh my god, what's going on?"

"Stay down there!" Christian shouted back. His pleas were inaudible.

Amy began to panic having never seen anything like this before. She screamed for Matt and Tina, turning back to look at Christian in the middle of the circle of whirlwinds, yelling his name as loud as she could. Her panic increasing, she prayed for someone to respond to her desperate calls.

Christian continued his struggle, slowly making his way through the whirlwinds that enveloped him when a bolt of lightning struck just in front of him at the head of the path leading down, stopping him in his tracks.

Blinded by the flash and thinking Christian was struck, Amy frantically screamed for him, "CHRISTIAN, CHRISTIAN!" She received no answer.

The commotion from the storm had roused Matt and Tina from their sleep, but when they heard Amy's muffled screams for help they sprinted from their tent and began running up the path. "AMY, AMY, what the hell is going on?" Matt yelled.

"Christian's up there!" she yelled frantically.

Looking up in shock, Matt saw the tops of the whirlwinds on the mesa with bright flashes from multiple lightning strikes. Matt told the girls to stay put and worked his way up to a point where he could see the mesa and the whirlwinds that were surrounding Christian. As if trapping him in a cage, bolts of lightning were now striking all around him as if intentionally preventing his exit from the mesa.

Amy and Tina nervously followed Matt further up the path. They could smell the ozone from the strikes. Once in view of the deluge confronting Christian, the girls became increasingly hysterical. "Calm down! Calm down!" Matt called out, attempting to calm the girls. "We need to be focused," Matt barked. "I need you to stay here and listen for my call. Got it? Wait for my call!"

He sprinted up the path to help Christian. As he reached the boulder just before the top of the path, a bolt of lightning shot down with amazing precision, striking directly in front of him. The explosive impact threw him backward through the air and up against the pines along the path. He crashed to the ground with a thud and began rolling back and forth in agony. His face was distorted from the pain, his eyebrows were singed, and his face flash-burned from the strike.

Tina and Amy were screaming frantically as they ran to Matt's aid with tears in their eyes. Tina picked his head up and put it into her lap, weeping while asking, "Are you okay? I'm so scared, please be okay. Please . . ." He had a trickle of blood coming from the side of his head where his face had struck a tree.

Matt opened his eyes, gathered his strength and sat up, supported by a sobbing Tina. "I'll be okay; we need to help Christian," he said while looking at Amy who was hysterically ranting on about getting up to the mesa. Tina, relieved that Matt was okay, hugged him tightly. Together they reached out, pulling Amy in and holding her tightly.

The three looked on helplessly as the barrage of wind, sand and lightning engulfed Christian. Matt was trying to figure out how to get to him to help, and calm the girls at the same time. Amy suddenly pulled away and started back up the path yelling, "We have to help him! We have to help him!" Matt and Tina quickly restrained her as she sobbed uncontrollably, reminding her of the targeted lightning strike that hit Matt.

Christian was centered in the in the melee of dancing whirlwinds and lightning strikes. Holding his arms up to protect his face and eyes, he blindly struggled to move about in the center of the melee. As Matt and the girls watched helplessly, a single bolt of lightning shot from the cloud striking Christian.

It was a continuous bolt, striking him directly on his chest as if carefully aimed, the sight of which stunned all of them and caused Amy and Tina to scream and cry uncontrollably. Amy dropped to her knees crying out, "I can't believe this is happening, why is this happening? Please God, Please God, Please God."

This strike was nothing like the others. The others were short duration strikes that had surrounded him over the past few agonizing minutes. It was unlike the targeted strike that sent Matt flying through the air. This strike was intense. It entered Christian's chest, passing through him and exited the small of his back. It was unlike anything they had ever seen or heard of before. A continuous, unrelenting, thick bolt of pure energy passing through him.

Amy, Matt and Tina watched helplessly, horrified as the undulating bolt slowly lifted Christian's now limp body off the ground, slowly raising him further and further above the mesa. Amy was chanting, "Please don't die, please don't die," as they watched in horror.

The bright light emitted from the bolt passing through Christian lit the mesa like floodlights in a stadium. The whirlwinds circling his position created an eerie wall of sand and light grey smoke illuminated from within by the continuous strike passing through him. The smell of ozone filling the air got stronger and stronger with each passing second.

Amy clasping her hands together looked up and started to pray. "Please God, please, let this end! Please God, please." She looked up in hopeful amazement when she noticed a figure on the mesa with Christian. Her teary eyes strained to focus through the bright flashes of light. Now fixed on the figure, she slowly motioned to Matt and Tina to look at the eye wall of the storm.

Within the wall Amy saw a shadowy image of what appeared to be an American Indian in full ceremonial dress, dancing within the wall that enslaved Christian's rising body. "Oh my god, do you see that?" Amy asked with her shaking hand pointing in the direction of the shadow dancer within the wall. Tina's gaze moved to the eye wall, briefly catching a glimpse of the shadow dancer before losing sight of him again.

"Oh my god, what was that?" Tina asked, trembling under her breath, turning to grab Matt's attention while still fixated on Christian's limp body which appeared to have stopped rising.

"He stopped, he's not going up anymore," Matt exclaimed, "He stopped!" Tina grabbed Matt's arm and directed his attention to the shadow dancer within the wall.

Matt looked in the direction Tina was pointing, seeing nothing at first. The dancer had just passed behind Christian's floating body, blocking Matt's view. A few seconds later the dancer slowly emerged from behind Christian, causing Matt's eyes to widened in disbelief as he viewed the spectacle playing out before him.

As the tense moments passed, additional shadow dancers materialized out of thin air, joining the dance that encircled Christian. Seconds seemed like hours as they watched helplessly.

The dancers moved fluidly, floating in and out of the wall of sand and smoke. More and more dancers appeared until they encompassed the entire base of the wall encircling Christian. They were dancing counter to the rotation of the wall, appearing to slow its momentum.

"Look . . . look, he's coming down," Amy cried. Christian was slowly floating back down to the mesa as the spear of light piercing his chest faded. The rampage of flashes and strikes were diminishing. The whirlwinds continued to slow and the wall began to dissipate.

The shadow dancers continued to dance, their ghostly chants and muffled drumbeats now audible as the sounds from the storm slowly faded. As the whirlwinds and strikes continued to fade, now barely visible, the shadow dancers began to slowly wisp back into the darkness of night, one by one rising into the night like grey smoke from a candle's wick. The final shadow dancer made its way to Christian and knelt down beside him briefly before he, himself vanished into the night.

Almost as quickly as it had started, it was over. The sounds of whipping winds and lightning strikes giving way to the silence and calm of the night. The smell of ozone dissipated and the songs of the night returned. The frogs and crickets were singing, filling the night with their calls. The storm cloud vanished without a trace, almost instantly yielding to the starry night sky.

Amy sprinted up the path, tears rolling down her face yelling, "Christian, Christian!" There was no response. Matt and Tina were on her heels. Amy cleared the boulder first, launching herself onto the mesa. Seeing Christian's still body lying on the ground, she once again broke into hysterics, "No, no, noooo," she cried as she ran to his side.

Matt arrived a second later, jumping down to check if he was alive. Placing his head on Christian's chest, Matt was relieved to hear a faint heartbeat. "He's alive!" he yelled, continuing to bark out orders to the girls for water and a shirt to use as a pillow. Amy positioned herself by his head. She picked up his head and placed it on top of her legs as she knelt behind him.

"We have to get him down! "Matt yelled excitedly, trying to process everything he had just witnessed.

Tina was nervously scanning the sky for any signs of the cloud. Slowly, Christian started to stir; his movements grabbed their attention, stopping them in their tracks. They couldn't imagine how he could be alive, much less moving after what they had witnessed.

First his fingers began to twitch, then his hands moved, followed by his head and arms. He tried to lift his legs, which moved slowly as if they were weighed down. Amy handed Matt some water then placed her shirt under his head, brushing his hair back as she moved to his side. "Christian?" she said softly attempting to gain his attention. Christian's eyes opened slowly and began to focus on Amy looking down at him, the tear running down her cheek dropped onto his face. He smiled. Amy let out a sigh of relief.

"What . . . what happened?" he asked sluggishly.

Matt jumped into say, "Don't move yet, let's check you out." Matt proceeded to check Christian out with the speed and precision of an EMT, checking his light reflexes and vitals as well as he could. Tina assisted, checking Christian for cuts, scrapes and gashes. "My god. There's not a scratch on him, not even a burn," she claimed with a puzzled look on her face.

Amy, looking down, put her hand on his chest. "His shirt, it's not burned either," she said, thinking she was in an episode of The Twilight Zone. Matt finished his checkup, finding nothing visibly wrong with Christian. They were all thinking the same thing; *How could this be possible?*

Christian slowly lifted himself to a seated position with some help from Amy, again asking, "What happened?" He had no recollection of the events that had transpired from the time the cloud was overhead. "The last thing I remember I was watching the storm roll in and—now I'm sitting here with all of you. How . . . when did you guys get here?"

Noticing that Amy's cheeks were wet from crying, "Why are you crying? Are you alright?"

"I'm fine," she said leaning in and placing her head on his shoulder, quietly repeating "I'm fine."

"How are you feeling? Do you feel strong enough to stand?" Matt asked, bending over to hear Christian's somewhat weak response.

"Yeah, I think so . . . but, what happened?" he asked again.

Matt responded, "It's a long story. Right now we need to get you back to the tent. You need your rest. Tomorrow we'll head back down and get you checked out."

"Checked out from what?" Christian asked.

Matt reached down grabbing Christian's hand to pull him up. "Ouch, what was that?" Matt asked, looking at his hand.

Christian groggily looked down at his hand. "Where did these come from?" he asked.

In his hand was an arrowhead, a bear claw on a tough old leather strand, and a beaded necklace. "What is that?" Amy asked. "Did you find that today?"

"No," he replied, "I don't know where it came from." Amy, Matt and Tina looked at each other with concerned curiosity.

Amy looked up. "It looks like the necklace around the—" She stopped herself mid-sentence so as not to alarm Christian of the events. Now wasn't the time, she thought. Tina and Matt knew exactly what she was going to say; it was the same type of beaded necklace the shadow dancers were wearing. Nodding to each other in agreement, they began moving slowly to the head of the trail, Christian in tow.

"It's too late to head out of the canyon tonight. We will settle in tonight and then walk out tomorrow morning," Matt said. The girls nodded their heads quickly in agreement.

The group stumbled back down the path, returning to the tents. After getting Christian settled in for the night, Matt suggested each of them take a shift watching him through the night, just to be safe. Amy offered to take first watch, asking that Matt and Tina stay close. She stayed with Christian through the night, only dosing off and on when her relief arrived a couple of hours later. She played the scary events of the night over and over in her head, remembering how frightened she was, yet grateful that Christian was alive. But how?

Matt and Tina retreated to their tent for some rest, discussing the events that had just played out, over and over. Tina quickly started sketching from memory what she had witnessed on a small pad. Matt began jotting down notes of the events while it was fresh in his mind. His notes ending in *Necklace, Bear Claw, and Arrowhead!!!* with scurried underlining.

- Eight-
The Old One

Morning arrived without further incidence. Tina was in the tent with Amy and Christian. They were all sleeping soundly. Matt packed up his site and prepped a quick campsite breakfast. He ventured to walk up to the mesa one last time to check the surroundings for evidence from the activities of the previous night and take some pictures. He searched the area carefully, finding no signs of lightning strikes, burn marks or disruption upon the mesa of any kind. His curiosity was peaked.

He headed back down the campsite to find Amy stirring slowly about the fire, looking at the coffee pot perking above the fire. "Hey, good morning," Matt said to Amy. "Coffee's ready, want some?"

"Please," Amy responded.

"How is he?" Matt asked.

"He seems fine, he didn't move all night," she said, holding two cups out for Matt to pour.

Tina appeared from the tent, following the smell of the coffee to the fireside. Mmmm, smells good. . . . May I?" she asked as she reached out to grab a welcome cup of coffee from Amy.

"Hell of a night! I've never seen anything like that and I hope I never see it again!" Tina exclaimed.

"Anything like what?" Christian asked. He had rolled out of the tent unnoticed just after Tina. He was sleepy eyed, stretching one arm overhead and holding the back of his neck with the other. "Anything like what?" he asked again. "And what happened to my neck?" he asked, head flexed forward while he continued to rub his sore neck.

Amy slowly walked to him, looking at him with her soft morning eyes, giving him a hug and saying, "You're not going to believe this."

Matt jumped in, "Buddy, you scared the living sh*t out of us last night!"

"You sure did!" Tina added, offering him a cup of coffee.

The three of them regaled Christian of the events on the mesa over morning coffee. They were amazed Christian continued to have no recollection of anything that happened. Matt was packing up the other tent as the discussion continued. He packed out the camp into three packs and a small knapsack for Christian to carry out of the canyon.

Christian listened to what happened the night before in disbelief. He agreed with the others that he should get checked out in Blandings at the Blue Mountain Medical Center before anything else, even though he felt fine with the exception of the soreness of his neck. He requested no one discuss the events with anyone until he decided to. He didn't want to fuss over it, but the real reason was he didn't want to take any chances of his parents finding out. He didn't want them to worry, especially his mom. They appeared to be under enough stress and didn't need the extra worries. All agreed.

All packed up and coffee finished, Matt headed up to the Big Pond with two collapsible water buckets. He returned shortly and extinguished the fire. Christian was watching him walk back down the path, and pointing behind him he asked, "Who was that?"

Matt stopped in his tracks with his eyes opened wide, turning quickly to Christian, "Who is who?" he asked.

"Him," Christian replied pointing up the trail.

Matt looked up hesitantly and saw an old Indian man up on the trail to the mesa. "Hold on!" Matt said, dumping the remainder of the water on the fire. He sprinted up to where the man was standing, finding no one was there. He looked around quickly then continued up the path, rounding the boulder and jumped onto the mesa. Again, nothing—no one was there. "What the hell?" he questioned, scratching his head. He hurried back down to the camp.

"Who was that?" Christian asked.

Amy and Tina anxiously looked at Matt, waiting for his response. "I don't know," Matt said. "Let's get down to the car."

"What happened? Who was up there?" Tina rattled off her questions nervously.

"I don't know where he went. When I got up there he was gone, vanished without a trace!" Matt said in nervous undertones. "C'mon, let's get out of here, it's getting freaky again."

The group headed down the trail, Amy closely watching Christian who continued to profess he was fine. They reached the car in about an hour. The girls passed their packs to Matt who packed the truck. Christian handed Matt his knapsack, grabbed a couple of waters and passed them to the girls. He handed a bottle of water to Matt and noticed over his shoulder the Old One standing on the ridge at the beginning of Trails End.

"Look who's back," Christian quietly said to Matt, not to alarm the girls. Matt turned to see the old man again, staring down at them with cold, dark eyes. "This is freaky," Christian said.

"Let's go," Matt responded. They jumped in the truck and headed for Blandings.

Christian entered the Blue Mountain Medical Center with Amy while Tina and Matt filled the truck with gas, picked up some supplies, and took the opportunity to use the cell signal that was available to make a few calls.

It was quiet in the medical center and he was taken back quickly. The nurse escorted him to the room to change. He removed his shirt and put on the gown, open in the back. Minutes later the doctor entered, an older gentleman with grey hair and a soft voice. He began his evaluation, asking the usual questions.

Christian explained what he had been told happened the night before. The doctor, looking on in disbelief, asked if he had taken any drugs or thought anyone would slip something to him. Christian responded, "I don't take drugs and I don't believe anyone I was with would do something like that." The doctor questioned him more about the events and began his examination.

Completing the exam, the doctor asked one more question. "You indicate on your forms that you have no scars. What is this?" he asked, pointing to Christian's right shoulder and chest.

"What is what?" Christian asked.

The doctor directed Christian to a mirror pointing to his chest and saying, "That!"

Christian stared in disbelief. On his chest was a massive scar. Three jagged claw marks, eight or more inches long, passing diagonally downward from his right shoulder across his right pec to the edge of the sternum. "I . . . I don't know how they got there,"

Christian stuttered, running his fingers across the scar with a shocked look on his face.

"Well it's obviously an old scar," the doctor said with a discerning look. "Is this some kind of joke?" asked the doctor.

"No, it's . . . it's not. I honestly don't know where that came from!" said Christian, still confused about how this scar got there.

The doctor, unimpressed with what he thought a joke, half-heartedly finished up his exam. Finding nothing else remarkable other than a circular redness of the chest and the small of the back, he released Christian with instructions to watch for signs of disorientation. He left the room, telling Christian to dress while he went to the waiting room to interview Amy about the events of the previous evening.

The doctor, wanting to confirm Christian's unusual statements, approached Amy. "Are you the young lady with Mr. Asher?" he asked.

"Yes, I am," she responded.

"Would you be kind enough to tell me what the hell happened last night?"

Amy started talking. She recapped the story for the doctor who was convinced this was more of a ruse than an actual occurrence after receiving the same unbelievable answers. He suggested a follow-up if Christian experienced any adverse effects and possibly a psychiatric evaluation for them both. Shaking his head he walked over to the nurse, tossed the chart in a bin atop the counter, then headed down the hallway and into another operatory.

Christian stood staring at the mirror and the scar on his chest in disbelief. As he dressed he focused in on the reflection in the mirror and saw something else that alarmed him. Anxiously spinning around, he was looking right at him—the weathered old Indian man with long, grey hair tied back in a ponytail staring straight at him from across the street.

Christian's inner monologue was off and running. "How is this possible? How could he know where I was? How could he see me through the mirrored windows? How did he know I was in this room? How the hell did he get here so quick?" The questions kept coming, and as they did his anxiety grew. His heart was pounding. Who was this strange old man who, as if by magic, kept popping up?

He quickly exited the exam room and headed for the lobby to meet up with Amy and pay his bill. He used cash so as not to involve his insurance and the paperwork he knew would eventually reach home. Then he grabbed Amy's hand and hurried her out to the truck where Matt and Tina had been waiting.

"How'd you make out?" Matt asked.

"Fine, let's get out of here," Christian replied abruptly.

"The diner?" Matt asked.

Christian quickly responded, "Sure, anywhere but here."

As Matt pulled out of the lot curious as to what was bothering Christian, he noticed the old Indian man standing across the street staring at the car as it turned onto the roadway. He refrained from saying anything but his face said it all as he looked over at Christian who acknowledged the old man's presence with an anxious look on his face as well.

"Got it!" Matt said, and off they went to the diner a few miles up the road. The front seat was quiet during the quick trip while the girls were occupied in the back seat making themselves up for the diner, none the wiser of the Old One's presence.

Matt pulled into the café parking lot. They exited the truck and went inside, taking a seat up against the back wall of the restaurant. It was a quaint little eatery, a clean place with tables reminiscent of high school cafeteria tables. The smell of fresh baked muffins and coffee filled the air.

The waitress, a fast stepping, busty, middle aged brunette with a perky attitude and a slightly crooked smile walked up and placed the breakfast menus on the table with a sunny morning greeting. "Coffee?"

A unanimous "Yes!" poured out from the table. While the waitress poured the coffee, Tina looked up saying, "Some storm last night, huh?"

"What storm honey?" the waitress asked.

"You mean you didn't have a storm here last night?" Tina asked with a bewildered look on her face.

"No honey, we haven't had rain for a while. What can I get you or do you need a minute?" she asked pleasantly.

They scanned the menu as the waitress continued asking them the standard questions; "Where you all from? Are you on vacation?" After responding, they all ordered and the waitress headed to the kitchen.

After ordering, Christian realized he left his wallet in the truck. "Back in a minute," he said, making his way to the truck.

"That was weird, don't ya think?" Tina asked. Matt and Amy agreeing.

"How is it possible that anyone could miss seeing the flashing lights and lightning strikes?" Amy asked.

"Yeah, what about the loud, rumbling sound? How could you not hear that?" asked Matt.

"You can hear a squirrel fart a mile away here," Tina giggled, "but you couldn't hear or see what we saw? What's that about?" Tina asked.

An older man, overhearing their conversation, slowly turned in his seat to face them. He had piercing blue eyes and his face was weathered from years of ranching in the area. He gently removed his cowboy hat and politely interrupted, "Excuse me," he said with a slight drawl." Are you referring to Mule Canyon?" he asked with an inquiring gaze on his face.

Amy and Tina immediately directed their attention to the rancher. Matt turned quickly to face him and replied, "Yeah, did you see that storm last night too?"

"There's always something strange going on out there at night . . . 37th parallel, you know," said the rancher."

"Well, what was it?" Amy asked.

"You know, a lot of people have a lot of ideas about that, but no one is really sure. If you listen to the old Indians around here, it's ancient Indian mysticism stuff, but you'd have to believe in all that. All I can tell you is that I saw it once from a few miles away and it sure seems strange that all that only happens in the middle of the night. Some folks say its government testing, that's why it only happens at night so folks can't see what's going on."

The rancher continued with the story of the night he saw all the commotion. In mid-stream of the rancher's story, Tina interrupted and started to ask, "Did you see the lightning on the mesa?" This heightened the rancher's interest before Matt could nudge Tina in an attempt to limit her questioning. He wanted to hear more from the rancher before divulging more of their experience to him or anyone else.

"You were there, weren't you?" the rancher asked looking at all three. "You were at the mesa last night when it happened?" he asked.

Matt reluctantly replied, "Yes sir, we were camped out just west of the mesa below the Big Pond." The rancher could tell by their faces that they actually witnessed this up-close.

"I'll be damned," the rancher said with a grin on his face. "Rumor has it that the folks curious enough to go up there at night when this happens usually don't come back. Sheriff probably has a dozen posters from the 1950s through today of folks gone missing. He'll probably want to speak to you kids about that."

The rancher's interest was roused even further, wanting to hear as much as possible about their experience. He mentioned he was a tracker on a number of the search teams that searched the canyon for past victims. "Did you ever find anyone?" Tina asked.

"Nope," the rancher replied. "All we ever found was belongings. Tents and such, but no people and no trace of them other than their stuff. It's the strangest thing to have so many people disappear into thin air like that."

They continued to compare notes for a while, each asking multiple questions about the experience. Matt omitted most of the details regarding Christian; he thought it best. He also thought it best to get going as soon as they finished eating in order to avoid a possible run in with the local sheriff for questioning, but kept that to himself for the time being.

Christian walked through the empty parking lot to the truck and opened the back hatch. He leaned in to search through his backpack for his wallet. Finding his wallet, he stepped back, closed the truck hatch and turned around, freezing in his tracks. He felt a coldness around him as fear built up inside him. He was face to face with the old Indian man, staring into his cold, dark eyes which were sunken deep in his chiseled face.

The old man, staring emotionlessly into Christian's eyes said, "You and I are as one," in the ancient language of the Anasazi.

Christian, startled by his sudden appearance blurted out, "What do you mean?" The old man's facial expression remained unchanged as he reached out to Christian with one hand, grasped his shirt and pulled it open slightly, revealing the scar on Christian's chest.

At the same time, he exposed his right shoulder and chest revealing an identical scar. "We are the same," repeated the old man, still speaking in ancient Anasazi.

Christian was startled and tried to pull away from the old man's grasp, stopping only when he saw the scar on the old man's chest. It was identical to his. "How . . . how can this be? How come I understand you?" asked Christian.

The old man continued speaking in his native language. "We are of the same tribe. My spirit guides led me to you on the mesa. They saved you from the grey ones. You must be careful with your gift or they will take you."

Christian, staring back at the Old One asked, "What gift?" The Old One continued to stare into Christian's eyes as if he was reading his very soul. Christian, totally captivated, stared back into the darkness of the Old One's cold, lifeless eyes. The old Indian raised his hand and opened it slowly, revealing a bear claw on a tough old piece of hide, a beaded necklace, and an arrowhead. Patting Christian's pocket, he gestured for him to remove the contents.

Christian reached into his pocket and pulled out the contents. He was staring at an arrowhead, bear claw and a beaded necklace. He stood in stunned silence, looking at the identical artifacts. He had completely forgotten about the artifacts they found in his hand the night before. Amy had put them in his pocket before heading down from the mesa. He continued to stare at his hand in stunned silence.

The Old One continued talking to Christian in his ancient dialect. "I am your guide. Keep these three pieces as one. When the time is right I will be summoned and we will stand together once again. Remember to always keep them together."

Matt, inside the café, was still talking with the rancher. Glancing over the rancher's shoulder and through the window he saw the old Indian man and Christian behind his truck. "Son of a . . ." He leaped from his chair, startling both the girls and the rancher and ran toward the door, throwing it open. His forceful push caused it to crash against the wall, making a loud noise that startled Christian. Christian quickly turned and looked in the direction of the noise by the café entrance to see Matt running in his direction.

"Where is he? Where did he go?" Matt asked excitedly.

Christian responded, "He's right h . . . e . . . r . . . e . . ." turning his head, only to find the old man had vanished into thin air. He ran around the side of the truck, looked up and down the parking lot and roadway. Nothing; he was gone. Christian and Matt stood in the parking lot for a minute.

"You saw him, right?" Christian asked, now more puzzled than ever.

"Where the hell did he go?" Matt asked. "I saw him from inside the café and by the time I got here, he was gone."

"I don't know," Christian responded. "He was here one second and gone the next," he said.

Matt hit Christian on the arm, gesturing for him to come inside. "This is one freaky place," Matt said as they quickly walked to the cafe door. "Let's ask the rancher," Matt said entering the café.

"Who?" Christian asked.

"You'll see," Matt answered.

The guys hurried back inside to ask the rancher about the old Indian. They sat down just as the waitress brought their orders.

"More coffee?" she asked.

"No thanks," they quickly responded, eager to ask the rancher about the Old One.

Back at their seats they picked at their breakfasts while Matt turned to the rancher. "Do you know the old Indian man we've been seeing since last night?"

The rancher stopped sipping his coffee, "What old Indian man?" he asked.

Matt explained in more detail the circumstances of the previous night and the pack out of this morning, making sure not to mention the artifacts placed in Christian's hand during the event. He mentioned the whirlwinds and lightning strikes, including the one that hit near him as if it was purposely aimed in his direction. He mentioned the wall of dust and sand created by the winds.

He thought it best not to mention the shadow dancers since the story seemed crazy enough without them, but he told him of the old man's sudden appearance and disappearance on the mesa and on the ridge near the parking area. He gave details about the man's appearance at the medical center. Christian filled in specific details from the most recent encounter, including an estimate of age, his cold, dark eyes, chiseled face with a small scar under his left eye, his strong stature, and emotionless facial expression.

Christian informed him about the conversation he just had with the old man out by the truck. The rancher leaned forward staring directly into Christian's eyes and asked, "What did he say . . . Exactly?"

Christian responded, “He spoke to me in some Indian language which, for some reason, I could understand.”

“But what did he say to you?” the rancher asked again sternly, sounding more demanding than curious.

“He told me, ‘We are one and the same’ and ‘We are of one tribe.’ Does that make any sense to you?” Christian asked.

“I’ll be damned . . . but it can’t be . . . Hhhhmmmm, it must be . . . true,” the rancher said in a mumbling undertone as he slid back into his chair. The rancher ran his fingers backward through his hair with a sigh, trying to get a grasp on this unbelievable tale. He had heard tales of the gifted ones here and there, but never thought the stories could be true.

It was like he just learned that leprechauns exist. "And you understood what he was saying?” the rancher asked with a now more serious look.

“All of it,” Christian replied.

The rancher sat back and said, “Well I’ll be damned!”

Amy and Tina were sitting quietly on the edge of their seats, listening carefully to all that was being said, occasionally looking at each other, amazed at what was going on. “It sounds to me that the legends might be true after all,” he said, unsure if he even believed it.

- Nine-
The Legend

he rancher began to tell a story of a young Indian boy who had special gifts from early childhood. His magic or 'medicine' as his tribe called it, was said to be powerful beyond imagination. It was said he could speak in many tongues and had abilities that far exceeded others around him, including other shaman.

As he grew he came to be called the 'Star Walker'. It was said he became the strongest of shaman at a very early age, feared by other tribes like the Apache and Navaho. He was thought to commune with the sky riders and possess their knowledge.

"What's a sky rider?" Amy asked.

"Well, I guess they would be what ahhh . . ." he paused for a long moment grasping for the right words. "What we call aliens. . . . Yep, spacemen," the rancher said with a controlled smirk on his face, suggesting disbelief. They all sat in the booth listening intently to the rancher's tale, hardly touching their food. They were mesmerized with the story and the possible connection to their experience.

The rancher continued, "It is told that when he was a young boy he was out with his father on a hunting trip. After tracking a deer his father shot earlier that morning they found the carcass next to a fast moving stream."

"His father was teaching him to thank the gods and animal spirits for the good hunt with traditional song and dance. They then began to prep the deer for transport when the horses spooked. Jumping backward, they came face to face with a large bear."

"The bear was said to be ancient, old from many years and just as big as the years would allow. It had followed the scent of fresh kill to the site."

"The spooked horses had run off with the hunter's weapons, stopping a short distance away and leaving the warrior to fight off the bear with only his bare hands and a small hunting knife. He fought fiercely while his young son helplessly watched his father do battle with the beast."

"The warrior cut and sliced at the bear with his hunting knife as the bear tossed him about effortlessly. The massive bear was far too strong to defeat and ultimately knocked the warrior to his back. He raised his left paw for the final blow meant to finish off the exhausted warrior who was looking anxiously at his son for the last time."

"The warrior, seeing his son charging the bear, cried out to him in a vain attempt to stop him from attacking the bear. The boy's courage was true, but it was too late. His father's attempt to stop him went unheard by the little warrior. His son's attack against the bear with a long thorny switch had begun."

"He reached the great bear at the very moment the bear released his death blow. The little warrior struck the bear in the eye with the thorny switch at the exact moment the bear's paw struck the child. His long, ferocious claws unsheathed, shredded the flesh from the boy's right shoulder and chest and knocked him into the waters of the fast moving stream. The boy floated downstream in and out of consciousness, never to see his father again."

"In a place where the river was calm, the boy came to rest on the shoreline. It has been told that before a tribesman fishing along the riverbank came across the injured boy, many animals had come to him. Nobody knows why, they just did. Next to him, among the many different types of prints leading to and away from the boy, were the large bloody foot prints of a bear with three claws on its left front paw. Clasped in the boy's hand was a lone bear claw."

"Some say it was a sacrifice offered to the boy by the bear, ripped from his paw by his own powerful jaws for killing his warrior father. Others say the father cut the claw from the bear during their battle, and yet others say it was the boy himself who cut the claw from the ancient bear's paw. No one really knows for sure."

"The legend says that from that day on his magic grew. It grew more and more each day until he possessed knowledge beyond the boundaries of civilization. He spoke in many strange tongues and used fighting techniques unknown to this part of the world. His powers of prediction many times saved his tribe from attack by outsiders, and himself from capture by Indians and Whites alike."

"Many years had passed and, as the story goes, he grew so strong that the tribal leaders themselves feared him and wanted to bind him to take his powers away."

"The chief, jealous of his abilities, planned to take his powers by killing him one night long ago as he lay sleeping. He realized that to take the power of a warrior shaman with such strong medicine would ensure his legacy as chief in this life and the next."

"The night came when they were to take the one known as Star Walker. The chief and a few selected tribal leaders and shaman quietly approached the young man's dwelling. As they approached, a large bear roared, waking the Star Walker. Call it fate, destiny or divine intervention, the bear's mighty roar was a warning. Now alert, he was aware of the pending attack."

"The assassins cautiously entered his dwelling, unaware the Star Walker was awake. As soon as they entered the room they heard a low, angry growling voice coming from a dark corner, cursing them for their cowardly actions and betrayal. There was a blinding flash and a clap like the sound of thunder. In an instant the Star Walker was gone, disappearing into the darkness of the night."

"The chief and his assassins searched for the Star Walker until morning without success. The best tracker in the tribe was unable to find a single sign of where he had gone. It was as if he magically disappeared."

"Rumors were heard from traders friendly with the Apache that Cicatrix had been seen in the wilderness. The Apache called him Cicatrix, which means scar. Tales of sightings from the Navaho, who called him Shizid or Deilzhizh or something like that, which roughly translated is the same . . . scar."

"Nothing was said among the would-be assassins, but they all knew their failure would bring big trouble. Then again, they didn't have to say it. It was obvious to all by the look on their faces."

"Folks believe that it was the one-eyed bear that roared to awaken Star Walker. The tribal leaders found large paw prints spread throughout the area outside of Star Walker's dwelling the following day. Paw prints from a bear with three claws on the front left paw."

"The legend says by waking the Star Walker and saving his life, the bear with one eye repaid his debt for killing his warrior father, who then wandered off, never to be seen or heard of again."

"Well, where did The Walker go?" Tina asked.

"The ancients believe he flew to the sky and lived among the sky riders, returning only to seek vengeance on his attackers. He is said to have returned each year to claim the life of one of the assassins on the anniversary of their betrayal until the last assassin was claimed," the rancher explained.

"His story and his legend grew stronger with each passing year, taking one assassin at a time and leaving the rest to suffer the torments of their betrayal. The strength of his medicine grew with the taking of each assassin's life. His victims were found lying in their beds next to their loved ones, one eye missing and two fingers cut clean off the left hand without a drop of blood. Each victim's throat was cut through and through with an object so sharp and fast that the wound was cauterized instantly, leaving only trickles of blood dripping down their throats, resembling a beaded necklace."

"This was bad medicine and the tribe suffered for as many years as there were assassins. Their crops failed, water was scarce, and the hunting and fishing were poor."

"Why did he cut off two fingers?" Amy asked.

"Well, my best guess would be to honor the bear with three claws for waking him, but I don't really know for sure. It's probably something like that."

The rancher continued, "Each assassin was tormented the year through with the thought of his own demise. You see, warriors want to die an honorable or glorious death in battle. The Star Walker's revenge was bad medicine and they believed that their betrayal and a bad death would torment them in the afterlife."

"It has been told that one year the chief had convinced the remaining assassins that the best way to rid the tribe of this bad medicine was to once again attempt to capture and kill the demon. The warriors all knew that in order to redeem themselves and lift the curse from the tribe, the curse they brought upon themselves, was to face and kill the Star Walker, so they laid out their plan."

"On the anniversary of the attempted assassination that year they planned to stay awake in ritualistic prayer with centuries around them. If the Star Walker tried to approach from any direction they could capture and kill him. In doing so they would have redeemed themselves in the eyes of the spirits which would release them from their self-imposed curse."

"What if he didn't show? I mean what if he came and realized he couldn't get to them and just did it another night?" Tina asked.

The rancher paused, "If he didn't show to claim the life of an assassin, his magic would have been broken which would also release them from the curse."

He continued his tale. "They gathered around a fire at sunset. The assassins began chanting and praying to their spirit guides. The chief was taking no chances. He had chosen the bravest and strongest warriors to stand vigil over the group of would-be assassins. He had them form a two ring circle around the group. The outside ring faced away from the fire so they could see anyone or anything that was approaching, and the inside ring was to observe the group and stand ready to fight with the chief and his men."

"The night passed slowly for the group. At sunrise the chief felt positive they had thwarted the Star Walker's revenge for that year and broken the curse. He could make out the silhouettes of the guards in the early morning light, still standing vigil over the group. With weary confidence he stood up, boasting their defeat of the demon Star Walker to his fellow assassins. The others smiled wearily, nodding in agreement with the chief and joined in the celebration of their apparent success."

"As they rose to their feet, the chief patted his brother on the back in celebration. His brother had been sitting directly to his right the entire night. No one had left the circle from sunset the night before, nor did anyone enter. With one touch, his brother's head rolled off his shoulders, bounced off his crossed legs and rolled up to the side of the fire pit, stopping face up and staring back at the chief with one eye, the glow of the red coals in the fire burning like the fires of hell behind it. His torso simultaneously fell backward to the cold ground, his left arm flopped to his side revealing a hand having only three fingers."

"The chief gasped for air and fell back, horrified as he cursed the Star Walker. 'How was this possible? How could the demon do this? He is not man! He is a demon spirit!' the chief said in disbelief. The remaining assassins panicked for fear they had made a bad situation even worse."

"The chief turned angrily and called to his handpicked warrior guards. There was no response, just an eerie silence. He stormed toward the warriors standing only feet away, freezing in his tracks just before them as the dim morning light revealed their fate. He trembled in fear as he stared horrified at the first, then the next and the next. Each was dead, standing unaided in front of him . . . dead."

"It is told that the guards were not killed in the same fashion. There were no cuts, blood, or missing eyes or fingers. Their faces were painfully contorted as if each had died of fright, and their eyes had turned black like polished doll's eyes. Their lifeless bodies stood erect at their posts with weapons in hand, still keeping vigil like sentinels from the abyss itself. It was a very unnatural death that alarmed the chief and his assassins, driving them to near madness."

"As the years passed, the remaining assassins were taken one by one. All were found lying in their beds with one eye gone, two fingers missing from the left hand, and their throats sliced through, each in the same manner. The chief was the last to be taken; however, the details of his death are unknown."

"It is said that on the night of the anniversary, the chief, being the only assassin remaining, bid his family farewell and laid down for the night accepting his fate. The following morning, he was nowhere to be found. A serpent lay next to his wife. As with the others, there was no sound or struggle in the night. His body was never found and could not be laid to rest in the traditional manner, leaving his tormented soul to wander the afterlife without rest for all eternity."

You could have heard a pin drop from the table. The group was in a trance, hypnotized by the incredible story the rancher was telling. Even Matt's attention was fixed on the rancher.

In that moment of dead silence, the waitress accidentally dropped a pan in the kitchen. The loud crashing sound it made when it hit the floor startled them so much that they all flinched violently, knocking over just about everything on the table. "Oh my god, that scared the sh*t out of me!" exclaimed Tina. They all laughed uneasily. It was funny, but that had triggered the last nerve of everyone except the rancher.

He continued, "For years brave hunters searched for the Star Walker, trying to claim his magic. The next generation of hunters were treasure seekers more than hunters, searching for his possessions, some of which were rumored to be from beyond this world if you can believe that," the rancher smirked, "As time passed, these too faded into memory, giving way to thrill seekers looking to get rich from stories of ancient Indian gold and silver hidden somewhere in the many caves and crevices of the desert."

"As the story passed from generation to generation, the true story about his gift was lost to tales of gold and riches, eventually morphing into something more like a pirate's treasure map. To the best of my knowledge no one has ever found a trace of the Star Walker or any riches buried out there."

"Well . . . how is it we saw him just a few minutes ago outside?" Matt asked the rancher.

"Well now that would be impossible wouldn't it? He was an Ancient. You may have seen another local Indian fella we call Old George. He's always wandering around here. Your description sounds like Old George," he said.

Christian jumped in excitedly, "But how could we see him on the trail to the mesa? Then on the ridge while we drove away from Trails End, then see him standing outside the medical center less than 30 minutes later, and just now in the parking lot not a minute after we got here when he was standing on the side of the road three miles away?"

"Ah, you're probably just confusing different old Indians. There's a dozen or more walking in and around town every day. Maybe they're different people altogether," said the rancher.

"I don't think so!" Christian said excitedly standing up to make his point. "This guy had a very distinct look. Not one you easily mistake for anyone else, that's for damn sure!"

A stack of magazines on an old wooden table in the corner of the room caught Christian's eye. "Wait . . . that's him! It's him!" he claimed. Reaching down, he grabbed an old wrinkled magazine. Christian picked up a magazine titled, Local Legends. It was a regional publication with the history of the area including local folk tales, Indian history and legends. "He's right here on the cover," he said confidently, passing the magazine to Matt.

On the cover was a drawing of the Old One. It was a younger version of him, but there was no mistaking him. A cold, dark stare from his sunken eyes, the chiseled face with a small scar under his left eye. His partially exposed chest revealed the claw marks from the one-eyed bear. Around his neck was a single claw hanging by an old piece of rawhide. Matt quickly identified the man's face on the cover of the magazine as the man he had seen three times from a distance and most recently up close through the café window. It was definitely the Old One.

"That can't be," the rancher said with a puzzled look on his face. "This is an artist's rendition of. . . . It's not possible." The rancher reached for the magazine and unfolded the edge of the page revealing Star Walker in faded ink.

The girls reached for another copy of the magazine and began to study the drawing on the cover. Tina pointed out what looked like a beaded necklace wrapped around the warrior's arm. It had a familiar pattern. They asked Christian for the artifacts from his pocket. Not thinking, he reached into his pocket and pulled out all three objects. He selected the beaded necklace and passed it to Amy.

They compared the drawing to the artifact and realized it was not a necklace, it was an armband. The extra un-beaded strings holding feathers at the end in the picture were missing on Christian's band. Tina reached up with the artifact and wrapped it around Christian's arm. "It's the same," Tina said with cautious enthusiasm.

The rancher's eyes opened a bit wider when Christian pulled out the artifacts and passed them to the girls, and even more so when Tina wrapped his arm with the band. He didn't ask about them right off, but all could tell he was very interested. This was proof that the legend existed. "How can this be?" the rancher asked. "It's not possible," he continued with a bewildered look on his face.

Christian, caught up in the moment, pulled open his shirt revealing his scar. "Not possible! Then how can you explain this?" he asked. Everyone stopped talking at once, looking at Christian's exposed chest revealing the jagged three claw scar.

"It's just like the picture," Amy said under her breath.

"Where the hell did that come from?" she asked uneasily while reaching out to touch the scars crossing his chest. "You didn't have a mark on you last night when we checked you."

"Checked him for what?" the rancher inquired.

They looked at one another apprehensively. "Listen, I think you should speak to the sheriff about this." The rancher continued with a serious look on his face, "This could clear up a lot of things with the others who disappeared."

Matt jumped in, "No, that's okay. I think we should just get on our way. We've had enough of this and I don't need to be involved with a 75 year-old missing person's case," he said, gesturing to the girls that it was time to go. "Christian, let's go," he said tugging on his shirt sleeve before walking to the counter to pay the bill. "It was nice talking with you. Have a nice day," Matt said.

The rancher, more curious than ever, watched as Christian and the girls exited the café at Matt's prompting.

They jumped in the truck and headed out of the parking lot, Matt turning the truck onto the road in the direction leading away from the interstate, which Tina picked up on immediately.

"Where're you going?" Tina asked. "We want to go the other way," she said anxiously.

"That rancher knew a lot more than he let on. He's probably calling the sheriff as we speak and I don't want to be tied up with some cowboy constable's missing person's case all day! Who knows, they may even try to charge us with removal of protected artifacts. These are real," he said pointing to the artifacts in Christian's hand. "And who's gonna believe how we got them. I hardly believe it and I was there!"

"Did you see the rancher's face once he saw them? He couldn't take his eyes off of them. There's a lot more to the story and who knows what's up with that. Let's not give them the chance to collect," he added.

Matt continued following his GPS up the road, telling the others, "If we go this way there is a turnoff we can use to backtrack to the highway a few miles up. Hopefully that will put enough distance between us and them."

They reached the highway without further incident. Matt checked the GPS to ensure it was programmed for Vegas. They continued to discuss what happened for most of the seven hour trip. They reviewed everything that occurred over and over so they were all on the same page as far as the details were concerned.

Christian couldn't believe what he was hearing. The things that happened to him on the mesa were still a blur and hard to believe. All he knew was that he now had a set of three artifacts that were part of a puzzle from an old Indian man. A story about an ancient medicine man and an eight inch, jagged, three claw, diagonal scar across his shoulder and chest that appeared out of nowhere and looked like it had been there his entire life.

The questions still remained; who was the old Indian? Was it somehow possible that he was the Star Walker? What did his words mean? What was the gift he spoke of, who was the rancher, and why was he so interested?

-Ten-
Rocking at the Rio

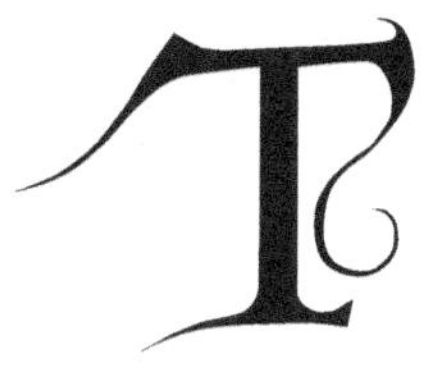

he drive to Vegas flew by. They pulled up to the valet at Rio All Suites Hotel and Casino about three in the afternoon. Grabbing their bags they checked in and headed up to their rooms to clean up. Matt opened the door to the room and walked in, Christian right behind him. "I'm going to jump in the shower," Matt said grabbing a toiletries bag.

Christian dropped his bag on the floor and flopped onto one of the beds and with a sigh of exhaustion he kicked off his shoes. "Nice room," Christian said.

"Yeah, it's great isn't it," Matt replied while heading towards the bathroom. "My uncle plays here a lot so they comp him rooms all the time."

"He must play a lot to get free rooms," Christian said glancing around the room asking, "Hey, where's the minibar? I could use a Coke."

"I don't know, why don't you take a look around? "Matt replied, one foot in the shower. "I'll be out in a minute."

Christian looked around the room for the minibar without luck, thinking to himself, "I guess we don't have one." He walked over to another door that he thought was another closet, thinking maybe it was hidden in there. As he opened the door, a magnificent room appeared in front of him. It was almost palatial. There were soft leather couches, twenty foot tall floor-to-ceiling windows, a fully stocked bar, a gaming table, and a formal dining table all simply finished in light colors.

He stepped into the room cautiously, thinking maybe this was someone else's room. The carpet was so soft it was like walking on air. He stood in the middle of the great room for a moment enjoying the luxurious surroundings and the view through the huge windows when the door on the opposite side of the great room opened slowly, making Christian a little nervous.

"Whew!" It was Amy.

"Oh my god, do you see this? This is incredible!" Seeing Christian standing in the center of the room she ran over to him, excitedly jumped into his arms giving him a big kiss—which Christian happily returned. "This is incredible, did you know about this?" she asked.

"No, I had no idea. I was looking for the minibar," he replied.

"Well there it is!" Amy said pointing to a fully stocked bar with a fresh basket of fruit and snacks on it.

"Is this ours?" Christian asked.

"Yep, it's all ours," Matt replied, standing in the doorway with a towel wrapped around him.

"Wow, this is incredible! Your uncle must really play a lot!" Christian said walking over to the bar and grabbing a snack.

"Yeah my uncle told me he'd set me up nice," he replied.

"Nice?! . . . Nice is an understatement," Amy added with a smile from ear to ear.

A moment later Tina opened the door to the great room, wearing her sweats and a Cal Poly tee. "Oh my god, oh my god, oh my god!" she blurted repeatedly, running into the room and launching herself onto the couch in front of the big screen. "Is this ours?" she asked.

The others looked at each other and all at once replied "Yes, it's ours!" and started to laugh. "C'mon, let's get dressed and head downstairs for a while, then we can hit the strip," Matt said. Everyone jumped at the idea. "We'll meet here in 30 minutes," Matt suggested. Tina and Amy to ran to their room to get ready.

"Thirty minutes isn't much time," Christian said.

"I know, it'll probably take an hour, but if I said an hour, it would take an hour and a half," Matt responded with a knowing smirk on his face." Christian laughed and headed for the shower.

Forty-five minutes had passed and Christian and Matt were watching a game on the big screen in the great room, enjoying a drink. Matt had ordered assorted appetizers that were sitting on the table in front of them when the girls made their entrance. Christian and Matt immediately lost interest in the game.

"Wow, you . . . you look amazing," Christian stuttered, unable to take his eyes off of Amy.

"Not so bad yourself," Amy responded. It's not that Amy was dressed to the max. She had a natural look and beauty about her but this was the first time Christian had actually seen her dressed up a little and wearing makeup.

Matt walked over to Tina, complimenting her on how nice she looked. "Why thank you sir," she replied, planting a kiss on his lips. "Ready to go?" she asked.

"Let's do it!" Matt enthusiastically replied.

They headed down to the lobby, deciding to find a restaurant before hitting the strip. "What do you feel like eating?" Christian asked the girls.

It was a quick decision; the girls looked at each other and replied in stereo, "Italian!"

"Italian it is," he smiled.

The elevator doors opened to the sounds of a thousand slot machines. The casino was jammed with hopeful patrons. Bells were ringing and change was clinking as payoffs hit the collection trays with the unmistakable sound of a winning pull. Lights were flashing throughout the casino and you could just feel the excitement in the air.

The occasional burst of cheers for lucky players erupted at different gaming tables across the floor stimulated even more excitement as they navigated their way through the players and up to the restaurant area.

Upon reaching the restaurant Matt gave his name to the hostess. They walked over to the bar for a drink, but before they could order the hostess came up behind them, "Mr. Henderson, I'm sorry for the wait sir, your table is ready. If you would please follow me." Christian looked at the line of people before them waiting to get into the restaurant.

"Matt, what's going on? There's like an hour wait for a table!"

"It must be my uncle somehow. This is great!" He said in a low tone with a subdued smile on his face. The girls, however, had smiles plastered across their faces. They had never been treated so favorably and they were enjoying it all as they casually walked into a private back room within the restaurant reserved for high rollers and their guests.

The hostess seated them at a large table in the corner of the restaurant. After they were seated she went over to the waiter, spoke briefly with him and exited the room. The waiter arrived at the table shortly after introducing himself, welcoming them to the restaurant and began reciting the specials of the evening before taking the drink order.

He spoke in broken English that was difficult to understand. While reciting the specials he mentioned the Saltimbocca, a veal dish that Amy had heard of before and wanted to try. "What is Saltimbocca?" she politely asked the waiter.

"Ah, Saltimbocca isa de veal witta the sayja, anda, anda, anda, how do you say 'lardo' ina d'english.

"Bacon, with bacon," Christian automatically answered.

"Oh! Il signore parla Italiano?" the waiter said with a smile.

"No, I . . . no, non parlo italiano, Parlo solo inglese," Christian answered the waiter with perfect pronunciation and inflection.

The waiter looked at Christian curiously, "Signore, si parla splendidamente."

Christian replied, "Grazie." The waiter continued reciting the specialties.

Matt, Tina and Amy were very impressed with Christian's ability to speak Italian so well. The waiter left to place the drink order. "That was amazing! Where did you learn to speak Italian so well?" Amy asked casually, reaching out to grab Christian's hand.

"What are you talking about?" asked Christian, "I don't speak Italian."

"But you were just speaking Italian with the waiter," Amy said looking oddly at Christian.

"Yeah man, you just had a conversation with the waiter," Matt repeated.

"Don't you remember?" asked Amy.

Christian sat there with a puzzled look on his face looking at them all. He had no idea that he just had a conversation in Italian. "No, I couldn't have, I never took Italian."

"Well maybe you just forgot," Tina said suggesting another topic. They blew off any further questions and comments on the Italian topic in favor of a great meal and night out.

After an incredible meal and a little R&R, they headed for the strip. Matt walked to the concierge requesting a taxi and went outside to wait. The girls were planning the clubs they wanted to hit when a long stretch pulled up. The driver stepped out and walked around the back of the car to the passenger door and opened it. Tina and Amy stepped back to let the passengers out when the driver said, "Mr. Henderson, your transportation has arrived."

The girls' faces lit up whispering to each other, "This is for us? This is amazing!" with a happy, shrill scream. They jumped into the limo, a smiling Matt and Christian followed behind.

Christian was impressed, giving Matt his look of approval uttering, "Impressive—very impressive."

Being first-timers in Vegas they wanted to hit as many of the clubs as possible, and they did. Arriving at their first choice Tina said, "Wow, look at that line. It's going to take us forever to get in." It seemed there were hundreds of people trying to get into the hottest new club in town. The driver smiled and requested they remain in the car.

He walked up to the entrance and had a discussion with management. Moments later he came back to the car and opened the door. "Your accommodations have been arranged." As they exited the stretch the chauffeur directed them to the club entrance where they were immediately escorted into the building.

"This is like being royalty!" Amy smiled at Christian.

"No—rock stars!" Tina interjected.

At each club they arrived at, the driver would request that they remain in the car. He would leave for a moment and then return and they would be escorted into the building. Of course between clubs the girls couldn't pass up the opportunity to frequently pop out of the sunroof, celebrating the strip. They ended up their incredible night dancing at the Marquee.

Exhausted, they headed back to the room around 3 a.m. They walked, in dragging their feet, plopping down on the couches in the great room while still talking about the night when Tina stood up, reached for Matt's hand, said goodnight to Amy and Christian while winking at Amy as she walked away. Amy and Christian talked a while longer then headed to the other room for the night.

Christian was restless, tossing and turning, so he decided to slip out to the great room early in the morning. He watched as dawn greeted the day through the floor-to-ceiling windows. The morning brought a beautiful sunrise climbing from behind the foothills. As he enjoyed the morning view, Amy entered, slowly walking over to him and sleepily wrapping her arms around his waist from behind. She gently kissed the back of his neck whispering, "Come back to bed, you need your rest."

Christian softly smiled, pulling her hands tight in front of him and sighed with contentment. "Okay, I'll be in in a minute." He stood there for a moment longer thinking of the early morning fishing trips he had taken with family and friends, watching the sunrise over the Atlantic just before the morning bite. It was the first time he felt truly relaxed since he arrived at Cal Poly.

It was late morning when they heard, "Breakfast is served." Slowly walking from their rooms and wiping the sleep from their eyes, they entered the great room one by one. Standing in the great room was a butler with a large cart carrying a magnificent breakfast assortment with a fold-out omelet station, "Compliments of Dr. Henderson. He has additionally taken the liberty to arrange en-suite massages for you following breakfast unless, of course, you prefer to use the steam, sauna and massage facilities in the spa."

"I am Martin and I will be preparing and serving your breakfast this morning." Martin poured coffee and tea water then prepared the morning meal of choice for each of them. They were on cloud nine and kept insisting Marty sit down with them and have some breakfast. He eloquently declined.

Shortly after the service was complete, Martin excused himself, removing the service cart and motioning the massage therapist team to enter. They entered with introductions and instructions for preparation before the massages. The couples exited the great room for hot showers as the massage team set up.

"My god, can you believe this? This is the most unbelievably fantastic thing that I have ever experienced," Amy said with the look of obvious excitement on her face.

"Yeah, it's okay," Christian said jokingly.

"What? It's okay, what's wrong with you?" Amy asked, playfully smacking Christian's arm.

He started laughing, "Yeah this is . . . very, very *okay*!"

After a welcome hot shower they re-entered the great room dressed only in the hotel's plush terry cloth robes to find a team of four massage therapists standing next to double stations separated by partitions that had been set up while they were showering. Matt looked at Christian giving him a wink, "Now this is the life, isn't it?"

Christian timidly nodded in approval and was directed to a table. "I've never had a massage before . . . I'm not sure what I . . . ."

Amy jumped on the table next to him, "Well, we wouldn't want to disappoint the doctor, now would we?" Christian smiled and followed suit.

Amy and Christian headed to the poolside party for the afternoon. Matt and Tina decided to meet up with them a little later in the afternoon. They lounged in the sun and enjoyed tropical drinks as they planned their evening. Christian wanted to try his luck in the casino before heading out on the town.

The energy around the pool was infectious. The DJ was cranking and hundreds of party goers were dancing in the early afternoon sun. Matt and Tina arrived and joined them on the dance floor. After working up a sweat dancing, Amy and Tina jumped into the pool to cool down for a while as Matt and Christian sat talking and watching the endless parade of people moving around the pool deck which seconded as a dance floor for the multitude of partiers.

Of course, it goes without saying that when two such attractive and shapely women are standing alone that they would draw the attention of other admirers.

After watching the girls turn down multiple advances from a number of studly party goers attempting to hook up, Matt and Christian hopped into the pool. "You guys jealous?" Tina smirked coyly. Amy laughed along with her.

Matt smiled snidely at Tina and then lunged forward playfully, dunking her in the pool. Amy wasn't going to give Christian the chance and jumped on him in a vain attempt to dunk him. He played along and fell backward into the water. Tina, by this time, had wrestled her way to the top and was holding Matt underwater, which was until he grabbed her legs pulling her under as well. They played around for a while before exiting the pool and headed back to the room to change.

After the pool party the girls went shopping for a few items as the guys rested on the couch watching a game and finalizing their plans.

Christian and Matt headed down to the casino as the girls prepared themselves for the night. They were going to meet them when they finished getting ready to go out. Matt and Christian wanted to surprise them by taking them to a show before hitting the strip. Avoiding the dramas and male reviews, the guys elected to go to a comedy show and, as luck would have it, *Fluffy* was in town.

Matt arranged for the tickets and they picked them up at the desk before hitting the tables. "What do you want to play?" Matt asked.

"What about poker?" Christian responded.

"Have you ever played before?" Matt asked.

"Not since I was a kid," Christian smiled.

"I don't think you want Vegas to teach you how to play poker. It'll be a hard lesson if you know what I mean," Matt suggested.

Christian laughed, "I just want to sit in for a hand or two and see what it's like."

"Okay if that's what you want, but you sure you wouldn't want to try Black Jack first?" Matt asked, convinced he was going to lose his shirt.

"No, I'm good. Let's sit at this table," he suggested to Matt.

"No thanks buddy, you're on your own. . . . Poker's not my game," Matt smiled, taking the opportunity to hit the nearby slots.

After making his deposit in the slots, Matt returned to see a crowd of people gathering around the table. He worked his way in, positioning himself behind Christian to watch. In twenty minutes he had compiled four stacks of chips and was playing double hands.

The girls were up in the room putting the final touches on the masterpiece that was them. Amy was dressing in her new clothes that they laid out on the bed while Tina was blowing out her hair. "Tina, how are things going with you and Matt? Things seem pretty hot between you two!" Amy inquired, talking over the blow dryer.

Tina replied, "Good—real good," she responded, smiling as she finished her hair, the high pitch whine of the blow dryer trouncing on every word.

Now dressed, they went to check the great room to see if the guys came back. Not finding them, Tina texted Matt, "Where are you?" and they headed to the casino as planned. They hopped onto the first elevator and headed south to the casino.

The doors opened to a packed casino. The sounds from all of the gaming machines seemed to blend together into a loud hum. Bells and buzzers were sounding everywhere. The strange sounds from the electronic games created an atmosphere more conducive of an arcade than that of a casino. An adult arcade, of course! Matt's reply came through as they exited the elevator, "Poker table to the right of the bar, YWBT!"

The girls headed across to the opposite side of the casino. They heard occasional outbursts from happy players at different tables as they passed through the main channels on the casino floor. As they approached they could see a large crowd around one table. Everything seemed to get quiet as they got closer and just before reaching the crowd, the onlookers burst into applause, cheering loudly as the last hand closed.

The girls were standing at the back of the crowd trying to look in at what was going on when Matt's hand reached out from between the patrons, grabbing Tina's arm while pulling her and Amy into the crowd. Tina was startled, jumping back and letting out a little yelp. "What the hell are you doing? You scared the hell out of me!" She blurted with clenched teeth in a suppressed voice. The viewers were still cheering. "What's happening?" Tina asked. Matt didn't hear her, he just pulled them in and pointed at the pile of chips in front of Christian.

Amy looked across the table to see Christian sitting in the fourth position with a pile of chips in front of him. The dealer was dealing him two hands. She was excited for him at first but then she noticed something different about the way he looked. As the crowd came to a hush, Amy whispered to Tina, "Do you see anything different about him? He looks different."

"He looks fine to me. It's probably just the lights. Can you believe how much money he's won?" Tina asked.

Christian played another winning hand before leaving the table with just shy of eighteen thousand dollars. Not bad for an hour's work! He passed the dealer two one-hundred dollar chips as he got up from the table. The crowd broke into applause as did the dealer. He nodded as if tipping his hat to the crowd in appreciation of their applause. As he stepped back into better lighting Amy's suspicions were confirmed.

He did look different, his eyes seemed dark. Matt and Tina didn't notice it because they were too busy celebrating his success. Her concerns wavered with all the excitement and she blew it off to lighting and fatigue, joining the others in applauding his success as he made his way through the crowd.

"I thought you said you didn't play poker?" Matt claimed, patting him on the back as he broke through the crowd.

"I only played as a kid with my parents and friends," he said smiling, looking at his pile of chips.

As he cleared his admiring fans, Amy came into full view. He couldn't take his eyes off of her. "You look gorgeous!" he said smiling. She was wearing a sheer party dress and heels. "I didn't know you were going shopping-shopping," he said admiring her. "You look incredible!"

Amy threw her arms around him and gave him a big kiss. His compliment diffused any concerns she had and her excitement for the moment returned. "I can't believe you won all that money!!!" she said, exhilarated. She examined his eyes closely. "It must have been my imagination," she thought to herself.

"Beginner's luck," Christian smiled. "Beginner's luck."

He cashed in his chips and the group headed out to hit the town again. They caught *Fluffy's* first show before hitting the clubs they missed the night before. On the way through the casino Christian insisted they all try their luck on some machines with some of the winnings he had. They resisted at first but Christian wasn't taking no for an answer. They played for a few minutes with nominal success then headed for the clubs.

Later that evening at one of the clubs they were standing at the bar talking when an overly enthusiastic partier bumped into Christian, spilling his own drink on himself. Christian automatically said, “Excuse me,” and returned to his conversation, thinking nothing of it.

The wobbly guest started talking loudly, “You bet your ass you’re sorry, you . . . you owe me a drink.”

Matt looked at Christian in laughable disbelief saying, “Don’t waste your time with this guy, he looks like he started early.”

Christian nodded in agreement as ‘Wobbles’ poked him, attempting to get his attention. After a minute he turned to address the overly enthusiastic partier. “Excuse me, you bumped into me and spilled your own drink. I don’t owe you anything and I’d appreciate you leaving us alone,” he said firmly to the partier.

As soon as he finished his statement, low and behold there were two obnoxious partiers. The second was a massive, big and thick type who was more obnoxious than drunk. He asked, “What’s going on over here?”

His friend regaled him with the slurring version of the events and surprise, surprise he sided with his friend and demanded Christian buy them both drinks.

Christian smiled, “I don’t think so. Why don’t you guys just leave us alone and let everyone enjoy the night?”

‘Big Heavy’ started poking Christian’s chest with his railroad spike stub of a finger. “Don’t you tell me what to do pretty boy, I’ll drop your ass where it stands,” a dribble of his beer dripping from the corner of his mouth. Now you owe us some drinks,” he said with ‘Wobbles’ grinning alongside.

Matt, anticipating trouble, moved the girls to his other side to distance them a bit further from their new friends. As he turned to support Christian he saw the big man slowly dropping to his knees. As he closed in he could hear Christian say, “Now apologize and leave.”

The big man slowly stood up with the look of fear in his eyes. He apologized and left the area, pulling his wobbly friend along with him. Matt stood for a moment, bewildered and trying to figure it out before asking, "What the hell happened there?"

As Christian turned to answer, Amy caught a glimpse of his eyes. Again, they looked dark and distant, just like at the casino. Matt stepped into her line of view and by the time she could see his face again his eyes had returned to crystal blue. She had a weird feeling and couldn't stop thinking how strange it was to see this not once, but twice.

"I'm not sure, but I don't think they were used to having people treat them like that," Christian answered.

Matt said continuing, "What the hell happened there?" he asked again. "One minute it looked like a fight was going to break out and the next Big Lou is apologizing and walking away. How'd you manage that?"

Christian smiled and said, "Manage what?"

Matt looked at him strangely and repeated, "How did you manage that?" Christian did not respond.

Morning came and so did Martin. He served breakfast to the weary group and asked if there was anything else he could do for them. He thanked them for staying at the hotel and departed with a generous gratuity.

Everyone got ready for the trip home. After showering, Christian started to dress, and while tucking his clothes into his duffle he saw an envelope. He reached in, grabbed it and folded over the flap to find a wad of cash. A little confused he asked, "Hey Matt, where did this come from?"

Matt looked at him holding the envelope full of cash, "You're kidding right?"

Christian thought for a moment, "Yeah, just kidding," he said with a bewildered look on his face.

The trip back to Cal Poly was uneventful. The guys shared the driving and talked about the weekend. The girls were unconscious in the back for most of the trip, waking up off and on and offering to drive to which Christian was quick to reply, "No, that's okay . . . we've got it," remembering Amy's imaginary high speed pursuit on I-40. Matt again enlightened Christian to some of the stranger events that had transpired. It was apparent to him that Christian was still fuzzy on the details. He urged him to get another checkup when they got back.

One thing was still bothering Matt. He still couldn't understand how Christian survived it all. A bolt of lightning that struck in front of him sent him flying into a tree almost killing him, yet for a few moments a bolt passed through Christian's body and didn't even leave a scratch. He kept his thoughts to himself so as not to stir up any anxiety in Christian.

- Eleven-
Connections to the Past

hey made great time back to Cal Poly. They unpacked the truck and went their separate ways. Tina and Amy thanked the guys for an incredible weekend. Even though she had the greatest time of her life in Vegas, Amy couldn't stop thinking about what had happened in Mule Canyon, in Blandings the next day, or the strange look Christian had on his face a few times in Vegas. Something just wasn't right with him since the mesa. She couldn't put her finger on it. He had somehow changed, but yet was still the same.

If it were up to her, Amy would have watched over Christian all night, but she couldn't. She had a tremendous amount of work to complete for the morning. She leaned into him, giving him a kiss goodnight. "Take care of yourself, I'll see you tomorrow. Text me!" She then yelled to Matt," Hey Matt, look after him for me tonight, ok."

Matt nodded, confirming he would watch after him.

Matt and Christian reached their dorm room and tossed their bags on the floor. "That was some interesting weekend, huh?" Matt asked as he changed into sweats. "How are you feeling?" he asked Christian.

"I'm fine, just a little tired from everything," Christian yawned.

Matt looked at him with curiosity, "What are you going to tell your parents?"

"I don't know yet," he replied.

"Well you're going have to tell them something. I can't see how you're going to hide that scar across your chest or the fact that you learned to speak perfect Italian overnight," Matt said with growing concern.

"We'll see, I just need to think about it for a few days. If I mention anything to them now they'll freak out and I don't want them to worry. I think they have enough on their plates without this. Besides, I've only been here for a few weeks."

"Well, you better think quick . . . we have Thanksgiving break coming up and unless you can get rid of that scar, you'll have some 'splaining to do," Matt jokingly added in his best Ricky Ricardo voice.

Christian smirked, "I'm sure I'll think of something."

An exhausted Christian sat quietly on the edge of his bed, thinking about the events of the weekend and wondering how he could explain any of this to his parents, or anyone else for that matter. Matt had already passed out from exhaustion. He needed to tell someone about everything that happened, someone close, someone he could trust not to say a word to anyone. Hailey popped into his mind, which brought a smile to his face.

He wanted to call her since it was still early California time. He wanted to talk about the adventure but second guessed that move and simply texted, "Hailey . . . miss you, I hope we can talk soon!" and hit 'send'. He had no idea where she was since she travelled regularly for work. He lay in his bed quietly thinking for another half hour before falling asleep.

It was about twelve-thirty a.m. when Matt was awakened by strange noises coming from Christian's side of the room. Sitting up in bed he whispered loudly, "Christian . . . Christian, are you awake?" A few moments had passed when he thought he heard a response coming from the darkness on Christian's side of the room.

The response was like nothing he had ever heard before. It was almost unnatural. It was a strange guttural sound with clicking and popping noises like some ancient bird language from the Librarian movies coming from the dark that was very unnerving. He wearily sat up on the edge of his bed, wiping the sleep from his eyes. He turned on a small nightlight and began quietly watching as Christian wrestled with sleep. He was tossing and turning as if he were doing battle with his blankets.

He heard Christian speaking multiple languages, often mixed with the unfamiliar guttural sounds that had originally woken him. He began to write in his journal what was happening, watching and listening intently for the next two plus hours as Christian cycled through periods of restlessness and calm. Matt listened as he changed languages between each active period like he was changing the channel on his TV.

He documented the languages he was sure of; Latin, German, Italian, French and an Asian dialect, among others. He was sure that it was an Asian language, but he wasn't sure which dialect. Others he described to the best of his ability before realizing he could record them with his phone. *Son of a . . .,* he thought to himself as he grabbed his phone to record the remainder of the event.

It was hours before Christian quieted down allowing Matt to try and get some sleep. He slept lightly in case things with Christian started up again.

Matt woke the next morning to see Christian sitting on the side of his bed. He was a mess with his hair wet from profuse sweating, looking like he'd been to hell and back. The bags under his eyes were pronounced. His color was paler than usual and he appeared sickly, like he had the flu.

"Hey buddy, how ya doing?" Matt asked apprehensively.

Christian slowly looked up and jokingly replied, "I feel like I got hit by a train."

"Yeah, you were pretty restless last night. Bad dreams?" Matt inquired.

"I guess . . . I can't remember much detail," Christian replied.

"Well you look like sh*t! How about I go get us some breakfast and bring it back?" Matt asked.

"Sure, sounds good, thanks," he replied. Matt got dressed and headed out the door, looking back at Christian. "Do you need anything else?"

"No, I'm good, thanks. I'm going hit the shower."

Matt returned 30 minutes later with breakfast sandwiches. Christian was already dressed and looking better but still a little green around the gills. He was ready to head out to classes for the day.

Matt tossed Christian's sandwich to him and placed a coffee on the desk, "So, how'd you sleep last night?" he inquired again.

"Not so good," Christian responded weakly.

"Tell me about it! You were tossing and turning all night," said Matt, forcing a laugh.

"I had the weirdest dreams," Christian said, peaking Matt's interest further.

"Oh yeah, what about?" he asked.

"I can't remember a lot about them, but I do remember they all ended with someone dying. It seemed as if I was there when it happened. They all seemed real somehow, one after another.

Weird, really weird," Christian answered in deep thought, trying to remember more details about each dream.

"Sounds pretty strange. No wonder you were tossing and turning all night," Matt added.

They finished breakfast and Matt suggested Christian stay in and get some rest for the day. "I can bring back any work after classes."

"No, I'll be fine, let's get out of here," Christian said grabbing his bag and heading out the door.

Christian, moving sluggishly at first, headed toward his first class with Matt. Crossing through the campus he and Matt bumped into Tina.

"Hey, what's up?" Tina asked giving Matt a peck on the cheek. "Wow, Christian you look like—" she interrupted herself. "Are you ok?"

"Yeah, I'm fine, thanks . . . just had a rough night," Christian responded. "Hey look, I'm going to head to class. I'll see you guys later," as he headed to his first class.

Tina and Matt continued. "My god, what the hell happened last night? He looks like sh*t," Tina asked.

"He just has the flu or something," Matt replied, avoiding the specifics and quickly changed the topic. "What are you and Amy doing this weekend?" he asked.

"No plans yet. Any ideas?" she asked.

"They've got a car show, Oktoberfest this weekend in Baywood Park. Want to check it out? It's supposed to be pretty good."

"Sure, sounds good, but can we do it Saturday? I'm busy Friday with some family stuff," Tina asked, thinking about what she really needed to do on Friday.

"Saturday works," replied Matt.

"Perfect, I'll check with Amy and get back to you," she smiled.

"Great then, you and Amy put it together and we'll hook up for the weekend."

"Sounds good, I'll talk to you later. . . . Gotta go, bye!" she said hurriedly, realizing she was late for her first class.

-Twelve-
Octoberfest

he week passed without further incident. Christian was feeling better and busied himself with his classwork which, for some reason, seemed to go easier this week, regardless of the increased degree of difficulty. He couldn't explain it, but somehow his mind was crisp and quick like a computer. He began to calculate difficult equations in his head. The plans he was drawing seemed to appear without thought, spewing from his mind to his hand and onto the paper. His only thoughts were, "My studying must be paying off."

Tina and Matt had firmed up the plans for Saturday at the Oktoberfest celebration. Baywood is a small community set upon a peninsula with a few shops, restaurants and local artist shops. The quaint town closes down its main street for the Oktoberfest celebration. Thousands of attendees visit the quiet town during the celebration and enjoy the shops, scenery, and autumn plantings. At the end of Main Street is a small pier jutting out into Morro Bay Estuary, providing photo hounds the opportunity to capitalize on the picturesque landscape, dunes, calm waters and a hilltop backdrop across the bay. The occasional sail is unfurled for an autumn cruise.

Christian and Amy planned to meet up with Matt and Tina around noon by the pier. By the time they met, the cool morning had given way to a beautifully warm and sunny October day. Tina was wrapped in Matt's arms on the pier when they arrived. Amy called to them, "Hey guys, what's up?"

They greeted each other and headed up Second Street through town. The street was festively decorated with autumn harvest fair and the girls were popping in and out of the local shops, checking out some of the street vendors and artists. Christian and Matt were following along, weaving in and out of sidewalk shoppers, talking about a few of the older structures within the town, but what Christian really wanted to do was to check out the cars that were set up in the town parking lot. Amy and Tina rejoined the guys, Tina talking about a jacket she was interested in that was in one of the shops.

Christian took the lead and started heading toward the cars. Amy playfully locked arms with him, "Let's go check out the cars." Christian smiled and picked up the pace a little.

As they walked up the short hill to the parking lot they heard a familiar voice, "Oh, hello Amy," she heard the sleazy voice say. Amy cringed, knowing the voice well.

Tina turned to see that it was RJ walking right behind them. "What are you doing here?" Amy demanded to know as Christian stared at him in defiance of his presence.

"I just thought I'd check to see if there was anything worthwhile around. Seems like I'm looking in the wrong place," he said snidely as his buddies Jesse and Simon snickered to themselves. Jesse and Simon were tagalongs. They were weak-minded, immature types that thought hanging out with RJ would somehow bring them status or respect. RJ used them like he used everyone else.

An obviously agitated Christian moved toward RJ and postured himself as if ready to make a stand. Matt stepped in between the two of them as RJ replied in kind, stepping up while asking in a gruff tone, "What, are you looking for another ass whooping? What are you a tough guy now? Right now, let's do it," RJ growled, pushing forward toward Christian as Matt strained to hold them apart.

Jesse and Simon started moving in to assist RJ just as Daniel and Hunter arrived. "What's the problem here?" Hunter asked with his strong accent, his inquiry stopping Jesse and Simon in their tracks.

The two cowardly sidekicks started shying backward as RJ glared over at Daniel and Hunter, obviously annoyed with their timing The odds no longer being in his favor, RJ reluctantly backed down as he answered, "Oh, there's no problem here, at least nothing that can't be handled later." RJ scowled at Christian, "We'll finish this later."

RJ watched Daniel and Hunter from the corner of his eye as he turned to walk away, pushing Jesse and Simon down the hill and mumbling, "We'll take care of this later. He won't always have that Euro trash around to save his ass." He turned back frequently looking angrily at Christian as the trio of misfits made their escape.

"What was that about?" Daniel asked.

"Oh, the three of them gave our buddy here a little beating one night," Matt explained, putting his arm around Christian and shaking him a bit.

"Really?" Daniel said inquisitively.

"Good to know," Hunter added with his strong accent. "I don't like people like dat. They act tuff together, but are voosies mitout each other."

"What's a voosie?" Tina asked then thought about it. "Ohhh." The girls looked at Hunter, trying to hold back their laughter unsuccessfully. Hunter's accent and vocal inflection added a special giddiness to the statement. Tina, on the verge of tears again asked, "What's a Voosie?"

"Day are," he replied, suggesting that the three delinquents were. This caused the group to crack up laughing. Hunter also joined in laughing as they made their way up to the cars.

Christian walked through the show explaining details of the cars he admired most to Amy with as much enthusiasm as a kid looking at toys at Christmas. He explained details far beyond Amy's interest level although she stood by and listened with as much enthusiasm as she could muster. He stopped at every Ford and discussed the rebuild he and his father had worked on for the past few years. He took pictures out of his wallet, proudly displaying his mistress from 1970.

While he was involved in one particularly long conversation with a car owner about compression issues, something caught Amy's eye. She excused herself and stepped away briefly, returning with a little brown bag. She didn't think he even knew she had left his side. They were still talking cars when she returned. She said, "Miss me?" and playfully urged Christian to move on.

As they moved through the crowd, Amy waved the little brown bag in front of Christian, ensuring she had his full attention. "Hey, look what I found," she said smiling as she reached into the bag jiggling the contents.

"What is it?" he asked.

"You'll have to guess . . . All I can say is that it's a present for you," she said playfully.

"Is it a taco?"

"No."

"A burger?"

"No."

"A pretzel?"

"No—what's with you and food today?"

"I give up. What is it?" he asked grabbing for the bag unsuccessfully.

"Ha, ha, ha," Amy laughed, withdrawing the bag quickly, preventing Christian from grabbing hold. She turned away coyly, pulling the bag close in and slowly opened it to look in. "I think you're going to like it. . . ."

Christian's interest was piqued further when his attempts to look over her shoulders to see what might be in the bag failed.

She slowly lifted the gift from the bag revealing a vintage Ford Mustang key chain. "That's awesome, where did you find that?" Christian asked.

"Well, while you were busy talking shop, I found this little baby!" she said proudly. "It's from the seventies, just not sure which year exactly. I thought you'd like it."

"Like it, it's perfect! It even has the same blue as my 302," he responded giving Amy a hug and kiss.

"Now you have to give me a ride in it!" she smiled.

They headed over to Matt and Tina who were more interested in admiring the dogs wearing sunglasses than they were the cars. "You guys hungry?" Amy asked.

"Brats and Beer?" Matt asked.

"Mmmm," Tina said rubbing her stomach. "That sounds good."

They made their way through the crowd to the food court. Daniel and Hunter had made their way there earlier to get something to eat along with a couple of cold beers. They were doubled up with beers like it was Happy Hour. Daniel directed Matt and Christian to the best beer and brat stand.

The afternoon passed quickly. They walked the park, relaxed for a while under some trees by the shoreline, then returned to the quaint village shops. Tina decided to drag Matt to the shop where she saw the jacket she wanted. "Hey guys, we're gonna head in here to check out that jacket again," she said with a touch of excitement.

Matt appeared as thrilled as any other guy going shopping. "Have fun you two," Christian said, razzing Matt with a smirk.

Amy, with a touch of the giggles said, "We're going to walk the boardwalk while you guys shop. I want to pick a spot to see the sunset."

"No problem, we'll see you there," Tina responded with a thumbs up, heading into the shop with Matt.

Christian and Amy slowly walked on the narrow wooden path running along the shoreline. They walked for a while, finding a nice spot next to a small beach with a couple of small catamarans. They sat on the sand at the edge of the boardwalk and looked across Morro Bay. The quiet setting was romantic and Amy couldn't resist—she leaned into Christian and started to kiss him.

The romantic moment was cut short only minutes later. Christian's sixth sense kicked in, telling him that something wasn't right. He paused for a moment, then noticed that RJ and his friends were standing around them, now with one extra tagalong. This was a muscle head named Garrett who RJ had dredged up, undoubtedly to offset the possible presence of Hunter and Daniel.

"Look who it is," RJ said grinning as he panned across his three accomplices. "I told you we'd settle this later." Jesse and Simon stood silently with the look of confident stupidity on their faces.

Christian leapt up. "What's your problem now? I don't think we—"

"That's right, you don't think!" RJ interrupted. "If you thought, you wouldn't be out here all alone about to get your ass kicked."

Christian smirked, "Ok, have at it," he casually responded with smooth confidence.

"No . . . just knock it off," Amy demanded, now angrier with RJ's persistence than nervous about the situation as she jumped in between Christian and the group.

Looking angrily at RJ, "What the hell do you want? It's over, let it go for Christ's sake!" Amy shouted.

"I don't think so! I'm going to give the champ here another shot, then I'm going to kick his ass across the beach. . . . Let's see what you got! Nobody's here to save your ass now!" RJ said as he leered at Christian with pompous arrogance, one corner of his mouth raised slightly as he started to slowly circle.

"What, are you high? It's four against one!" Amy shouted.

RJ pushed Amy backward into the hands of Jesse and Simon. "Hold this bitch!" RJ growled while he started moving toward Christian with Garrett close behind, and Jesse and Simon coaxing him on.

Amy's frantic attempts to break free yielded little success. She watched nervously as RJ pulled back to throw his first punch, a miss. Christian easily evaded the haymaker. He tried again, another miss. Christian easily evaded each of his attempts. "Not so easy this time!" she shouted, grinning.

RJ, now embarrassed having thrown his best and missing, started throwing a volley of uncoordinated punches, trying to land at least one as Christian continued to skillfully block and evade them. RJ became increasingly enraged with each miss, his anger causing increased awkwardness in his attempts to strike Christian. He motioned for help from his friends.

Jesse and Simon tossed Amy down on the sand and all four started to close in on Christian. Amy jumped up, grabbing Garrett's arm from behind in an attempt to restrain him, and was again shoved to the ground.

The activity startled a couple of girls walking by on the boardwalk. They nervously ran past the scuffle as Amy shouted frantically to them, "Get help. Please!" The girls ran back toward the fair.

The four closed in on Christian, RJ shouting orders to block any escape route. "Grab him!" he yelled. Jesse grabbed Christian from behind as RJ lunged forward with a punch. Christian spun Jesse around into the path of RJ's swing, the punch connecting with the back of Jesse's head with a thud.

"Ouch, what the . . .?" Jesse said as RJ shook the pain from his hand.

Christian, in an instant, simultaneously grabbed Jesse's groin and pulled down hard with his left hand while raising his right shoulder and stepped out with his left foot, placing it behind Jesse, allowing him to duck out of the bear hug. He tagged him with a restrained ridge hand under his jaw.

The shot to Jesse's throat lifted him off the ground and sent him flying backward, laying him out flat. He gasped for air as he rolled on the ground holding his throat. RJ looked at Christian with a look of bewilderment, "Get him—kick his ass," he angrily shouted to Simon and Garrett.

Together the three remaining men ran at Christian. He began blocking and throwing punches, moving in between his three assailants with grace and speed, tossing them about like they were rag dolls. He tossed RJ against one of the boats. He turned to the others, redirecting their punches into thin air and occasionally into each other while playfully striking them with lightning speed.

Matt and Tina had just started up the boardwalk, Tina sporting a new jacket, when they saw the excited girls running toward security. His interest piqued as he listened to the girls frantically telling their story to a security guard. When Matt heard that there were four against one he knew immediately it was RJ. He and Tina went running up the boardwalk.

They had a good head start on the crowd and were in eyesight of the melee when Matt stopped dead in his tracks with his jaw wide opened "What the hell is this?" he questioned curiously under his breath.

Tina, panting by his side from the run up the boardwalk, coughed up an, "Oh . . . my god!"

They watched for a moment in amazement as Christian skillfully fended off repeated attempts by his attackers. He placed Simon in a wrist lock, pulling him around with him as he countered Garrett's attempts to connect. Christian ducked one of Garrett's left hooks that connected with Simon's face, taking him down for the count. Garrett's final rush quickly came to an end when Christian dropped him with one strike to his solar plexus. He stood breathless with arms folded across his chest as his knees buckled beneath him.

Christian was standing in stunned victory, admiring his handiwork when RJ raised himself from the ground and picked up a long wooden paddle. Raising it up overhead, he rushed toward Christian from behind. Amy shouted, "Watch out!" Christian quickly spun around, catching the paddle in its downward thrust with one hand, the other striking it hard in the midsection, splitting it in two.

RJ, completely dumbfounded, stared in disbelief at Christian before he sprang forward with the remaining section of the pole for another attempt. Christian, with perfect timing, launched himself, twisted into the air executing a perfect sweeping kick that connected with the side of RJ's head. With a loud slap, he sent both him and the pole flying for the last time.

He turned back to the two remaining assailants, looking at them with unforgiving eyes as if to warn them not to proceed. Simon edged forward, then hesitated, taking the hint, unlike Garrett who moved in for one more attempt. He grabbed half of the broken paddle that RJ had dropped and lunged toward Christian, ready to strike. Christian evaded the advance and proceeded to drop his assailant with a flurry of strikes and a spinning kick, dropping him to the ground. It was over.

Christian directed his attention to the boardwalk where Matt and Tina had watched the melee with amazement. Tina rushed over to Amy, helping her up from the sand. They all looked on in wonderment as Christian stood triumphantly in the center of the four would-be assailants with a glazed stoic look on his face, his eyes dark and emotionless.

Simon nervously looked at Christian and backed away. He pushed Jesse over to RJ saying, "Help him," and bent down to pick up Garrett who was reeling on the ground. Amy hesitantly moved toward Christian, looking curiously at him as she approached. Christian had a blank expression on his face as if he wasn't present. She slowly reached for his hand. "Are you okay?" she asked, lifting the hand that split the pole to look for signs of injury. Christian nodded to communicate that he was fine. He was only slightly winded and without any other noticeable injury.

"What was that? I thought you didn't know how to fight," she said, relieved that it was over. "Where did you learn how to do that?" she asked.

"I don't know," he responded searching for the answer. "I don't know," he said faintly and a little dazed.

Matt and Tina jumped in, "Holy crap, that was amazing!" Matt said, patting him on the back.

Christian looked at him with a baffled expression. "What was amazing?" He seemed more confused than ever. Matt looked oddly at him.

It was as if he had completely forgotten what had just happened. Hearing the noise from the crowd heading up the boardwalk he insisted, "Let's get out of here," as he pulled Christian to the boardwalk. They passed fair security who were making their way to the fight scene. Matt quickly pointed up the boardwalk telling them, "It's just up there, four guys just playing around."

Security looked them up and down, pausing extra-long while observing Christian's blank expression before proceeding up the boardwalk. "Whew! I thought they had us," Tina said nervously.

"It's probably not a good idea to hang around," Amy said. "They're probably going to rat us out first chance they get."

"I wouldn't worry about that," Matt said. "I'd be more worried about his next try. You know as well as I do that his father isn't going to like this and RJ will twist it all around making you out to be the bad guy." He looked at Christian.

"Probably," Amy agreed. They started their walk through the town back to the cars as fast as they could without raising suspicion.

Christian's senses were kicking in again. He couldn't shake the feeling that he was being watched since the time they left the boardwalk and started to walk through town. He casually looked around the crowd and didn't notice anyone specific, but he felt sure he was being watched.

By the time they reached the car Christian was back to his usual self. The heightened senses had subsided. Better to be safe than sorry, they elected to go elsewhere for dinner. Matt, Tina and Amy regaled Christian with their respective versions of the altercation over dinner. Christian absorbed their renditions, comparing them with his foggy memory. After dinner the girls wanted to head out to a club and tried to coerce Matt and Christian to come along. Christian made his excuses and had Matt drop him off at the dorm before going off to meet up with the girls.

Matt and the girls headed out to one of the many clubs in the area. They grabbed a table and ordered some drinks. Amy started off the conversation with her concerns about Christian and his immediate memory loss following these remarkable events. "It's weird. How can anyone forget something like this a second after it's over?" she asked.

"I don't know, but it can't get any stranger," Matt chimed in. "I mean, we've witnessed some amazing things over the past couple of weeks, and as strange as it is to us, how do you think he feels? He knows something happened but he can't remember the details, even after we tell him what happened. . . . That would drive me nuts."

"Maybe we need to give him some time," Tina interjected. "Let him figure it out."

Amy objected, "I don't think that's a good idea. We need to watch him more now than ever. After the fight he just stood there with that glazed look on his face. It was kind of like he was catatonic or something."

"I agree." Matt added, "We can't leave him on his own for too long until he gets a grip on this. Here comes Daniel and Hunter. We'll talk more later. "

Daniel and Hunter walked up to the table and dropped a tray of shots down. "Hey guys, where's Christian?" Daniel asked.

"Oh, he had some work he wanted to catch up on," Amy responded.

"We heard he had some problems at the fair. What happened?" Daniel asked. Amy provided them with a brief rendition of the events before steering the conversation to the activities in the club. Amy joined in halfheartedly as they danced and partied for a couple of hours longer, her thoughts remaining on Christian.

Christian paced back and forth in his room, growing ever more frustrated with his lack of recall. Exhausted, he lay down and slowly drifted off, his frustration yielding to sleep and another night of relentless dreams.

As always, Christian liked to catch up with family on Sunday. Making calls home to family and friends to stave off that homesick feeling was easy as Matt was always off somewhere on Sunday, giving Christian the time he needed. After speaking with Mom and Dad and answering their usual line of questions, including some extras they had regarding his camping trip, he called Connor, Tweet and Maddy to get caught up. They all asked the same questions: How are you doing? What are you doing? What did you do this weekend, anything good? When are you coming home?

He didn't mind the repetition—he was grateful to have such great friends to talk with and find out what they were up to. He purposely avoided discussing specific details of the events that had transpired over the past few weekends. He was sure everyone would think he was crazy, and until he figured a way to share it with his mom and dad he figured it best to keep quiet. He preferred his parents didn't find out through the grapevine.

After the calls he sat quietly looking at the classic Ford keychain Amy had bought for him and thinking about all of the strange new things he was experiencing when his ringtone chimed in. He checked his caller ID. It was Hailey. "Hi Hailey," he answered excitedly. "It's so great to hear your voice. Where are you?"

"I'm in Dallas," she sighed. "I had to pick up contracts for this deal and I have to hand deliver them in Tokyo by Tuesday." After the initial formalities were complete they began their hour and a half long conversation.

Christian unloaded the whole story on her; Mule Canyon, the old Indian man, the scar, speaking Italian, the card game and club, as well as yesterday's fight. Hailey listened with trepidation as he continued telling his tale.

In the middle of his describing the blow-by-blow details of the fight as he was told by Matt and Amy, something clicked. He felt a wave of enlightenment and realized he had total recall to the smallest detail of all the dreams he'd been having over the past week since his return from the canyon. All of them, down to the finest detail.

He began to spew details of portions of each and every dream. Hailey silently listened on the other end, absorbing every detail described by Christian and chiming in on occasion, "Well it was just a dream, right? It sounds like the script of a sci-fi movie."

Christian could sense uncertainty and concern on the other end of the phone, as he professed, "I'm not crazy, this is really happening to me!"

They finished their talk and Christian thanked her for listening, "I'm so glad to get that off my chest. I wanted to tell someone, anyone so badly, but I couldn't trust anyone not to slip and let it out. That's why I'm so glad you called. You're the only one I can trust not to repeat it."

Hailey responded, "Well you know I'm always here for you, and don't worry, your secret's safe. Buuuut . . . this is kind of big you know. It may cost you for me to keep this one quiet," Hailey said jokingly, and then forced herself to emit something close to a laugh. "Listen, I've got to go, but I'll see you soon, okay."

"Okay great," he responded adding, "Hailey . . . thanks again."

"No problem, you just take care of yourself and don't forget, I'll see you on Thanksgiving. Take care!" Click.

Christian sat for a moment trying to get a grasp on things. He was happy to finally tell someone what was going on, but for some reason he couldn't quite put his finger on, it was the first time in his life he regretted sharing something with Hailey.

He lay there on his bed reviewing his dreams over and over in his mind's eye, searching for any link or answer to what was going on with him, especially everything Matt explained had happened the first night back from Mule Canyon.

His memories of those dreams had come back to him and were as vivid as any real life experience. He remembered each of them down to the smallest detail as if they had just happened. These dreams were vivid and had taken him across the globe and beyond. He wondered how all this was possible. Was it the old Indian? Was it from the mesa event? Could it be supernatural or was it something else? It was still a little unsettling for him.

He hadn't mentioned to Matt or Amy that he was still having dreams. Each new dream was now as clear in his mind's eye as the first. They all seemed so real and life-like, as if he experienced the content firsthand. But how? The topics of his dreams varied widely.

He dreamed of ancient Rome and Greece, walking the cobblestone roadways with his servants following along. He could taste the wine, olives, fresh breads and fruits. During the dreams he could somehow feel every sensation and emotion associated with life in ancient Roman times; the pains as well as the pleasures.

He dreamed of sailing as a captain of a British Man O' War. He felt the salt air on his face, the pain of scurvy and the nauseating smells associated with living on a ship at sea. He experienced, as if firsthand, the horrors of battle, the smell of the air pink with the mist of blood following a direct hit from a cannon ball. He could smell the rum soaked breath and rotting teeth of combatants with whom he was dueling, and the flash powder from his muzzleloader.

He dreamed of fighting hand-to-hand combat as a warlord from the Shang Dynasty, as well as being an officer in the German army responsible for rocket development with Huckel and Winkler in pre WWII. He dreamed of cowboy times and even what he could only imagine to be Atlantis, with a population mixed with people who looked as ordinary as today and others who were like nothing he'd ever seen before.

One of the most exhausting dreams he had was of him being a sailor in the early and mid-sixties. Whatever the reason may be, this particular dream, although without the violence associated with most of his other dreams, was the most exasperating.

In this dream he was on the deck of a ship with some shipmates soaking in the sun. It was the mid 1960s. He felt the cool air coming from the icy waters blowing across his face, then panic. A sense of terror coursed through him and then nothing, blackness.

Of all the dreams he had up to this point, this was the one he most wanted to get a handle on. What was it that caused so much fear and why couldn't he remember this one?

What puzzled him more was his ability to understand the dreams. Each dream was in the language of its setting, and yet he understood all of them. He didn't dare admit this, even to Hailey. He was curious if and how these dreams tied in with his newfound skills but most of all, since his new talents showed up without warning, he was concerned that one of his new talents might slip out in front of his parents or friends before and if he was ready to let them in on his secret. He knew he had to somehow gain control of them, sooner rather than later.

Christian embarked on weeks of trials, trying to learn how to consciously unlock the secret to his newfound talents. First he concentrated on speaking Italian. He attempted to read an article in Italian off the internet with no luck. He tried the same with Latin, German and French with the same results. Then he tried focusing on the fight with RJ and his friends, and tried to repeat his movements from the fight.

One afternoon when he attempted a simple spinning back kick, his foot slipped out from under him and he went down, hard, face first just as Matt entered the room. "Hey, what's up?" he said laughing as he looked at Christian sprawled out on the floor holding his crotch and groaning.

"Nothing, I was just trying something," Christian painfully replied.

"Guess it didn't work, huh?"

"No, not really," he responded as he pushed himself off the floor with a painful grunt.

"Well whatever it was, maybe you should try some padding next time and maybe even a cup," Matt smirked. "I never thought I'd see the day when someone kicked his own butt. Can I get you some ice?" he laughingly asked.

Christian just looked at him with that, 'Okay, you can stop busting my balls anytime now' look and crawled onto his bed.

Christian became more frustrated over the weeks leading up to Thanksgiving break. He spent most of his free time searching for the triggers that would free these hidden skills and bring them to conscious availability without success. Nothing he tried up to this point had worked and his concern still lay that something may happen in the presence of his parents, which was growing with each passing day. *What am I missing?* he thought.

-Thirteen-
Smokin' 'Em Up

On Tuesday after classes Christian and Amy met up to do some shopping in town before they each headed home for the long holiday weekend. They met in the parking lot by Amy's car, a Camaro her father had bought her for school. Her father was a bit of a gear head and passed his love of cars along to his daughter as well. Amy was waiting by the time Christian got there with his duffle in hand. "Hey, sorry to keep you waiting," he apologized. "I forgot to pack up my laptop."

"No problem, do you mind driving?" she asked, tossing him the keys.

They headed off campus and into town. Christian wanted to pick up some gifts for his parents and friends and Amy needed to grab some items for her trip home as well.

After shopping they were running late and decided to head for the airport. As they were leaving the mall parking lot they unknowingly passed RJ and his friends who were pulling into the lot. RJ quickly noticed the two and turned to pursue them. He sped down the street, recklessly weaving in and out of cars, catching up to them at a red light.

Pulling close to their car, he sneered at Christian and Amy who were busy talking about the holiday and beeped his horn to get their attention. Amy glanced over Christian's shoulder to see RJ's sneering face come into view. "Oh sh*t!" she said as Christian turned to see RJ scowling at them both

RJ yelled across his passenger, "Hey butthead, where you think you're going?" RJ seemed more angry than ever and Christian knew he didn't have the time to deal with him now.

Instantly he felt his senses heighten. His face glazed over as he turned and smiled devilishly at RJ then calmly back at Amy. She instantly noticed his strong, gentle face had changed. His glazed over eyes were dark, fearless and focused. Now looking straight ahead and still smiling he simply said, "Here we go again. Hold on."

Amy's eyes opened wide, "What do you mean hold—" and before she could finish her question, Christian downshifted and hit the gas.

The throaty V-8 screamed, the tires dug into the pavement and they took off, turning right. He moved through the gears, skillfully hitting the gas even harder through the turn, breaking the back-end loose as he continued to power slide through the turn. With the tires screaming and smoke curling up from the wheel wells he sped down the side street.

RJ pushed his car to follow, turning awkwardly and almost hitting the car that was moving into the Camaro's now vacant space. Simon's arm was frantically waving off the oncoming cars through the turn. "Are you crazy man, you almost hit that car?" he asked.

RJ responded by smacking him across his face and telling him to "Shut up" crossly.

RJ hit the gas trying make up distance between the two cars. Christian hit the next light green and quickly turned left entering into another power slide. He expertly guided the Camaro sideways through the turn and down the street. He straightened her out partway down the block. RJ, also making the light, was less successful in negotiating the turn and sideswiped a couple of parked cars, causing him to lose some distance. He recklessly continued his chase through the streets as Christian evaded him, skillfully moving in and out of the downtown streets with Amy holding on, nervously pointing out potential hazards with the high pitched tone that often accompanies fear.

RJ pursued with total disregard, driving on both sides of the street, swerving in and out of cars and crossing sidewalks, forcing pedestrians to flee for their lives.

Christian looked back through the rearview mirror noticing the path of destruction RJ had created with his angry pursuit and calmly said, "Time to end this before he hurts someone." He looked at Amy, giving her a wink. Amy said nothing in response, her eyes widening as she braced for whatever was coming next.

Christian continued to easily evade RJ until he saw the perfect opportunity. He timed his entrance into the next intersection with perfection. He entered just as the light turned from yellow to red, cutting the wheel hard left and hitting the gas.

Amy's Camaro started spinning like a top in the middle of the intersection. We're not talking a large round circle with a little noise and smoke—we're talking spinning like a top with the nose in the center of the intersection and the tail spinning with tires screaming.

Amy could only stare out the passenger window as the smoke billowed from her tires, hoping the waiting cars didn't enter the intersection. With tires spinning aggressively he smoked up the intersection completely before he exited, leaving traffic snarled in zero visibility. RJ was, to say the least, pissed; he was stuck in the pack of cars blocked from the intersection just as Christian had planned.

He got out of his car shouting a multitude of obscenities while kicking and banging the car in defeat. He dropped his head, disgusted and disgraced as the smoke drifting from the intersection slowly enveloped him and drifted further down the street, lifting slowly from the roadway.

RJ's anger was understandable to Simon and Jesse who had witnessed firsthand the physical and verbal abuses at the hands of his father, George Oswald Wellington. Growing up he watched his father belittle workers and colleagues alike. He rarely missed an opportunity to publicly humiliate RJ, making him feel small and insignificant, a practice which he continued to this day.

It was easy to understand why RJ was the way he was and the ease of which he could transfer his anger to other people who were less threatening than his father. They dare not say anything to him for fear of what he might do to them; after all, he is his father's son.

By the time he was seven, RJ enjoyed making people cower under his own threats, a behavior well taught by his father during his many trips to his office. The employees knew all too well to mind themselves when RJ was around or risk losing their jobs. They had to show him respect in his father's presence no matter what mischief he was up to, but behind Mr. Wellington's back it was a different story. He was openly called 'The Little Turd' by the masses. He would walk through his father's office and threaten people with their jobs if they did not comply with his childish demands.

On one occasion a secretary, after making repeated requests for RJ to stay out of her bag, yanked his greedy little hand out of her pocketbook telling him to 'Stop it' in a raised tone, and was immediately fired. Mr. Wellington ordered she literally be tossed out of the front door.

Upon her ejection from the building, RJ stood laughing with his father. He enjoyed this power over the adult staffers and exploited his control every chance he had.

It didn't matter to Mr. Wellington that RJ was invading her privacy and pulling her personal belongings from her bag. If he wanted it, he got it. The Little Turd latched onto this mentality and treated people with the same disregard that his father has always displayed.

It was no surprise that many in Wellington's staff brought small gifts or candy to work on the days they suspected he was to be there, some to gain favor and others to get some satisfaction by altering the candy in one form or another.

One particular genius on more than one occasion went as far as removing the juice from chocolate covered cherries and replaced it with cherry flavored liquid anti-histamine. He would smile and offer a handful of the wrapped confections to the Little Turd. Shortly after gobbling up the treats, RJ would fall asleep for most if not all of the afternoon. The staff snickered as they enjoyed their peace and quiet, maybe a little too much.

Wellington noticed the unusually uplifted spirits of his employees on one of those sleepy days. Curiosity got the best of him and he began making inquiries in his usual intimidating manner. It wasn't long before Wellington found a weak link. Having attained the information he was seeking, it was business as usual.

One night, a couple of weeks after Wellington's discovery, the architect of this ingenious plan who had been asked to assist with a project that required he stay late at the office for a few nights, was severely beaten while crossing the parking lot on the way to his car.

Mr. Wellington, with a smile on his face, reportedly had RJ watch part of the beating to show him how the Wellington's deal with people who cross them. He was hospitalized for fractures to his jaw, the supraorbital ridge above the left eye, multiple rib fractures and a compound fracture of the right tibia.

While in the hospital he filed a police report documenting the beating and placing Wellington at the scene. When the story broke in the local newspaper, the police report confirmed it as a hit and run by an unknown vehicle driven by an unknown assailant. Needless to say, after he was released from the hospital he did not return to Wellington Enterprises.

The staffers knew the story well because Wellington had the article pinned to the message board in the staff room under Get Well and seemed to enjoy glancing at it every once in a while with a smug look on his face. He used it like a trophy—pointing it out to employees with intent to intimidate and prevent anyone from even thinking about messing with him or his family.

RJ enjoyed the spotlight that was associated with the Wellington family name. His victories and successes were grandly rewarded; however, the humiliation and punishments for failure were equally as grand.

His father had once made him stand out in the cold rain for an hour after tearing the shirt off of his back because a classmate ripped his jacket in retaliation to RJ's bullying. It was a hard lesson from an equally hard man. RJ knew all too well what his father was capable of. He knew he had to rectify this situation with Christian the way his father would or his father would be on his back, pushing his buttons until he ended it.

It was apparent to everyone who knew him that Mr. Wellington was embarrassed by RJ's defeat at the Oktoberfest. The first he knew of the fight was when he read about it in the local newspaper and he was less than thrilled. He slammed his office door closed and called RJ immediately. He ranted and raved for half an hour while slamming some office furniture around behind his closed door.

Wellington's anger increased exponentially each time he heard the story. Business and community members discussed the altercation openly and enjoyed it more if Wellington was within earshot. Most knew very well that hearing the topic of his son's ass kicking was a real sore point for him. They also knew all too well that Wellington would make RJ's life a living hell because of it.

Maybe they considered it payback as most had worked in one capacity or another for the Wellingtons and had experienced George and the Little Turd's merciless antics and cruel behavior first hand. It felt good to them to use the 'kick a guy while he's down' angle that Mr. Wellington had used on so many, so often over the years.

The owner of the local paper, Henry (Hank) Fargus, had no love for the Wellingtons and could not be bought. He rejoiced with each newsworthy tidbit he could print about them, and RJ was a constant provider of material. RJ was always in trouble with the law, not that that mattered. Wellington was powerful and had powerful friends, or more likely than not 'off the books' employees, if you know what I mean.

Fargus preferred to print firsthand accounts from witness statements as opposed to paraphrasing the police reports or interviewing the police directly in order to ensure greater, more accurate disclosures of the events. This was a well-known source of aggravation for Mr. Wellington. Fortunately for him he had the money and contacts to make all but the embarrassment go away. Wellington, for some unknown reason, had never acted against anyone associated with the newspaper.

Mr. Wellington persuaded RJ to relinquish all the details of the fight, professing he was tired of hearing all the different renditions through the rumor mill. Afterward he expressed his feelings verbally as well as physically, and made it perfectly clear as to what needed to be done.

He continued to humiliate RJ both privately and publically following the fight, assumedly to separate himself from the situation in the public eye. It didn't matter who was present; friends, family, co-workers or other businessmen. It was his demented sense of pride. If the topic came up, he let RJ have it. He always had to win and this is how he did it; humiliation and intimidation to the point of compliance. He never stopped going after his enemies until he was victorious and he expected his son to do the same.

On many occasions in the past he had successfully used this tactic to varying degrees on his employees and business associates, not to mention his friends and family members, in order to manipulate them into doing exactly what he wanted. That's how he got his father out of the business early on. RJ witnessed this first hand on more occasions than he wanted to and knew his father would be relentless until he "avenged this embarrassment and restored the family's honor," one way or another.

-Fourteen-
In Aliis
(Latin–The Others)

Leaving RJ and his friends behind in a cloud of smoke, Christian headed to the airport. His driving reverted back to his casual laid-back style, driving at or below the speed limit, stopping at every yellow light, and signaling to change lanes even when no other cars were around. His eyes were no longer glazed over and dark, his demeanor was calm.

Amy stared at Christian for a moment as she calmed herself down. "Christian are you alright?" she asked, trying to determine if he was present and aware of where he was.

"Yeah, great!" he responded with a big smile and nodding.

"What the hell are you smiling at? That psycho almost got us killed and you're smiling! And where did you learn how to drive like that? I've never seen you drive like that . . . Christ, you always drive like a little old lady. Where did that come from?" she asked.

"I honestly don't know. It just came to me, just like the fight and the Italian, but this time it's different . . . I remembered it and now I think I know how it works."

"What are you talking about?" Amy asked.

"Listen, for the past few weeks since the fight I've been trying to recreate the events that have happened since Mule Canyon. It really bothered me that I couldn't remember what had happened. I want to be able to consciously control these things or at least remember them like I remembered today. I couldn't figure it out till now. I think I know what it is."

"What WHAT is?" She curiously inquired, "What are you talking about?"

"I've been trying to figure out what triggers these things, the things that I have been doing. I don't know where it's coming from, but I think I know how they come out now.

"How?" she asked.

"Each time this happens there is one thing that is there."

"What is it?" she asked.

"Stress . . . I'm always stressed when it happens. Once I feel pressured, stressed or nervous it happens. Just before the fight I sensed something wasn't right, and seeing RJ and his friends and knowing what was going to happen stressed me out. And just now, I felt the same sensation just before RJ pulled up, and I got stressed and it happened again."

"Yeah, but at the restaurant when you spoke Italian, you weren't stressed," she said.

"I thought about that too. I *was* stressed. I was totally stressed from everything that happened at the mesa, the doctor's office, and the freaky old Indian, not to mention hours of talking about it afterwards. And when the waiter couldn't explain the dish, Italian just flew out of my mouth. It's got to be stress, and all I have to do now is figure out how to control it." Amy urged him to be careful testing his theory.

Christian pulled up to airport departures, parked the car and jumped out. Amy met him at the back of the car where he was grabbing his duffel. She wished him a Happy Thanksgiving with a big hug and kiss. "Promise me you'll take care of yourself," she said, playfully smacking him on the butt. "Don't worry, you'll figure it out. Just be careful this weekend."

"Thanks, I will. You have a Happy Thanksgiving too."

Her thoughts were on Christian as she drove away, hoping that he would be able to gain control over whatever was going on inside of him and not have any episodes while he was home with his family and friends. At least he was beginning to remember the details from the events on the mesa, Vegas and the fight at Oktoberfest. He seemed to be remembering more every day and for the first time he had total recall following one of his episodes. Still, she thought, it's pretty freaky how everything about him changes. Her curiosity grew. What is it that takes over?

Christian boarded the short flight to LAX. It was a small jet with two seats on either side of the aisle and was only booked to half of its capacity. He set himself up with a window seat and sent a final text to advise his mom he was on his way. As the remainder of the flight boarded he noticed a gentleman with slight Asian features looking at him intently from the front entrance of the plane. He appeared to be on edge as he walked down the aisle surveying the plane and the other passengers boarding, and frequently brought his gaze back to Christian.

Christian thought this was strange because even when he made direct eye contact with the stranger he did not change his gaze, he continued staring at him. Most people look away when a stranger makes eye contact, this stranger didn't.

The stranger slowly passed Christian's row and nodded to him in acknowledgement, his eyes remaining fixed on him as he took a seat a couple of rows back and across the aisle. Christian had no idea what was up with this guy and he wasn't about to take any chances. He swiveled around in his seat a bit to keep an eye on him.

He noticed that he felt no sense of urgency or threat from the edgy stranger. His newly acquired internal alarm was not going off as it had in the recent past, but he wasn't ready to trust the absence or presence of his internal alarms just yet as they were all so new to him. He thought it best to stay alert for the time being.

The flight attendants did the cross check as requested by the captain and prepared the cabin for takeoff. The plane taxied to the runway and shortly after was cleared for takeoff. The plane rolled down the runway, gaining speed and lifted off, slowly banking as it climbed to cruising altitude.

Once they reached cruising altitude, Christian started reading a classic auto magazine he purchased for the trip. He was just getting into an article about a '65 Mustang rebuild when the strange man approached him and introduced himself.

"Hello, I am Channarong. May I please sit?" he asked, continuing to survey all passengers in the cabin.

Christian answered him with a curious expression thinking, *This guy is a little out there.* "Well there are plenty of other seats, why don't you take one of them?"

"Because it is you I am here to see." He repeated, "May I please sit?"

Curiosity getting the best of him, Christian reluctantly agreed and the man sat down and introduced himself again.

"I am Channarong," the man said again, studying Christian carefully.

"Interesting name, where is it from?" Christian asked.

"It is my Thai name, one of many. It means experienced warrior in my native language," he answered continuing, "Please call me CB."

"Experienced warrior?" Christian asked inquisitively. "What do you mean you are here to see me?"

"May I ask you a question?" CB requested.

"Sure, go ahead," Christian answered, interested in what he would hear next.

"If I were to say to you, 'we hebben ein', Dutch for 'we are one' what would you respond?"

Christian's interest piqued as he felt his senses heighten and automatically he responded, "'Nos sunt a caelestri tribum', Latin for 'we are a celestial tribe.'"

Channarong continued, "'Es eu pesente', Portuguese for 'and our gift.'"

"'Traverse le temps et l'espace', French for 'crosses time and space,'" Christian automatically replied.

CB smiled happily and said, "It is you," with a noticeable expression of joy in his face.

Christian felt taken back and a little confused, "Wait, how did I understand your questions and how could I answer them?"

CB just sat there with a smile on his face as Christian launched a volley of questions at him. "Who are you and how do you know me? And why exactly are you here?" Christian continued throwing question after question at CB. He softly urged Christian to lower his voice and avoid drawing the attention of the other passengers.

CB finally calmed him down and started to explain. "I asked the question in that way to determine if you had truly been Awakened."

"What do you mean Awakened?" Christian asked "Is that what happened to me? I somehow got Awakened? Awakened to what?" he asked.

CB continued, "The languages used in the question are not important. It is how they are answered. The languages spoken in response to my question needed to be in a language that you were, up until this point, totally unaware you were able to speak or understand. This is only a small part of your gift and can only happen after you have been Awakened."

"What gift? What do you mean Awakened?" Christian asked with alarmed interest.

"When we are Awakened, our gifts begin to develop within us. I have watched you through your experiences since we were young children. I did not know the importance it would play until now. You have recently had a few unusual experiences, am I correct?"

"Yes," Christian replied.

"I too have had similar experiences. And now you find strange things are happening to you, things that you cannot explain but are helpful in certain circumstances, correct?"

"Yeah, but how do you know?" he asked.

CB continued, "I will get to that soon enough, but before I go on, do you have a Mark?"

"What do you mean, a Mark?" Christian asked apprehensively.

"Each one of us has been given a Mark, a Mark that is passed on to you when you are Awakened. The Mark is a symbol passed down through the generations along with your gift," he replied. Christian looked around the cabin making sure no one was looking and slowly pulled open his shirt, partially revealing the three claw scar running across his chest.

"Is this what you mean?" Christian asked.

CB looked closely at the scar and smiled, reaching into the recesses of his mind in thought, "Mark of the bear. That's big medicine, very big medicine."

"How did you know that. . . . Did Matt put you up to this?"

CB smirked responding, "I do not know Matt; forget Matt for now."

Just then the captain's voice came through the speakers, "Ladies and gentleman, we have begun our descent into LAX and we should be on the ground in about twenty to twenty-five minutes, just a few minutes ahead of schedule. I'd like to thank you for flying with us. We hope you enjoyed your flight today. . . ." The message seemed to go on and on as far as Christian was concerned. He wanted to get back to his conversation.

CB continued speaking softly so as to not be heard by others seated nearby. "The Mark is a symbol, your symbol. It identifies you as one of us. We who are Marked have access to things that others will never understand and it is important that they do not learn of this."

"From the beginning, each time we are Awakened we will be Marked with the same symbol. Some feel the stronger the Mark the greater your powers will be. Your Mark, the Mark of the bear, is very strong. It always has been." Christian listened intently. It all seemed so strange, yet familiar to him.

Channarong continued, "You have carried your gifts with you since you were born. They were suppressed in you as a child and that is why they are only just beginning to Awaken. Did you ever notice how so many things came naturally to you? How you knew things?" Christian nodded affirmatively.

"Our gifts are the experience and memories carried through time from each of our pasts. We all have this ability. There are some of us with stronger Marks who are capable of tapping into the memories of the others, all memories past and present. Only a chosen few ever develop the ability to see lives that have not yet been lived, if they live long enough."

Christian interrupted, "Hold on, you mean—" CB chimed in quickly before Christian could finish.

His concerns lay with anyone that may be eavesdropping on their conservation. "Yes, this is possible too, but this gift takes time to develop and many of us do not survive that long."

"What do you mean we don't survive that long? Why not?" Christian anxiously inquired.

CB paused for a moment, scanning the passengers one more time before explaining, "In the past some of us openly used the gift for gain, ego or ambition, drawing attention to themselves. You do not want this kind of attention. . . . Trust me. This rarely works out well for our kind. They are eventually captured and held prisoner or killed by their captors."

"Killed?" Christian said with suppressed alarm.

"Yes . . . killed, but at least you won't be burned at the stake for being a witch this time. Ha, ha," CB chuckled. Christian looked at him oddly. "That's why I am here. To teach you not to be stupid and end up like the others," CB laughed cynically.

An anxious Christian sarcastically asked, "Gee thanks, and how do I do that?" There was a moment's pause before CB's comment struck him, "And what do you mean, burned at the stake?"

CB continued, "When you have learned and are fully Awakened you will know when you are in danger. You will know how to do amazing things; your body will tell you. You will feel a rush of adrenalin that makes your heart pound. Your senses will sharpen beyond your imagination and you will know things that until now you could not possibly explain or even imagine."

The plane was descending quickly through the low lying cloud-bank. CB, knowing the flight would soon be landing, hurriedly continued, "You cannot let anyone know of your gift! It is rare to be Awakened so late in life. Some like yourself are surprised by new skills like you were surprised with your fighting skills at Oktoberfest. Unfortunately you were seen by your friends, not to mention the four guys you left on the ground. That was one of your first mistakes. They will tell the tale of the fight and people will come to know of your skill. Fortunately it happened three thousand miles from where you live so it will be slightly less problematic. Another mistake was speaking Italian at the restaurant. How will you explain this if it were to happen in front of your family?"

"Wait, if you were there, why didn't you approach me then?" Christian asked.

"That was not the time or the place. We would have been too exposed to potential threats at Oktoberfest and to be quite honest you looked like sh*t in the restaurant after the events at the canyon," CB chuckled.

"You were there too?" Christian asked with a baffled expression. "How is that possible? No one else was there, just me, my friends and the old Indian, and you're definitely not the Old One," Christian stated with surety.

CB smiled at Christian, "Past, present and future. I saw the canyon through the Old One's eyes, a shared experience or memory. I watched as you were Awakened. That is how he knew where you were and how I knew where to find you. He was there to protect you through the Awakening."

"What do you mean, protect me?" Christian asked.

"Being Awakened so late in life is dangerous. Not because of your age, but because there are others who are interested in learning why you Awakened so late in life," said CB, peering out the window, watching as the ground started to come into view through the broken cloud layer.

"Others, what others?" Christian anxiously asked.

"Not to worry, that part's over. Let's keep our eyes on what's in front of us not behind, at least for now. Now it's important that you learn who you are and what your gifts are," CB said knowingly.

He continued, "In my case, like many others, I was Awakened early in life. I did not have the knowledge to control or protect myself from my own inexperience and from others who would use me for their own benefit. This happens to all of us and will happen to you as well if you are not very careful."

"I was Awakened at an early age, about five or six years old. The people of my village witnessed my body floating in the air with a fiery spear passing through me as if Mother Earth and the gods were having a tug of war over my body. My body crossed over the water, passed through a waterfall and came out the other side."

"I was found lying on the river bank, my Mark etched in my side. I remember the people of my village saying my body was smoking like hot meat from a fire. The villagers said I was anointed by the gods because I survived. Some revered me, others saw me as a threat, and yet others saw me as a demon. They all had one thing in common; they all came to fear me, even my family after time."

"The stories of my skills and knowledge foolishly used openly for the good of the village spread quickly until the wrong people heard of my gifts."

"What I'm going to tell you will save you a lot of trouble and possibly your life, if you listen. You have a lot of learning to do. First you need to accept the fact that your family and friends may come to fear you, your government will want to lock you away for fear of the knowledge and secrets you have access to. Others, bad people, will want to use your skills and the knowledge you possess for criminal activity."

"Wait," Christian said. "How can a criminal use me for anything?" he asked.

"CB looked around carefully and then stared directly at Christian's eyes, instructing him to, "Think about the combination to the safe in your president's office."

"The Oval Office?" Christian skeptically laughed.

"Just think about it," CB replied firmly in a low register. Christian closed his eyes and started to think, "What is the combination to the safe in the Oval Office?" A few moments after Christian began focusing on the question, CB sharply smacked the top of his hand.

Christian jumped, grabbing his hand, "What the hell are you doing?"

CB smiled calmly and confidently asked, "What's the combination?"

Christians eyes widened, "Eight, two, seventy-six."

"Not that one," CB added to further make his point. "What is another, more recent combination?"

Christian continued, "Five, twenty-nine, seventeen."

"And what does that represent?" CB asked.

"Oh my god, that's the actual date of the signing of the Declaration of Independence and, and the other is JFK's birthday. How did you do that?" Christian asked as the plane touched down.

CB smiled, "I didn't—you did. You will learn how to bring the gift out with time. Pain is one way, peril another, even something as simple as an elevated emotion. You will grow to learn the ways to use these gifts and bring them to your conscious mind without effort. But you must learn to control it, especially your ability to heighten and control your senses. This will exponentially increase your strength, skills and ability to survive. Without control you will quickly attract unwanted attention—and never—let anyone know of your abilities, although if past experience repeats itself, I think they'll find out soon enough."

"I have many people hunting me because of my abilities." CB lifted the side of his shirt revealing a discolored raised scar shaped like an elephant with a man holding a spear atop the elephant. CB's Mark was almost as defined as a tattoo; however, it was apparent what it was as he briefly explained the history of the warrior sitting atop his elephant. "This is how you will always know it's me; you will come to know the others by their Marks as well."

The plane arrived at the gate and the attendants were preparing for disembarking. "We will talk again soon. DO NOT follow me off this plane or you will endanger the both of us," he said standing up and entering the aisle.

"But I have so many questions. . . . What about my questions?" Christian pleaded.

"Later and remember. . . . Do not follow me. I'll be in touch with you soon," CB firmly stated as he waited for just the right moment.

He timed the opening of the plane's door perfectly. Once open he skirted past everyone in order to be first off the plane, leaving Christian trailing behind with his heightened curiosity. He tried to follow, but was immediately blocked by exiting passengers standing in the aisle. He knew it was against CB's wishes but he needed to find out more about his own Awakening, the gifts and the potential danger he may someday have to face. It all seemed to make sense to him however alarming it was.

Immediately after CB left the plane Christian heard a commotion on the gangplank. He pushed his way as far as possible to the front of the plane to see what the commotion was about. Reaching the halfway point between his seat and the door he could see the flight attendants blocking the exit and preventing the passengers from disembarking. A few tense minutes passed before the all clear was given and the attendants allowed the passengers to disembark. As Christian reached the exit he could see the flight attendants talking to airport security and looking at him as if to point him out as CB's companion.

CB was smart enough to realize Christian's excitement and inexperience might lead him to be careless at first and attempt to follow him from the plane. His escape, although simple, was flawless and designed to put distance in between the two of them. He knew he had stimulated his thirst for knowledge and was hopeful that he could help Christian develop his skills before anything bad happened to his friend again.

Nervous and with sweaty palms, Christian crossed through the exit onto the gangplank. As he made his way up to the terminal the security guard clicked on his radio mic and said something indiscernible as he passed by. He entered the terminal, passing a trio of security guards who looked him up and down carefully allowing him to pass without question. "Whew!" he sighed as he passed into the terminal.

Christian was frustrated, nervous and more curious than ever as he walked through the terminal looking for any sign of CB, but he was nowhere to be seen. He walked to his connecting gate with heightened awareness of his surroundings. He could hear the conversations of everyone around him. Each and every detail was loud and clear. His vision was so acute he could see the wings of a fly overhead. He noticed his internal alarm was sounding. His adrenaline level was on the rise. He could feel it but there was nothing he could see that was a threat.

He continued to make his way to his connection gate when he heard the speaker's overhead requesting security go to the departure exit area by the very gate he just left. A nearby security guard's radio squawked an announcement about the apprehension of a man fitting CB's description.

He picked up his pace to the gate, keeping an eye out for any activity out of the norm. Making it to his gate he sat inconspicuously behind one of the large terminal support stanchions, anxiously waiting for his zone to be called for boarding. He could feel his heart pounding and was sweating like he had run a marathon.

Others from the San Luis Obispo flight were on this connection to New York. Christian, with his senses heightened, was concerned that CB may have been followed by someone else on that flight and decided to pay close attention to them for the duration.

Just as Christian boarded the flight and found his seat he received a text. His caller ID showed no name or number. He opened the text to see to a lengthy message from CB simply signed C. "How did you feel at the airport?" he texted. Christian thought of what he just experienced in the terminal, the heightened senses and feelings of urgency then continued to read, "That was your second lesson . . . Shared experiences. You were able to tune into me at the airport, and as you develop, your abilities will grow and you will learn to tune into the collective knowledge of the tribe. This is how you connect."

He continued, "First, concentrate on me, not the airport. You will begin to see everything that happened when I left the plane through my eyes. You will see, feel and hear all that occurred as if it were you experiencing it all."

Christian was a bit unnerved as he thought about the prospect of this ability. If he can see what's happening to others, then they can see what's happening to him. He began to think, "How will I react to a shared experience? Do they just pop into my head?"

He paused this thought process momentarily and started to think, "What was the first lesson?" His cell eerily chimed in, "Your first lesson was to listen to me and don't be stupid. And you failed. You tried to follow me. Next time listen!"

This freaked Christian out, "Oh my god, can he read my mind?"

His phone chimed in again, "No, I can't read your mind. It's just common sense."

Christian stared at the message in disbelief as his phone chimed in yet again. Just then the flight attendant tapped him on the shoulder, startling him. He jumped nervously in his seat. "Sir, you're going to have to turn that off for takeoff." He acknowledged the attendant with a nervous smile and shut down his phone.

He glanced over to the women sharing the row of seats with him to find her staring oddly at him. "Nervous flyer," he said with a forced smile.

As the plane left the tarmac and climbed he began to focus his thoughts on the events at the terminal, concentrating on CB rushing off the plane and everything he felt in the terminal. Nothing was happening, he couldn't connect. He tried off and on for over an hour. Nothing!

Feeling a little tired he laid his head back and closed his eyes, slowly drifting off to sleep. He was out for about an hour when he was abruptly awakened by his arms slamming down on the armrests.

The captain's voice came over the cabin speakers, spewing his announcement as fast as his lips could move, "Ladies and gentleman we will be experiencing some strong turbulence for the next few minutes as a result of a severe weather front. We will try to get back into smooth air as soon as possible. Please remain seated with your seatbelts on until the seatbelt sign is turned off. Attendants secure the cabin and take your seats."

Christian watched as the attendants locked everything down as quickly as they could before sitting down themselves and strapping in. One of the four attendants was talking with the captain on the cabin phone and had a very uneasy look about her. She advised the other attendant strapped in beside her what they were in for in a low voice with her hand covering her mouth. "Not very comforting," he thought.

The plane started to bounce as the bumpy air greeted the fuselage, passing the impact energy through the superstructure. At first they were small, rapid jolts that felt like a car going over small bumps or grooves on the side of the road. Then the hits progressively increased in severity, making the flight seem more like a ride on a rollercoaster.

The passengers anxiously gripped their armrests as the plane dropped aggressively in the turbulent pockets of air. The intensity of the strikes continued to increase as the captain piloted the plane further into the weather system.

The plane started to jostle about violently, pitching up, down, right and left. Each new impact of turbulent air shuttered through the plane, sounding like a bomb going off as the unstable air slammed against the fuselage. Anything not tied down was thrown about the cabin. The inside of the plane appeared to be twisting with each blow. For those who dared look, you could see the wings flexing dramatically as the plane dropped and then caught air.

Christian felt the floor shift more than a few times making him feel uneasy. Some passengers started screaming, others crying and most praying as they were violently jostled back and forth in their seats. The overhead bins were shaking and rattling with each assault of unstable air, some popping open from the violence of the impacts. The insulated walls were creaking as the plane's polished aluminum skin was repeatedly assaulted.

Even the most seasoned flyers had white knuckles as the plane quickly dropped through the unstable pockets of air, falling hundreds of feet before catching air and quickly rising again.

The headrest video screens displaying course, altitude and distance travelled slowly registered the loss of altitude. One particular drop registered a loss of altitude of almost seventeen hundred feet which was enough to cause a handful of passengers to grab their little white bags.

Christian had never experienced turbulence to this degree; he was uneasy but not as much as the lady sitting next to him. She was terrified, her face frozen with fear. Christian graciously reached over and took her hand in an attempt to calm her. She was white as a ghost with watery eyes, a stream of tears running down her cheek, and her lips moving to "Our Father".

Her hand locked onto Christian's like a pair of vice grips. She glanced at him with a quick sweep of her eyes as if trying to thank him, her head frozen, facing forward. He spoke softly to her in a vain attempt to calm her down, his words sometimes elongated and distorted as the plane dropped rapidly before catching lift.

It was like a fast moving elevator coming to an abrupt stop, but this was no elevator. The lady could only squeeze his hand and stare forward, paralyzed with fear. Christian continued talking to the lady, trying not to reveal his own anxiety.

The plane soon found its way to smoother air and climbed back to its desired altitude. The captain's voice again came over the cabin speakers informing the crew and passengers that the worst was over and he didn't anticipate any additional turbulence of that severity, although he recommended people remain seated until he turned off the seatbelt sign.

The flight attendants composed themselves before beginning to clean up the cabin. One attendant helped to clean up a passenger who had a cut on the top of her head from a laptop or something that fell from the overhead bins. The others attended to the cabin and other passengers with lesser maladies.

It took a few minutes for most to gain their composure and a few more for Christian's row mate to release her grip on his hand. As his blanched fingers welcomed the return of arterial blood flow, she looked at him with grateful eyes and whispered, "Thank you" to him softly as she wiped the tears from her eyes with trembling hands.

Christian scanned the cabin as the attendants busied themselves picking up coffee pots and cups and clearing the aisles of debris. The unmistakably rancid smell of vomit was permeating the air. Most of the passengers had gained their composure with the exception of a couple of crying children and a few of the unluckiest that required the little white bag. These passengers were easy to locate. They were surrounded by other passengers covering their noses with anything available to block the pungent odor.

The attendants escorted the unsteady green passengers to the lavatories to clean up while the other attendants sanitized their seats. The smell of air sanitizers and cleaning fluids mixed with the remnants of lunch the passengers left behind created a medley of aromas that was even more nauseating.

Passengers turned on their overhead fans in an attempt to clear the air which only helped to circulate the odor. The smell lingered on for about fifteen minutes before all accommodated to the diminishing odor and the cabin settled down for the remainder of the flight.

Christian reclined his seatback and leaned back, emitting a sigh of relief while watching his hands and fingers return to color. He closed his eyes to relax for a moment and dozed off quickly. His catnap ended as quickly as it began when he felt his senses fire up. His internal alarm was going off, his pulse rate was rising, adrenalin was pumping and he started sweating profusely. "What is it now?" he asked under his breath, opening his eyes to scan the cabin for any signs of danger. There was nothing he could see to be alarmed with.

He leaned backward in an attempt to calm himself down and closed his eyes again. In an instant, in his mind's eye, he began to experience the events at LAX. His mind was replaying the events, following CB's departure from the plane.

He watched with his mind's eye as CB exited the plane and walked up the gangplank. It was like being there himself, as if he were CB, seeing through his eyes. It was amazing. As he reached the top of the gangplank, security was waiting for him, standing on each side of the exit doors. Security immediately attempted to take him into custody.

Christian, feeling his heart pumping stronger, was now sitting in his seat wide-eyed as if he were watching the climax of an exciting movie. He could somehow understand CB's thought process through the event. He sensed CB's desire to get as far away from the gate and Christian as possible. He easily evaded the inexperienced security guards blocking his exit and slipped into the crowd.

Christian could feel him laugh at the overaged and overweight security guards as they rolled down the gangplank, grunting and groaning as they bounced loudly off the walls. They immediately called for back up to cover the gate and exits and provided a brief description of their assailant.

Christian could feel CB's heartbeat as well as his own pounding heart; CB's was strong and steady. He could hear his thoughts and see his actions as he made his way to the exit, ducking security and police along the way.

He watched as he started to descend the staircase to the airport exit and ended up face-to-face with a wall of police. He quickly spun around finding the same closing in from behind. Then he noticed something strange, or sensed it. CB wasn't a bit nervous, nor was he panicking as he faced a half dozen Tasers and twice as many drawn pistols. He was actually smiling and calmly said, "I'll talk to you soon."

"Who was he talking to? Me?" Christian questioned internally.

CB headed down the stairs toward the wall of officers. It was as if he were leisurely skipping along. Reaching the bottom of the stairs he was ordered to stop by police, but before he stopped, the bank of nervous security guards unloaded their Tasers, hitting him with a barrage of high voltage electrically-charged probes.

Christian, seeing this from CB's eyes, jumped in his seat as if he himself were struck by the probes. He didn't feel it, but he saw them coming toward him as if he were the target. CB only twitched slightly when multiple probes impacted his skin, which amazingly did not affect him as they should have.

Most people drop to the ground with one Taser hit and CB was hit with at least a half dozen probes. He simply grabbed the wires, pulling the probes from his chest, arms and stomach and threw them to the floor before he was inundated by police and taken into custody without a struggle.

Christian even heard CB's thought process which seemed to be another lesson. It was strange that he could even sense the difference between his thoughts and when he was speaking. "Never fight back with authorities. If you hurt one of them, it is my experience that they will hurt you more. Accept it until the time is right and the odds are on your side."

After seeing Christian flinch and pull away from an invisible attacker, the lady he calmed moments before reached out to Christian asking, "Are you okay?"

Christian responded, "Yes, thank you, just a bad dream I guess." He closed his eyes and once again was immediately back at LAX.

He witnessed with all of his senses CB's arrest, from the pat down to the cuffs. He heard him say, "Don't worry, I will talk with you soon."

Then he heard the escorting officer's response, "Who are you talking to? You ain't gonna talk to nobody but the judge, buddy."

The policeman walked him to a waiting police car and placed him in the back. The officer grabbed a pad from the front of the car, locked it and moved to the crowd of security officers standing by the exit, providing the opportunity CB was waiting for.

Christian could sense CB laugh as he pulled his hands from behind his back—he had slipped his cuffs in less than 20 seconds. Within an instant he somehow unlocked his door and was out of the squad car, slipping past security as if he were invisible. He hopped into a cab and began to text Christian, "How did you feel at the airport?"

Christian's only thought was, "Oh my god, how is this possible?"

-Fifteen-
Thanksgiving The Feast of St. Katheryn

New York welcomed the weary travelers with cloudy skies and a misty rain. The remnants of an early season snowfall added to the chill. Mrs. Asher waited patiently with Maddy for Christian's exit from the airport. Maddy texted their location to Christian after seeing the flight had landed on the Arrivals board. Christian exited the terminal finding it a bit colder than he was used to in Cali.

As he exited the airport the cold misty rain sprayed him from head to toe sending chills through his body. He located his mom and Maddy standing by Mom's Mercedes ML550. It wasn't very hard with Maddy and Mom jumping up and down waving. He hurried over to them. Mrs. Asher greeted Christian with a crushing hug and kiss, leaving the mother's mark on his cheek. Maddy jumped in making it a group hug. They began to barrage Christian with questions about his school, classwork, friends he had made and how he was coping so far from home. The very same questions he had answered each Sunday since he had left for college.

Maddy, half joking, expressed interest in any cute California men that Christian might introduce her to. He slowly wiped the lip prints off of his cheek as they climbed into the car. "How's Dad?" he asked.

"Fine, he's at the office today. He has a couple of post-surgical follow-ups he has to take care of," she replied smiling and added, "He's got a surprise for you when you get home."

Christian smiled with restrained excitement, rubbing his arms and legs to get the chill out of his body. He began to answer their questions one by one, in detail on the long trip to the Hamptons. He told them about Matt, Hunter, Anton and Daniel with only a brief mention about Amy and Tina. He was tired and didn't think he had the stamina for the inquisition that would follow once he mentioned his budding relationship with Amy.

The Ashers had, for as long as Christian could remember, always enjoyed the holidays at the Hampton's home. It was a tradition that started when Christian was young. Family and friends gathered at the large table enjoying good food and drink as they laughed at familiar stories, played games and watched the ball games on the big screen. It was often referred to as the feast of St. Katheryn.

The day after was always reserved. While the entire U.S. ran crazy with Black Friday deals, the Ashers trimmed a tree and ate leftovers with family and friends. The home was the heart of the family during the holidays. It was quieter at this time of year with fewer tourists, unlike the summer months. The locals celebrated the upcoming holidays with simple country-like traditions and holiday harvest festivals often hosted by the farms and wineries in the area.

Dr. Asher was home by the time they arrived and greeted them at the door. He stretched his hand out to Christian with a serious expression. Christian responded in kind. Once he had a good grip he pulled Christian in for a hug and excitedly welcomed him home. He too asked a number of questions about college life which Christian happily answered.

They moved to the kitchen, continuing the conversation over a mug of hot chocolate. "Maddy, would you like to stay for supper?" asked Mrs. A.

"Love to!" Maddy enthusiastically answered. "What are we having?"

"Christian's favorite, Italian takeout!" she jokingly responded. Mrs. A. pulled out the menu for the local Italian restaurant. After everyone had made their choices she placed the order while everyone caught up with current affairs.

After catching up for a while the doorbell rang and Christian jumped up to answer it. He opened the door to find Tweet and Connor standing there holding the delivery order. "Hey buddy, how's it going?" Conner asked as Tweet put away his phone and playfully grabbed Christian.

"It's great to see you man."

"You too! Why are you delivering the food? Do you work at the restaurant now?" Christian asked.

"Nah, we were at the restaurant when your mom placed the order. Since she put it on her account we figured we would bring it over. Tony didn't mind. He's pretty slammed with pre-Thanksgiving orders so he was actually happy for the help," Connor explained.

We hope your mom doesn't mind, but we brought our food along too. That okay?" Tweet playfully inquired.

"No problem, I'm sure she'd be happy to see at least one of you," Christian replied jokingly.

Mrs. A. and Maddy set the table as the guys got reacquainted. All the usual questions were addressed until Tweet asked, "Do you have a girlfriend out there?" Christian jokingly attempted to evade the topic, unsuccessfully.

The whole house fell eerily silent like those E.F. Hutton commercials, especially the kitchen where Mrs. A. and Maddy were talking. "Well there are a lot of attractive ladies out there but there is one I really got to know. We've gotten really close and we're actually thinking about taking it a step further and getting married the next time I come back. I thought it would be a great surprise for everyone," he said seriously.

You could've heard a pin drop. Maddy and Mrs. A., having heard only bits and pieces of the conversation, stopped in their tracks, automatically tuning in to the conversation. "What?" a shocked Maddy asked.

Mrs. A. looked up waiting for his reply. "Yeah, I thought it would be a fun surprise. She can't wait to meet everyone. I told her all about you guys."

"NO WAY!" Connor blurted. "You're full of it! Where is she then?" he asked.

"Since her flight was landing a couple of hours after mine, she planned to rent a car and drive out. She thought it would be best for me to break the news first. Here, look."

Katheryn and Maddy, although sensing Christian was joking, were a little concerned. They knew all too well Christian wore his heart on his sleeve. In the past when he dated he would fall hard, usually making grand gestures of his affections and usually ending up heartbroken.

This was something that Katheryn had not considered. What if he actually fell in love while he was away? Or thought he fell in love like he had in the past. Growing up, when he got this way he was easily taken advantage of. They listened intently.

Christian showed a text received from Amy, a response from a text he had sent to her from the airport asking how close she was to being home. Her response was, "I'm almost there!!! Can't wait!!!" Connor's mouth dropped to the floor. Maddy, curious, started to slowly make her way over to see the text when Christian said to Connor, "In fact, she should be here any minute now. Why don't you go and see if she's outside yet."

Connor was most gullible and started for the door. Christian's giveaway was his telltale smirk that always popped up on his face when he was joking.

Two steps away from the door Connor stopped and turned, noticing the smirk on Christian's face. "You—are—sooo — full of it!" Christian broke into laughter, followed by his relieved mother and the rest of the gang. Dr. A. smiled approvingly of the ruse, shaking his head back and forth at the always gullible Connor.

They talked for hours, catching up on every last detail of life on Long Island versus life at Cal Poly. Of course, one of the first questions Maddy asked was about the text he showed Connor. Christian blew it off by saying that it was from his roommate. Christian avoided talking about girlfriends as much as he avoided talking about the unusual events he had recently experienced.

Tweet was very interested to hear about the camping trip he had taken to Mule Canyon, especially the part about Vegas. Christian had told everyone of the plans they had made to go camping and shared the Vegas part with them a few days after returning. They knew Matt by name and that he was his roommate and had surprised him by stopping in Vegas on the way home. For obvious reasons he omitted the events that took place on the mesa and the strange events that followed.

"Did you win any money?" asked Tweet.

Christian smiled, "Yeah, I walked away from the poker table with eighteen thousand."

"No way, that's awesome," Tweet gleamed with delusions of grandeur. Christian smiled. He didn't think anyone would believe it and he was almost right. "Oh, you're full of it," Tweet blurted, playfully shoving him. "Yeah, first time in Vegas and you walked away with eighteen thousand dollars. I've played poker with you and you stink," he laughed.

Dr. A. was less convinced that he was kidding. He studied Christian as he told the story. Katheryn, noticing her husband's mental inquiry, asked Christian if he had pictures from the trip.

He showed them the pictures he had taken, explaining the glyphs and their locations on the rock wall as he talked about the dwellings and how the Anasazi reportedly lived. He did get questioned as to why there were two tents which he easily explained by stating his roommate was a slob. All knew that Christian was a borderline neat freak.

"Any pictures from Vegas?" Tweet asked. Christian carefully pulled up the folder that contained only scenery shots; driving in, up to and through The Strip and a few from Fluffy's show plus a selfie of him and Matt with the Eiffel Tower in the background.

He had separated the group photos to a different folder for the time being, figuring there would be fewer questions without them. He disliked deceiving his family and friends but rationalized it as a simple omission of details. Once he figured out the best way to tell them about Amy and explain what had happened he wouldn't need to hide anything anymore.

The guys and Maddy headed home about ten-thirty and an exhausted Christian said goodnight to his parents and headed up to bed. On his way up he remembered he received another text from CB just before takeoff. He opened his messages and scrolled down through the list. The final message read, "Not a mind reader. Obvious you were going to try and follow me. Now you know it's important to listen, CONTROL YOURSELF! Talk soon." Christian laughed to himself and headed to bed.

He slept well that night. He had little or no recollection of any dreams that he may have had during the night. He rolled out of bed about eight o'clock and worked his way down to the kitchen, greeting his mother who was prepping for the next day's feast. He spent the day playing around with the Mustang, taking care of little odds and ends he noticed that needed attention.

While sitting in the front seat he placed the key on the keychain Amy had gotten him at Oktoberfest and placed it in the ignition He was sitting quietly, thinking about her when his father knocked on the window startling him. "Hey sport, what are you thinking so hard about?" he asked.

"Oh, nothing, just school and stuff. What's up?" he asked.

"Your mom needs some things from the store. Would you mind picking them up for her? I have some work I need to get out of the way."

Christian pulled the key from the ignition, "No problem. I'll take care of it."

"Thanks! Hey where did that come from?" Dr. A. asked pointing to the keychain.

Before thinking he spewed, "Amy found it at Oktoberfest. It's great isn't it?" Just then he caught himself. He paused for an awkward moment before Dr. A. chimed in.

"Oh, Amy huh, the same girl from the text?" Dr. A. smiled confidently having just proven his instincts were correct.

"I thought you seemed a little pre-occupied. I'll assume you haven't mentioned Amy to your mother yet."

"No, not yet," Christian replied. "How do you know?" he asked.

Dr. A. laughed as he answered, "Remember when you started dating that girl Donna from school?"

"Yeah," Christian answered reflecting.

"Remember how Mom was?" Dr. A. asked, remembering as well.

"Oh yeah, it was like The Inquisition," Christian laughed half-heartedly. "Dad, do me a favor . . . don't mention it to Mom yet. I'm not ready to answer a bunch of questions about this. It's all pretty new."

"No problem. After all you're not the only one affected. When she's finished with you I get to hear the recap later. If we're lucky she's past that now." Dr. A. said knowing it would probably be worse now that he was older.

"I hope so," Christian replied making his way to kitchen.

Christian entered the kitchen and was promptly handed a list of items needed from the store. Katheryn was already prepping for Thanksgiving dinner. She enjoyed the holidays. It was one of the few times of year she had to pursue her passion for cooking and one of only a few times of the year she prepared everything not on a cardiologist's approved food list.

"Honey, are you sure you don't mind picking this up for me?" Mrs. A. asked.

"Not at all Mom, glad to," Christian replied with a smile. He grabbed the keys to the Mercedes and headed for the door.

Dr. A. quickly interrupted his exit, "Hey, why don't you take the Mustang?" he asked smiling.

Christian stopped in his tracks. He turned to his father, "Excuse me?"

"Why don't you take the Mustang? Take that new keychain for a test drive," Dr. A. repeated, tossing a thin wallet holding the Mustang's papers and giving him a wink. "I was able to get it registered while you were at school. Thought it would be a nice surprise for your return."

Christian's eyes lit up. "Awesome!" he said excitedly as he ran out the door.

He was ecstatic. There couldn't have been a better surprise to take things off his mind. He flew out the door and jumped into the Mustang. His mom yelled, "Don't be too long, I need those things from the store."

His dad was right. He was preoccupied earlier, and with all that was going on he hadn't noticed that the registration and inspection stickers were on the windshield. He started her up and pulled out of the garage with a smile from ear to ear. Mom and Dad looked on shouting simultaneously, "Take it easy," as he pulled out of the driveway.

He made it to town in no time and returned with the supplies his mom needed. "How'd you like it?" she asked.

"It was incredible, she handles really nice," Christian replied. "Better than I thought it would," he continued. "Do you think Dad would mind if I took her out a little more?"

"Of course not honey. I'll let him know when he's finished in the office," Mrs. A. answered. "Just be careful, okay."

"Don't worry, I'll be careful, thanks," Christian said, kissing his mom on the cheek as he headed out the door.

He spent the remainder of the afternoon driving around and getting a feel for how the Mustang handled. He found his mind was clear while he was driving and he could forget, at least for a while, all that had been going on. The afternoon passed quickly and he returned home after meeting up with Tweet and Connor and making plans to hang out for the night.

Another night passed without incident. He awakened to the smells of Thanksgiving morning. Mrs. A. was busy in the kitchen finishing up the preparations for the holiday meal. She had twenty plus guests arriving around two o'clock for Thanksgiving Day. Her appetizer menu alone included crispy shrimp and artichoke hearts in lemon butter served in filo cups with lightly browned bread crumbs; caviar pie; the perfect combination of chopped hard boiled eggs topped with a sour cream, mayo and Dijon combination with caviar thinly spread across the top; grilled split baby artichokes served with a variety of dipping sauces; and bacon wrapped shrimp and jalapenos.

The turkey was butter-rubbed and seasoned, potatoes were sitting rinsed in the colander waiting to transform from simple stem tubers to mashed potato pie. A buttery combination of mashed potatoes, mozzarella cheese and breadcrumbs baked to stringy golden perfection. The yams were prepped and ready to slow bake until they released the sticky sweet sugar from within. The broccoli was steamed and sitting in the baking tray covered in garlic lemon butter and sprinkled with breadcrumbs. The sweet potato pies covered with pecans and brown sugar were sitting on cooling racks aside the stovetop waiting to be baked to perfection. The cucumbers were sliced and salted, filling the air with their fresh, crisp scent, waiting to be drained and mixed with mayo, yogurt and dill.

Mrs. A. greeted Christian with her hands full of her homemade stuffing ready to pack into the turkey. "Good morning honey, how did you sleep?"

"Great Mom, how about you?" he asked, yawning.

"I'm glad you're up. Dad has another surprise for you."

"Oh yeah, what is it?" he asked. "It can't be as good a surprise as the Mustang was!"

"I'll let him tell you about it—he's out in the garage."

Christian grabbed a glass of OJ and headed for the garage. "Morning Dad, how's it going?" he asked.

"Couldn't be better, it's a beautiful morning," Dr. A. responded.

"What's this surprise Mom is talking about? Bet it can't beat the Mustang surprise," Christian said with interest.

His dad smiled, "Well, this one probably won't excite you as much," Dr. A. replied. "You know that peach pie you like with the sugar crystals and drizzled chocolate and caramel on top?" Dr. A. asked.

"Yeah, you've got one?" Christian responded.

"No, no, nothing like that but were going to take a ride to get one. Are you up for that?" asked Dr. A.

"Sure, sounds good," Christian replied. "I'll go get dressed."

As Christian headed for his room to change, Dr. A. placed a call. "We're on, see you in about thirty?"

Christian and his father headed out the door bidding Mrs. A. farewell. They drove for about 10 minutes before Dr. A. turned onto Daniels Hole Road. Christian was so engrossed with their conversation about the Mustang and how it handled that he paid no mind to where his father was going. By the time he knew it they had arrived at the airport.

Dr. A. tapped his horn and waved to Hal Porter, an old acquaintance of his. Hal was a retired Air Force Colonel, a veteran pilot who had served with the Armed Forces in and over Vietnam and up through the Gulf War. He was a highly decorated pilot who had flown just about everything there was to fly. He worked closely with government agencies in procurement of aircraft and appeared to know just about everything you could know about aircraft, both old and new.

Christian looked at the planes with the excitement and enthusiasm of a kid on Christmas morning. "We're going up today? I thought we were going for pies?" he asked excitedly.

"Yes Sir! We are going for pies . . . to Martha's Vineyard!" Christian fought hard to hold back his excitement. He loved the thrill of being in the air, especially in small planes. His dad had taken him on a puddle jumper to Virginia when he was younger and since then he had always dreamed of when he could go up again.

They pulled up next to a twin engine Piper Seneca. Dr. A. walked up to Hal, shaking his hand and introduced Christian. "So you like to fly?" Hal said with a smile. "Well you're in for a treat today. She's only a few weeks old," he said continuing his preflight-check, and pulled the chocks. "What do you say, let's get her up there?" he continued, motioning for them to follow him aboard.

Dr. A. and Christian followed Hal onto the plane. He directed Christian to sit in the co-pilot's seat. Christian happily obliged and climbed into the seat.

Hal fired up the twins and completed his checklist review. As he taxied to the runway he reviewed the particulars of operating this type of craft with Christian, making sure to include basic piloting; rudder control, angle and rate of climb, aileron function and throttling. He briefly explained pitch, roll and yaw as he taxied out to the runway.

Having clearance, he throttled her up and they took off. As they climbed, Hal monitored the avionics and scanned for other traffic in the vicinity.

Shortly after lifting off Hal looked at Christian and said," Well, she's all yours if you think you can handle it. Take her to 3500 and level her off," as he tapped on the instrument panel, specifically the altimeter to indicate where Christian's attention should be as they climbed. He would monitor the rest. Christian happily followed orders, taking control of the yoke. He felt a rush of excitement as he piloted the plane to altitude. He could feel the power of the twin engines pulling him through the air.

After about a minute into the climb he looked at Hal and made a suggestion that Hal did not expect from someone who had never flown. He suggested he trim the throttles to improve engine sync. Hal was impressed with the suggestion, more so after he noticed the sync was slightly off. "Have you ever done this before?" he asked.

"No, first time," Christian replied. Hal and Dr. A. looked at each other curiously.

Christian leveled the Seneca off at thirty-five hundred feet. Hal was amazed at how relaxed he was in the seat. Christian, as if on autopilot himself, reached over and made some minor adjustments to the avionics. Hal watched intently with building curiosity. Christian was flying by the book.

He adjusted the elevation to twenty meters for MVY, Martha's Vineyard airport, from the seventeen meter setting for HTO, Hampton's airport, a minor change often overlooked during visual flight standards, but none-the-less it was by the book. He double checked the GPS coordinates that Hal had entered and then confirmed his compass heading before jumping into the conversation, splitting his time between the instrument panel and the stunning view afforded by a clear fall sky.

Neither Dr. A. nor Hal said a word to him, they just observed as Christian unknowingly demonstrated flying capabilities more associated with veteran pilots. Christian glowed behind the yoke for the next twenty minutes as they crossed over to MVY.

As the Seneca approached Martha's Vineyard, Christian clicked in, contacting air traffic control. "MVY tower this is November-Zero-Five-Two-One-Lima . . ." He was advised to enter a holding pattern at fifteen hundred feet prior to receiving clearance to land.

Hal and Dr. A. looked on with interest piqued. Hal was amazed as he continued to monitor his actions, ensuring proper procedure and handling of the aircraft, ready to jump in at a moment's notice.

After receiving clearance and without direction he lined up with the runway glide path for visual landing using VASI, Visual Approach Slope Indicator, a set of red and white lights at the end of the runway. Hal watched as Christian set the flaps for the approach and landing, ready to intercede if and when necessary but that time never came. It never did.

Christian landed the Seneca like a pro, and then without instruction taxied over to the FBO. The FBO is where pilots can dock, or park, their planes, and refuel themselves and the plane if need be. FBO's generally handle all aircraft associated business, soup to nuts.

"Nice job," Hal said as he shut down the Seneca's twins.

"Thanks, that was a blast," Christian responded glowing. They disembarked the plane and headed for the Black Dog Bakery. The owner makes the peach pies special for the holidays. Dr. A. called and special ordered a few for the holiday. They reached the bakery and grabbed their pies plus some additional goodies with some coffee and headed back to the plane.

With the plane topped off and ready to go, Hal spoke briefly with the FOB operator and they boarded for the trip home. Christian moved to jump in the co-pilot's seat but was redirected by Hal. "Why don't you jump in this seat," he said, pointing to the pilot's seat.

"Really?" Christian replied looking back at his dad with a smile.

"Okay, let's take care of the pre-flight checklist and crank her up." Hal was curious just how far Christian's natural ability would take him.

Christian busied himself with the checklist and fired up the engines, Hal carefully observing his comfort with the process. He was amazed with Christian's abilities with the plane. He and Dr. A. were both baffled by it as well, and still nothing was said.

Hal thought to himself, "This is not possible. Someone with no flight training doesn't just jump into a plane and fly like he's been in the cockpit all of his life."

Dr. A. had a look of concern on his face in the back seat. He forced a smile when Christian turned to look at him with a smile from ear to ear before looking at Hal for the go ahead. "Ready to roll?" he asked.

"Good to go," Hal responded giving him the thumbs up.

Christian notified the tower and moved out of the FBO. He taxied to the runway, waiting briefly before the tower cleared them for takeoff. Christian thanked the controller and throttled up the twin continental engines to a throaty roar.

The Seneca accelerated down the runway reaching velocity quickly. Christian pulled back on the yoke and lifted off without a hitch. They climbed out to thirty-eight hundred feet and leveled off for the flight back to HTO with Christian loving every minute of it. Hal continued discussing the attributes of his new toy; max altitude, RPMs and just about every other stat he had on the plane while Christian absorbed it like a sponge.

As they approached HTO Hal told Christian to hold off contacting the tower, that he would do it. Christian completely understood as Hal continued to explain. The controllers see the same planes coming and going and are familiar with the pilots. There might be questions to answer if Christian communicated with the tower in Hal's new plane and he didn't want that kind of attention.

Christian lined up for the approach, adjusted for the light crosswind with aileron and rudder and landed with the finesse of a professional. Hal complimented him on yet another textbook flight and landing. "You're a natural," he said, dumbfounded at the skill Christian had demonstrated.

Christian smiled, "Thanks Hal, it's been a long time."

Hal turned his gaze to Dr. A. sitting in the passenger seat behind the pilot's seat thinking, "Maybe a little too natural."

Hal was impressed although somewhat puzzled after hearing Christian's statement, "It's been a long time" after they had already established that he'd never had a lesson. Dr. A. halfheartedly smiled back at Hal with a look more akin to concern than elation. "You might consider a position as a pilot in the Air Force; you'd probably go a long ways," Hal smiled.

Dr. A. and Christian disembarked and packed the goodies in the car. Thanking Hal one last time they headed for home. "See you later, right Hal?" Dr. A. asked.

"Wouldn't miss it," he smiled.

Christian started talking about how great the flight was and thanked his dad for setting it up. "Happy to, I'm glad you had a good time," Dr. A. said then abruptly changed the topic to the Mustang and the guest list for Thanksgiving dinner. He had noticeable concerns about Christian and his demonstrating his ability to fly—and fly well.

"Hey, we're back . . . How's everything going?" Dr. A. asked.

"Fine thanks," Katheryn answered greeting them with kisses hello. "How'd it go? Did you bring back any surprises?" she asked.

"It was great," Christian jumped in. "I got to fly Mr. Porter's plane."

"Really," she said inquisitively glancing at Dr. A. "That sounds like fun. How'd he do honey?" she asked.

"Well," he said clearing his throat, "It was if he was flying his entire life."

Katheryn's eyebrows rose with the news and without missing a beat she switched topics. "Well then, what did you bring me?" she asked.

They laid out the boxes and opened them one by one, six in total. "Oh my god, what did you buy?" she asked. "It looks like a little of everything."

Dr. A. smirked, "Of course, never can have enough around the holidays." Christian couldn't resist but to grab a few cookies before getting chased out of the kitchen. Dr. A. looked at Katheryn, "I'll tell you about it later. I think it's happening."

Christian headed up to his room to check his emails and give Amy a call. She answered on the first ring, "Happy Turkey Day!"

"Hey, how's it going?" Christian asked.

"Great, just helping Mom get everything ready, how about you? Anything exciting to report?" she asked.

"Well," he paused.

"Oh no, don't tell me . . . It's only been a day, what could happen in a day?" she paused a moment, "Oh yeah, I forgot who I'm talking to. Spill!"

"I got to fly a plane today. It was wild," he said with a smile from ear to ear.

"What do you mean, fly a plane?" she asked.

"Yeah, my dad's friend took us to Martha's Vineyard and he let me fly his plane!" he responded.

Well that doesn't sound so bad Amy thought . . . "Did you just grab the wheel for a while or was it like Tuesday in the car?" asked Amy.

The phone fell silent as Christian compared the events. Amy chimed in, "It was like the car wasn't it? I told you, you need to be careful."

"No, It wasn't like the car at all, I didn't feel stress or anything strange, I just flew the plane when he offered the yoke to me," Christian answered not wanting to go into the details.

"That doesn't sound bad. Just remember you need to be careful not to have one of your episodes in front of your parents. Hey, I'm sorry, Mom's calling me. I've got to get back to the kitchen. I'll see you on Monday, right?" she asked.

"Yeah, I'll see you on Monday . . . Have a great Thanksgiving."

"You too."

After hanging up Christian thought about the flight and his abilities with Hal's plane. It all came so naturally yet he never had a lesson. He wondered what else he could do.

He started to play around, trying to speak different languages for a while, again without success. He thought about CB at LAX, the fight at Oktoberfest, the car chase and even tried smacking his hand just as CB did on the plane to no avail. He even closed his fingers in the dresser drawer once; it just wasn't happening. All he got was a sore hand.

Before he knew it, the bell rang and Christian heard his mom welcome the first arrivals, his Aunt Janice and Uncle Mac. They were the close family friends who earned the title of Aunt and Uncle early on.

Janice, originally from California herself, had longish, straight, strawberry-blonde hair, light freckles, and was the epitome of the healthy California look. Mac was a retired Naval officer with a gruff voice and was brutishly strong. They were Hailey's parents and it was easy to see where she got her good looks and her temperament.

Christian quickly dressed and headed downstairs. He greeted his aunt and uncle each with a hug and kiss and proceeded to light a fire log in the see-through wall fireplace, more for the ambiance than the heat as Mom's cooking had filled the house with warmth and the fragrance of the holiday feast.

The ladies were talking by the kitchen and Edward and Mac were headed to the Mustang for the update and a ride. Christian answered the door repeatedly over the next hour until all but one had arrived.

He mingled with the guests, listening to the wide variety of stories they had to offer. Giorgio and Anna, close family friends, were planning their trip to their winter getaway in Argentina. They had remarkable stories about their life experiences. Giorgio, to the best of his knowledge, was the first man to ride an independent suspension motorcycle over the Andes. He had travelled the world over many times, including most of the countries that are no longer safe to visit.

A favorite story of Christian's was when Giorgio and Anna went to dinner following a Frazier fight. Giorgio was friendly with the owner of Madison Square Garden and regaled us with stories of attending the fights in the Owner's Box. He had seen the greats of his time; Ali, Frazier, Foreman . . . the list goes on and on.

There was one occasion when they had gone to eat at a nearby restaurant after the fights. Shortly after being seated one of the pugilistic artists walked in to join them. They greeted the group and sat down.

They appeared relatively unmarked considering they had just gone through multiple rounds of punishing blows to the face and head during the evening's main event. Giorgio greeted them and chatted with them briefly, watching as their facial features began to slowly morph into the unrecognizable.

He remembered how amazed he was to see a person's appearance change so dramatically over the course of a dinner. He had a firsthand view of what others rarely see following a prize fight.

He described the facial metamorphosis by the course. During the appetizers their eyes swelled to puffy slits. By the time the salad arrived their lips had half-filled with fluid. By the end of that course they were completely filled, stretching the skin to its limits. As the entrée was served, the remainder of the head and face started to swell and distort; ears, cheeks and foreheads puffed out under the pressure of tissue fluid pushing its way into the thin layer of subcutaneous facial tissue. Of course, the hands responsible for the punishing blows didn't escape the wrath of combat. They too swelled to more than twice their already enormous size.

Giorgio commented on how difficult it was for them to handle a fork with stiff and swollen hands. As for dessert—well, they skipped dessert; after all, they're professional athletes.

Christian had heard these stories on many occasions and always enjoyed hearing them again. To hear history straight from someone who was there made him think of all the opportunities in the world that could and would present themselves in his lifetime. It was exciting for him to think about what the future may have in store for him, but that's another story. If he only knew . . .

The holiday was a little different this year. Although there were many family friends and relatives, both old and new, including Hal and his wife Addie that he could talk with, something was missing. All of the cousins and friends his age were busy with their current significant others. He missed the interaction with them that he had become accustomed to. He had a hollow feeling inside without them.

Before long the guests were seated at the dinner table waiting for the feast to begin. Two long tables were put end to end that could accommodate the twenty plus people. It was an amazing setting. Among the numerous place settings on the table there were decorations fitting the holiday.

Autumn colored floral bouquets, figurines and horns of plenty. Mrs. Asher came in from the kitchen and started fussing around one of the appetizers when she asked, "Christian... Could you please get the other trays of appetizers for me?"

"Sure Mom," he answered as he headed to the kitchen, making his way past the lingerers that hadn't yet seated themselves. He pushed open the door and without a thought grabbed two trays of shrimp and artichoke appetizers from the counter, paying no mind at all to the guest standing next to the oven. Half way through his turn he stopped and looked toward the stovetop, "Hailey, when did you get here?" he asked, surprised that she was there. He couldn't be happier to see her.

Looking at the clock on the wall as she stirred the pumpkin soup Katheryn had simmering, "About ten minutes ago. Your mom put me right to work," she answered with her usual smile. Christian, with an ear to ear smile that magically appeared whenever Hailey was around, sidestepped over to her and pecked her on the cheek.

"Great to see you, I'll be back in a minute," and made his way to the dining room. He repeated the process several times, spacing the bounty of appetizers equally across the table. Each trip into the kitchen gave him the opportunity for small talk with Hailey.

Katheryn, having finished fussing in the dining room, came in to inspect the soup. Tasting it with a wooden ladle that looked as if it were used to stir an old witch's cauldron, she gave her final approval and motioned for Christian and Hailey to bring the soup dishes. Christian opened the cabinet to grab the dishes and Katheryn blurted, "Not those honey, they're in the pantry." She scurried over to the pantry door and pointed to the trays she needed.

Christian and Hailey headed to the pantry to find two dozen hollowed gourds complete with lids that had been prepared for the soup course. Each gourd was fashionably decorated by hand with a turkey on one side and the name of each of the guests on the other. Hailey looked at Christian with a silly look of approval on her face. They laughed and brought the gourds over to Mrs. A. who promptly ladled the perfect portion into each, sprinkled some lightly toasted and salted pumpkin seeds on top before having Christian and Hailey serve the covered gourds to the guests one by one to start the holiday feast. "Make sure you give everyone the right bowl," she said as the first round left the kitchen.

Christian and Hailey were able to catch up with each other about their activities over the past few months in between the seemingly never-ending stories crossing the table. He avoided the topic of the mesa and the strange things that had been happening over the past months, and Hailey, as promised, did not mention it either. The table was loud with laughter. The guests were talking over one another, the noise only softening with the beginning of each new course that was served.

After what seemed an eternity of feasting, the guests withdrew from the table. Some resumed their conversations, others admired Mrs. A.'s new additions to her almost famous Coca-Cola collection, and others resumed their ongoing pool game.

Christian and Hailey joined together with a few of the guests to clear the table and began prepping for the final course of the day, dessert. Everyone's favorite.

The group made quick work of the cleanup following the meal. During the hour long hiatus all was cleaned and put away. Coffee and tea were made and the table was set yet again with desserts of every kind. There were cakes, cookies, pies and custards as well as two platters of fruit and cheeses, not to mention the pastries.

Mrs. A. had placed snifters and dessert wines on a side table along with a couple of bottles of port and three different cognacs to complete the setting.

The guests were called back to the table. Some having worked off a little of the feast approached the dessert table with an enthusiastic gate. A few of the others, however, were overcome by the L-tryptophan blues. They sluggishly dragged themselves to the table, slow and irresponsive. They were the first to receive a reviving cup of coffee.

Anna, making her way to the table asked Giorgio, "Amore, donde esta mi cartera?"

Giorgio responded, "No lo sey."

Christian looked at Anna blurting his response before thinking, "Su cartera esta en la cucina."

Anna replied, "Gracias," and headed for the kitchen.

A surprised Giorgio asked, "When did you learn to speak Spanish so well?"

"Oh, recently," Christian replied. "I have some friends that speak Spanish all the time so I'm picking up bits and pieces from them and from high school."

Christian turned to see Hailey glaring at him. "You never took Spanish in high school, you took French. How did you learn Spanish?" she asked.

Christian looked at Hailey, "It's all part of that long story I told you about, remember?"

Hailey looked at him in disbelief, "Well you're just going to have to fill me in a little more."

"Okay, but not now," Christian replied. "We'll talk about it later."

Meanwhile, without even realizing it, Anna was letting the cat out of the bag. In the kitchen she was putting on some lipstick when she commented to Katheryn how well Christian spoke Spanish. Katheryn, busy cleaning, stopped wiping the countertop, a sense of disappointment and sadness coming over her face. She forced a smile as she turned to thank Anna for the compliment. Without any further mention of it she continued on with cleaning the counter for a few moments more before, with a sniffle and watery eyes, she made her way to the first available door, ending up in the garage where she began to quietly weep. A few minutes later, after composing herself she rejoined the party.

Katheryn noticed Edward's curious stare when she re-entered the dining room. To him it was apparent she had been weeping. She directed her attention elsewhere, joining in as the party continued.

The desserts were devoured. Dr. A., looking to break the apparent tension Katheryn was feeling jokingly said, "See, I told you so. Never can have too much dessert," forcing a smile. The party finally broke up around ten with the last of the guests heading home shortly after.

Exhausted from the day's events, the Ashers all headed upstairs for the night. Tomorrow was another big day.

Katheryn and Edward had come to a crossroad. It had been many years since they had to face what they were almost certain was beginning to resurface. They both realized the problems this could lead to and what would have to be done if it continued.

They quietly sat in their bedroom, softly talking about the signs that once again were beginning to surface. At Katheryn's urging, they both agreed not to jump to conclusions and hold off until after the holidays before confronting the situation, if need be. Edward agreed not to pursue the issue directly although it was quite apparent to them both what was happening.

Christian lay in bed reading one of his many magazine articles devoted to Mustangs. He slowly drifted off to sleep; however, it was not as restful as the previous two nights. Once again he started having dreams that were as lifelike as any memory he possessed. The only similarity with the dreams he experienced following the canyon was that he felt present as if he were actually there. It was the same feeling he had with the others although, unlike his prior dreams, the most memorable of his dreams this night was what appeared to be a flashback of a childhood memory, or so he thought as it seemed so real and familiar. But unlike the wide variety of dreams, languages and geographical settings following the canyon, this dream repeated itself over and over throughout the night.

It involved a small boy about the age of five or six years old. In the dream the boy's parents were arguing. Christian could feel the anxiety and fright the little boy was experiencing as he hid himself behind his bedroom door, peering out to watch the argument become increasingly louder and more physical. The parents were arguing about the little boy, unaware he was watching the confrontation. Their argument was about something that he did or had done more than once.

In this dream the boy's father was becoming increasingly distraught. About what exactly was unclear to Christian, yet it made him feel as anxious as the little boy. What was clear was the sadness the boy felt and the fear he experienced with each object that was angrily thrown against the wall or floor, each impact causing the boy to nervously flinch. He stood behind his door trembling with tears running down his cheeks.

The final moments of the dream were of a women with a red nose and puffy eyes from crying putting him back in bed, reassuring him that everything was alright with a goodnight kiss and, with a sense of urgency, softly asking him to promise never to do it again so his daddy wouldn't get mad. "Do what again?" he thought. What could this little boy have done that could cause such an angry response by his father? Christian's curiosity was piqued.

He attempted to re-enter the dream to find out what was so enraging to the little boy's father. His attempts were futile. The morning sun was piercing through the windows and he could hear his parents moving about. He'd have to wait until tonight to try again.

Trim the tree Friday was here. Following a late breakfast the Ashers started organizing the trimmings for their tree, a magnificent ten footer Dr. A. brought into the center of the entrance foyer. Katheryn was deciding where it should be placed as Dr. A. and Christian waited patiently, listening to her monologue of the pros and cons of each location she was considering for the tree's placement.

Every year the tree was set in a new location, representing a fresh start to the holidays and promise for the New Year. Katheryn decided the tree should go in front of the French doors stating, "It will look nice there with the snowy background, if we have snow this year."

Christian and Dr. A. set the ten foot Blue Spruce in its stand and carefully centered it in front of the doors. As they started stringing the lights, the doorbell rang. Maddy and Connor were standing at the front door with bells on, literally. Katheryn opened the front door to a loud and cheery, "Happy Thanksgiving" and the sound of bells jingling.

"Come in, come in," she said stepping back from the rush of damp cold air pushing past her. "It's freezing out there! Can I get you some hot chocolate?" she asked.

"Please!" Maddy shivered.

Connor chimed in, "Absolutely, thank you."

"Where's Chris?" Christian asked, happy to see his friends.

"He'll be by in an hour or so," answered Maddy.

"He's helping his dad with something," Connor said shaking off the chill.

The group grew larger as the day went on. Chris arrived as stated about an hour later. Mac, Janice and Hailey popped by around half past two as well as a few of the neighbors who also stopped by for the holiday preview party, each bringing a dish to contribute to the feast.

With the fireplace roaring, the growing group enjoyed trimming the tree, each other's company, and snacking on leftovers. Connor and Christopher were playing a game of pool with a couple of other friends that had wandered in while Maddy was busy helping with the tree.

With everyone occupied, Hailey was able to sequester Christian and inquire further about his recent activities. Christian once again explained the events at the canyon to her. "It all sounds so strange . . . how can something like this happen?" she asked.

"I don't know how or why, it just did," answered Christian.

"To be honest with you, I really didn't believe you at first," said Hailey, continuing, "You sounded so confused and out of it, I didn't know what to make of it."

"I know, I couldn't believe it myself," Christian added, "At first it was all a blur. To me it sounded like something out of science fiction when Matt and Amy told me what had happened, but when I was in the doctor's office—"

"What doctor's office?" asked Hailey?

"The one in Blandings," he replied.

"You didn't give him your real name did you?" she asked.

"Yeah, why?" he asked.

"Because you don't want him posting this on any medical blogs or whatever they do!" she said with suppressed alarm.

"I wouldn't worry about it," Christian added, continuing, "He thought it was all a hoax. After he saw . . ." Christian paused.

"After he saw what?" Hailey asked. There was another moment of silence.

Christian was contemplating telling Hailey about the scar but he kept hearing CB's voice in the back of his mind as a million thoughts went rushing through his head. "Saw what?" she asked again.

"A scar," Christian softly replied.

"What scar? You don't have any scars that I know of," Hailey questioned. Christian scanned the room, stalling for time to make a decision.

"At the doctor's office, I told him I didn't have any scars and while he was checking me out he opened the front of the gown and said, 'I thought you said you didn't have any scars? What's this?'"

"What's what?" asked Hailey.

"This," said Christian as he slowly opened the front of his shirt revealing the jagged three claw scar.

Hailey covered her mouth gasping, "Oh-My-God" and stepped back in stunned silence.

Christian continued, "After he saw this, he thought I was messing with him and the exam was over."

Hailey, still taken back by the sight of the scar sputtered, "Oh my god! Where the hell did that come from?" Re-gaining her composure she stepped forward and placed her hand on his chest, gently running her fingers across the length of the scar.

"I don't know," said Christian as he closed his shirt.

"The first I found out about it was at the doctor's office. You're the only one who knows about it and I'd like to keep it that way for a while."

"You have to tell your parents about this," she urged. "They have to know all about this!"

"No, not yet," Christian pleaded. "There are things I need to work out before I tell anyone. Besides, they have been uneasy about something the past few months. I think they might be having some issues or something. I don't know. I'd just rather keep it to myself for now, ok?"

"Sure," Hailey responded apprehensively. "If that's what you want, but promise me you'll tell them when the time is right." Christian nodded in agreement. Hailey hugged him supportively.

Realizing they had been away for a while they decided to rejoin the party and headed down the stairs. Connor seeing Christian called out to him to let him know he was up next on the pool table.

Dr. A., who was not one to miss anything, noticed the unsettled look on Hailey's face as she walked down the stairs to the living room. "Everything ok?" he asked.

Hailey smiled, "Yes, fine, thanks," and headed to the ladies room. Edward carefully observed her as she made her way past.

The party wound down and Christian headed up to his room to prepare for his morning flight back to school. He was checking the morning train schedule when his dad knocked on the door. "Hey Dad, what's up?" he asked.

"I had a last minute meeting re-schedule and have to head into St. Francis for a 10:00 a.m. I can drive you to the airport if you like."

"That would be great, thanks," Christian replied.

"We should head out about eight then. See you in the morning," Dr. A. said while slowly closing the door. Christian finished packing his duffel then slowly drifted off to sleep.

It wasn't long before he began to dream of the little boy again. The dream opened with the happy little boy sitting in the back of his mother's car and smiling as he played with a small toy his mother had gotten for him for being a good boy. They were on their way home from shopping when they approached a bridge undergoing construction.

The crew had closed one lane of the two lane Dalton Bridge and the boy and his mom had to wait a couple of minutes for their turn to cross. Christian could see the boy in his car seat had stopped playing and was eerily peering out at the river crossing. After being waved through, his mother slowly began to cross the bridge. Traffic was stop-and-go crossing the bridge and as they approached the opposite end of the bridge the little boy said, "Mommy, this is where I died . . . Remember?"

His mother, not sure of what she thought she heard asked, "What did you say honey?"

The little boy was staring blankly over the bridge railing into the icy river water. "This is where I died . . . Remember?" he said calmly.

Hearing her son say this sent a chill down her spine. Hesitantly the boy's mother asked, "What makes you say that honey, you are safe in the car with me?" with a cracking in her voice.

"No, not now, last time. Don't you remember?" the little boy professed.

"Honey, what are you talking about?" the unnerved mother asked.

The little boy began to tell his story. "I was helping Daddy change the tire. It was dark and I was cold. I saw the car coming and then I died." The boy's mother started to tremble and with an unsettled voice assured the boy he was alive and well. The boy persisted, "But I did . . . that's where I died."

He could see how upset the boy's mother looked as she peered nervously through the rearview mirror at her son with an unsettled look on her face. With a raised and anxious tone she ordered him to, "Stop it," and continuing in her fearful tone, "You're not dead, you're safe here with me," and hastily headed for home.

Christian woke in a cold sweat, panting, his mind racing trying to interpret this dream. How is it possible? Is this one of my dreams or just a regular dream? He couldn't get a hold of this dream that had repeated itself over and over again.

He lay awake for a while trying to grasp the significance of what he witnessed through his dream. What seemed to be only moments passing was actually hours. Dawn quietly broke with the sun's rays breaking the horizon.

Hearing his dad moving about the house he knew it was time to move. After washing up he grabbed his duffel and sluggishly headed to the kitchen. Mom and Dad were seated at the breakfast nook looking out the large windows enjoying the morning. Mrs. A. wasn't quite herself this morning. Christian noticed she was a little unfocused, bordering on sadness and did not greet him with her usual perkiness. He attributed it to the exhausting work she had done preparing for the two days of holiday festivities.

Following a quick breakfast Christian said goodbye to his mom with a hug and kiss. “Love you Mom,” he said to her softly, causing her to squeeze a little tighter. Katheryn’s eyes welled up as she stood by the door, forcing a smile over her underlying sadness as they pulled out of the driveway and headed to the airport.

Katheryn went inside and sat on the couch in deep thought. Her welling eyes released her sadness and she began to sob uncontrollably. She continued to sob as she considered the situation for close to an hour before finally composing herself. Her hopes that everything would work out were dwindling and if things didn’t work out, nothing would ever be the same. She again wept.

As Christian and his father shared the long drive to the airport Dr. A. noticed Christian was pre-occupied. “How’d you sleep last night?” he inquired.

“I was a little restless,” Christian replied in a low tone.

“It sure sounded like it,“ Dr. A. agreed.

“What do you mean?” he asked.

“Your mother and I heard you tossing and turning last night. She checked in on you about 2:00 a.m. and said you were bouncing around in your sleep.”

“Really?” Christian paused. “I don’t know why that is. I guess I was a little restless about the flight back after the bouncy ride I had coming here. Dad, why did Mom seem so sad this morning?” Christian asked.

“Mom, sad? No, she’s just very tired. She worked like a dog for the past few days and I guess it finally caught up with her,” he answered evasively. Christian processed his reply as he watched his dad fumble with a wrapper from a piece of gum.

"Yeah, that's probably it."

Dr. A. continued, "You know her, always giving 110%." He chuckled, then continued, "Anything you want to talk about?" he asked.

"No," he reflected, "all's good," Christian replied before quickly changing the topic for the remainder to the drive to JFK.

Arriving at JFK, Dr. A. handed Christian a bottle of prescription meds. "Oh, before you go, I picked up a refill for you." He handed the bottle of meds to Christian.

"Thanks Dad, I appreciate it, but . . ."

"But what?" he asked. Christian paused for a moment. It had just struck him that he hadn't been taking his meds since the canyon.

"Oh nothing, I was just going to say that I had plenty at my dorm room."

"Excellent, I spoke to Dr. Mitchell last week and he called in the script for us. I thought it might help with those night terrors," he smiled. Christian thanked him and with a handshake and hug he was off.

-Sixteen-
The Learning Curve

Christian was exhausted and slept through most of the first leg of the trip. Well rested, he hopped on his connection headed to San Luis Obispo. He was relieved the flights were uneventful. The majority of his thoughts focused on Amy, but as much as he wanted to see Amy he was hoping to hear from CB again. He had so many questions to ask. He again tried to focus on CB, just like at LAX, in an attempt to connect with him but he drew a blank.

His frustration grew during the short flight and as the plane touched down he gave up his attempt to connect with CB and prepared himself to exit the plane. He moved through the small airport quickly and exited by the taxi stand. As he approached the stand a taxi quickly sped up and pulled right in front of him cutting ahead of the other drivers. The driver threw open the front door telling him to hop in.

The cab concierge started going ballistic because the car had cut in front of the line of cabs waiting for fares. He was jumping up and down waving his pad at the driver and shouting all sorts of explicatives.

Christian, aware of what the cabby did, was surprised when he bent down to tell the driver he would wait for the next cab and saw CB behind the wheel. "You rang?" he asked smiling. "Hurry up, get in before this guy has a stroke." Christian was elated and jumped in the front seat with CB.

"Where did you get the cab?" asked Christian.

"Oh, the cab. . . . I borrowed it from a friend," CB chuckled. "Don't worry, he won't miss it."

CB hit the gas and drove away from the agitated taxi concierge as Christian started in with his questions. "I don't know where to begin. There are so many questions I have, things I need to know."

CB, sporting a grin from ear to ear, glanced over at him stating, "I'm happy to see you survived. You hungry?" he asked.

"No," he said asking, "Survived what?"

"Okay then, let's start with your plane trip home," CB said. When we first met, what was the first lesson I taught you?"

Christian grinned, "That I should listen to you and not be stupid."

"Okay, now we both know you failed miserably at that and that you are still failing," CB smirked.

"What do you mean I'm still failing?" Christian asked.

"I warned you to be careful and you weren't. You were careless and have raised suspicion in your mother and father. What did you think, flying a plane like a pro in front of your father wasn't going to bring up any questions?" CB asked.

"Oh, that. You saw that, huh? Christian asked.

"Yeah, I saw that. And what about you speaking perfect Spanish with your parents' friends? Did you think that went unnoticed?" he asked.

"Look, keep going like this and you'll have more problems than you can imagine. And what the hell were you thinking showing your Mark to that girl? What's wrong with you? I'm risking my ass to help you and you keep drawing attention to yourself."

Christian paused in reflection for a moment. "This freaks me out a little. How can you know all of this?" he asked.

CB looked at him as if he were looking at a hopeless case, shaking his head back and forth. With a smirk on his face, "You were always slow from the gate. Why do you always ride the back end of the learning curve when we start?"

Christian a bit confused thought, "Learning curve?"

"Look, I know this is all still a shock to you, and if I were you, I probably would have walked away from me on the plane, but you didn't, never have. And you have to understand, I am your friend and we have been friends many times before in one way or another."

"We agreed to seek each other out each time we Awaken to help each other survive. That's why I am here. It's your choice. . . . You can listen and learn or wait and see what happens. Just do me a favor and let me know now. I don't want to die trying to help you if you don't want my help. I'm kind of enjoying this life."

"No, I do want your help. I have to know what this is all about . . . I need to know," Christian answered.

"Are you sure?" CB asked seriously.

"Absolutely, I'm in!" Christian said enthusiastically.

"Ok then, get ready to have your mind blown," CB smiled.

They headed down by the local eateries close to campus and found a remote spot to drop off the car. "What's going on?" asked Christian. CB gave him a wink while getting out of the car and scanned the area. Christian watched as CB opened the back door and pulled back a blanket. Under the blanket was the owner of the car, sleeping like a baby, a chubby balding man with a bad comb over. "What the... Oh my god! Is he . . ."Christian stuttered.

CB looked down at the man, "No, just sleeping. Thank you for the use of your car my friend." With a smile on his face he pulled two thin needles out of the man's neck and gave him a pat on the head.

Christian looked on as the man slowly came to. His eyes slowly opened as he grunted and pushed himself up to a seated position asking, "Where am I? What happened?"

CB gently shook him once or twice and asked, "Are you okay?"

The man responded, "I'm a little confused."

CB simply said, "You'll be fine, just drink this." He handed the man a cup of coffee and fifty bucks for the fare which read twenty-eight dollars on the meter. With a smile on his face he said, "Thanks for the lift, and be careful. Falling asleep behind the wheel like that is dangerous, especially with a passenger. Maybe you should see someone about that," CB added to add some confusion to the unknowing man.

He started walking toward the eateries that lined the street, a stunned Christian in tow. "What the hell was that?"

"What?" CB asked.

"You know . . . the guy, the car? What's going on?" he asked.

CB smiled, "Oh, that's an ancient Chinese technique used to put someone to sleep." He paused briefly. "Well it's more like temporarily paralyzing an opponent. You'll remember it as soon as I open you up."

Christian jumped in, "Not that, the whole car thing?"

"Oh that. Well, you kept trying to connect with me on the plane so I thought I would meet you."

"Yeah and?" Christian questioned.

"So I needed a car," CB smirked, "And I got one."

"But what did you do to him?" Christian asked.

"Oh, you want to know what I did to him," CB laughed. And you can't remember? That's funny."

"Why is that funny?" Christian asked.

"Because you, my friend, were the one who taught me how to do that!" CB chuckled thinking to himself, "This is always the best part."

An excited Christian continued, "How could I have taught you? I don't even know what you did?" he huffed.

CB looked at his confused face and said, "Past, present and future . . . past, present and future."

The driver, fully recovered but still a bit sluggish, got behind the wheel, sipped his coffee and headed up the street. He tooted his horn as he passed the boys and thanked them for the coffee. Christian looked at the driver with his hair sticking straight up on the side and a confused look on his face, then at CB and they both broke into laughter.

CB continued walking while trying to decide what he wanted to eat as Christian started in with his questions. "How is it you can tune into me and I can't tune into you? I tried what you told me on the plane and it didn't work."

CB interrupted a growingly frustrated Christian. "Let's grab some burgers first and then head back to the dorm," CB said, turning hard left and entering a burger house as Christian stumbled behind. They took their order to go and headed to the dorms. Once out the door CB resumed his explanation.

"The reason you could connect with me but not open the connection on your side is because your mind is full of crap!" laughed CB. "You were able to connect on the trip home, right? CB asked. "Why was that?"

"I don't know," Christian said, thinking.

"When I first left the plane your senses, although clouded, were heightened. I had just dropped a bombshell on you and opened the door to your abilities. Then you heard the commotion when I left the plane. I opened myself to you and you, being nervous and on alert, I was able to get in. You could feel your senses expand. You were knocking on the door but not Awake enough to open it. You probably were amazed at how tuned in you were to your surroundings leaving the plane but still frustrated that you couldn't connect with me, right?"

"Yes," Christian answered.

"That's because your mind is full of thoughts that cloud you, so basically you're full of crap," CB laughed again.

"After all that had happened, you were still nervous as you boarded your flight to JFK. Being nervous kept your senses heightened and allowed you to stay open and connected to me. I could see where you were in the process and what you were doing. That's when I sent you the texts. I thought they might help you along. You know, to help you focus a bit more. Technically speaking, you need time to develop your Trans Neural Telepathic communication skills."

"Oh, is that all," Christian said sarcastically.

"The problem you're having is everything else you were thinking about clouded your mind and blocked you from connecting. You were right there. I felt you jump when the flight attendant tapped your shoulder to tell you to turn off your phone." Christian continued to listen intently. "Your senses faded as you relaxed on the plane and by that time you lost your ability to connect completely. You lost focus, closed the door if you will. You turned off your connection to me until you hit the bumps."

"Bumps? Bumps my ass. If I weren't strapped in they'd still be prying me off the ceiling of the plane," he said adding, "I couldn't feel my fingers for a half hour!" he ranted.

CB laughed as he continued, "Yeah, that lady really put the squeeze on you." Laughing, CB said, "It was the roughest flight I've seen in a while, but not as rough as the time you . . ." CB paused a second, electing not to continue with his thought. "Glad I wasn't there."

"But you could see it?" Christian asked, intrigued.

"Sure, I could see it, I saw everything, just like I was there. The only difference was that I could turn it off and on like a TV if I wanted to, while you were living it firsthand. And the fact that don't have smell-a-vision, that was a plus," referencing the smell of vomit in the cabin. That's when you were able to connect again."

"How?" Christian asked.

"Because you were completely relaxed, with a clear mind when the plane started bouncing around. When the turbulence caused your arms to slam down on the armrests and woke you up, your internal alarm sounded and your fight or flight reflex kicked in, which triggered the increase in your senses. The only difference is, our senses increase far beyond others. It has to do with—"

Christian cut in, "The physiological response to a perceived threat or danger causing the release of hormones like; norepinephrine, epinephrine, testosterone and estrogen . . ." CB just listened patiently as Christian rambled on about the physiological response that occurs during the fight or flight reflex. When he realized what he was doing he stopped, paused and reflected on the moment and began to smile. "That's amazing."

"Yes it is, and it's also the thing that can get you killed," CB said nonchalantly.

"How exactly can that get me killed?" he inquired doubtingly.

"We were just having a simple conversation about your experience on the plane. As I started to explain what helps trigger your ability to connect, you started a five minute rendition of the physiological responses that occur during the process. Don't you think that would draw attention? Especially by your parents who know you have little interest in medicine or physiology," CB said seriously. "Back to the plane."

"Your only focus was on the turbulence. You didn't have all that other crap floating around in your head and interfering. That's when you opened the door connecting on your side and you could see my experience clearly. But this was now a shared memory, not an actual shared experience."

"After you have practiced clearing your mind and heightening your senses, you will be able to connect instantly and see, first-hand, things that are happening at that very moment . . . a live experience connection. And not just with me, but with the others as well as long as they are willing to open up to you."

Christian pondered for a moment, "Ok, how do I do that?" he asked.

CB continued, "Well you already know how to keep the door closed, right?"

Christian looked at him unsure of what to say, "Yeah, I guess so."

"What do you mean you guess?" asked CB. "For now, you clutter your mind with everything and anything you can think of. That will interfere and block anyone trying to connect. Don't worry, it gets easier with time and once you can do that we'll move onto blocking your memories and experiences."

"Now as far as connecting with others, my friends Akachi and Hwei-ru are already aware of your Awakening and looking forward to meeting you. They will connect with you when I give them the go ahead to do so . . . . These are two of my most trusted friends."

Akachi is from Nairobi, Kenya. His Mark, or calling card, looks like a pair of hands cupped together with rays of light coming down from above. His name roughly translated means, 'God's hands'.

Then there is Hwei-ru. She's the second oldest one of our group, a real strong spirit. She lives in Mandalay."

"The Casino?" Christian joked.

CB rolled his eyes, "Burma, or you may know it as Myanmar." Her name means 'Wise One or 'Intelligent One'. She will reach out as well," he smiled.

"Does she have a Mark?" Christian asked.

"Yes and no," he said. Christian focused curiously. "Her Mark used to look like a dragon," he reflected with some sadness.

"What do you mean, used to?"

"Hwei-ru grew up in a time and place where it was dangerous to be a woman and deadly to be a woman noticed. She was born in a small town in Jiangxi province. Once Awakened, her Mark made her famous. Rumors of her talents spread throughout China, drawing unwanted attention from everyone up to and including the Emperor himself. We've talked about that, remember, drawing attention to yourself?"

"The Emperor's minions had reported hearing of a magnificent young child with uncommon knowledge, skills and abilities. He ordered them to seek out the child and report back to him. The Provincial Minister had her brought to him under protest from the family and villagers who saw her as a heavenly gift. He had her examined, her abilities tested, and reported his finding to the Emperor."

"Upon hearing the reports, the Emperor concluded that her abilities may give the people of her province hope and ordered his Provincial Minister imprison her. She was six years old."

"To make sure his point was firmly embedded, his guards ordered everyone in the village to stop work. Workers were ordered out of the rice paddies and the local shops. The young and old were pulled from their homes and moved into the center of the small village where the Provincial Minister read a proclamation;

Let it be known; by direct order of his Imperial Majesty,
That the family known as Jian have conspired in treasonous
activities against the Emperor and the people of China
and are hereby ordered to be put to death.
Anyone caught aiding and abetting the family of Jian
Will be put to death.
Any mention of the name Hwei-ru Jian
Will be cause to be put to death.

"After reading the declaration the guards were ordered to execute the sentence. Hwei-ru was forced to watch as they brutally murdered her family, her entire family; mother, father, brothers, sisters, aunts, uncles, and cousins. All she knew were dead. The horrified villagers were also forced to watch helplessly at gunpoint. They knew to react or show sympathy would result in their own deaths."

"Hwei-ru once told me of a neighbor who was very kind to her, pleading in an attempt to convince the Minister to release her. The Minister sneered at her angrily, forcing her into submission before he pushed a sword through her throat. Hwei-ru remembers her caring eyes staring at her sympathetically as blood gurgled from her mouth and poured from her fatal wound."

"She suffered terribly at his hands. While in custody she was starved, tortured and whipped, flaying the skin from her in an attempt to remove the Mark. And then, after fifteen years of disfiguring torture she was released."

"She wasn't sure why the Minister or Emperor didn't just kill her along with her family until some time had passed. Initially the Emperor wanted to learn of her gifts and wisdom, just like everyone else, but he also feared her magic, believing he would somehow be cursed if he killed her, so he let her live."

"Over the years she avoided using her abilities in front of the guards and the Minister until they believed she possessed no more of the magical gift she was born with. The Minister visited the cell where she was held daily to question her and report her activities to the Emperor. On one particular day he gazed upon her in disgust of himself."

"The once beautiful child full of life was now an abomination to the eyes at his hands. Her lifeless eyes stared hopelessly through him. Filthy, unkempt and scarred for life, he felt pity for the first time in his life."

"At his urging, the Emperor was convinced that she was no longer a threat. The memory of her was successfully suppressed and she was thought to no longer possess any special skills and did not present a threat to the Emperor or to China. Rumor has it that the now elderly Emperor still feared being cursed for his involvement, especially if he were to kill the girl. By the Emperor's decree the Provincial Minister released her."

"The guards were not so sympathetic and tossed her into the street, naked, for all to see their dirty work. Anyone seen trying to help her was beaten on the spot. Her gift became a death sentence to anyone who dared speak of it. She was badly scarred and broken but not beaten. She was stronger," CB welled sympathetically for his friend.

"What happened to the Minister?" Christian asked shaking his head in disbelief of the atrocities committed against Hwei-ru.

CB regained his composure and continued, "No one knows for sure. As with any government official they attempt to hide the truth by making up stories, but rumor has it that the years of brutality, torture and the murder of hundreds if not thousands of people finally got to him."

"It was told that he slowly went insane. As his insanity progressed so did his paranoia. He became afraid of shadows for fear the spirits of his victims lay in wait for him there to drag him to the underworld. Villagers would get an occasional glimpse of him flinching and twitching as he walked the veranda of his home, talking to himself and pleading for mercy from the torments of unseen souls."

"He refused to leave his home and was often found wandering the halls at night talking and pleading to his victims for forgiveness. He refused to sleep for fear of the nightmares his tortured conscious brought to his dreams. Toward the end he stopped eating, fearing that he was going to be poisoned, and eventually died in madness by mistakenly drinking the very poison he feared."

"Hwei-ru said he died of a self-imposed curse brought on by years of brutal acts against the people of China. His acts caused a madness in his soul that consumed him like a cancer. She felt sympathy for him."

"She what?" a shocked Christian asked.

"Hwei-ru felt sympathy for him."

"You're kidding?" Christian questioned.

"No, I told you, Hwei-ru is a very special person, a strong spirit. She learned while being held captive that hating this man for what he did was eating her up inside, taking her strength away. So she accepted what he did and her circumstance and moved on, at least mentally."

"Her ability to exercise her body was limited because she was always under the watchful eyes of the guards. She stretched to prevent her joints from freezing by moving so slowly the guards couldn't tell she had moved at all. She developed skill and knowledge far beyond anyone's imagination. She had spent almost fifteen years inside of her mind, connecting with past, present and future. You'll learn that as you get to know her," CB smiled. "Enough about that. . . ."

"Now they already have access to your past memories as you have access to theirs. Always have, you just didn't know it. That's why so many things came easy to you growing up. Your full potential for accessing our cumulative knowledge is building faster than most. Soon enough you'll be able to access this information instantly. As for connecting, you will simply choose to or not to open the connection, and more importantly who you should or shouldn't let in."

"Wait a second," Christian interrupted, "Did I just hear a compliment?" he asked jokingly.

"Maybe, but don't get a big head," CB said smirking.

"This is more important than you realize. Now that some of the others know you have been Awakened, they will try and connect with you. Each one has their own calling card."

"What do you mean?" Christian asked.

"When you connected with me and my memories you knew it was me, right?" Christian nodded affirmatively. "Well you will know who's trying to connect with you once they try. . . . It's kind of a telepathic calling card. You will sense their presence, and you can choose to open the door or not, like blocking a call."

"You will know Hwei-ru and Akachi because we will reach out to them. You will meet the others and learn who they are as they connect. As you progress you will be able to access each of them. Remember, every one of them has access to your past memories, experiences and skills to access at will and use for themselves. But you have to open the door for them to see where you are in real time."

"Okay, so what you're saying is that everything I can do, all the others can do as well?" Christian said contemplating.

"Yep, that's pretty much how it is with one or two exceptions," CB answered.

"What exceptions?" he asked.

"Okay, the skills you have access to like the fighting styles and flying the plane are all shared by everyone but . . . How can I explain this so you'll understand?"

"It's like being on a baseball field. Each player knows the game, the rules and strategy, yet they all have different skill levels. Some are stronger in hitting, others in fielding. Some are good at both, so even though you know what everyone else knows, you all have different skill levels. In some you're strong and in others you're not going to be so strong. Like anything else, it's all based on practice."

"It is possible to block your memories and skills, but you are nowhere near ready for that. That takes a lot of control. First you will need to master the basics and then we can get to the advanced stuff," CB smiled reassuringly. "The main thing you must learn is that if you sense something bad knocking at the door, don't open it."

"What do you mean, something bad?" Christian asked.

"Do you remember I told you that others knew you had finally Awakened?"

"Yeah," he replied.

"Well, as I had mentioned there are a few of us out there that have gone to the dark side, if you know what I mean. They have tried to recruit others to join with them and try to block the rest of us from connecting or accessing their memories completely."

"Who are they?" Christian asked.

CB became very serious, "There were three or four of them. It's hard to tell if they're all still alive. They have learned to block us from their recent memories and live connections completely. Connecting with them could be very dangerous."

"They can block all their memories?" Christian asked.

"No, not all of them. We still have access to their past memories, it's just that they somehow learned to block us from most or all memories in this lifetime. I think they do it to prevent anyone from seeing their long-term plans as they are developed. It's difficult to accomplish and takes great concentration and skill to keep everyone out; however, their past life memories are easily accessed and trust me, the further away from them you are the better," CB assured.

"'Pwunu' roughly translated means 'Ruler'. This guy is bad news. He deals in anything and everything illegal. He's like 'Murder, Inc.' of Armenia and basically controls the black market in half of Europe. Rumor has it he was captured and tortured to death, but I don't know for sure.

"That's the problem, the delay thing again. It's like memories become memories after a short time. It can be immediate if you are openly connected in real time. If not it usually takes a few minutes to a few hours. But it can be up to a few days or even months if the person successfully blocked them up to and through death. But these guys somehow continue to block out memories even after they are reborn. I'm not exactly sure how it works but Hwei-ru will know, she's on top of everything."

"How can that happen if the guy's dead?" Christian asked.

CB continued, "When we die we are still a conscious energy. We see ourselves floating away, entering the tunnel and then experience our own rebirth."

"So that was real?" a shocked Christian interjected, "I dreamt that the other night."

"I know," CB said moving back to the original topic. "Since we are focused energy in this state we can continue to control our prior life's memory for a short time after being re-born, longer if you know what you're doing."

"Wow!" Christian blurted, amazed.

"Then there's a guy from North Korea, 'Myung-Suck'"

"Nice name," Christian laughed.

"Yeah, it's funny here, but in Korea it roughly translates to 'Foundation of Ages'. A fitting name for one of us. He is well up in the political hierarchy and is ruthless in controlling the masses. To them he is known as 'Ag-hana' or 'Evil One'. He lives like a king in a government funded castle. Definitely on the terror 'A' list."

"Then there's 'Kutsal-bir' the 'Unholy One', a Turkish rebel. If possible, he may even be more ruthless than the rest. He's known for using old world torture before he beheads his victims, if they are lucky. The unlucky ones usually get impaled and left to suffer for hours or even days. He enjoys watching his victims suffer as wild dogs tear the flesh from their feet and legs. Most of his issues are political and localized to his immediate area, but if he ever joined up and combined forces with the others, he could be extremely dangerous."

"There is another one from somewhere in Peru. His name is 'Adriano' or the 'Dark One'. Another fitting name. He's high up in the cartels. It took him a while to learn how to block his memories and a few of us got to see what he was capable of. It wasn't pretty. He's a heartless bastard."

"Each of us has a unique calling card. I can only tell you that by the end of today you will know to who and how you should respond."

"Fair enough," Christian said. "Let's get started."

-Seventeen-
La prise de contrôle
(EnFrancais–Gaining Control)

There are many methods of gaining control of one's mind. The method I use most brings me to a place where I have zero thoughts in my conscious mind. A state of mind where I am present and fully aware of my surroundings, but have no active thoughts. . . . It's called 'artori.'"

There is a process to clearing out the junk before you can reach this point. I will show you step-by-step how to clear your mind and help reprogram how you think. Over the years you have learned many things from many people. Unfortunately these lessons are more often wrong or inapplicable over time as all things change. They clutter your thoughts and need to be cleared before you can succeed in controlling your mind. As I remember, you used to call it "Mother, Father, Teacher, Preacher."

"When did I call it that?" asked Christian.

"A long time ago. You'll see when we open you up completely."

CB commenced with teaching Christian to clear his mind of clutter in preparation for him to connect. Once completed, they spent the remainder of the afternoon practicing connecting. CB taught Christian how to bring up connections and how to effectively block them. He introduced him, via connecting, to a few of the other members of their private fraternity. Akachi and Hwei-ru are two that graciously offered to help the newbie at the request of CB.

Akachi was first to connect. It was early in the morning in Nairobi. Christian could see firsthand, through Akachi's eyes, Akachi's penthouse apartment. He was given a tour of the elaborate home with a spectacular view overlooking the city. Every one of his senses were alive. He could smell the flowers on the table, see and hear every detail surrounding Akachi as well as feel what he was touching, and taste the piece of fruit he put in his mouth. It was like being there in the present moment, sharing a body through a conscious connection. They shared memories and Akachi showed him how he blocks an active memory by cluttering his mind with random thought. It was a trip. An awestruck Christian thanked him for sharing the connection.

CB continued teaching Christian the dos and don'ts of connecting and shared memory for another hour or so until it was time to connect with Hwei-ru.

It was about seven-thirty in the morning Hwei-ru's time. CB introduced the two and the connection was made. Hwei-ru was very impressed that Christian was able to connect so effortlessly. She shared her morning experience with him as she went through her routine. She lived in a small home overlooking a valley. The song birds were singing as the sound of moving water from a gentle stream next to her home echoed inside. She gave him the tour of her home which was modest in comparison to Akachi's.

Hwei-ru had just started to boil some water when she started laughing out loud for no apparent reason. It was strange to Christian because he sensed nothing funny. "First time being a woman?" she asked.

Christian turned red in the face, "Yes," he replied.

"I can sense your uneasiness. Don't worry I won't pee in front of you," she laughed. Hwei-ru was a character but possessed a tremendous amount of knowledge which she openly shared with Christian. She gave him pointers on how to block connections, thoughts and memories and enlightened him about the three remaining Dark Ones. She couldn't be sure about the fourth; she picked up nothing on him.

Before breaking off their hour long connection she shared a memory. A future memory that she asked he not share with anyone, including CB. He agreed, thanking her many times over before disconnecting.

CB looked at him while he was glowing with excitement. "That was amazing! She's amazing," Christian raved.

"I know," CB smiled.

He was astonished he could see firsthand where each was in real time with the added bonus of being able to see most all of their memories and experiences. Plus having the ability to draw on skills shared within the group didn't suck, as well as the fact he could miraculously understand and speak their language and most any other language. He thought quietly for a moment, astounded by this gift when the Ah-ha moment came. He suddenly realized he could do anything, absolutely anything. Solve highly complex mathematical equations in seconds that take the greatest minds a month to perfect, interpret poetry, read music, paint like Rembrandt, da Vinci, Picasso, Van Gogh, and Vermeer. He could operate just about every type of equipment on the planet from the most delicate surgical tools to giant construction and military vehicles. The list seemed never ending. It appeared there was nothing he couldn't do now that he was able to tap into the world's database of knowledge. He was glowing with aspiration.

CB interrupted his blissful moment of realization. "Incredible feeling isn't it?" he asked smiling.

"Yeah, I feel incredible. Do you know how many things I can do? There are so many things that need fixing in the world and I can help," Christian imagined.

"Hold on a second," CB interjected. "Remember, you do not want to draw attention to yourself. Revealing your knowledge to the world will bring more than you bargained for."

"Yeah, but . . ."

"No buts," CB answered quickly and sternly. "Doing something like that could endanger all of us."

CB continued explaining why it was unadvisable to be so ambitious. "Look, I understand your desire to help the world, it's just not to your advantage to do so. Becoming famous for inventing, curing or fixing any of the world's problems is what we all wish to do at one time or another. I know it's tempting to want to be famous, successful and a hero for any cause, but there are repercussions for doing so.

The more involved you get, the more attention and scrutiny you draw to yourself. Next thing you know, you've lost your freedom. Look up Edgar Casey, the famous mystic. He was one of us; see what his capabilities did to him. The path you're thinking of heading down is similar in many ways. I know you don't or can't understand it, the how's and whys right now. I only ask that you wait to see it for yourself firsthand before acting." CB's statement wasn't out of greed or selfishness, it was for self-preservation and he hoped he got that across to Christian. He would know soon enough. "You can help the world quietly from behind the scenes, but you don't need to be the hero."

"I was wondering. You told me all Hwei-ru had been through, but why didn't I see that in her memories?" he asked.

"That is a very personal thing to her. She accepted what happened for what it was and has released all or as much of her resentment that she could." CB continued, "I witnessed part of her experience once, and it's best to never ask or mention it again unless she offers it to you as a lesson." Christian agreed.

Christian had a long list of questions, some of which could be answered by shared memories and others CB needed to explain. CB touched lightly on the history of how they came to be and moved on to Christian's inquiries about his dreams. He focused mainly on the first set of dreams, pulling together the knowledge from past lives and experiences and the skills he could draw from those memories. It was all very obvious to Christian now that he was learning quickly and could access his own past on command.

CB intentionally avoided discussing Christian's most recent dreams. There was still more for him to learn and CB didn't want him upset by what he may find if he looked in the wrong place. Not yet, it wasn't time. They had only scratched the surface of the world of resources now available to him. Most of it was good and some of it, well, some of it was bound to cause some pain.

Christian was mesmerized as CB carried him in and out of his past. He could see details of each life experience as if he were living them firsthand. CB helped him connect more deeply with the places he had dreamed of the first night back from the canyon. They laughed at experiences they shared in real life a few lifetimes ago. Christian absorbed everything he could like a sponge and before he knew it, he was accessing everything on his own.

He travelled back in time in his mind's eye to ancient Rome and Greece as a business man, to Germany as a rocket scientist with

Huckel and Winkler, back to the Midwest during cowboy times where he was a wealthy businessman hiding his fortune from thieves. He connected with his past as a warrior in the Shang Dynasty.

It was amazing. He could taste the foods, smell the fragrances in a garden and feel all forms of physical contact. Pain and pleasure from the gentle touch of a lotus blossom being caressed against his neck and chest to a soldier's blade slashing him in battle. He could pull the knowledge and skills from the past to the present to use at will.

CB had him get used to seeing a few of his own deaths from past lives. It was surreal to say the least. Experiencing one's own death is hard enough to think about, but having to see multiple deaths across the millennia was unimaginable. Christian, although freaked out a bit, adjusted quickly. They even had a laugh or two about some of the circumstances that brought death to his door as they viewed the backdrop of surreal experiences from the past in his mind's eye.

CB was watching Christian carefully as they relived these memories again. He looked like a kid at Christmas. CB brought Christian back to the present. He was glowing with excitement. "Did you notice anything from that last one?" CB asked.

"That's where we first met! I remember now, we trained together as students," Christian answered, and then together as if on cue they both said, "and we've been together ever since!"

"That's when you taught me the needle trick," CB added. A strong sense of connection came over Christian. He felt a sense of relief and newfound trust in CB, knowing that they had guided each other many times in the past.

CB explained to Christian that with time he would have access to the entire string of life experiences and not just the bits and pieces that he can see now. He explained, "Because you have only just opened your mind, you will need time to adjust. Your mind needs a little time to reboot."

They continued to discuss the memories to which they had access, laughing at some, and mourning others. CB brought to light interesting facts to help Christian connect more deeply with his past and open him up to the memories and past lives of others. This was all part of the learning process.

He told stories of famous public figures as Christian spurted names out of thin air. Most of their lives appeared benign, but some were real shockers. It was the stories from these lives that CB used to confirm to Christian just how careful he really needed to be.

He explained, "The temptations we've had in the past to use our gift for gain was strong and for most of us, yours truly included, at one time or another did things we were less than proud of, out of necessity."

One of the notable stories was about Howard Carter, the founder of King Tut's tomb. Christian asked, "Was he one of us?"

CB responded, "No, but Lord Carnarvon was."

"But wasn't Carnarvon the first to die from the curse?" Christian asked.

"Well, that's what most people think."

CB paused as Christian chimed in again, "What do you mean?"

CB continued, "Everyone thinks Carnarvon died from infection as a result of the curse which was more media hype than reality. But it was a little more than that. You see, Carnarvon was feared in certain circles because of his abilities. He did not flaunt them, but let's say he had a knack for knowing the future. A lot of good that did him," CB chuckled in remembrance.

"What do you mean?" asked Christian.

"Well, I told you some of us can see the future, but I didn't tell you that you can change it to a certain degree. You only need to change one little thing in the present to create a whole different future."

"Is that what he did?" asked Christian.

"Not so much what he did, as what the others did. The future he envisioned prior to the actual find was remarkable. It was filled with extravagant celebrations and award ceremonies and lectures surrounding the find which would have superseded the rumors that were being laid about, but that all changed when he remained on the dig site instead of returning to England as planned. He insisted on staying even after growing weaker and more fatigued from working long hours. He should have returned home as planned or at least taken a respite as he was advised. If he did that, then the future he viewed would not have changed."

"You see, you can view the future today and see one outcome and then if something changes you can see a completely different outcome the very next day, hour or even minute."

"Wait, I don't understand. . . . Wouldn't you be able to see the change coming?" Christian asked.

"No, not necessarily." CB continued, "He changed his own plans after he looked forward. By changing his plans and deciding to stay in Egypt at the dig site he changed his future. Well anyway . . ."

"In his absence, the people that feared him most set about the rumor mill all sorts of nasty lies. These rumors quickly spread among his peers because he wasn't there to defend himself. It wasn't long before he was under suspicion for a multitude of charges to which he was unaware until he received a communication from one of his allies, Lord Bentley. Having been made aware of these rumors he began communications with his other allies and they opened communications with George and May in his defense."

"George and Mary?" Christian asked.

"Oh sorry, King George V and Queen Mary. As there was no urgency to return by command, he elected to stay on at the site. He refused to let the smearing campaign dampen his discovery."

"Then comes the supposed curse of King Tut's tomb. The perfect opportunity."

"For what?" Christian asked. "If you can see the future then you pretty much know what's going to happen, right?" he inquired.

"Yes and no. If he had taken the time to look again he would have seen it coming but connecting with the future takes a lot out of you, so most of us that can, only connect when it's absolutely necessary. It's exhausting when you're strong and healthy, but it's downright dangerous when you're not."

"Carnarvon was so enthralled in the discovery and was working morning through night on the documenting and cataloguing of all of the artifacts associated with the find that his health started to fail. When you're sick or weak you don't even consider looking forward."

"What happened?" asked Christian.

"Like I said, Carnarvon didn't take the precaution to look ahead to see what was coming or what may have changed, allowing the opportunity for his undoing. Knowing that he was under no royal command to return home, his accusers set to the task of eliminating him instead."

"How'd they do that?" asked Christian.

"The pathologists on site had discovered the walls of the tomb were covered in a yeasty toxin. It was kind of an ancient germ warfare painted on all surfaces of the tomb that was meant to be inhaled or pass through the skin to sicken or kill anyone who dared enter the King's tomb. The Curse."

"The head pathologist and discoverer of this spore-ridden toxin was secretly associated with Carnarvon's adversaries and withheld information about the lethal substance from the diggers, Carter and Carnarvon. His plan was perfect. As the workers got sick, the media hyped The Curse of the Tomb of King Tut."

"So is that what he died from?" asked Christian.

"Yes and no." CB continued, "You see the pathologist, Carter and a select few had access to Carnarvon's quarters. After the curse reached its peak in the media, the pathologist mixed a deadly solution of poisons, including the yeasty spore infested toxin from the tomb. He covered anything in Carnarvon's tent that he could get his hands on in an attempt to eliminate the weary Lord."

"What happened next?" Christian asked.

"Well you know the rest of the story. . . . He cut himself shaving. The cut got infected and he died a slow painful death with aches, fever, chills and swollen lymph nodes choking off his airway. Not a very glamorous death for such a noble archeologist and philanthropist."

"What most people don't know is that his hands were gnarled and twisted from working long hours at the site. A deformity that made even a simple task like shaving difficult. That was pretty evident to the pathologist who saw him daily with fresh shaving nicks and cuts on his face. And that's how he did it. One of the items he covered with his poisonous brew was Carnarvon's shaving soap, brush and straight razor."

"But didn't those Lords and other nobles have attendants to shave them?" he asked.

"Yes, and he did too, but he preferred to do it himself on site because he was always in a hurry to learn what they may find next in the tomb."

"It's funny, in all of your American movies people are looking for the perfect crime. If there was ever a perfect crime this was it. Covering his murder with a Curse."

"That's amazing! How do you know so much about this?" asked Christian.

"It's easy . . . I was Carnarvon," CB smirked as he looked at a stunned Christian.

"Oh my god—this, that, this is . . ." Christian stuttered trying to find his words.

"I know, pretty cool right," CB responded.

"I was thinking more messed up than cool," Christian replied. "You mean, if I can see the future I can see how I die too . . . " Christian gulped.

CB smiled, "You can see potential for death. It's a little freaky at first, but once you can fully differentiate between future shared memories and your direct future, you'll see it all. At least you'll know which ones involved you directly; however, if and when you become one of the lucky few who develops the ability to see into the future, you will not be able to see your own death clearly. You will only be able to perceive dangerous situations, or at least those that are life threatening which show you potential end of life scenarios. Once you're dead, you'll be able to see your death.

After all, who wants to know when they are going to die. Now that would be freaky!"

They headed to town to grab something to eat. They hit an out-of-the-way place so as not to be interrupted. CB, when in public, was always on alert, especially with Christian by his side. Even with being extra cautious, that didn't mean they went unnoticed.

RJ and one of his friends saw them enter the eatery and continued on to another location but not before snapping a pic of Christian and the stranger with his cell phone, a request his father had made of him—or more like demanded. Mr. Wellington wanted to see for himself who brought embarrassment to the family. He should have only looked at RJ for the answer but was too proud or stubborn to admit his son was the cause.

RJ's weak character would never consider any attempt to approach Christian and the stranger unless he had the upper hand. And two on two wasn't his idea of having the upper hand, especially after feeling the effects of Christian's skills firsthand. Like his father, he was searching for an edge, one that his picture just may provide.

After dinner Christian offered up the extra bed in his room but CB graciously declined. "I should get going, I don't think your roommate would understand seeing me as your guest when he returns in the morning," CB chuckled.

Christian reflected back to earlier in the night, "Hey CB, explain to me again. If I have all the experience and skills of all the others and they have the same abilities as I do, how are we different?"

CB reflected, "Slow from the start," he smiled.

"Our connection to the others and their pasts is like being on the internet. We all have access to the same information, but all of us do not apply that knowledge to develop ourselves fully. In our case our minds are the computers and we can connect with energy produced from within us. Eastern philosophy calls this energy 'Chi'."

"Like being on the internet, you have the same resources as everyone else. The resources of the world are at your fingertips. The only exception is that our knowledge base expands far beyond that of the net, and our Chi, the vital energy or your life force, is many times greater than that of the average person, allowing us the ability to do remarkable things," CB explained.

Our differences come from here and here." CB pointed to Christian's head and patted him on the chest.

"Our Marks?" he asked.

"No, not the Mark itself. It is the knowledge and skill you develop over time and how you apply it. The Mark and its strength are a symbol of your specific development over that time, in our case millennia, as well as the strength in your heart."

"The strength of your heart grows through each Awakening. It is this strength along with your character which is reflected through your sign. The stronger the Mark, the more potential you have. I once told you your sign was strong and always has been. This is because you have always proven yourself to be, well, to be you. And for that we are grateful." CB smiled, taking his leave, leaving Christian with his questions.

Christian had no idea of the potential he possessed. Even with his newly strengthened abilities to connect and access information, his gift was only just beginning to bud. CB was well aware of his friend's capabilities which is something that caused great concern for him. Being so powerful and yet vulnerable at the same time placed Christian in a very dangerous position developmentally.

Christian woke to the sounds of birds chirping and a beam of sunlight hitting him in the face. He sat up finding Matt had not returned just yet which gave him another opportunity to connect with his past. Like a kid in a candy store he opened the vault containing multiple lifetime's worth of memories and experience.

Christian looked into his mind like scrolling through a library of events, memories and lifetimes. He quickly connected with a memory from the mid 1800s in the Midwest. He laughed to himself, seeing how he was dressed. He felt the rush of a chase as he and a group of men pursued three men that had robbed a local merchant who traded gold for credit. He was amazed at how crisp and fresh the memory connection was. The sights, smells, and sounds as well as the feeling of exhilaration. He knew each and every detail of what had transpired during the robbery.

Tom Atkins, the store owner, was as greedy as they came. He apparently shorted the three men on their gold deposit and when they tried to take it back, Tom pulled his gun. After arrogantly threatening that he could shoot the men on the spot and be within the law, he started waving his gun around in a threatening manner.

The three men threatened to go to the law just before Mr. Atkins pulled the hammer back on his gun, pointing it in their direction. And that's when one of the men shot him point-blank in the chest.

A customer who was watching from another room provided her account of what had happened to the sheriff. The men would have been within the law according to the witness' statement, but they got scared and ran; but not before they got greedy and pulled the remainder of the gold from the open safe. Now it was up to the law.

In all, the three had grabbed six hide bags at twenty-five pounds each and a couple of bags of gold coins before they left the dead merchant's shop. They ran into the street filled with curious onlookers who had heard the shot before they headed south out of town on their aging horses.

The chase wasn't hard. The three men were weighed down by the gold and their horses were old and running weary from double shifting as prospecting horses. As the posse caught up with the men they split up in a last effort to escape. One took to a path to the left, headed to the base of the foothills outside of Oatman and the others followed the main trail.

Christian, who was at the time named William Hand, split left to follow one man while the remainder followed the other two travelling straight on the main trail. When he finally caught up with the man, he was standing next to his exhausted horse with his hands up in the air. William arrested him without a struggle just before another member of the posse arrived. While tethering his hands together with a leather strap he noticed they were covered in dirt and some fresh blood from scratches. Thinking nothing of a prospector having dirty, cut up hands he had his partner retrieve the two bags of gold from the back of the man's horse and placed them on his own horse. He helped put the prisoner back in the saddle and the three headed to meet up with the others.

It was only when they got back in town that they realized the hide bags filled with gold coins were missing . . .

Just then there was a noise at the door. It was the sound of Matt's key being inserted into the lock. He was back from his Thanksgiving break.

Christian broke the connection immediately and greeted him, "Hey, how's it going?"

"Excellent," Matt replied. "How was your Thanksgiving?" Matt enthusiastically inquired as he entered the room burdened with two overstuffed satchels.

"It was great!" Christian exclaimed.

"Did your parents see the scar?" Matt asked.

"No, but I did show it to Hailey," he answered.

"Oh, Hailey, that good looking cousin of yours," Matt smiled.

The two got caught up with the events of each other's short holiday. Christian shared most of the events, leaving out certain details as advised by CB, after which they both busied themselves with prepping for the next day's classwork.

Once they finished their prep work they decided to head out for a bite to eat. Christian picked his jacket up from the bed and tossed it over his shoulder. While swinging his arm around, the jacket hit the chair and the prescription his father had given him came flying out of the pocket. "Oh, I forgot about these," he uttered.

"What's that?" Matt asked.

"The prescription my dad got for me. They're for my allergies and headaches," he said while carefully reading the label.

"But you don't get headaches, do you?" Matt asked.

"No, not for a while," Christian replied.

"Not since the canyon," Matt said inquisitively.

"Yeah, not since then," replied Christian, reflecting.

Christian started to think about the medications he had been given since early childhood. He always thought they were for allergies and to help with headaches associated with allergies. But why change the medication and increase the dosage? He hadn't complained to his parents of any problems. In fact, since the canyon he had completely forgotten to take them. He put the pills down on his desk, deciding to look into it when he returned from eating.

On the way out the door Christian's phone chimed in. It was Amy texting, "Just got back. Are you doing anything?" Christian responded telling her their destination with an invite.

"Perfect, see you there," she replied.

They met up at Firestone Grill a few minutes later. It was close to the campus and served excellent BBQ and burgers, the perfect college fare. Amy was especially happy to see Christian and made that apparent with her amorous greeting. Matt waited patiently before asking, "How is Tina?"

Amy smiled replying, "I don't know. Why don't you ask her yourself?" Amy looked over Matt's shoulder smiling. Tina expressed her feelings equally passionately. It was clear she missed Matt's company as well. The Four Musketeers sat for a couple of hours catching up.

-Eighteen-

Montaña de Oro

he first couple of weeks back in class had heavier than usual workloads as professors pushed to finish up the semester's curriculum and prepare for exams. In the little spare time he had, Christian sequestered himself from his friends and navigated his way through his new skill set. He travelled in time with his memories and connected with others from around the globe. It was an amazing journey. When he had a question he connected with CB who was keeping a watchful eye on him, ensuring he did not venture where he did not belong.

Of the seven remaining people he could connect with, two of them were children with whom he did not connect. CB was kind of the big brother, looking in on the kids from time to time to make sure they weren't having any problems. He was able to connect with two of the five remaining; a Brazilian woman named Doroteia which means 'Gift from God', whose Mark resembled a dove; and an aboriginal gentleman from Australia named Orad whose name means 'Earth' and his Mark was of a 'Star' as drawn by aborigines; a circle with smaller circles drawn around the perimeter. They were both very helpful in sharing with Christian and he shared in return. He was forming bonds with new friends and allies.

Of course in his eagerness to develop his skills he distanced himself from Matt and Amy as well as others in his study group, a fact that produced curiosity in Matt and concern by Amy as this was more apparent to them than the others. After all, finals were almost here.

Thursday following classes, Christian again went missing for a couple of hours. Before Matt headed out to meet the girls he texted him, "Hey buddy, where are you? Meeting girls in twenty . . ."

Christian replied, "Meet you there." Christian arrived thirty minutes later. As he walked into the restaurant he noticed Amy, Matt and Tina at a corner table. Tina was first to notice him walking up to the table and shook Amy's leg to get her attention. Amy and Matt were deep into it about Christian. It was apparent from the look on their faces that they had concerns. "Hey guys, how's it going?" he asked as he leaned over to give Amy a peck on the cheek.

"Where ya been?" Amy asked.

"Studying," he replied.

They continued with idle chatting for a while before Matt asked, "What's been going on the past couple of weeks?"

"What do you mean?" Christian asked.

"Well, you disappear after class and to be honest, you've been kind of distant. Is everything ok?" asked Matt.

"Yeah, everything's fine, I've just been busy," he replied.

A curious Matt continued to inquire about his recent activities for a while longer before moving onto other topics. There was an obvious tension about the topic and Christian's responses were less than satisfying to them.

During their evening out, Amy would occasionally glance at him as if trying to see what he was thinking, curious to know what was going on inside of him. Was he distancing himself because of her? His schoolwork? Something at home? Or was it the events at the canyon? Maybe the pressure is getting to him. Whatever it was, she set herself to finding out.

As the evening came to a close, Matt and Tina headed off on their own. Christian walked back to the dorms with Amy snuggling under his arm in the cool night air. She coyly continued to pry about his activities and why he'd been so distant. Although he loosened up a little while hanging out, he relaxed even more on the walk back to the dorms. It was easy to relate to Amy, but he wasn't going to tell all. He was trying to heed CB's advice and carefully chose his words regarding his activities on the walk back.

After a few awkward moments regarding his recent behavior, the topic changed to the upcoming weekend. "I was thinking, since this warm front is only supposed to last until Sunday that I'd like to go hiking on Saturday. Would you want to join me?" he asked.

"That's a great idea. Where do you want to go?" she asked enthusiastically.

"Montaña de Oro. I thought we could hike the coastline. What do you think?"

"That'll be perfect," Amy said leaning in for a deeper hug, happier now that he appeared to be opening up a little. "Were you going to ask Matt and Tina?" she asked.

"No, I thought it would be nice if it were just the two of us," he said glancing at her with a gentle smile.

"Even better," she smiled in approval, tightening her hug a bit more.

Saturday morning arrived and the weather couldn't be better. There was an early morning chill in the air but the unusual warm front promised to push temperatures up by almost twenty degrees above normal to about seventy degrees. The two headed to Montaña de Oro State Park in Los Osos which was about twenty miles away, stopping along the way for breakfast. The extra time allowed the cool oceanfront air to warm a little before starting their hike.

Arriving at the park, they both grabbed knapsacks and headed for the coastline. It was the perfect day; blue skies with the occasional tuft of cotton white clouds. The air was crisp, chilled by the light breeze drifting across the Pacific and keeping them cool as they made their way. "I forgot to look at the tides, I hope we can see some caves," he said.

"Why wouldn't we get to see the caves?" Amy asked.

"Well it's a Moon Tide," he replied.

"What's that?" she inquired.

Being from Jacksonville, a small town in Southern Oregon, Amy had little experience with the beach and lunar effects on tidal changes. She spent most of her childhood climbing trees, mountains and following streams and rivers when she wasn't working with her mom and dad tending to the many animals on her family's large farm.

"Moon Tide happens when there's a full moon. The gravitational force makes the tides higher and lower than normal. If it's high tide we won't be able to get close to the caves."

"Don't worry about that, we can always hike the ridges. They're pretty exciting and they have small caves, I think," added Amy.

"Oh, you've been here before?" Christian asked.

"Not exactly here, but I've walked the ridges a little further down before," Amy responded pointing to an area further down the coast.

The tide was on its way out when the pair reached the coastline. They slowly worked their way along the waterline for a couple of hours as the surf retreated, exposing more of the rocky flats. They had hit the tide just right. As Christian and Amy walked along the slippery rocks, hopping over the small pools of water they were able to access some of the smaller caves and hollows in the rugged coastline. They took photos of tidal pools and rock formations on their way to the caves as well as some curious wildlife.

Amy questioned Christian about his interests in exploring. He regaled her with tales of his exploring adventures as a child, including how his mother never knew what to expect when he came home. "There was always a creek or something I could explore. Winter or summer, it didn't matter. I was always checking on something or checking some theory out," Christian said. He told her about the time he tested the ice on his way to school.

"In a shop demonstration the day before, my teacher showed the class that long boards were weaker in the middle than short boards. They could hold less weight because of the increased distance between the support on each edge. So on my way to school the next day I looked at the width of the lake, frozen over but not enough to walk on. Then I looked at the swollen creek that fed into the lake, also frozen over and only ten percent as wide." Christian smirked in remembrance.

"Well, what happened?" Amy asked.

"Needless to say, the theory of long and short boards didn't apply to frozen water."

"Twenty minutes after I'd left for school in my brand new pants, I reached the back door to my house, with my mother standing there just glaring at me. 'What happened this time?' she asked, continuing, 'Those are brand new pants!' Well I told her the story and she freaked out a bit. I mean it's understandable. I never thought of the possibility of drowning! Then out of the blue she started laughing, telling me not to move. She ran and got her camera and took my picture. I didn't understand what was so funny at first until she showed me the picture later. I was covered head to toe in icy mud, with small twigs and icicles hanging from my hair. Sticks or twigs or something were caught in the laces of my shoes and I had a bright red nose to boot. As she put it, I looked as if I were dragged through a pile of wet, muddy leaves."

Amy laughed, "Sounds like you and I had something in common. I must have explored every crack and crevice within a mile of my house. And I was always covered in dirt. Mom never knew what to make of me. I'm sure she would have preferred me playing with dolls instead of having to buy me work boots and coveralls to go climb the hills in, but that wasn't me. I used to freak her out on a regular basis."

"How'd you do that?" Christian asked.

"Let's just say Mom wasn't a fan of anything creepy-crawly. I'd always come home with something in a jar that I found, and put it on the counter for all to see."

"That doesn't sound too bad," Christian said.

"Yeah, but how would your mom feel if a five inch centipede ran up her arm from the kitchen sink?" Amy asked, smirking.

"No way, what happened?" Christian asked laughing.

"I found this centipede, biggest I ever saw and I didn't have a jar, just a small box, so I put it in the box and brought it home. When I got home I put the box in the sink and went looking for a jar. Mom walked into the kitchen, picked up the box and took the top off," Amy chuckled remembering.

"What'd she do?" Christian asked anxiously.

"She freaked. . . . She screamed so loud the neighbors heard her down the road. When I ran out I saw her flapping her wings, grabbing at her top just before she ripped it off and threw it to the floor. She ran into the yard screaming my name until my father came out and calmed her down. She punished me for a week, but Dad got me off for good behavior the next day."

"She must have been pissed!" Christian laughed.

"Yeah, but it was funny seeing her standing in the yard in her bra jumping up and down and yelling at the top of her lungs. The dog even looked at her like she was nuts!" she smiled.

"After she calmed down a bit the story came out. She thought my dad had bought her a gift and put it in the sink. When she opened the box the centipede ran up her arm and into her blouse," Amy said laughing. She continued, "To this day you can't bring that story up without giving her the willies. She get the shivers, stands up, looks at me and Dad with our smirks on and says 'Funny, real funny,' before she leaves the room mumbling to herself. I guess it really did freak her out," Amy reflected.

They had gone about as far as they could go when they reached the end of a small flat. The outgoing tide being at its lowest allowed them to travel much further than anticipated. The rock wall towered straight up above them on one side and the crashing surf pounded the rocks just below the shelf on which they were standing. "Do you think we should head back?" asked Amy. Christian didn't respond. Stepping closer to him and grasping his arm she asked again, "Do you think we should head back? It doesn't look like we can go any further."

Christian hesitated, his eyes were fixed on something familiar. He felt somehow drawn in the direction he was looking. "Yeah, I guess we should. We still have a few minutes. There's something I want to check out."

"What else can you check out? We can't go any further . . ." Amy said as she followed his gaze to a small ledge that wrapped around the rock wall.

The surf, although at its lowest, was still pounding the cliff face just below. Amy, now well aware of his adventurous side, looked at him as he studied the cliff face. A confident smirk appeared on his face. She looked again at the ledge and knew what he was thinking, "No way, you're not thinking what I think you're thinking. . . . Are you?" Christian nodded affirmatively, his smirk now a smile stretching across his face.

"Wait here, I'll be back in a few minutes," he said as he made his way to the ledge.

Amy nervously looked on, "Are you crazy? You're out of your freaking mind!" she said shouting over the sounds from the pounding surf as she followed him closer to the edge of the flat where he had access to a small ledge. The sound of the turbulent water slamming into the cliff was almost deafening. The ocean spray was filling the air with a cold mist.

A confident Christian reassured Amy he would be fine as he climbed out onto the ledge and started carefully working his way around the point. Amy inched herself closer to the edge and anxiously watched him work his way around as she shouted for him to, "PLEASE BE CAREFUL," but the pounding surf was louder.

Christian disappeared from view as he worked his way further along the path. He reached a point where a six or seven foot section of the rock ledge had broken away from the constant assault of the pounding surf. His reasonable self told him to turn back, but there was something so familiar with this spot and something, let's call it his curiosity, pushed him forward.

The narrow ledge he was standing on was slippery with algae and wet from the ocean spray. He grasped hold of a rock protruding out of the cliff face just in front of him and lunged, making a grab for the other side. Barely clearing the gap, his left foot landed on a small flat on the ledge. Struggling to maintain his balance, he pulled up his right foot which was dangling over the broken edge of the gap and wriggled it onto the ledge. As he grabbed hold of a rock jutting out from the cliff face just above him, the ledge beneath him cracked loudly and collapsed, crashing into the torrent below.

He could feel his grip slipping from the icy cold rock face as his feet scraped frantically along the wall, trying to get a foot hold on any protrusion that would support him. He struggled, using all the strength he could summon in his hands and arms to work himself across the slippery rock wall, his fingers straining to hold the full weight of his body as the waves crashed relentlessly below.

After what seemed an eternity he reached the ledge on the other side and let go a sigh of relief. His heart was pounding as he calmed himself. He could feel he was close to something, but close to what? His curiosity continued to push him further. As he cautiously made his way around the next point he entered the shadows, a cold, dark spot where the rock wall was angled out over his head and was blocking the sunlight. He sensed he was almost there. But where? He could see that the ledge widened a few feet away from where he was standing. It was hard to see with the salty mist burning his eyes. As he anxiously inched his way along he reached the point where the ledge widened and found himself standing at the entrance to a cold, dark cave. His excitement was building, but still. . . . What was it that brought him here? It all seemed so familiar, as if he had seen this place before.

His eyes adjusted to the darkness as he slowly made his way into the cave. The fairly well lit entrance was large, about ten foot high, and he could see to the back of the depression forming the cave, which was about thirty feet deep. Working his way to the back of the cave he noticed a much smaller opening. He pulled his LED light from his carabiner and shone the light into the opening. His excitement grew; it was like looking into the past. He continued to ignore his reasonable side telling him to turn back, and instead elected to follow his adventurous curiosity. The entrance was small, only three to four feet in diameter, and led to an even deeper cave. It was deeper than any other cave he'd seen before, appearing to go back another thirty or forty feet.

He crawled through the opening and stepped into a large vault. The front of the cave had a sloping twelve to fifteen foot high ceiling. He felt as if he had entered a tomb. It was eerie. His heart was pounding even harder now than it was when he was hanging from the cliff face.

Light in hand, he worked his way further back, carefully watching his step as he studied the interior walls. The floor was covered with a slimy growth making it difficult to move without slipping. The width of the tortuous cave grew narrower then wider then narrow again as he moved closer to the back of the dark cavern. He could feel his heart pounding in his chest.

Water was dripping from the walls, making an eerie sound as it dripped into small pools where the rock had been hollowed out by the spinning vortex of water created over centuries of surf rushing into the cave. The sound of the pounding surf, loudly noticeable in the outer cave, was growing faint as he moved further into the cave.

After a few minutes exploring the back of the cave he decided it was time to turn back, still a bit curious as to what was driving him to take such a chance to reach a cave that he had no idea was even there. Was it curiosity, intuition, or something else?

He started moving toward the front of the cave, working his way in and out of the chambers formed by the cave walls, periodically narrowing along its path. He entered one of the wider chambers and noticed a steady stream of water dropping from a jagged ledge about seven or eight foot up. His curiosity kicked in again and he worked his way up to the shelf. Poking his head above the edge of the shelf, he shone his light across it. There was nothing remarkable, just a little slime and a slow stream of water falling into what appeared to be a small depression in the shelf. He inched his way closer to the depression and shined his light down into the pool.

It was dark and murky. As he moved the light across the pool he noticed something. It looked like a rope covered with a floating dark green slime. Whatever it was, it looked out of place.

He reached in behind the ledge and into the depression, pushing his hand deep into the icy water. His fingertips, desensitized from digging into the cliff wall, worked their way into the slimy bath and started probing the depth of the depression. He felt something sharp and hard wrap around his arm and instinctively withdrew his hand as quickly as he could, falling backward to the cave floor with his heart pumping from the scare.

Summers in Long Island had taught him if you feel something hard and sharp in the water, especially if it wraps around your arm, it usually bites.

He chuckled nervously and climbed back up to the shelf. Pushing his hand deep into the slimy, dark pool he felt the strange object again. Whatever it was, it was something he just knew didn't belong there. His excitement grew as he pushed his hand in deeper and grabbed a hold of it. He pushed, twisted and pulled, trying to wriggle it free from the natural casing that had entombed it. Finally he loosened it up enough to remove it from the watery time capsule.

As he pulled his hand from the depression, he couldn't believe his eyes. In his hand was a slime-covered, barnacle-encrusted cross, complete with a slime-covered ropy chain. He carefully worked the length of the chain free from its attachment to the bottom of the pool and with one final tug, released it from the calcific tomb. He stared in awe of what he had found, but his time was running out. The tide had changed; his curiosity had to wait.

The sound of the rising water crashing against the outside cliff face reminded him where he was. He quickly checked the pool on the ledge for any other treasures with a quick swipe of his hand at the bottom of the depression before placing the cross in his back pack and hurried out of the cave and back to Amy.

He was gone well over twenty minutes before she could see him rounding the point. She was relieved to see him but at the same time, she—was—pissed! Before he reached the flats where she was standing she started yelling, "What the hell is wrong with you? You climb out on a freaking ledge and leave me here by myself for over twenty minutes . . ." This time he heard every word, pounding surf or no pounding surf. She continued her rant, "You disappear around the point and I can't see you . . . I kept looking into the water to see if you fell in. What would I have done if you fell in the water? You crazy son of a bitch!"

He reached the flat and walked up to her with a smirk on his face like a kid with a bag full of candy on Halloween. "What the hell are you smirking at?" she asked loudly as he reached into his pouch and pulled out the cross. Amy's eyes widened, "Oh my god. What is that?" she stuttered, covering her open mouth with one hand and smacking his arm with the other. "That's for scaring the hell out of me you crazy S.O.B."

They didn't know it yet, but the cross, partially covered with slime, dirt and small barnacles was in daylight for the first time in almost two centuries. The two admired the find closely. Areas of the cross that had been attached to the wall of the cave, now exposed to the sunlight, revealed the glittering of gold. "Oh my god! How? Where did you find that?" she excitedly asked again.

"I don't know how. When we started out I only wanted to see the coastline and some caves, but when we got here I felt something pushing me to continue around the ledge."

Amy looked at him curiously, "Is this something that happens often?" she asked.

"No, first time I can remember," Christian smiled adding, "I'm glad it did."

"Me too," she smiled.

Christian started peeling back some of the crusty grime on the cross. As he tried to peel off what he thought was a large barnacle, a layer of slime wiped off, unveiling another little secret concealed by time. The crusty covering was hiding precious gems. They uncovered one of them from under its dirt casing. An emerald, bigger than they had ever seen, sparkling in the bright mid-day sunlight for the first time in centuries. They continued to examine the treasure for another few minutes, still stunned by the find, before realizing the tide had turned and was quickly rising.

Christian hurried to pull a tee shirt out of his bag and moistened it in a pool of water. He quickly wrapped the cross and placed it in a plastic bag and back into his knapsack. The first wave of the rising tide had just crested the edge of the flat, crashing loudly close to where the two were standing. Christian said, "Let's go this way," pointing up.

Amy looked at him like he was crazy, but her adventurous side kicked in. "Let's go," she said as another wave crested the edge of the flat. They looked at each other with the excitement of adventure and began to push their way upward and inland to avoid the quickly rising surf. They climbed the treacherous rock face until they reached the trail at the top of the cliffs and headed back to the car.

Sitting in the car they couldn't help but to take another look at the cross, pouring bottled water onto the tee to keep the cross moist. He slowly unwrapped it, double checking that it was real. It was magnificent! Well over twelve inches tall and heavy with a number of large barnacle-like protrusions, suggesting it was heavily jeweled. "Why do you keep wetting it?" Amy asked.

Christian explained, "I don't know why exactly, but on all the treasure hunting shows I used to watch, they always put stuff in trays or buckets full of water to keep them wet. My guess is it's to stop the slime and crusty stuff from drying out and becoming too hard to remove."

Christian started thinking about cleaning up the cross as quickly as possible. "Hey, is Tina going to be back at your room when we get back?"

"I'm not sure, why?" Amy asked.

"I want to clean this up tonight and check it out. This definitely has a history," he smiled in admiration of the find.

"Definitely," Amy added.

Christian continued, "I'm sure Matt will be back at my place tonight. . . . Hmmm, I think it best not to tell anyone about this yet."

"I agree. I'll check with Tina and see what's up for tonight. She did mention something about dinner. I'll find out."

Shortly after returning to her room, Amy texted Christian, "Tina's going out with Matt for an early dinner. She wanted to know if they could have our place to themselves tonight."

Christian thought for a moment before texting, "That's perfect, come over after Matt picks her up, we'll order in."

"Ok, C U L8R," Amy replied.

Matt was sitting at his computer when Christian walked in and gently placed his bag on the floor next to his bed. "Hey, what's up? How was the hike?" Matt inquired.

"It was amazing, a perfect day to hike," Christian replied trying to hold back his smile.

"No doubt," Matt responded, "By the way, I found this on the floor when I came in."

"What is it?" asked Christian.

"It's a note. 'Remember Lesson 1.' Know what it is?" he asked.

Christian responded evasively, "No . . . I don't."

"Well, I thought you might know. There's a number written on it in your handwriting."

Matt handed the paper to Christian, "Oh, that's the number to where Hailey was working the other day." Placing the note on his desk he changed the topic. "What's up for tonight? Where are you and Tina headed?" he asked.

"How do you know about that?" Matt asked. Christian didn't have to say a word. "Amy?" Matt asked, receiving the affirmative nod from Christian. "We're headed out for a quiet dinner. She insisted on taking me out for my birthday," Matt explained.

"It's your birthday? Happy Birthday! I didn't know it was your birthday," Christian said cheerfully.

"It's not. My birthday isn't until next week, but she wanted to take me out tonight for some reason," Matt explained.

"It sounds like you're going to have a great night," Christian added.

"Yeah, it should be," Matt smiled.

A couple of hours had passed before Matt headed over to Tina and Amy's. Christian hustled to grab a Tupperware container and fill it with water. He placed the damp tee-wrapped cross in the water bath to soak before heading to his computer for tips on how to clean the cross.

While waiting for Amy to swing by he started to prep the cross for cleaning. He soaked it in a tepid bath of soapy water. He gently began to clean the top of the cross and the attached chain with an old toothbrush and some gauze he had lying around. After applying a little elbow grease, the greenish, grey slime encasing the treasure slowly started to separate and peel away, revealing that unmistakable luster of gold.

He turned his focus on the large stone he and Amy had partially wiped clean while standing on the rocky shoreline. A close inspection suggested it was one of many skillfully set into the cross. He started carefully cleaning the crevices around the setting that had cradled the large emerald for over two centuries. Just as he moved on to polishing the stone with Q-tips and a soft polishing rag from his sunglass case, Amy arrived.

Christian opened the door, greeting Amy with the childlike grin on his face. "This is incredible, you have to see this," he said pulling her over to his makeshift cleaning station. He lifted the cross out of the soapy bath and handed it to her as the suds slid off the stone, revealing the most magnificent emerald she had ever seen. She stood stunned with amazement, staring at the emerald with her mouth wide open. “Oh my god, this is . . . the most amazing thing I have ever seen!”

“I know, right!” Christian said, exhilarated.

Over the next couple of hours they worked on freeing the cross and chain from the layers of slime and growth that accumulated over the centuries. Sand caught in the intricate braiding of the chain had allowed a slimy growth to build up, making for tedious work. Amy made use of a small eyeliner-type makeup brush to clean the inside loops of the braided chain and pipe cleaners to polish them to a luster. Christian went through a box of toothpicks, half a box of Q-tips and destroyed his toothbrush cleaning the settings on all the stones.

All totaled there were fifty-three stones. Five large stones; three emeralds, one on each side and one on the bottom of the cross, one diamond on the top of the cross and the most magnificent of all, a heart shaped ruby centered on the cross. In addition, each side of the cross was embellished with multiple smaller stones running the length of the cross, twenty-four on each side. There were diamonds, sapphires, rubies, emeralds, and amethysts as well as others. It was spectacular!

Christian took to the computer to continue his research on the cross as Amy completed some final touches on the chain. It wasn’t long before he had a hit. “Amy, you were right. This cross does have history . . . big history,” he said intriguingly.

Amy ran over to the computer, “What is it?” she asked excitedly.

The two started to read the story behind the cross. The Cross was a gift from King Ferdinand VII to the commander of the regional Presidio and Church of Spain missionary built on the Monterey coastline. The mission had since moved to Carmel, but the stone church on the Monterey coastline that was built in 1794 still stands today. It was used as a Royal Chapel for soldiers at the new Spanish presidio of Monterey.

It is believed The Cross was an advance payment for the development of the region under Spanish rule and to build fortifications and a stronger military presence.

The Cross remained at the Monterey facility until rumors of an impending attack by a Corsair named Hipolyte Bouchard and his troops started to spread throughout the ranks.

Bouchard was a French pirate or privateer working for Argentine, Peruvian and Chile's patriotic forces fighting for their independence from Spanish royalists. He was well known for attacking Spanish settlements along the west coast of what is now California and South America, and had travelled as far west as Hawaii.

The rumors soon turned into reality when Bouchard, with two ships and 350 men, attacked Monterey in 1818. Prior to the attack, in an attempt to protect The Cross from Bouchard, the commander in charge ordered The Cross be moved to the mission in San Juan Capistrano for safekeeping.

Bouchard was a skilled tactician. His assault on Monterey was victorious and shortly after the assault on Monterey, Bouchard and his men proceeded south and quickly overran the troops protecting San Juan Capistrano. The Cross was neither seen nor heard of again.

Some say that Bouchard was unaware of The Cross' existence until a cowardly officer traded knowledge of its existence for his life. He was slain mercilessly after divulging The Cross' whereabouts.

Furious of the loss of such a prize, King Ferdinand placed a large bounty on Bouchard's head. Bouchard was pursued by many, but most never returned. He was never found and as for the bounty, it was never collected.

They read the article through to the end. It provided a detailed history of The Cross and its origins. At the bottom of the article was an artist's rendition depicting Ferdinand VII receiving The Cross from two angels that had come down from above on rays of light from heaven itself.

It was the very same Cross, one and the same. They had found a piece of history made over two hundred years ago. After their initial moment of shock had passed they both became very excited. They started jumping up and down around the room. Amy jumped on and off the beds. "Let's go celebrate, what do you say?" Amy asked excitedly.

"I'm in!" said Christian grabbing his jacket. They packed up The Cross and hid it as well as they could and headed into town to celebrate the find. On the way they began discussing what they should do with the prize.

As the two celebrated they listed all of the ideas that they could think of on what to do with The Cross and then wrote down the pros and cons of each idea. By the end of the evening they both had agreed the best idea was to bring it to a collector/appraiser of historical artifacts to determine its value and the best course to take.

Morning came and Amy awoke to Christian sitting at his desk. He already had the names of two highly credentialed historians in the immediate area, both associated with the San Luis Obispo Historical Center. "I'm going to call them this morning," he said smiling.

"Well don't get your hopes up, it's Sunday," Amy smiled.

"Not a problem," a confident Christian stated, "The Historical Society is open from ten to four today so we'll be able to get in touch with someone." Amy smiled, giving him a hug from behind.

Christian was way too excited to wait for the center to open at ten so he picked up his phone and dialed the number for the first name on the list. Four rings later he heard. "Hello, you have reached Theodore Anolick, at the tone please . . ." Christian ended the call. "What happened?" Amy asked.

"He wasn't home and I really don't want to leave a message about this," he answered. "Next," he said, dialing the second number. "Hello," a raspy voice answered.

"Is this Dr. Arthur Balzack?" he asked.

"Yes it is. Who may I ask is calling?" asked Dr. Balzack.

"My name is Christian Asher and I—"

Before he could finish, Balzack interrupted him gruffly, "You do know it's rather early on a Sunday morning son . . . Don't you?"

"Yes sir, but I'm sure you'll want to hear what I have to say," Christian responded, continuing, "Dr. Balzack, I found something I believe to be extremely valuable and I'd like it if you would look at it for me."

"Well I'm heading over to the center at ten, can you bring it there?" Balzack asked.

"I'd rather not sir. You see, I'm sure it's extremely valuable and I'd prefer not to."

"Ok, well what is it that you found that you think is so valuable?" Balzack asked, interrupting with a tone of doubt.

"Well, we believe it's the Ferdinand VII Cross from Monterey."

The phone went silent. "You can't be serious. . . . Are you?" Dr. Balzack asked in disbelief.

"Yes Sir, one hundred percent," Christian said with confidence.

Balzack, believing this to be impossible, requested that Christian describe the cross. Christian replied smiling, "I'll do better than that. Why don't you take a look at your email?" Christian urged, having taken his email from the historical society's web page.

Balzack started to talk, "Okay, but this . . ."

Christian interrupted him stating, "This will be worth your while . . . trust me."

Balzack walked over to his laptop and opened his email just as Christian's email arrived. "Hold on, it just came through," Balzack said apprehensively, clicking through the email. Christian could hear the doubt in his voice. Balzack opened the email and the attached picture.

As the computer slowly revealed the picture of the cross, Balzack's mouth dropped in stunned silence. He was staring at a pair of hands holding the cross over today's Sunday paper. Christian heard him say under his breath, "I'll be damned, that sure looks like it, but it can't be."

Christian broke the silence, "Would you like to look at it for us?"

"Are you kidding! If this is what I think it is, this will be one of the most incredible . . ." Balzack started to stutter a bit continuing, "Of course, of course, I'd love to. When can you bring it over?" Balzack asked, getting caught up in the excitement. "Can you bring it now?" he inquired.

"Sure, but don't you have to go to the center?" Christian asked.

"Oh right, I'll have to take care of that. Not to worry," Balzack answered, pacing.

"Great, I'll bring it over now but under one condition. You have to promise not to talk about this with anyone," Christian demanded.

Balzack reluctantly agreed admitting, "I think that would be best for the time being." He gave his address to Christian and set plans to meet in a half hour.

Balzack had lived on the west coast his entire life. His interest in the history of the region began in childhood when he himself would play pirate and search for buried treasure. He became a teacher in the public school system teaching history, a field that allowed him as much time as he desired to research the region.

He had worked on multiple dig sites in the area searching for historical artifacts. Hipolyte Bouchard was one his favorite topics as he was the only real pirate known to frequent the area. Balzack had found many artifacts from dig sites over the years and some that were believed to be Bouchard's, including a gold ring with the initials 'HB' in French script which proudly resided in a display on his desk with a historical document suggesting its ownership.

Balzack anxiously prepared for Christian and Amy to arrive. He called his assistant at the center to advise her he would be late. He pulled historical reference books from the shelves by his desk and cleaned the dust off before he opened each to the pages with reference to The Cross, quickly skimming over the articles to refresh his memory of its history; not that he needed to.

Amy and Christian arrived at Balzack's house and started walking toward the front door. Balzack opened his door and excitedly walked out, greeting them. Introductions were made on their way into the house. Amy snickered at his quirky excitement. He was no

Indiana Jones but he did have that in-the-fields weathered look from spending years on dig sites.

"Thank you for seeing us!" Christian said as they entered Balzack's home.

"Wow," Amy said walking into the entrance foyer and gazing into his home. Balzack's house held a multitude of historical finds from the world over. It was a mini museum. There were wall cases and shelves filled with artifacts, fossils, pottery, jewelry and the like everywhere the eye could see. His adventures had followed Bouchard's trail. Bouchard's efforts were helpful in bringing independence to these regions.

Balzack's collection was a snapshot of his travels; there were wacos and jewelry from Peru, pottery from Chile, spurs and armor from Spanish conquistadors. He had silver and gold leaf Bibles from Spanish churches established in South America. The North American versions had been absorbed by collectors and were long gone.

Each and every item was sorted neatly and displayed in oak cases that were lined with velvet trays. There was also a Spanish officer's uniform, sword, and parade saddle in the corner. He had bows and arrows, spears and arrowheads used by the indigenous tribes from each region, and a shrunken head that made Amy cringe. All were neatly catalogued and labeled with dates of discovery, the estimated age of the artifacts, region of the find and his catalogue number at the base of the label. It was all very proficient.

He led them over to a table and asked excitedly, "Do you have it? Did you bring it?" Christian replied affirmatively as he lifted the tee-wrapped Cross from his bag and placed it on a table next to a felt pad. Amy watched Balzack's face as Christian slowly unwrapped The Cross. As he flipped the final fold of the tee away from The Cross, a flicker of golden light bounced across his face. His eyes widened as he pulled a lamp in closer asking, "May I?" as he reached to pick up The Cross, his knees shaking. Christian smiled, nodding affirmatively. "It's beautiful, absolutely beautiful," Balzack said as he held The Cross closer to the light. "I can't believe this is really it. How . . . Where did you find it?" he asked. Christian just smiled, watching him as he carefully handled The Cross.

Balzack started examining The Cross. His hands trembling at first as he took measurements of The Cross and chain then weighed them together and separately as well as he could. He asked question after question about how and where they found it as he studied each of the magnificent stones through a jeweler's eye loupe. Balzack's questions were answered cautiously so as not to give away too much detail.

Before arriving at Balzack's house, Christian and Amy had both agreed not to go into too much detail about the location of the find. Like every other treasure hunter, it's location, location, location. Although Christian wasn't planning a return trip to the site anytime soon, he'd rather not see a massive influx of would-be treasure hunters in the area, more for fear of someone getting killed trying to reach the cave.

They answered the questions as cautiously as possible but Balzack was good, real good. He quickly pointed out, "I can understand you not wanting to tell me exactly where you found this, but it is fairly apparent," Balzack smiled confidently.

"What do you mean?" Amy asked.

"Look, I understand that revealing the location might seem like a bad idea to you. I of all people understand. I hated it when uninvited guests came to my sites and poked around. The bastards would camp on the outskirts of my digs all the time. They would dig for themselves, not to document history, but for whatever they could find to sell.

They destroyed countless artifacts and have stolen history out from under us. It's all about the money to them. They're no better than tomb raiders and treasure whores, if you'll excuse my French. But if you don't want anyone to know this came from the caves over by Montaña de Oro State Park we'll have to clean it up a bit more.

Christian and Amy looked at each other in shock. "How did you know that?" they asked simultaneously.

Balzack chuckled. "You cleaned it up pretty well. Probably used dish soap, am I right?" he asked. Amy nodded in confirmation. Balzack continued, "The soap mixes with the organic growth resulting in a cloudy film. Now as for how I know where you found it, under two of the larger stones there are pieces of calcium. The most likely source around here would be from crustaceans like barnacles, mussels and things like that. Under this one," he pointed to one of the emeralds, "this one still has algae under it. Hard to notice because the stone is green. This stringy type of algae grows in dark places out of sunlight. That, plus a few encrusted grains of sand, leads us to the caves along the beach."

"Okay, I understand that part, but how did you know we found it at the park?" Christian asked.

"That was the easy part," he said. There are tiny shards of stone in the bottom of your bag from the park. They stuck to the shirt when you pulled out The Cross. I'd know that rock anywhere. I used to explore there myself, and if I know it, others will as well."

For three hours they examined and talked about The Cross. There was no doubt in his mind it was Ferdinand VII's cross. The excitement was almost too much for him to handle. Balzack opened a cabinet filled with beakers and containers containing various products used to clean artifacts. Grabbing two of the containers, some cloth and a few pointed dental instruments he began cleaning The Cross, chain and jewels as he further discussed the history of The Cross with them. Amy and Christian watched the sheer joy he was experiencing doing this. Fifteen minutes later, The Cross was so clean it almost glowed in the dark. It was truly magnificent. The three of them stared in silence, admiring its luster.

Balzack had to get to the center for an afternoon presentation but not before taking a few pictures for his records. They agreed to keep quiet about the find and meet again over the next few days. The extra time would allow Balzack to determine the best course of action. To start, he suggested having a jeweler appraise The Cross with emphasis on the fifty-three stones. Balzack knew of such a jeweler, one he had worked with in the past who dealt with antiquities. "I'll think about it," Christian said as he started to pack The Cross up in the tee.

"Hold on, wait a second," Balzack said, stopping Christian from wrapping The Cross in the dirty tee. "You don't keep a find like this in an old tee shirt." He walked over to his desk covered with dust and old papers and opened a drawer, pulling out a black crushed velvet wrap and bag.

"Nice desk," Christian commented.

"Yeah it is," Balzack grunted, bending forward to reach the drawers. "I never use it. . . . I'm a field man, not a desk guy." He grunted again as he looked through a few more drawers and shelves before pulling out a yellowed box about the size of a picture frame but a little thicker. "This should do," he smiled. "Let me show you how to do that," he said as he took The Cross from Christian and removed it from the tee shirt.

"First, wrap the chain this way," he instructed, wrapping both sides of the chain in the velvet blanket, folding them over onto each other and placing rubber bands in three locations along the length of the chain. "This will prevent additional damage to the chain from rubbing against itself and it will also prevent it from bouncing up against The Cross and scratching it, or worse, dislodging one or more of the stones.

He explained the need to protect the original condition of The Cross and chain as he carefully placed pieces of cotton in the loop on top of The Cross where the chain passed through. He showed them the wear caused by the chain rubbing on the loop. "This will help prevent further wearing of the loop and the chain as well."

Christian and Amy watched as he opened the box. It was filled with a light Styrofoam impression material that was faded from the years it had spent on his shelf. Balzack centered The Cross and pressed it into the foam, forming a perfect cast of The Cross and providing a temporary protective casing. Then he lay the wrapped chain next to it, depressing it slightly, and secured the lid. He placed a thick rubber band around the box before putting it in the black velvet bag. "Okay, now you're set," he said patting the bag gently and handing it to Christian with a grateful smile and a final, "Unbelievable!"

"Thank you," Christian smiled.

"No, thank YOU," he said. "It's not often dreams come true, but this really is a dream come true. Thank you!" he said most sincerely.

Christian and Amy headed back to Cal Poly. On the way Amy asked, "How did you know where The Cross was?"

"I don't know, I just knew—I had a feeling," he said semi-evasively.

Amy continued, "I mean, just before you climbed out onto the ledge you had that strange look on your face again."

"What do you mean?" Christian asked curiously.

"It's hard to explain," she said, thinking about how to best approach this.

"Listen, I know you've been distant for a reason. You have a lot on your plate with school and this canyon thing and all the stuff that's been happening. I can understand that, but when certain things happen now, you become a different person and it's a little scary for me," she said confiding.

"I haven't noticed anything," Christian responded.

Amy continued, "Since the canyon strange things have happened to you. Remember the first time RJ started with you—at Taco Tuesdays—you were you. Sweet, normal you, and you got your butt whipped?" she chuckled uneasily. "Then while we were walking the fair and on the boardwalk everything was fine until all of a sudden just before we saw RJ and his friends, your face changed. It's hard to explain. It's like one minute I'm with you and the next I'm with someone completely different." Christian listened closely.

"Your eyes get dark and serious. You get this hard, stoic look on your face and you look more confident than I've ever seen in anyone before. Then you do these incredibly amazing things that you don't even remember as soon as it's all over."

Christian chimed in, "Well in my defense I did remember the chase through town," he said smiling at her.

"Yeah, that's another example of when your face changed," she said with concern in her tone. "We're talking in the car and as soon as RJ pulled up, you changed."

"I'm just afraid that something is happening to you that you can't control or that may be hurting you," Amy said with concern. "I don't want you to change," she confided. "At first whenever something stressful or bad was about to happen, you changed. This time you changed and it wasn't because of anything stressful, you just did. I just think that whatever it is, might be getting worse and I'm afraid for you," she said with concern.

Christian stumbled for a moment trying to think of a way around this conversation, unsuccessfully. He opened up to Amy about his heightened senses. "It's like this," he said, Amy looking on anxiously, "Since the canyon, anytime I'm in a stressful situation or something bad is about to happen, my senses become heightened and for some reason, as you have seen, I can do things. Things I've never been able to do before, like the fight, the car and even flying the plane at home. But I never noticed any change, it just happens," he said omitting all of how and why. "At least now I can remember what happens."

Amy looked at him for a moment. "But at the park there was no stress. How did you know about The Cross?" she asked.

Christian pulled over and paused for a moment, "I didn't. Something told me to keep going," he said.

"Yeah, I know. I was there too, and I saw you keep going. You scared the sh*t out of me," Amy blurted.

"No, you don't understand. Something told me I was there before."

Amy looked at him strangely. "What do you mean you were there before?" she asked.

"This is going to take a little faith on your part. I don't want you to think I'm crazy," he said. "Do you remember the dreams I was having?" he asked. Amy nodded affirmatively. "Well, those weren't just dreams, they were memories.

"Memories?" she questioned.

"When I think of those dreams, I can remember things. Things like where I was, who I was and what I did for a living. I can even speak and understand the language, kind of like the restaurant in Vegas. I get this flashback, like a string of images racing through my mind and I remember."

"So . . . you're talking some kind of reincarnation thing?" she asked hesitantly.

"Yeah, I guess it's something like that," he said continuing, "I'm not exactly sure."

"When we were on the flats and I saw the ledge, something connected. It was so familiar. That's why I climbed out on the ledge and followed it around. There was something inside telling me to keep going, so I followed my instincts."

"So, you had a dream about this. . . . The Cross?" she asked.

"No, that's the funny part, no dream or flashbacks. It was just something pushing me forward. Call it intuition or whatever, I don't know. All I know is it led me to The Cross."

They sat quietly for a while longer before Christian started the car and headed for the campus. The conversation had left Christian with as many questions as it had Amy.

-Nineteen-
Being There

hat night Matt was again woken by strange sounds from Christian's side of the room. Sitting up, he grabbed his pad and his phone. He videoed Christian's night terrors, as he called them, and jotted a few notes down. The sequence was shorter than most of the previous episodes that had lasted up to and sometimes over three hours. This episode was just shy of an hour long.

In the morning Matt inquired how Christian was feeling. Unlike the initial dreams, he did not wake exhausted and feeling ill. He woke refreshed and full of energy. Enlightened, if you will. "Great!" Christian responded. "How'd you sleep?" he asked.

"Pretty good," Matt said. "You sure you're alright? he asked hesitantly. "You were at it pretty good again last night! You know . . . dreaming."

Christian smiled. "I'm fine," he responded before changing the topic. "Last week before finals. You ready?" he asked.

"No problem," Matt said, accepting the topic change reluctantly. "I need to study up on Leone's class and I'll be set."

"Excellent!" Christian replied. "I'm going to meet Amy for breakfast, want to come along?"

"No thanks, I'll catch up with you in class," Matt said, reflecting.

Christian grabbed his jacket and left the room texting Amy, "Good Morning. On my way for breakfast, want to meet?"

As soon as Christian left, Matt downloaded and reviewed his video from the night before, studying it carefully. He picked up his phone and texted, "Zeus in full motion!"—Send.

Amy met up with Christian, noticing he was excited about something. "Hi," she said kissing him on the cheek. "What are you so excited about?" she asked.

"I was there," he said.

"You were where?" she asked.

"It was me that put The Cross there," he said excitedly.

Amy looked at him pausing, "What do you mean it was you? How could you put The Cross there?" she said with concerned curiosity. "And stop smiling like that," she ordered.

"Look, I had a dream last night showing me everything that happened," he assured her.

"Wait. . . . So you're telling me in some previous life, if that's even possible, that you somehow put The Cross in the cave and that's how you knew it was there?" she inquired skeptically and continued. "I mean, how do you know it was you? Just because you had a dream? How can you tell the dream was real or if the dream was caused by finding The Cross?" she questioned.

"I know it must sound crazy to you, but I swear I put The Cross there," he said persuasively.

The two sat down with breakfast as Christian began to tell her about the dream. "Do you remember when I told you some of my dreams are actually memories of past lives? Well, that's what this is . . . was . . . is. It was a memory," Christian said seriously.

"Well how can you be sure?" she asked.

"I'm just sure of it. When I started having these dreams, they were different, unlike any other dreams I've had. They were full of details complete with sights, smells, tastes and feelings." Amy listened intently. "I could taste foods I've never eaten and feel the pain and stiffness in my back, arms and legs from a long day's work. I could feel the heat from my tea cup. I could see my kids playing in the field of wheat and the smell of fresh baked bread.

"Kids?" Amy said inquisitively.

"I can see everything I was doing in each life and it was just like sitting here, right now, but faster. All I can say is this dream was like that," he assured her before continuing.

"In 1818 just before Bouchard sacked Monterey, all valuables were ordered taken from La base militar."

"From where?" Amy asked.

"The military base at Monterey. The majority of the valuables were moved north with most of the gun powder, and The Cross was ordered taken to San Juan Capistrano. Remember the history we read?" he asked. Amy responded with an affirmative nod. "Well, during the trip to San Juan Capistrano I was the lieutenant who was charged with the safe delivery of The Cross," he smiled.

"You were the lieutenant?" Amy asked skeptically.

"Yes, Lt. Juan Carlin, posted at Monterey under Governor Pablo Vincente de Sola."

"Were you married?" she asked with a hint of jealousy.

"Yes, my wife's name was Flora," he smiled.

"What are you smiling at?" Amy said playfully.

"Bouchard knew the governor was going to strip Monterey of all valuables and any additional weapons and gun powder that may be lost to the corsairs. It was a common tactic used by many to reduce the potential for loss, so he had ordered small raiding parties north and south of Monterey to intercept any attempts to hide the valuables."

"Why just north and south?" Amy asked.

"Because there were other Spanish controlled settlements up and down the coast that offered protection. It made sense to send the valuables there for protection."

"So even though the governor was aware of Bouchard's two corvette class ships approaching to attack Monterey, he was not aware of a third ship with a crew of raiders that had been ordered by Bouchard to land and scout our activities a month earlier. The governor thought it prudent to move valuables as soon as he heard of the impending attack. He knew if he waited too long to move them the chances of losing them to his attackers increased. He planned to use this to his advantage."

"The governor had surmised that a large group of soldiers with ten or twelve wagons would draw more attention and be a more tempting target than three soldiers headed south with no wagons. He couldn't have been more wrong."

"His plan was well thought out. He would move The Cross immediately as far away as possible and then take half of the remaining valuables and payroll and bury them in the desert, a last minute idea. As for the other half of the valuables, weapons and gun powder, he would use them as bait and move them just before the attack to draw attention away from The Cross."

"The governor did not realize the information Bouchard possessed regarding his ruse. To say the least, the raiders were well informed of the plans to split the valuables and planned accordingly."

"Bouchard ordered his men north and south, even he didn't think to go further inland. There were no posts and no one would consider sending valuables into such an open, unprotected area at the time," he said knowingly.

"It was a long trip to San Juan Capistrano. We pushed our horses hard the first few days to get some distance between us and Monterey. On the fourth day we slowed down to give the horses a break. I remember feeling confident we were far enough away from any danger when my men and I were ambushed by seven of Bouchard's men. They sailed through the night and landed a raiding party with fresh horses. Our horses had no chance, they were near exhaustion. The raiders caught up to us with little effort."

"My men and I were less than half way to San Juan Capistrano when we were attacked, just north of Montaña de Oro."

"The park?" Amy asked. Christian nodded.

"During the attack my men were captured and tortured for information. When they failed to provide that information, they were brutally murdered. I was cut pretty bad. I had multiple cut wounds across my arms and side and was grazed by a musket ball, but was able to slip away with The Cross."

"Oh my god," Amy said under her breath.

"I found a spot where I could climb over the edge and hide. I heard them laughing when they found my horse. I could see them getting closer and I knew it wasn't going to be long before they found me so I climbed as far down the cliff face as I could and that's when I stumbled upon the cave." Christian paused.

Amy, now totally into the story asked, "What happened next?"

"Well it was dark, so I had to feel around inside the cave and along the walls until I found the ledge and threw The Cross up there. I remember it was cold and dark and the pounding surf crashing against the cliff face was deafening. Cold water was dripping from everywhere and I kept hitting my head on rocks protruding from the wall as I pulled my way to the back of the cave

Everything I touched was slimy and cold. I remember thinking that it felt like death. I was so tired and scared. The misty damp air chilled me to my bones. I could feel myself shaking from the loss of blood."

"Then what?" Amy interrupted.

"On my way out of the cave one of the corsairs had made it down the cliff face and surprised me when he jumped down off the ledge next to the opening in the cave as I was coming out. He pulled his knife and we started fighting. While we were fighting I could see some of the others cheering him on and yet others starting to attempt the climb down from above."

"I remember the nauseating smell of his breath, rank from rotting teeth as he was attempting to yell to his companions, 'THE CROSS IS IN THE CAVE', but the sound from the waves crashing on the cliff face below was too loud and no one could hear him. I remember being there, worried what might happen if more of them made it down to the flat in front of the cave with me being out numbered. I worked my way onto the ledge, trying to escape but the raider followed. I can't understand why; he knew I didn't have The Cross any longer, but he still followed, swinging his blade at me."

"All that the others could see from the top of the cliff face was me and the raider fighting on a small ledge. They could not see the opening to the cave from above because of the angle of the cliff face. They must have stopped climbing down after seeing us fall. That's the only way I could see why The Cross was still there. They probably assumed The Cross went down with me."

Amy sat with a sad look on her face before blurting, "Oh my god! You actually saw yourself die?" Amy gasped.

Christian looked at Amy, "Yeah, it's pretty freaky."

"So, what you're telling me is you can see all of these past lives and experience everything, including how you die; each time?" Christian nodded affirmatively. Amy looked at him empathetically. "How did you fall?" she asked.

"Well, during the fight I climbed on the ledge next to the cave and the raider followed, swinging his blade at me. He connected with my arm as a huge wave hit the rock face and he was pulled into the pounding surf."

"But you said you both . . ." Amy started to say.

"Yeah, I know. I thought I was safe on the ledge after he fell off, but only seconds after that another wave crashed into the cliff face and the ledge I was standing on cracked loudly, broke free, and fell into the crashing surf, taking me along with it."

"So you drowned?" Amy asked.

"I drowned," Christian said reflecting. "The weird part is when I was climbing around the ledge, I came to that spot where the ledge was missing and I could see how it happened somehow . . . I thought it was my imagination showing me what could have happened, not my memories showing me what actually happened. It's creepy. I mean, pieces of me could still be down there stuck under that rock."

"Oh gross!" Amy blurted.

A couple of days had passed before Balzack contacted Christian. "Hello Christian. I've set up an appointment with Eric Trudeau; he is the jeweler I discussed with you. Will you have time Thursday afternoon?" he asked. "We'll meet at my place if you'd like."

Christian rattled off a few questions to ensure anything discussed would remain confidential until he was ready to release the news of the find. Balzack assured him all would be kept in the strictest of confidence. "Ok then, I'm free after one on Thursday. Does that work for you?" Christian asked.

"Yes, Eric knows of your wishes and has agreed not to discuss this with anyone as well. I forwarded the picture you sent me to him. He was quite enthused to say the least." They agreed to meet at two-thirty at Balzack's house.

Christian met up with Balzack and Trudeau on Thursday. Trudeau's eyes lit up when Christian pulled The Cross from the box Balzack provided. "I told you so," Balzack said smiling confidently. "It's the Ferdinand VII Cross."

Trudeau put on white cotton gloves and started his examination of The Cross. Over the next one and a half hours he examined each of the fifty-three stones, sketched and documented shape, clarity and an estimated size. Christian and Balzack listened as Trudeau rattled off the stats on each stone finishing each with, "Amazing! Absolutely amazing."

Trudeau completed his examination, finishing up with a few calculations. "Well, what do you think?" Balzack asked eagerly with Christian looking on.

"It's Magnificent! Truly Magnificent! The Cross itself is a work of art, not to mention the intricate twisting braid on the chain. Do you know how hard it was to extrude continuous long strips of gold to the length required to braid this chain? There's not even a visible braze mark. This is the work of a true artisan," Trudeau boasted admiringly of an unknown colleague.

"The stones are flawless," he said calmly, admiring them. He continued with his appraisal, breaking down the total carat weight of the stones. "I estimate each of the forty-eight side stones to be one carat each, each flawless in its own right. As for the large stones, the emeralds are between twelve and fifteen carats apiece. The diamond too is flawless and is about twelve to fifteen carats as well, but the winner is the heart-shaped ruby. The skill required to cut this stone today is possessed by only a few men in the world but to do it two hundred years ago. . . . Almost impossible. It's more of a miracle. I think this one's about eighteen to twenty carats. Again, I'll need to do a little more research on it."

"That in mind, there are one hundred sixteen to one hundred twenty-eight carats of flawless gems held on a magnificent cross of gold weighing over eleven pounds," Trudeau said.

"Eleven pounds, fourteen ounces, to be exact, not including the pound and a half the chain weighs," Balzack smiled.

"Oh, without the chain," Trudeau agreed, continuing, "The chain alone is a masterpiece. Long extruded lengths of gold intricately braided by hand over and over without a visible break. Total mastery. There's no doubt, it's authentic," Trudeau said smiling.

Christian looked at Trudeau, hesitating to ask. "What is your estimate of the value?" he inquired.

Balzack briefly glanced at him and looked back to Trudeau. "Hmmm," he thought, "this is definitely a museum piece," Trudeau said with surety, knowing Balzack would want to hear that. "In gold and jewels alone it's probably worth twenty to twenty-five million or more, but in historical value—It's priceless."

Christian flopped back onto the couch mumbling, "I've been carrying over twenty million dollars in my backpack."

Trudeau questioned Christian of his intentions for The Cross. Balzack listened intently, hoping to hear what he believed would be the right answer. He was hoping Christian would offer it to a museum as opposed to selling it to a private collector. Christian assured them that he would let them know what his final decision was once it was made.

Christian, still stunned at the news he had just received, made a quick stop to withdraw money from his account before heading back to the dorms. When he reached his floor he noticed Anton and Matt arguing. As he approached they stopped their arguing and went about their business. Christian didn't give it a second thought as he greeted the pair and excused himself, passing between them and entered his room. The two continued their heated discussion in the hallway, using hushed tones as he busied himself prepping for his final classes of the semester the following day.

The next day on the way to classes he ran into Amy. "Hey, what's up?" Amy asked kissing him on the cheek. "How did your meeting go yesterday? What did the jeweler have to say about The Cross?" she asked cautiously, surveying the area to ensure they were out of earshot of anyone.

"You won't believe it," he said smiling.

"I thought you were going to call me after the meeting?" she said curiously.

"I know, I know, I'm sorry about that," he said continuing, "I had to make a few stops on my way back. I got salt water in my phone and the battery connections corroded and crapped out so I had to go to the Apple store and pick up a new phone."

As they walked toward their classes, Amy looked at him, "So what did he say?" she asked anxiously.

"Oh, Trudeau said the gold and jewels were valuable but the historic value was priceless."

"So, what's valuable?" she asked.

"In his opinion it's worth about twenty to twenty-five million," Christian said calmly, smiling.

"Oh my god! Twenty five million! What are you going to do?" Amy asked.

"I don't know. Balzack and Trudeau are pushing toward getting it into a museum," he said.

"Yeah, I can see Balzack wanting that. He only mentioned it at least a dozen times when we were there. When are you going to tell the rest of the world about it?" she asked.

"I don't know . . . I'm calling my parents today to tell them, then I guess I'll decide when to tell everyone else after I tell them," he answered.

-Twenty-
Weltschmertz
(German–Things are Not What They Appear to Be)

After classes Christian found a quiet spot on campus and called his parents to tell them the great news. He told them of the hike he and Amy had gone on the weekend before at Montaña de Oro. They seemed preoccupied as he told his tale although Mrs. Asher did not pass up the opportunity to jump in and ask all kinds of questions about Amy. “Who is she? Where is she from? What is her major? How did you meet?” Finally after the mini inquisition was over, Christian was able to continue the story of how he came to find the cave and The Cross. He told them how he cleaned it up and how he had brought it to Balzack to check it out and that he said it looked like the Ferdinand VII Cross.

His excitement in telling the story was short lived. At first his parents sounded excited, but he could sense something else. Instead of elation he sensed a sadness overshadowing their excitement, especially in Katheryn’s responses. “Are you guys ok?” he asked inquisitively, I thought you’d be more excited.”

“No, no. This is fantastic news,” Dr. Asher answered with forced enthusiasm. “Have you told anyone else?” Dr. A. inquired.

“No, other than Balzack and, of course Amy, no one else knows.”

“Good, it’s probably best to decide what you want to do first before letting the cat out of the bag,” Dr. A. said.

Katherine jumped in, "Are we going to meet Amy any-time soon?"

Christian was puzzled at the lack of interest on his parents' part. He responded to his mother's question." I was thinking of driving back for Christmas break with her. I don't want to bring it on the plane. It might attract attention so I thought we'd drive and make a couple of stops on the way. Besides, I'd rather have it there if that's ok with you guys?" he asked.

"Sure, sounds like a great idea. We'd love to meet her," Dr. A. said.

"Of course, that'll be perfect," Katheryn added. "I'm really excited for you, honey," she said all but halfheartedly.

Edward and Katheryn cut the conversation short, telling Christian they were late for a medical conference dinner and they had to run. "We'll talk to you soon honey," Katheryn said before hanging up on him.

Amy was walking up to Christian as the conversation ended. "Hi, what's up?" she asked.

"I don't know," he said.

"Did you call your parents?" she asked.

"Yeah, I was just talking to them," he said

"So what's wrong?" she asked.

"I don't know," he said, reflecting on the conversation. "Something's not right. They weren't as excited as I thought they would be," he said.

"Well don't stress over it. It's pretty big news. Give it some time to sink in. I mean, it's a pretty big bomb to drop on someone, 'Hey I just found twenty-five million dollars worth of cross. . . . They're probably in shock," Amy said supportively.

"I didn't tell them what Trudeau said, you know, what he said it was worth. It was odd, the whole conversation. I can't explain it but, you're right, I'm probably making more out of it than I should," he smiled.

Amy noticed Daymond running across the campus straight toward them. "I wonder what's going on," she said inquisitively.

"Christian, Christian," Daymond huffed.

"What's the matter? Is there something wrong?" Christian asked.

"You got tossed," Daymond said, trying to catch his breath.

"Tossed?" Christian said.

"Yeah, someone broke in and ripped your room apart. Campus security is there."

"Oh my god . . . what about The Cross?" Amy blurted.

"Don't worry about it, they won't find it," he said jumping to his feet. "I've got to get back there," he said, rushing off.

"I'll catch up," Amy said, grabbing their bags.

Daymond and Christian ran toward his room. "There's something I think you need to know about your friends," Daymond huffed, running alongside.

"What's that?" a preoccupied Christian asked. "They are not who you think they are," Daymond continued.

"What do you mean?" Christian asked.

"You've got to go. I'll talk to you later. Watch your back," Daymond said stopping at the building entrance.

Security allowed Christian to pass. He made his way up to his room. Security and Police were everywhere. "What happened?" he asked an officer exiting his room.

"It looks like a B&E. Is this your room?" asked the officer.

"Yeah," Christian responded, winded.

"Is your roommate with you?" he asked.

"No he's not," Christian answered.

"We're gonna need you to see if anything was taken and fill out a report," the officer said.

"No problem," Christian replied, taking a first shocking look at his room.

It was tossed. Closets, cabinets and drawers were open. Their clothes were thrown on the floor. Papers were everywhere. The kitchenette area was torn apart and the mattresses were even flipped. Everything in every cabinet was pulled out. Christian surveyed the room noticing nothing of importance appeared to be missing, not even his laptop which was on top of a pile of clothes on the floor.

An officer approached Christian saying, "This doesn't look like your standard college dorm room B&E. Usually the first thing they grab are the computers and I see two of them. Anything missing? Jewelry? Watches? Drugs? Anything?" the officer asked snidely.

Christian gave the suggestive cop a look, then took a quick survey of the room. "It doesn't look like anything is missing. . . . It's just a mess," Christian said as Matt entered the room.

"What happened?" he asked.

"Nothing was taken that I can see," Christian said, "Help me look around."

The two looked around the room for anything that may have been taken while the police finished up their report and left them to clean up the mess. "What do you think this was about?" Matt asked.

"I have no idea," responded Christian, continuing, "Well, I think the cop was right. Somebody was looking for something. . . . They didn't take anything valuable." Matt agreed, placing his laptop on his desk.

Matt turned to pick up the remainder of his clothes from the floor and stopped dead in his tracks, dropping the clothes he had just picked up and rushed to his desk. "No, no, no," he said as he leaned down to look under it. "Damn it!" he said as he slammed the top of his desk.

"What's the matter?" Christian asked, bending down to look only to see a piece of tape hanging from the bottom of the desk.

"What was there?" he asked.

Matt stumbled in his response. "Son—of—a –"

"What was it?" Christian asked again.

Matt picked up another shirt and threw it across the room. "My work files. It was a memory stick with all my work files on it."

"Work files?" Christian said inquisitively.

"Yeah," Matt paused, realizing he almost slipped. "It had all of my class work on it, everything I've worked on for the last few months," he said angrily. "I know who did this . . ."

Matt stormed out of the room and down the hall and started banging on Anton's door. Christian stepped into the hall when he heard the commotion Matt was making. As Anton opened the door, Matt lunged at him and grabbed him by the throat, pushing his way in. He pushed him backward and shoved him onto the bed, causing his head to bang up against the wall.

Anton's roommate interceded, pulling Matt off of a stunned Anton. "What the hell is wrong with you?" Anton asked, grabbing the back of his head.

"Where the hell is it?" Matt asked angrily.

"Where's what?" Anton asked.

"You know, you son of a bitch. . . . The memory stick," he yelled angrily.

"I don't have it. I've been here all day, ask Jake," Anton yelled in response to the accusation.

Jake confirmed they had been studying all day and didn't leave the room until the police knocked on their door to ask them if they had heard anything. Matt pushed Jake away and angrily stormed out the door, bumping into Christian. "You guys ok?" Christian asked. Matt didn't acknowledge him and stormed down the hallway.

Christian followed him out of the building and was stopped by some curious friends talking with Amy near the entrance. He caught her attention and gave her the ok sign. She blew a sigh of relief and excused herself from the conversation. Christian kept his eye on Matt as he hurried toward the parking lot.

Hunter was among the spectators seemingly trying to find out what happened. He had his back turned to the group and was talking to someone on his cell phone. He hadn't noticed Christian standing there. Christian overheard him say, "Ich habe den USB. Kein problem."

Christian knew exactly what he said and curiosity got the best of him. He started talking with another student standing close to Hunter. As soon as he started talking, Hunter looked over his shoulder, saw him and ended his call immediately. Christian's suspicion was roused.

"Christian, what happened? he interrupted.

"Someone tossed our room looking for something," Christian replied. "You wouldn't know anything about it would you?" Christian asked suspiciously.

"No, I just walked over when I saw the crowd. Are you ok?" he asked.

"Yeah, I'm fine, thanks," Christian said suspiciously. He excused himself and moved away with Amy.

"Is everything ok?" she asked.

"Yeah, everything is fine," he said still watching Hunter out of the corner of his eye.

"Did they get The Cross?" she asked.

"No, it's right here in my bag," he said, reaching over and pulling his bag from her shoulder and opened it up.

"Oh my god! Where is it?" he said looking at Amy with a frantic look on his face.

Amy's jaw dropped. "Did you drop it crossing the campus?" he asked.

"No. . . . No, I don't think so," she said starting to panic.

Christian started to smirk, his giveaway when he was kidding, and something Amy had learned quickly, "How could you?" Amy said playfully smacking him. "You are so freaking bad! How could you do that to me? You creep! You scared the crap out of me." Christian laughed, wrapped his arms around her and apologized. He explained that following his meeting with Balzack and Trudeau he thought it best to place it in a secure place so he opened a safety deposit box.

"Thank god," she said continuing, "I wonder if that's what they were after, don't you?"

Christian shook his head, "I don't think so. I think it was something else, something Matt has. I'll explain it later when we meet," he said, giving her a kiss.

Christian went up to his room and began cleaning up the remainder of the mess. He grabbed a pair of jeans that belonged to him that were tossed under Matt's chair and when he pulled them he saw a glimpse of something oddly familiar. He rustled through the clothes under the desk and located the missing memory stick under a pile of clothes on the floor. He realized it must have fallen when the room was being tossed.

He looked at his find curiously. Is this what he was so pissed about? What schoolwork could be so important that would enrage him so much? Christian turned on his laptop and took a quick look in the hallway. The coast was clear. He copied the contents of the stick onto his computer, placed the USB back on the floor under the shirt where he had found it, and finished cleaning up his stuff.

Matt came in thirty minutes later apologizing for his outburst. Christian told him not to worry and proceeded with prepping his study materials for finals the next week. An obviously irritated Matt began to clean up the area around his desk. Christian sat waiting for it . . . "Yes!" a resounding "Yes!" came from Matt.

Christian smiled and asked, "Find something?"

"Yes, I found the stick. Thank God they didn't get it," Matt said happily.

"What's on that thing that would make you think someone would want it?" Christian asked.

Matt stalled awhile before responding. "It's just a lot of work stuff. Hey, thanks for cleaning up," he said, referring to the cabinets, closets and everything else Christian had already cleaned up. I'm sorry I stormed out like that."

"I wouldn't worry about it," Christian answered, "but I think you might owe Anton an apology . . ." Matt looked at him blankly.

Later that evening the Four Musketeers headed out to a club to stave off what appeared to be some pre-final jitters. The mood was semi-tense at the beginning. Christian hadn't had a chance to review the contents of the memory stick but knew something was up. And, of course, there was that whole cross thing that he and Amy were trying not to let slip out just yet.

They loosened up a bit as the night went on and celebrated the end of classes. Amy could tell Christian's heart wasn't into being out, but he stayed on with the group until it was time to leave a couple of hours later. Matt and Tina went off to stay at Tina's for the night and Amy and Christian walked silently toward the diner for a post party snack.

After reaching the diner Amy broke the silence asking, "What's going on with you tonight? Something's up?"

"Yeah, I'm not sure yet," he responded. "Listen, some strange things are happening with Matt."

"Matt?" she said with curiosity. "Yeah, when I got back from the meeting yesterday he and Anton were arguing."

"So they were arguing, we all argue," she said.

"It's not like that. They looked like they were ready to kill one another, and as soon as they saw me, they stopped. Then when I got into the room and shut the door they started again. Then today after the break in, Matt stormed into his room and started fighting with him."

"About what?" she asked.

"I don't know, but whatever it is, Matt keeps it on a memory stick. When I asked him he said it was classwork and became evasive, then he changed the topic . . .

"So, don't you have any secrets in your closet?" Amy smirked, suggesting all that had happened over the last months.

"It's not like that. I mean, what classwork could be on a memory stick that if he lost it would literally enrage him? Everything we have is backed up or available online," Christian continued, "No, there's something else and I'm going to find out what it is," stated a determined Christian, calling for the check.

The waitress came over to the table, "Are you ready to order, sir?" Amy was covering her mouth, snickering. He was so preoccupied with everything else, he forgot to order.

Amy jumped in, "Would it be ok if we placed an order to go?"

"Surely," the waitress smiled. Amy ordered for both of them and they headed back to the dorms.

Once in the room Christian turned on his laptop. "Where's the stick?" Amy asked.

"He keeps it taped under his desk," he said.

Amy bent down to look for it, finding a half stuck piece of tape. "Not anymore he doesn't," she smiled.

"Don't worry, I made a copy," Christian said, clicking through his folders.

"Oh, so you're a spy now are you? Do you need to frisk me before dinner or have I cleared security?"

"Ha, ha, ha," he said, shaking his head.

Christian scrolled through the files, opening the ones without names he would normally associate with classwork. A few minutes into his search he came across a file named 'Zeus'. This was a big file, bigger than anything else on the stick. He clicked on it and it opened to a bio sheet on project Zeus. They scrolled through documents and articles that were scanned to the file. Most of it was about a kid. It had pictures of the kid and his parents. There were articles about the boy and his parents. As he scrolled down they came across an article about the boy's father committing suicide and another about the mother being committed to an institution. It seemed a nicer way to say her ship had sailed and left her on the dock. "Do you think this is Matt and his parents?"

Amy asked. "This is terrible, he must have had a really hard life," Amy said empathetically. "This is kind of personal, I don't think we should be looking at this," Amy suggested.

Christian agreed, just as the next set of pics opened up. It was pictures of the boy, now about six years old with his new adoptive family. His face grew pale as Amy continued to urge him to end his investigation. His eyes welled up and a single tear rolled down his cheek. Amy was watching the screen and hadn't noticed Christian's sudden sadness. He stared at the screen, attempting to hold back his tears. His lips started to quiver. Amy glanced at him and noticed his tears, "Oh, it's okay, and look he's doing fine," she said rubbing his back. He didn't move, blink or say a word. The tears continued to roll down his face as he quietly stared at the screen. "Really hon, it's ok to feel bad for him . . . It's a sad story but he's fine now."

Christian opened his trembling lips and started to speak slowly, "It's—not—Matt. It's me." For the first time since the canyon, Christian didn't have a thought. He sat in silence.

"Excuse me?" Amy asked apprehensively.

"It's not Matt. . . . It's me," he repeated softly. "That's a picture of me, my mother and my father in front of our house in the Hamptons. It was the first time I had gone there after they bought it," he said with crushing sadness. "The entire file—is about me."

A single tear rolled down Amy's cheek as she softly hugged him from behind. Her attempts at reassuring him went unanswered. He was devastated. He walked away from the computer, excusing himself from Amy and walked out of the room. "Wait, I'll come with you." Amy said following him out the door.

"I'd like to be alone for a while . . ." he said heartbroken, as he turned away from her and walked down the hall.

Amy didn't know what to do. She saw the heartbreak in his face. She'd never seen him like this and she was afraid something might happen so she decided to follow him from a distance.

Christian had made it as far as the parking lot when he heard a familiar voice from the shadows, "So how you doing, buddy? You okay?" It was CB standing under a tree in the shadows.

"I guess you knew already, huh?" Christian asked. "Why couldn't you tell me?"

"I'm sorry, I'm really sorry, but this was one thing I knew you needed to find out on your own."

"It's not easy, it never has been. We've gone through this a dozen times over and there is no easy way to find out about it when it happens this way," CB said with a sympathetic look and a pat on the back. "What can I do for you? Anything?" CB asked.

"Can you explain what happened?" Christian asked. "I need to know—the whole story. . . ."

CB started to explain, "Remember the dream about the little boy you started to tell me about? Well, I knew it was you, but I couldn't tell you at the time. I knew it was something you would need to find out about yourself. The mother and father you know are your adoptive parents. Your dad was active in the military when you were brought into the hospital late one night."

"Your biological mother had a breakdown after your father . . . well, you know. One of your neighbors saw you in the yard playing by yourself late at night and went to your house to find out what was going on. Once they saw your mom wasn't doing well they called the police and sat and played with you until they arrived. The police found your mom in bad condition and decided to take you both to the hospital to get checked out. They had no idea how long you had been locked out of the house."

"As I remember, you were about five years old at the time and you were sitting in the hospital playing with some little toy the nurse had given you."

"It was a G.I. Joe," Christian added.

"That's right, it was a G.I. Joe . . . with a missing hand," CB remembered. "While you were sitting there, an accident victim was brought in. Mrs. Espinosa I think it was. She was making all kinds of noise. None of the doctors could understand her. They didn't even know the language she was speaking was Portuguese. "

"They were working frantically trying to stop her bleeding, but she keep fighting them off, refusing treatment and repeating the same question over and over again, 'É o meu bebê está bem–É o meu bebê está bem . . . ' The doctors ordered she be restrained for her own good."

"The look on their faces," CB reflected, "when you hopped off the chair and walked over to the nurse and tugged on her dress."

"I remember she shooed me away."

"You tried again, and she did the same. Then you just came out and said, 'She wants to know if her baby is alright' and you turned around, G.I. Joe in hand, and walked away."

"The doctors and nurses, your father included, fell silent. They didn't know what to think. After all, your genetic pool doesn't swim in Latin waters, if you know what I mean," CB smiled, getting a little smirk from Christian. "The woman on the stretcher was still struggling and rambling in Portuguese, 'É o meu bebê está bem—É o meu bebê está bem'. They just watched your little butt waddle its way back to the chair and climb up to sit down."

"Your father came over to you and asked if you understood her and you said, 'Yes' nonchalantly and continued playing with your

G.I. Joe. He asked for your help and brought you to her side where you acted as a translator for them. They were amazed with how calm and mature you were acting. You were fearless, almost indifferent to the bloody mess around the table where she was lying and fighting off the doctors."

"Once you told the woman her baby girl was safe with her family and that she would be fine, she stopped fighting. You could see the relief on her face. The doctors and nurses stepped back and watched as you put your hand on her head and whispered, 'É bonito no outro lado.'"

"It's beautiful on the other side," Christian repeated.

"She smiled and a tear ran down her cheek. She was at peace. She pulled you closer and placed her bloody hand on your cheek and then kissed you on the forehead, just before life left her body. You gave her peace of mind, and she let go."

"I remember her," Christian reflected.

"After that happened one of the admitting nurses cleaned you up and was watching over you when her replacement came in. The woman asked who you were. The nightshift nurse told her what had happened with your mom and how you had helped with the Portuguese woman. She looked at you with disregard and said in Spanish, 'Well I have a lot of work to do, he better not be any trouble.' That's when you smiled and said 'No voy a ser ningún problema.'"

"I won't be any problem," Christian again repeated softly, remembering.

"The night shift nurse choked on her coffee. She immediately paged your father and told him what had happened . . . again. He hurried down to the nurse's station and had the nurses speak to you in Spanish and you responded in flawless Spanish. Not five or six year old Spanish, but flawless Spanish."

"I remember that," Christian said softly.

"Your father was both amazed and dumbfounded. Realizing you had a gift, he brought you to his office and proceeded to check your abilities further. He had people from all over the hospital who spoke different languages come in and talk to you, and you conversed with each of them in their languages. He was most impressed when you spoke Mandarin to one of the staff nurses."

"You were sitting in his office as each person he summoned entered and was instructed to speak to you in their native language. As he tested your language abilities he noticed your attraction to the Rubik's Cube that was on his desk, a gift that he played with often and was unable to solve for years. He handed it to you and you solved it in about 30 seconds, then gave it back to him with a big smile on your face. That's when he placed the call."

"The call?" Christian asked.

"Your father called Dr. Martin Stedwell, the hospital psychiatrist. He knew Stedwell would have to recommend that your mom be institutionalized. It was the middle of the night but he called and told him about you. The psychiatrist wanted to meet you and arranged to come to your father's office the next morning and have his own discussion with you. That was just after you fell asleep on the couch in his office. You know, he sat in his chair staring at you all night, making sure you were comfortable and were not disturbed by anyone."

"The next day, your dad was right there with you having a GI hospital breakfast when Dr. Stedwell arrived. After your dad introduced you, I remember Stedwell asking you an increasingly difficult series of questions, starting from 'Do you know where you are' to 'Can you solve this equation.' I think it was, 'What is the square root of pi,' and you did it, in your head in less than a second and said . . . 1.77245385091. Stedwell almost soiled himself. He continued with a line of increasingly difficult questions until your father put a stop to it. If Stedwell was allowed to continue he would have sat there asking you questions for a year. He was amazed with you and the knowledge you possessed. After your father put a stop to the questions you just looked at him, smiled and picked up playing with your GI Joe."

CB continued, "Your dad stayed on at the hospital to watch over you, making sure you were comfortable until arrangements were made to bring you home later that day. He and the psychiatrist realized that you would have to be put up for adoption because of the situation with your biological mom so they made some calls and arranged for your adoption. He took you home that afternoon."

"The following weeks proved trying for Dr. Stedwell. He was baffled by your abilities. Stedwell thought it best to keep your gifts under wraps and even came up with a way to suppress them with the medication you have been taking your entire life, thinking it was for allergies. Your parents have given them to you ever since."

"But they're not my parents," Christian said with an upset tone.

"Yes they are," CB said assuring him. "The two of them have committed themselves to you. They gave you everything in life you could ever want from parents and they loved you . . . and still love you. That's a lot more than most get. They have protected you from day one and even gave you those stupid meds to try and prevent exactly what's happening right now. You need to at least honor them for that." Christian was silent as CB continued.

"What your father didn't realize at the time was that Stedwell was involved with a government program that involved all of us. They had been aware of our existence since 1964 when it began. He was the lead doctor in charge of what we call the Original Fourteen."

"He was ordered by his superiors to bring your father on board the program since he was both your guardian and an officer in the Army. They tested you for a year with every test they could think of before releasing you to your father's care. It was fortunate that they only tested your knowledge and rudimentary skills and not your memories or past experiences. Otherwise they would have locked you up in a cage. You actually did better at hiding your gifts then, than you've done since the canyon," CB smiled before continuing.

"The good doctor prescribed the psychotropic meds you are taking to suppress your abilities and your parents told you they were for allergies."

"I know, they just changed the meds and gave me a higher dosage when I was home for the Thanksgiving weekend," Christian said, depressed. "So that's why they always gave me meds. To keep all of this . . . everything that's happening . . . suppressed?" he asked. CB nodded affirmatively. "I wondered why my parents were acting so strange over the past few months."

CB continued, "They were nervous because you decided to go to school in California where they would have no control over you and they were right to think that way. It's very important that you control your abilities around them and don't let on to your roommate that you know about him and his file, although that might be a moot point by now as I saw Amy running in the direction of her room just after you got here."

"You need to remember, even though he is your father, he is a soldier and he already knows your abilities are increasing, as you already know, thanks to regular reports from your roommate Matt; who, by the way, is Army intelligence. But more importantly, Dr. Stedwell knows. And if he knows it, the government knows it."

"Yeah, but Stedwell's got to be a hundred years old by now," Christian stated.

"No, he's actually about 62 years old, and he is still the head consultant for the program based on the Original Fourteen."

"Wait until you see his successor. This one's a piece of work. And she's aggressive."

"She?" Christian questioned.

"Yep . . . and she is going to be trouble if she takes over for Stedwell."

"Why do you think that?" Christian inquired.

"She only graduated a couple of years ago. She is young and hungry to prove herself to Stedwell and her superiors."

"Superiors?" Christian said with a curious look on his face.

"Yes, Superiors. The United States Government. We are just like every other government's best kept secret, which means every agency has teams looking for anyone who might be connected with the Original Fourteen. You are now considered a threat to national security," CB smiled.

"For now, Stedwell is still in charge of analyzing you and he thinks you are the link to the Originals from '64."

"Thinks?" Christian questioned.

"Yes, he's kind of put two and two together but hasn't been able to confirm his theory. I'm not sure how much his successor knows about us though."

"Back in '64 he interviewed the fourteen of us and made some headway while some of us were under narcotic-induced hypnosis and started discussing previous lives and memories of their almost instantaneous rebirth following death. At first he didn't think the stories were possible. That's when he started using the narcotics, and each of us told him the same stories. He was getting close until his program was interrupted because of some political issues. Something with government experimentation on humans. I think it was more of an ongoing fallout from the issues created by Timothy Leary's studies with psychotropic drugs at Harvard in '62."

"Ever since then he has been tracking the Original Fourteen and attempting to find a way to locate us as we are reborn, and you were the first he came across. He thinks you are his proof. He asked you specific questions to link you to the Original Fourteen, and based upon your answers, he concluded that you, my friend, were somehow linked to them."

"Now that you are out, the government will stop at nothing to get the information they want. This is what I was trying to help you avoid. Because of the knowledge we possess, we have been deemed a threat. Not only to this government, but all of them," he said seriously.

"They have entire networks of people scanning resources for stories of children with incredible talents."

"Just like Hwei-ru?"

"Yep, just like Hwei-ru. And just like her family, your father or mother won't stand a chance at protecting you once the government wants you. They will treat you like a lab rat with the plague and lock you away until they get what they want . . ."

"And then what?" Christian asked. "Oh, sorry, stupid question. Geeze, you really know how to cheer a guy up," Christian forced a smirk.

The two of them talked for a while longer as they walked toward the dorms. Christian was still noticeably upset by the news but had come to grips with the situation, and started thinking about how he should handle it moving forward. He offered for CB to come up for a while but CB declined. "I have something to take care off," he said. "You okay?" CB asked.

"Yeah, thanks . . . I'll talk to you soon," Christian said, walking into the building.

Amy had reached the parking lot just as CB and Christian walked off into the shadows, missing them by a minute. She turned her attention to finding out why Matt had a file on Christian and stormed over to her dorm. When she arrived at the room, neither Matt nor Tina were there so she headed back to Christian's, stopping at her car first to grab the charger for her phone. After finding the charger, she locked her car and turned to go back to the dorms when she heard that all too familiar voice.

"Hey Amy, where's your boyfriend tonight?" She turned to see RJ, Simon and Jesse sitting in a smoke filled car. It was apparent to her from their lewd comments, slurred words and gestures that they were all very high. Amy grimaced and started to walk away quickly. "Hey, where you going? We want to have some fun," Simon laughed from the back seat as Jesse started the car and pulled in front of her, blocking her exit from the parking lot.

She listened nervously at the barrage of drunken inquiries from the car, "What's the rush? Do you wanna hang out? Where ya goin'?"

"Knock it off you guys, this isn't funny. I've got stuff to do," she barked nervously as they got out of the car.

RJ approached her, pushing his sweaty hair back out of his blood-shot eyes. His nose rimmed with white powder, he grabbed her arm and pulled her in, forcefully trying to kiss her as Jesse and Simon drunkenly cheered him on. She could smell his breath, rancid from booze and weed. "Cut it out, this isn't funny," Amy said fighting his advances.

Jesse started softly chanting, "Do her, do her, do her . . ." as he circled the two of them with a demented gleam. Amy realized RJ wasn't backing down and started to panic. He had an evil determination in his eyes. Fearing for what may happen next she instinctively kneed him hard in the groin. Hard enough to cause him to drop to his knees in pain.

"You freaking whore," he gasped, doubling over as he fell to his knees.

"You think this is funny, huh? How did that feel you son of a bitch?" Amy asked angrily.

Simon and Jesse's drunken glee turned ugly. They lunged for her, grabbing her arms to prevent her escape as an angry RJ groaned, then slowly and painfully got up from his knees, holding his crotch in agony. "Drag her ass over here," he growled, hobbling over to a small fenced in area used for concealing a small dumpster and landscaping containers.

Amy started fighting back frantically. She was kicking and yelling for them to let her go but RJ would have none of that. He smacked her hard in the face and shoved a towel in her mouth, "Drag that bitch over here, I'll show her funny . . ." he snarled as he walked behind the fence.

RJ ordered the guys to hold Amy down. "So, you like it rough, huh? We'll see about that. Let's finish the game. You touched me, now I'm gonna touch you," he snickered perversely as he glared down at her. Jesse and Simon, sneering with anticipation, started clumsily tearing at her clothes.

Amy was fighting them off with every ounce of effort she had, twisting and kicking as she pushed the rag from her mouth and started to scream for help. RJ put his bottle on top of the dumpster and climbed on top of her, pinning her legs down, grinning with depravity and ordering Simon to keep her mouth shut. "So, you like it rough?" he said smacking her face.

Then from out of the darkness they heard an answer, "As a matter of fact I do."

Amy, struggling, strained to look up to see a stranger come out of the shadows and approach them. RJ jumped up, "Who the hell are you?" he demanded. "Get the hell out of here before I beat your ass," he barked.

"I can't do that," the stranger said calmly, walking past an indignant RJ and up to where Amy was being forcefully held down.

Simon and Jesse released their grip on her and backed away from the approaching stranger as he extended his hand out to help her up from the ground. They were quietly cowering as they nervously looked at the stranger and then to RJ, waiting for his orders. "Well buddy, you just made the biggest mistake of your life," RJ said, grabbing his bottle from the dumpster and swinging at the back of the stranger's head.

As soon as he swung, the stranger turned, catching RJ's wrist with one hand, the bottle just inches from his face. He started to squeeze RJ's straining wrist, causing him to grimace in pain. He had a look of disgust in his eyes as he glared at RJ. "People like you really make me sick," the stranger said, squeezing hard enough to make RJ's knees buckle in submission. "I should kill you right where you stand," he snarled. RJ started to tremble. He pulled hard, trying to release his hand from the angry stranger's grip without success. Simon, seeing fear in RJ for the first time, leapt over Amy who was still sitting on the ground, and lunged at the stranger. A very big mistake.

The stranger threw a lightning quick side kick hitting Simon so hard and fast that he lifted him off the ground. His body flew back past Amy and landed at Jesse's feet. Jesse cringed at the cracking sound he heard when the stranger's foot made contact with Simon's face. He looked at his friend, out cold, laying face up with his nose flattened and bleeding, and flew into a nervous rage.

Amy pushed herself up from the ground, trembling from her experience and tried to gather herself. As she looked down to fix her shirt she noticed it was torn and that there were a couple of buttons missing. Her nervousness started to turn into anger as she glared at Simon and then at Jesse.

Jesse's insecurity and nervousness caused him to hesitate, pacing back and forth in a nervous, drunken rage, trying to summon the courage to attack. His hesitation to attack the stranger provided Amy just enough time to realize the full extent of what had almost happened and turned her fear into anger. Just as Jesse summoned the courage to make his move, she punched him square in the throat. He grabbed his throat gasping for air, "Ohhh!"

The stranger winced, "Nice shot!" he smiled, then turned his angry stare back to RJ.

Amy scowled at Jesse for his participation in the attack, then she turned her attention back to Simon. She looked down at him as he started to stir. He cupped his bleeding nose with both hands and started whining. "You broke my nose . . . you broke my nose . . ." She started thinking how cruelly he had just treated her as he sputtered "I'm sorry, I'm sorry," repeatedly.

She looked down at him with contempt and said, "Wrong end," angrily, and kicked him hard in the groin. Jesse, holding his throat, winced as Amy delivered her pay back.

The stranger smirked with approval again, turning his attention back to RJ and said, "If I ever see you again, the last thing you'll have to worry about is if your balls will ever drop back down again," the stranger glared.

RJ, ever defiant, stared back at him as he released his grip and turned to Amy, ready to walk away.

As you have already surmised, RJ is not the brightest and never did learn when to keep his mouth shut. His ego was hurt and he couldn't have anyone, much less this stranger, make him look bad in front of his friends so he continued with his threats, "Yeah, you better walk away. When my father gets a hold of you . . . you've had it you bastard," RJ whined like a child while rubbing his wrist.

The stranger stopped in his tracks. "I was hoping you'd say that," he said, smirking as he turned to face RJ.

"Whaaaat?" RJ asked with a confused look on his face as the stranger released a lightning fast kick that connected with RJ's groin with the crack of a whip, lifting him off the ground and knocking him out cold, his limp body folding to the ground.

The stranger turned and offered his hand to a grateful Amy and helped her step over RJ's motionless body. They looked back at Jesse whimpering against the fence as they walked away.

"Thank you so much," a teary-eyed Amy said as they walked from the lot.

"You are welcome, I was happy to help," he smiled. "I am CB, it's nice to meet you Amy."

"How do you know my name?" she asked curiously, fixing herself.

"Oh that! I assumed it was your name after they used it ten or twelve times . . ." he smiled again. "Allow me to walk you to your room."

"Thank you, but I'm not going to my room," Amy said gratefully.

"I know . . . you are going to Christian's room," he said, handing her the phone and charger she had originally gone to the parking lot to retrieve.

"You know Christian?" she asked.

"Yes, we have become very close over the centuries," he smiled.

Amy looked at CB oddly as she continued to put herself back together, "You mean years, right?" she asked curiously.

"Yes, of course," CB replied as they proceeded toward Christian's room.

Amy looked at the stranger and thanked him again as they slowly walked toward the dorm rooms. "May I ask if you saw Matt and Tina tonight?" CB inquired.

"I'm sorry, do you know them too?" Amy asked.

"Not personally, but I know of them. I only ask because it is important to Christian."

"How is it important to Christian?" she asked.

"Because you are the only three people that know what happened to him . . ." Amy stopped walking and looked at CB with surprise.

"You know what happened?" she asked.

"Yes," he replied. "Christian trusts you, so I have to trust you, but you should know that both of you will be in danger now that he's been Awakened."

"What do you mean, danger?" Amy asked.

"We both know he is developing special skills, skills that, against my wishes, he told you about. What we didn't know was that his roommate and yours both work for the government."

"No way, Tina? She doesn't . . ."

"Yes she does, for the NSA, as a matter of fact," he interrupted.

"Bu,t I would know something like that, wouldn't I? I mean we live together!"

"Not necessarily, they are trained very well to hide who they are. It's like the college version of '21 Jump Street' except the movie was funny. They are here to keep an eye on him and if they find out he is developing his skills, they will take him and they will most likely take you as well."

"Why me?" she asked anxiously.

"Because you two spend a lot of time together and I'm sure that Tina and Matt both have a file on you as well. That is why it is important to know if you confronted them tonight after you followed Christian to the parking lot. Did you?"

"No, they weren't there when I got there," Amy replied.

"Good, you must not let on that you know about this. Do you understand? If you do they will do what they have to," CB warned.

CB continued to discuss with Amy the situation that she and Christian were in. He pointed out the potential danger for her and Christian alike if he revealed more of his newly developing skills. They were talking outside of Christian's dorm when he came down and met them.

Amy greeted him with concern, "Hi, I think you two have met," she smiled weakly. "CB was just telling me about . . ."

Christian interrupted speaking quickly, "About Matt and Tina and that they work for the government and that you knowing me is putting you in danger and that if I let them know my gifts are growing we are in for trouble . . ." he grinned.

"Yeah, how'd you know?" she inquired, surprised that he already knew. "CB told me at the same time he told you."

"How is that possible?" she asked.

"Just another little trick we have," he smiled.

"Wait, so you and he are . . .?" she started to ask before Christian interrupted.

"Like brothers. . . . We've been together for many years and in many places. What do you guys say; let's get out of here before Matt and Tina show up. We can talk on our way into town," Christian suggested.

"Why are we going to town?" Amy asked.

"I'm hungry," replied Christian, "and our food is ice cold."

The three of them went to town and got better acquainted along the way and during the meal. They laughed at stories CB told of their sillier exploits together in different times. Amy finally started to relax as they all got acquainted, asking for CB to tell more stories. One story CB started to tell caused Christian to blush, even after a few centuries of telling it.

CB looked at Christian and smiled devilishly. "Was is Rimnik or Martinesti? I can never remember."

Christian looked at CB as if pleading, "No, please not this one, not 'Old . . .'", and before Christian could finish his sentence CB chimed in, finishing the sentence for him, "'Blood and Nuts Petrov,'" CB laughed.

"Are you ever going to forget this one?" Christian blushed.

"Old Blood and Nuts. I have to hear this one," Amy said urging him to continue.

"Well, we were set up in camp during the Russo-Turkish War. Our friend here, who was known as General Aleksandr Petrov at the time, as well as 'The Naked General' and 'The Bare Ass General' among other less polite names,"

"Really, you're really going to tell this again?" Christian asked.

"Yep," CB replied, snickering as Amy urged him to continue. "He was a strategic genius and a very accomplished general, highly decorated and all that. This one day he was . . . Hmmm, how do I say this?" CB questioned himself as Christian turned his head away with a smirk, embarrassed. "Let's just say the good general here was getting a personal massage from one of his many interests . . ."

"You slut, you," Amy said laughing. Christian blushed, shaking his head in playful disbelief that CB was telling this particular story.

"Well the good general was in the middle of his 'massage' when a band of Turks raided the camp." Amy listened intently. "So Old Blood and Nuts, hearing the commotion, ran outside half dressed with his sword in one hand and holding up his pants with the other. He was in such a hurry to get out of the tent he put his pants on backward."

Amy glanced at Christian, "Blood and Nuts," she said laughing.

"As he ran out of his tent he came face to face with a Turk running through the camp, or should I say he ran into him head first. They both fell on their backsides and the Turk discharged his musket into the air when he fell back. Which was good news for the general because the good general dropped his sword as he fell on his backside, and started crawling around looking for it.

His pants kept falling down as he crawled around. Meanwhile, the Turk jumped up and started pulling his sabre while watching bare ass Petrov over here crawling around trying to find his blade."

"To kill the famous General Petrov would mean military fame. The Turk could only have been thinking how easy it was going to be to kill him. . . . After all he was crawling around on the floor with half his ass hanging out looking for his sword." Amy started to laugh, picturing the scene. "Fortunately for our friend here, he found his sword just as the Turk tried to strike."

"Blood and Nuts was stumbling through the fight trying to hold his pants up with one hand and fight off this rather large Turk with the other. It was comical."

"So, he was holding his own so to speak," Amy said laughing.

CB laughed, nodding in agreement. "Right in the middle of the fight his pants dropped to the ground. Tired of picking them up he decided to kick the pants off."

"There he stood in the middle of camp bare ass naked. I don't think the Turk knew what to do. He was shocked to say the least. The expression on his face said it all. Unfortunately for him, the distraction provided ample time for Blood and Nuts to end the fight. Thank god for him, the raid only lasted ten or twelve minutes."

"Why is that?" Amy asked still laughing.

"Well it was kind of cold that late in September," CB joked.

"Ohhhh," Amy blushed.

Christian, of course, retaliated with a story about CB as Amy listened intently. She was enjoying the 'story war' that was going on between CB and Christian. She could tell the relationship they shared by the stories they had to tell. Besides, each story was funnier than the next. She wondered what it would be like to have this gift herself; what she may find out about herself and if she would be different somehow.

Christian began telling the story. "Who was it this time? Alessandra, I think." CB rolled his eyes as Christian smiled, beginning to tell the tale. "One day we walked miles through southern Spain to get to a certain buxom maiden that CB had been eyeing for months. When we arrived at her farm he found his way into the house and made his advances."

"It was a peaceful, quiet day. The birds were singing, you could hear the occasional mooo of a cow and the baaaah of a goat. Horses were whinnying and neighing in the field and the chickens were scratching around the yard. It was perfect . . . almost."

"We were unaware her father was on his way home at the time his advances were being well received by the maiden," Amy snickered, anticipating the outcome.

"I was taking a nap in a shady spot under a tree close to the house when I heard something hit the fence and looked up to see her father entering the house. He had just laid his tools up against the fence."

"Couldn't you warn him?" Amy asked.

"I tried to. I threw a rock into the open window and hit him with it."

"It hit him?"

"Yeah, I knew I hit him because he stood up in the window, rubbing his head and threw the rock back at me and flipped me off Spanish style." CB looked at Christian and expressed his feelings with the very same hand gesture for telling the story. They laughed.

"I was jumping up and down and waving my arms at him to let him know that her father was home but I guess he thought I was messing around with him or he just didn't want to hear it. My guess is he probably didn't want to hear it . . ."

So, what did you do?" Amy asked.

"I laid back down against the tree and waited. What else could I do? I couldn't walk up to the house and knock on the door. I–j-u-s-t waited."

"What happened next?" Amy asked.

"Well, as you could imagine, I didn't have to wait long. What I didn't know was that her father was looking for her. He didn't see her in the field or out back tending to the animals so he went inside to look for her. When she wasn't in the kitchen preparing dinner he got curious. He wanted to ask her to prepare chicken for dinner."

"C'mon, how can you know that?" Amy asked, looking at CB who shook his head in agreement.

"By now a good ten minutes had passed since the father had gone into the house. He had gone out back and grabbed a chicken for her to prepare for dinner and when he came back into the house he could hear the two of them socializing energetically. She was very vocal. I remember, I could hear her from across the yard and that's when all hell broke loose."

"He ran up to her room, chicken in hand, and threw the door open. I'm sure he wasn't expecting to see what he saw, but when he did, he went ballistic. And of course he reacted like any father would if they walked in on their young daughter socializing so loudly. He tried to kill him..."

"Oh my god," Amy said thinking about the situation.

"And he almost succeeded," Christian added.

"The peace and quiet ended with a roar, 'A-L-E-S-S-A-N-D-R-A,' followed by the squawking of a chicken and a whole bunch of yelling and screaming. Her giant father yelled every curse word he could think of in as many languages as he knew."

"CB was yelling too, or should I say pleading, but all he could say was, 'Ouch. . . . Ouch. . . .' each time her father hit him . . . with the chicken."

"With the chicken?" Amy laughed.

"With the chicken," CB replied adding, "That was one crazy-ass son of a bitch."

"The father?" Amy asked.

"No, the chicken!"

Christian continued, "You could see a cloud of feathers flying inside the room. The chicken was squawking and flapping its wings trying to get away every time Señor Somero swung the chicken at him. There were feathers floating out of the window and drifting across the yard," he laughed, remembering.

"By now other workers were starting to gather to watch the excitement as Señor Somero continued yelling. Every fourth or fifth curse word he yelled you could hear CB get a few words in, trying to get himself out of his predicament, 'You don't understand sir. . . . Ouch, I love her. . . . Ouch, I want to marry her. . . . Ouch,' he said, pleading with this seriously pissed off giant of a man. But all of his pleading meant absolutely nothing to her father. He just kept beating him with the chicken and telling him to get up," Christian said still laughing.

"The next thing I see is the chicken come flying out of the window, hitting the ground and running for the hills."

"Lucky chicken . . ." CB mumbled.

That's when he grabbed young Lucho, that was his name then, by the neck and yanked him off of his daughter. When he spun around to defend himself He-Man picked him up by his you-know-what . . . and tossed him out the window. Backward."

Amy winced and looked over at CB simply saying, "Ouch!"

"I always thought he was trying to rip it off," Christian said, thinking.

"He probably would have if he had a better grip," CB added.

Christian continued, "So, now everyone who had gathered sees this naked man come flying out of the window backward, bouncing off the roof, then the fence, and into a pile of dirty straw . . . right on top of Señor Somero's pitchfork."

"Double ouch," Amy winced.

"He yelped like a kicked puppy, trying to climb out of the pile of straw with the pitchfork still stuck in his backside. Somero was cursing him from the window and decided to climb out onto the roof. He jumped into the pile of straw and started grabbing for him."

"As Lucho was twisting and turning, trying to stand up and get away, the pitchfork handle kept hitting Señor Somero in the head. He was having a hard time getting out of the straw pile as well. Señor Somero finally got ahold of the pitchfork handle and tried to ram it further into our friend's backside, but instead of pushing he fell back into some pig slop and pulled the pitchfork out of young Lucho's butt."

"Lucho jumped up and started running through the yard with one hand covering his front and the other holding his bleeding butt."

"By now the whole community had heard the commotion and were standing outside watching. When he reached me I cleared my throat and looked down at him, asking him if he forgot something. 'Damn it,' he said and turned around and ran back to the house, pushed Señor Somero back into the pile of slop and had the maiden throw his clothes out the window to him. He blew her a kiss and we both ran off to the applause of the curious crowd."

"Oh my god, that's terrible," Amy said.

"Tell me about it! I can still feel that pitchfork," CB said.

"No, I was thinking about the chicken!" Amy corrected him. They all laughed.

After a couple of hours of telling stories they decided to head back to the campus. On their way out the door they came face to face with a snarling George Wellington with two of his henchman, "Who did it?" he growled as he grabbed Jesse by the collar, almost lifting him off the ground, and pulled him forward. "Which one of these little punks put RJ in the hospital?"

Christian was surprised and a little confused as Jesse pointed to CB with a trembling hand saying, "He did."

"What's this all about?" Christian asked. Wellington just ignored him and motioned for his guys to grab CB. Christian started to step in between CB and Wellington's henchmen but was held back by CB.

Christian looked at CB for the explanation, which he provided without a word and without specific details about the attempted assault. "When I left you I came upon his son and his friends harassing Amy and I stepped in and helped her out a little. That's how we met."

Christian smiled at his response and replied in his thoughts, "Thank you," in the same manner. "Wow, what did you do to him?" he thought with curiosity.

His question made CB snicker, "Just a little kick."

Wellington didn't see or hear them talking, of course. In his eyes, their snickering was mocking him, which enraged him further. "You think this is funny, you little bastard? My son's in the hospital having one of his nuts removed because of you," Wellington growled again, motioning for his men to attack like a pair of rabid pit bulls.

As Wellington's men moved to grab CB, Christian again stepped forward, blocking the two gorilla-sized henchmen from CB and offered his warning, "I don't think you guys want to do that."

"Stay out of this, it doesn't concern you," Wellington ordered.

"Okay, it's your funeral," Christian smiled, stepping back out of the way.

CB looked at Christian, "Thanks for trying." The two men rushed toward CB, trying to grab him. He redirected their forward motion, dropping them to the ground while Amy watched, in awe of his ability to evade them.

Wellington stood frustrated as he watched his men being tossed around by a man half their size, repeatedly. He pushed Jesse into the melee ordering him to, "Get him." Wellington's push caused Jesse to bump up against CB who turned quickly, ready to strike. Seeing Jesse's frightened face, CB smiled and pushed a relieved Jesse gently backward.

Wellington, increasingly frustrated, started to move in himself just as two police cars arrived. "Hold it right there," they heard over the speaker. Wellington stood looking at his men with derision as they grunted and groaned, picking themselves up off the ground, mumbling something about them being useless.

The officer stepped out of his car. "What in God's name is going on here?" he asked in a commanding voice as he approached the well-dressed men dusting themselves off. Once closer he noticed it was Wellington. "Oh, Mr. Wellington, I'm sorry. I didn't realize it was you. What's happening?"

Wellington's demeanor became somewhat softer as he spoke to the officer. "This little son of a bitch put my son in the hospital tonight."

"He did what?" the officer asked.

"He put him in the hospital. He's having surgery right now," Wellington said in a strong voice.

"For what?" the officer asked.

Wellington, embarrassed, started to speak in a low tone, "They're removing one of his—testicles." But his answer was too low for the officer to hear.

"They're removing what?" asked the officer.

"They're cutting off one of his balls," Wellington growled. Out of the corner of his eye he saw Amy snicker, covering her mouth.

"I want him locked up," Wellington demanded, pointing to CB.

The officer heard very well the first time Wellington spoke, he just wanted to hear it again. He was one of the many who had no love for the Wellingtons. His family had seen and felt the effects of Wellington's cruelty. He bit his lip in an attempt to hold back snickering himself.

The officer turned to CB who was standing quietly watching. "Well, ok then. Is this true son?" the officer asked, holding back a grin.

"Yes sir, I saw him tonight," CB replied calmly.

"Did you two have some kind of fight or something?"

"Yes," CB answered calmly.

"Did you break one of his balls?" The officer wanted to look at Wellington but couldn't as he strained to hold back his laughter.

"Probably," CB smiled, looking directly at Wellington.

Wellington burst in, "Well, are you going to arrest him or not?" he asked demandingly.

The officer glanced at Wellington and then back at CB, "It looks like you're going to have to come with me son."

"I know," CB smiled.

Amy jumped in, "Wait, you can't arrest him, he was only protecting me."

The officer looked at CB, "Is that true?"

"Yes sir," CB replied.

"Well, why don't we all just take a ride and get this straightened out then?" he suggested.

The officer motioned for them to go to his car, turning to Wellington, "I'll take care of this Mr. Wellington." Wellington acknowledged him with a nod, disappointed that he was unable to carry through with his vengeful intentions. He would have preferred to have his two gorillas beat the hell out of CB, but knew all too well that he would need additional help if that were going to happen after watching CB toss them around effortlessly.

The officer placed CB in handcuffs and opened the back door of the patrol car, placing CB inside the car, then told Amy to go around and get in on the other side. "Does he have to have handcuffs on?" she asked.

"Yes ma'am, that's procedure," the officer responded.

"Well, what about him?" she asked, pointing to Jesse.

The cop looked over at a cowering Jesse. "Him? He was involved too?" he asked. But before she could answer, CB got her attention from the back seat and looked at her, winking and slowly shaking his head 'No'.

"No, I guess he's fine," she answered.

CB knew the more people involved, the longer the process. Besides, he already had a plan which he had shared with Christian.

Christian took Amy's keys and said he would meet them at the station.

The officer got into the car and radioed headquarters that he was inbound. As he drove away from the scene he apologized for putting CB in cuffs. "Sorry about the cuffs, it's just procedure."

CB smiled. "No worries," as he pulled his hands out from behind his back, already free from the handcuffs, but making sure not to let the officer see he was free.

Amy looked at him with amazement. "How did you do that?" she asked.

CB smiled placing his finger over his lips, "Shhhhhh," he whispered softly. She smiled.

The officer, having finished up his radio transmission to headquarters, looked at CB and Amy through the rearview mirror. "So son, you really broke one of RJ's balls?"

"Probably," CB smiled.

"Damn, I would have loved to have seen that. I always thought he was a ball-less wonder. Now I know he's a one-balled wonder," he laughed.

The officer explained what needed to be done before they could be released, telling them he had to follow procedure, especially because of Wellington's involvement and his connections on the force—but not to worry because his boss, who is friendly with Wellington, was out of town.

When they arrived at police headquarters they got out of the car. By then CB had Amy place the handcuffs back on his wrists for appearances. On their way into the building they passed Wellington standing at the front desk. He had arrived moments before to file a complaint as recommended by his friends on the force. He thought his presence when they walked in would somehow be intimidating. He was on his phone, impatiently attempting to locate the chief of police.

CB and Amy were escorted to separate rooms where they provided identical accounts of what had occurred earlier that evening. Amy was reluctant to talk about the experience, but the officer convinced her it would be best. He asked Amy if she wanted to press charges against RJ. She advised him that would not be necessary if no charges were brought against CB.

The officer approved of her reasoning, stating his concerns, but not before turning off the voice recorder. "If I know Wellington, he's not going to let this go. You and your friend need to watch your backs," he advised her in a low voice.

"I know," she said with some concern. He finished his report and placed it into a large folder that contained what looked like dozens of complaints against RJ from over the years.

"You can go if you like, your friend will be done in a minute," he smiled. Then he leaned in close to Amy and whispered, "I hope they take both of his nuts off. The world doesn't need any more of him running around." Smiling, he stood up and opened the swinging gate for Amy to exit.

Amy held back her urge to chuckle, knowing that other officers in the viewing room might be loyal to Wellington. They had kept a close eye on her since she had arrived. "Thank you. Please tell him I'll be waiting outside by the car," she said, confident that this was all cleared up.

Amy went outside to meet up with Christian.

"Hi," she said hugging him. "That was fun."

"I bet," Christian replied, motioning for her to get into the car.

"I'm glad that's over. CB should be out in a minute."

"No, not yet, he's being held."

"That can't be! The officer told me he'd be out in a minute."

"Unfortunately it's not up to him anymore," Christian advised her.

"Once you left he was told that CB was to be held indefinitely. But he wasn't wrong, CB will be out in a minute," Christian smiled.

"This is BS, I'm going in there," Amy stated, annoyed as she started to climb out of the car. She was already half way out of the car when Christian grabbed her arm, stopping her.

"Don't worry, he'll be out soon," he assured her, then he pointed at Wellington walking out of the station house. "Better to keep your distance from him."

Wellington walked past them with a confident grin on his face. "Don't bother waiting for your friend, you won't see him again any time soon," he smiled with derision as he strode arrogantly to his waiting car.

"What the hell does that mean?" Amy asked. Christian again pointed to the front of the building.

The four cops who had followed Wellington out of the building were gathered on the steps to the station house staring at them. "What's going on?" she asked.

Christian smiled again, "It's just a show of force. Wellington wants us to feel intimidated and see that he has power in this town. It's not too hard to see who's under his control."

"That's why he's sitting in his car waiting to see our reaction when CB isn't released." Amy turned to see Wellington smiling arrogantly with cocky contentment. He lifted a glass as if he were toasting his own success.

"What can we do? We have to do something." she stated.

"Nothing," Christian smiled as he started the car.

"You can't leave him here," she said.

"We're not . . . we're going to pick him up now. Hold on," Christian said while quickly backing the car out of the parking space, intentionally missing Wellington's car by only inches.

Christian looked through his rearview mirror and saw George jump nervously, spilling his drink as he fumbled to move across the seat in fear that he was going to get hit. Christian laughed.

They headed out of the lot as Wellington cursed him, wiping the drink from his clothes. The four officers who seconds before had been staring at them with sinister grins now stood with blank faces, not knowing how to respond to Christian's bold maneuver. They stood quietly on the steps with eyes glued on them as the car pulled out of the parking lot and headed down the street.

"What, are you nuts?" Amy chuckled, "And what do you mean pick him up? Pick him up where?" she asked. "How can we pick him up when he's in jail?"

"Not anymore," Christian said grinning, "Not anymore.

"What do you mean not anymore? How could he possibly get out?" Amy asked sighing, "You guys are driving me nuts."

The pair drove out of the parking lot and headed down the road until they were just out of sight of the station house and made a right turn, entering into a quaint, dimly-lit community. They turned right at the next intersection, heading deeper into the quiet neighborhood. Christian drove slowly down the poorly lit street, looking between the homes. "What are we doing?" Amy questioned. She didn't get a response. "Christian . . ." she said tapping his arm.

"Oh, we're just making a pick up," he smiled, pointing to a man walking out from between two houses.

Amy was shocked to see CB walking up to the car. "Oh my god, how did he get out of there?" she asked, happily opening the door for him. "How did you get out of there? We were told you were being held," she inquired.

CB smiled at both of them as he climbed into the back seat and patted Christian on the shoulder thankfully. "What happened?" Amy asked again with increasing curiosity.

"Everything was fine, I was on my way out to the car until what's his name—"

"Wellington," Amy said.

"Yes, Wellington, had his private police force come in. They took over and locked me up again." CB explained the hows and whys.

"Well, what about the guy that brought us in?" Amy inquired.

"His boss called just after you left and he was sent on an urgent errand."

"But he said his boss was out of town," she stated.

"He is. I guess Wellington has a far reach. One minute I was on my way out the door, then the phone rang and the next thing I know four cops are pushing me into a holding cell," CB explained.

"But that still doesn't explain how you walked out of a police station full of people without being noticed," Amy said, still curious.

CB smiled and said, "A magician has to keep some secrets, doesn't he?"

"It's probably best we get away from here," Christian added.

"No rush, they won't know I'm gone for a few minutes," CB said.

"How do you know that?" Amy asked. CB smiled and pulled two pins from a wristband and showed them to Amy. Christian chuckled. "What is that?" Amy asked curiously.

"The cure for insomnia," CB replied, putting them back into the wristband he carried them on.

The next morning, George Wellington was in the hospital berating the nursing staff for not catering to his still unconscious son and ordering they do more to help, or else.

The nurses weren't all that bothered by his loud demands with the exception of his disregard for other patients, because the few minutes of having to listen to him was nothing compared to the enjoyment they received by seeing the Little Turd get a taste of his own medicine. Many on staff at the hospital had treated a long list of people that the Wellingtons took a disliking to.

Wellington grabbed hold of one of the residents doing rounds and angrily ordered him to wake his son up. The doctor stood his ground, defending his answer, "NO, it is too dangerous. Your son had drugs in his system when he came in last night . . . a lot of them. He's lucky to have survived the procedure."

This, of course, infuriated Wellington who called the chief administrator to push his request through. The administrator agreed with the doctor; it was too risky. He explained what might happen if RJ was given a stimulant to wake him up, but George didn't care, he wanted him awake. While on the phone arguing with the hospital administrator, RJ started to stir. Wellington looked at his phone and said, "Forget it, you useless piece of . . ." and angrily ended the call.

He stood by his son's bedside, almost like a caring father waiting to greet RJ as he woke from his chemically induced sleep. RJ's eyes opened slowly. George was relatively compassionate. "How you feeling son, you okay?" he questioned. RJ nodded affirmatively even though his head was pounding with hangover-type symptoms. He knew never to show pain or weakness in front of his father. "I don't want you to worry about anything, we're taking care of that SOB that did this to you right now and we'll get that little bitch later," Wellington smiled confidently. RJ attempted to return a smile but could only muster enough energy to raise one corner of his mouth.

Wellington was consoling his son in his own gruff way when his phone rang. It was the chief of police. "George, I have some bad news for you. That kid you wanted me to look after last night is gone," the chief said apprehensively.

"W-H-A-T?" Wellington roared. "You had the little prick locked up last night. How the hell did he get out? I'll bet it was that guy that brought them in. What's his name?"

"No, George, it wasn't. I sent him on an errand that took all night, he couldn't have," the chief assured him.

"Well you tell me, how the hell does someone who is locked up get out without someone letting him out?" he roared.

"I don't know. . . . None of our guys remember anything. Hell, even the video from the station was blank, inside and out. There was nothing on it from the time Officer Cruchek drove into the lot until he was found missing."

"That's impossible!" Wellington exclaimed.

The chief continued, "It gets worse. All surveillance inside and out and within a five block radius of the station house was affected. All blank."

"So basically you're telling me everything we have on this guy is gone?" Wellington asked continuing, "There's nothing; no prints, no reports, paper or electronic, and no images. Nothing?"

"Nothing," the chief said.

"So, we don't even know who the hell he is then," Wellington mumbled.

Wellington started throwing a tantrum. He swiped at the tray of hospital food on the table and sent it flying against the wall. He kicked the equipment carts. One kick dislodged the leads from RJ's monitors, causing the alarm to go off. The nurses ran in to check what had happened. Finding the equipment and furniture was newly relocated by his ongoing tantrum, they escorted Wellington out of the room. He rudely shrugged them off and stormed off the floor and out of the hospital, intent on finding out how CB got away. . . .

-Twenty-One-
The Undesirable Invitation

It was mid-week during finals. Christian had two more exams on Thursday to finish up the semester. He had reserved a small storage unit on the outside of town to store his belongings while he was on Christmas break. The university was planning maintenance on their building over the holiday recess and requested all students remove their possessions before leaving for the holiday break. He and Matt were packing up of the last of them when Christian asked, "Where are you putting your stuff?"

He was having a hard time not letting on that he knew who Matt actually was and why he was there. "Oh, I'm just bringing it home with me. I don't think I'll be needing all of it next semester," Matt said.

"That's probably best. Are you and Tina getting together over the holidays?" Christian asked.

"No, I don't think so. I'll be back in Iowa and she's going back to D.C. She said she would be pretty busy working on some family project. I figure we'll talk and text but that's about it. How about you? You going to see Amy over the holiday?" Matt asked.

Christian paused, thinking of his response. He had to decide what to tell Matt. He knew if Matt was in communication with his father that he probably knew the plan to travel cross country with

Amy and if he said something different. . . . Well, then he would be suspicious.

"Yeah, Amy is going to come back to New York with me for the Holidays," he said.

"She's not going to see her family?" Matt inquired.

"No, not until after New Year's. Her mom and dad are going on some holiday cruise with her aunt and uncle," Christian wisely answered.

"That sounds like fun! Any special plans?" Matt asked.

"No, we're just going to hang out with friends and family, you know, have a little fun," Christian replied, shutting the cover on his last storage container.

"Ok, this stuff is ready to go," he said.

"I'm not busy this afternoon, did you want help bringing it over to storage?" Matt inquired.

"No, I'm good, I'm going to bring it over tomorrow after our last exam. What about you?" Christian asked.

"I'm going to head out tomorrow right after the last exam so if you want to use the truck to bring your stuff over we'll have to do it now," Matt said.

"Thanks, I appreciate it; it's only a few boxes. I can bring them tomorrow after exams. Thanks anyway," Christian replied.

"Okay, I was going to pack the truck tonight, but I guess I'll do it now," Matt said.

In an attempt to maintain normal appearances, Christian offered his assistance and carried a couple of boxes out to the truck with him. The conversation was limited as Christian devoted most of his thought on trying to appear as if nothing had changed between them. "Thanks for the help, I appreciate it," Matt said, continuing, "Do you need anything from town? I've got to pick a few things up if you'd like to tag along."

"No, I'm good, thanks. I'm just going to meet up with Amy," Christian replied.

Matt watched as Christian walked away. He sensed something was different about him, he just couldn't put his finger on it. He jumped in his truck and started texting one of his weekly reports. "Zeus prepped for return to Olympus. Departure Friday. Keep you posted."

Thursday's exams passed quickly. Matt said his farewells to Christian and headed to the parking lot. Christian met up with Amy to grab her car keys. Amy helped him to bring two of the six boxes he had to the car. Together they squeezed them into the back seat. "Thanks for the help," Christian smiled.

"No problem," Amy replied continuing, "I needed a break from studying anyway."

"Are you ready for tomorrow's test?" he asked.

"Mostly. Professor Lowry is known for giving brutal final exams. I'm a little nervous but I think I'll do fine as long as I get a few more hours of study time in."

"Why don't you take off? I can finish this and I'll meet you when I'm done. We'll grab something to eat and I'll leave you alone to study." Christian offered.

Amy paused, "I was thinking I would just stay in tonight and study. Lowry's test has me a little nervous."

"Ok, I'll talk to you later then. Call me if you need anything," he said giving her a kiss. "Don't worry, you'll do great," he said as he was getting into the driver's seat.

"By the way, where's Tina today?" Christian inquired.

"I think she's still taking one of her tests," Amy stated with uncertainty.

"Does she have any plans for the holidays that she mentioned?" he asked.

"Nothing specific, she just said she was heading back to D.C. to see her family. Why?"

"No reason. Matt said they aren't getting together over the holiday and I was wondering if she was doing anything specific."

"No, she didn't say anything," Amy said, curious why he was asking.

"Matt told me she was going home to help her family on a project. I was just curious if she mentioned anything to you."

"No, nothing special as far as I know," she said.

Christian said his goodbyes and headed up to his room to grab another box. He shoved it into the front seat of Amy's Camaro before heading off to the storage facility for the first of two trips.

As he drove up to the facility he thought how eerily quiet these places always seemed. On occasion you would see a few people driving in and out of them, but rarely did you see anyone, especially at this one. It was an enormous facility with a few long rows of doors and emptiness. Nobody ever seemed to be around.

He located his door and unloaded the car. It was a small locker about 5x5. He really didn't need much more. He locked up and headed back to campus to pick up the remainder of his belongings.

After loading up the remainder of the boxes he headed back to the storage facility to drop off the next load. Again, there was no one to be seen. It felt strange. He grabbed the first of his boxes and surveyed the area before he entered the storage room. He had a weird feeling. As he placed the container on the floor in the back of the storage room, the strange feeling he had suddenly changed to a sense of alarm. He felt his senses starting to heighten. His heart was pounding, he started to sweat, and he could see, hear and smell everything. He caught the scent of a man's cologne which prompted him to turn and exit the room, but he was too late. When he turned to leave the room the door slammed shut, trapping him inside.

His heart was pounding. He felt like an animal trapped in a cage as he tried forcing the door open, but it wouldn't budge. He tried to open an instant connection with CB and started to panic when he couldn't connect. He was banging on the door, calling out to whoever was on the other side. There was no answer. Just then streams of gas started filling the small storage room. The sweet and sour smell nauseated him as he continued pounding on the door, frantically trying to get out. He covered his mouth to no avail, the gas had already started to shut him down. He became disoriented and slipped slowly to the floor as he faded out.

Christian started to stir as the effects of the gas began to wear off. He found himself lying on a couch, looking up at ornate decorations painted on the ceiling some thirty foot above his head. His vision was blurry and the room appeared as if it were spinning. He tried to focus his thoughts but they were clouded from the effects of the gas. As his faculties slowly came back to him, his senses again started to heighten. His eyes slowly focused.

"Good, you're awake," he heard a strange voice say. His senses peaked and his face changed, taking on the chiseled, dark-eyed characteristics that Amy had described to him . . . except this time he could feel the change. The chiseled features and dark eyes now dominated his appearance as he focused.

"Now, now . . . there is no need for that," he heard the stranger say, walking from behind a large desk. You are not restrained and you are in no danger," the stranger said calmly, continuing, "Here, take these. They will help with the headache." Christian pushed his hand away, "Who the hell are you, and where am I?" he demanded to know. The stranger's assistants moved in, prepared to subdue Christian if necessary, but were motioned to stay where they were.

"I am Van Dunne, and we have a lot in common," Christian's senses softened. It was strange to him that his kidnapper, Van Dunne, didn't alarm him. There was something regal about him and his mannerisms. Christian pushed himself up to a seated position. His head was pounding. Van Dunne offered the aspirin to him again. "Are you quite sure you do not want these? They will help," he said calmly.

Christian looked up at him and reluctantly took the aspirin. Van Dunne removed a crystal glass containing water from a servant's tray and handed it to him. He motioned for his assistants and servants to leave the room, pausing until all had removed themselves.

"So you are 'Cicatrix' he said in a soft, confident voice. It is nice to finally meet you—again. My apologies for the undesirable invitation. It was, however, necessary."

"Necessary?" Christian questioned. "You kidnapped me. How is that an invitation?" he said, rubbing the back of his head and neck. "Where am I?" he asked.

"You are in one of my family's estates."

Christian surveyed the opulent room, "One of them?" Christian said still rubbing his neck.

Van Dunne smiled, "Yes, and as for the necessity of this rather rash invitation, you have attracted attention to yourself and I could not risk having any of the people following you know that you are here with me. Once again, please accept my apologies."

"Oh, and by the way, I hope you don't mind, but I took the liberty of having my men remove this from your girlfriend's car." He tossed the car cigarette lighter to him.

"Why, it's just a cigarette lighter?" Christian said.

"Remove the top." Van Dunne said, continuing, "We must always be careful. There are tricky people who have great interest in us."

Christian popped the top from the cigarette lighter finding a small transmitting device, flashing red LED and all. "You may also want to discard the green memory stick you have in your laptop carry case as well. I think your roommate provided that for you It is similarly equipped."

"I'm almost afraid to ask how you know about that," Christian inquired.

"I took the liberty of having my men check your laptop and other belongings when they, how do you say, tossed your room."

"That was you . . .? The police put it down as a possible drug related break-in," Christian said with a raised tone.

"They are not the neatest, but they are extremely efficient."

"You think?" Christian replied. "They unrolled all the toilet tissue."

"Yes, again my apologies. My men were searching for the file that your roommate kept regarding your upbringing. The one documenting all of your activity since childhood. It was quite enlightening, especially the video footage of your Awakening. That's not something you get to see every day, especially under such spectacular circumstances."

"I am sure you are aware that he was working in a double capacity, reporting to his superiors as well as to your father and Dr. Stedwell, his uncle I believe. Fortunately, his loyalty lay with his uncle and the reports he forwarded to his superiors were censored as to the extent of your activities."

Christian interrupted, "But I found the memory stick when I was cleaning up . . . "

"Of course you did. We wanted you to find it," Van Dunne said continuing, "We took the original and copied it onto a special memory stick."

"A special memory stick?" Christian questioned.

"Yes, . . . once the information on the replacement is accessed it triggers a timing mechanism that will destroy it."

"Destroy it? Destroy it how?" Christian asked nervously. "I copied that file onto my laptop," Christian said anxiously.

"I wouldn't worry about that. It was our desire that you find it and read it to see what was going on within your life that you were unaware of."

"As I said, we anticipated your curiosity, your desire to find out what was on the memory stick that had upset your roommate, so we placed the copy where you could find it. It was quite simple really. When you copied it you activated the timer and the next time your roommate, Matt is it? Or anyone else for that matter, tries to access the information in the 'Zeus' file, the memory stick will destroy itself and wipe out the Zeus file on any computer to which it is attached, and on any computer database the file was forward to. Rather ingenious I thought."

"What if Matt had found it before me?" Christian asked.

"We arranged that as well. He received a text just after his assault on Mr. Orlov who, by the way, is the only one of your little group who is not watching you on orders by governmental superiors. The text summoned him to contact his office and in order to do so, it was necessary for him to leave the building or risk being discovered." Van Dunne smiled, "It's fun to play the players."

His girlfriend, however, was a bit more difficult to deal with. She reports directly to her superiors at the NSA."

"How did you handle her?" Christian asked.

"We accessed her email account and cell phone. All communications come through us before sending or receiving and as for calls, we handle them directly," Van Dunne explained.

Christian's interest was piqued. "Okay, but that doesn't explain who you are and why I'm here," he said trying to rub the pain from his forehead.

"Getting right to business . . . I like that. Since our beginnings we have searched each other out. In years past it was done to form alliances of the likeminded for both business and to protect our kind. In my case it was to gather with the descendants of the Original Seven."

"You mean fourteen?" Christian inquired.

"Oh, I see you have not been made aware of the Original Seven... Curious, I wonder why your friend Channarong hasn't mentioned that yet. As time has passed and technology has improved we have found it increasingly dangerous for more than two or three of us to gather in one place. We feel it is an unnecessary risk, especially with increasing interest in our kind by every major governmental agency on the planet. Separation has become the best way to protect ourselves," Van Dunne said.

"What kind is that?" Christian inquired.

Van Dunne smiled, "I see you prefer proof rather than words."

Christian nodded affirmatively, "Well it's been a strange few months for me and right now I'm not feeling all that trusting."

"Of that I am sure," Van Dunne stated as he slowly removed his jacket, folding it crisply and placing it on the sofa next to Christian. "I can certainly understand why. After all, you have just found out that your roommate is actually working for the government. Army Intelligence, isn't it? You have also learned that your girlfriend's roommate works for the NSA, not to mention what you have learned about your guardians. This I'm sure, was most distressing to you."

Christian sat patiently and listened as Van Dunne continued, "You, unlike myself and the others, Awakened late in life. The medications Dr. Stedwell and your father provided you with were certainly effective. They interfered with your ability for higher brain function, effectively blocking you from us, making it difficult to locate and track you. But that no longer matters. The cat is out of the bag so to speak." He smiled as Christian scanned the room.

"I believe this is what you are looking for . . ." Van Dunne removed his shirt exposing a Mark. It was in the shape of a pyramid with an eye at the top and rays of light being emitted from around the peak of the pyramid. It was separated slightly from the base. Christian recognized it as one of the signs of the illuminati, and the same pyramid that is seen on U.S. currency. Van Dunne smiled, "I'm happy to see you recognize it."

"Tell me again why you couldn't just connect with me. Wouldn't that have been easier than going through this . . . this whole thing?" Christian asked.

"Unfortunately that was not an option. By the way, there's no sense in trying to connect with your friend CB either," Van Dunne said putting his shirt on. "This room is lined with a paint that contains a specific combination of lead mixed with a small amount of iridium plus other elements which, for all intents and purposes, shall remain unknown. We find it quite useful. It prevents others from connecting with us, eliminating the need to constantly expend energy-blocking connections. The whole house is painted with it, as a matter of fact. It's how we protect ourselves and our businesses."

"So, is that why I have no memory of you, no connection to your past? I thought it was impossible to block everything?"

"Not exactly. It can be done, it is just that it requires a tremendous amount of effort and energy to block constantly. Right now I have no need to block anyone from connecting. The mixture we developed in the paint is doing it for me. I have had the process applied to every home, vehicle, yacht and especially my private jets."

"Jets?" Christian rolled his eyes at the plurality of the statement.

"You of all people should know that blocking everyone continually on a daily basis is exhausting. You are trying to block me right now. That's why we use it. It allows us to save energy and relax without having to worry about connecting with someone with whom we do not wish to connect."

"And you do this just to protect yourself from the others?" Christian asked.

"Let me show you why I do this. Why don't you step over here with me," Van Dunne motioned for Christian to join him by his desk.

As he walked around the desk Van Dunne pushed a button and a large monitor rose from the desk with the word 'Genesis' written on it. Using an optical scanner to scan his retina, Van Dunne accessed the files. He waved his hands around in the air, pulling up various bits of information in holograms. One of these files was a map of the globe with dozens of dots. "This is why I block the others," Van Dunne said while watching the monitor.

"What's all this? " Christian asked.

"This map shows the location of each and every one of our kind on the planet, represented by the illuminated dots you see. As you can see, there are a lot more than fourteen," Van Dunne said peaking Christian's interest. "We each possess a unique and specific brainwave frequency that follows us through each of our lifetimes."

"This frequency functions at such a high level it is traceable if you know what to look for, and it is different for each of us. This is how we can track the whereabouts of any of our kind globally and beyond if need be," Van Dunne replied.

"And beyond?" Christian said inquisitively. Van Dunne nodded affirmatively, monitoring Christian's reaction. "What do the different colors represent?" he asked.

"The different colors show us what your current location is and more importantly what your affiliation is."

"Affiliation?" Christian questioned.

"To put it simply, we are all tracked and categorized base upon three factors; Location, political affiliation, and moral character."

"The green lights represent those of us that have sound intellect with non-threatening political beliefs or affiliations, and are of strong moral character. Let's call them 'The Good'."

"The red lights are the exact opposite. These people are akin to the likes of Attila the Hun, Hitler, Mussolini and, most recently, Bin Laden. They affiliate themselves with anarchists, terror groups and the like. They prey on the weak and most are ruthless killers, masters of genocide and are determined to destroy all who do not live by their fanatical ideals. They are capable of creating tremendous turmoil in the world. They are 'The Bad'."

"What are the blue lights?" he asked.

Van Dunne looked at him directly in the eyes as he explained, "The blue lights are people just like you . . ."

"Like me?"

"Yes, like you. And hence the reason you are here with me now," Van Dunne said, waving his arm to zoom in on their location.

He pulled up satellite imagery of the property and pointed to a green and a blue light side by side, standing in the east wing of what, from the satellite view, was an enormous estate. "This is you and I."

"Wow, this is amazing. Can you do that for everyone?" Christian asked.

"Of course," Van Dunne smiled at Christian's curiosity and with a few waves of his arm he pulled up CB's location and zoomed in on him. The imagery was so crisp and clear you could see the hair on his arms moving in the breeze. "Here is your friend CB. It appears as if he is looking for you at the storage facility. I will have someone let him know where you are," Van Dunne said looking at the door with focus. "Ok, now that that is out of the way..."

"Most in the blue group are quite a bit younger than you and have yet to be capable of influencing the world politically or socially for either good or bad. You, however, have the capability to do so without knowing it. Our major concern is that this does not happen by accident. That is why it was important that I meet with you today."

"Why, exactly?" Christian asked.

"It is only by me meeting with you that I could determine your fate."

"My fate? What gives you the right to determine my fate?" Christian inquired seriously.

"You, my friend have nothing to worry about. If I sensed that you were leaning the wrong way affiliation-wise you would already be dead. I am sure Channarong has discussed with you the importance of anonymity. Without anonymity we become the hunted and this cannot be allowed."

"So, you're telling me if one of the blue lights is a child 'leaning' in the wrong direction, you would kill him?" Christian questioned sternly.

"Oh no, quite the contrary. Children are provided mentors who can carry them through the developmental stages and set them on the right path. Channarong is your mentor. You have been together for so many lifetimes we thought it best to allow it to continue."

"You, however, are a rarity. An enigma of sorts, having been Awakened so late in life. In your case I was prepared to do what was necessary had that moment arrived."

"You mean you would kill me?" Christian asked.

"If need be, yes," Van Dunne said with calm certainty.

"How could you do that? How could you just kill someone, anyone, because they have different views than you have?" Christian questioned.

"It is not a matter of their views, it's a matter of the application of those views. Had you had the opportunity to eliminate Hitler before he committed the atrocities associated with his reign, would you? How about Bin Laden?" Van Dunne asked.

"But I'm not like them," Christian stated firmly in defense of the comparison.

"No, not at the moment you aren't; however, they weren't 'them' either as children. They became what they became because they were allowed to. They were seen only to have different social and political views early on. Those views, once acted upon, turned into fanaticism, murder and genocide of countless numbers of people. Their acts destroyed lives, families and property, and disrupted commerce on a worldwide level. Now if you could prevent that . . . would you?" Van Dunne asked, observing Christian.

"Yes, I guess I would," he replied. "But how do you know that is what will happen?" Christian asked.

"Have you forgotten your lessons so quickly? Past . . . Present . . . Future," Van Dunne replied.

"No, actually I haven't. What I remember is the story of Lord Carnarvon and how the future can be changed by a simple decision," Christian retorted.

"Yes, I see your point; however, you are forgetting one thing that occurred during the events of that story. Carnarvon failed to look forward following his change of plans, which of course, resulted in his demise. We do not make that same mistake," Van Dunne assured.

"But what if one of these people that you exterminate at your discretion would have changed their plans after you looked to their future. Wouldn't that mean that they had the potential for good? And if so, if that happened or would have happened, wouldn't that mean you took the life of an innocent person?" he asked.

"Ah, always the barrister," Van Dunne smiled, remembering a connection from an earlier time. "I prefer to look at it as removing a cancer from the planet. The only difference is that we can re-educate the emerging larvae, nurturing it to emerge from its cocoon as a butterfly as opposed to a gypsy moth," Van Dunne replied.

Although he wasn't thrilled with the idea of this practice, Christian reluctantly agreed to Van Dunne's defense. He was removing the bad from society and rehabilitating it in its new form, but that still didn't mean he had to like it. "So you have the last word on whether we live or die and you are willing to terminate someone at your discretion," Christian said without apprehension.

"Yes, we do what is necessary for the good of society and to protect our kind and our way of life," Van Dunne replied.

The corner of Van Dunne's mouth raised slightly as if he wanted to smile. He was impressed with Christian's verve. He was fearless, straightforward and protective of his thoughts, which he accomplished well for being so new to his Awakening. But what impressed him the most was that he had a pure spirit. He was uncorrupted and direct.

"You keep saying our kind. What exactly is our kind?" Christian inquired.

Van Dunne paused dramatically before explaining, "We are The Chosen. The few who hold the knowledge of the universe. The knowledge of this world, and worlds beyond our own. We are the architects of life as you know it, and have been since the beginning of time on this planet. We are a culmination of billions of years of evolution combined with technology that is far beyond the average man's abilities to comprehend or conceive. Everything that has been created can be traced back to our chosen lineage. We are the Creators. God gives life and we command it. It is by our rule that humanity flourishes. You may not realize this now as you are only beginning to learn of your capabilities, but you will see soon enough and we will be watching."

"You mentioned the first seven. Why don't I know about them?" Christian inquired.

"You have only just begun your development. I am sure Channarong will educate you further as your abilities increase. Listen to him and learn well."

The monitor on Van Dunne's desk started to chime. It was a strange sound that appeared to cause Van Dunne concern. "Our time is through for today. It was my pleasure to meet you," Van Dunne said ending the meeting abruptly. He extended his hand which Christian accepted.

"I will have my driver return you to your car." Van Dunne walked Christian to the door where he was greeted by the driver. "I look forward to our next meeting," he said.

"Likewise," Christian replied, following the driver out to the car. Van Dunne closed the office door.

He returned to his desk and viewed the alert. It was distressing news regarding a situation involving one of the Original Seven and a close personal friend, something that required his attention. He walked to the bookshelf behind his desk and pulled a book from the shelf and returned to his desk. He read the title to himself 'Awakenings' and held the book up to the monitor which scanned it. Once scanned, the side panel of his desk opened and a drawer slid out. The drawer held dozens of long crystal rods. He lifted one from the container and placed it directly in front of him on top of the desk. With a few movements of his hand the crystal started to glow bright green and projected a holographic file in front of him as it stood up on end.

He reviewed his options for a moment and then with a wave of his hand completed the task. He alerted his team to act, reminding them to follow protocol. The transmission ended. He sat quietly contemplating his decision and his longtime friend with a rare show of emotion as he watched the bright green crystal fade. It was done.

As he reflected, there was a knock on the door. A well-dressed man entered the room and nodded affirmatively to Van Dunne. The task was complete. He excused himself and left the room.

Moments later he took to the task of updating Christian's file. He returned the green crystal to the drawer and removed another . . . Christian's. He placed it on the desk in front of him and with another wave of his hand it started to glow, a bright blue color. With another wave the crystal stood up on end and projected Christian's holographic file.

Van Dunne communicated with the computer telepathically. He commanded the computer. . . . Rename file—Zeus. And his command was carried out. Then he ordered, 'Download Interview—Zeus.

The computer confirmed, 'Download Interview—Zeus.' The rod started to glow brighter and brighter and as it did, Van Dunne's facial features started to change. His eyes darkened and widened. The outside corners of his eyes lifted and the inside corners dipped. His features became more defined as bits of data were moving from his eyes to the crystal on bands of light and then projected onto the holographic file.

As the crystal received the download, the file updated on the monitor. Only moments after he started, it was complete. The computer shut down, lowering itself back into the desk. Van Dunne returned the crystal to its position in the sliding drawer and sat back in his chair in deep thought, fatigued from the transfer of data.

Christian arrived at the storage unit to find CB waiting for him. CB appeared nervous, watching the driver's every move as he pulled up. He was very relieved to see Christian as he exited the back of the black Rolls Royce Phantom limousine. CB greeted him nervously as Christian began to tell him of his 'meeting' with Van Dunne and how he received the invitation. The details of the invitation did not appear to concern him. "You don't seem all that concerned that I was kidnapped," Christian said with curiosity.

"No, I was nervous at first, but once I received the message from one of the elders, that's when I really got scared."

"I don't understand. Why would that scare you?" Christian asked.

CB stood there with a shocked expression on his face, "You're kidding, right?" he asked. "You don't understand. You met with Van Dunne. He is not just an elder, he is THE ELDER. Number One."

"I know, he's one of the Original Seven," Christian said nonchalantly.

"He told you that? What else did he say?" he asked in awe, continuing, "No one, and I mean no one, meets with him. Let me put it this way. If there was a King of the Earth, he would answer to Van Dunne. When a country needs to borrow a cup of money, they go to him. He makes Gates and Hathaway look like paupers. He controls everything and nobody makes a move unless they have his approval. I almost pissed myself when I received the message. I thought you were done," CB declared.

Christian stared at CB like he was nuts. "C'mon, you can't be serious. With the exception of the kidnapping, he seemed alright."

"Listen to me!" CB preached, "This guy is life or death. And I don't mean life or death for us, I mean life or death for everything. He is the first, the original one of our kind, and I mean original. Everything we know, everything you see is directly influenced by him in one way or another. When Emperors, Kings and Presidents need something, they ask him. And they don't even get to meet him. No one gets to meet him. H-O-L-Y—C-R-A-P!" CB said excitedly. "You have to tell me everything that happened . . ."

Christian told CB the details of the meeting, why he wanted to meet, as well as what he was told would have happened to him if Van Dunne had taken a disliking to him. He told him about the holographic desk and the colored lights, as well as how many there were. CB listened in stunned silence, amazed at what Christian was telling him. He told him about their conversation and his question to Van Dunne, "What gives you the right to kill anyone who has different opinions?"

CB's mouth dropped when he heard that, "YOU SAID THAT TO HIM? What? Are you crazy? You don't argue with Van Dunne! You're out of your mind!" he said excitedly. CB followed up with a barrage of questions, following each detail of Christian's story.

Christian couldn't understand what the big deal was, but he enjoyed seeing CB act like an excited kid for a change. He continued to discuss with CB every detail of his visit to Van Dunne's estate as they drove back toward the campus.

Since Matt had left town already, Christian invited CB back to the room to crash for the night. He wanted to learn more about Van Dunne and this new fraternity he belonged to. CB declined stating he had something to do.

"Are you saying no because of the rule?" he asked.

"What rule?" CB inquired.

"You know, the one where we can't gather in groups of three or more or stay together for long periods of time," Christian explained.

"No, I'm saying no because I have things to do tonight," CB answered. "Hey, you can drop me off here, thanks," CB told him abruptly.

Christian pulled over to drop him off in front of the diner, then looked at him with curiosity asking, "What is it that you do anyway?"

CB smiled as he got out of the car, "What, you don't know?" he asked continuing, "Have a good night. I'll be in touch before you leave tomorrow," he said and walked through the doors of the diner.

Christian, ready to drive back to campus, remembered he was going to pick something up for Amy to eat while she was studying. He hopped out of the car and hurried toward the entrance to the diner, pulling his phone out to text Amy to see what she wanted.

He walked through the entrance only moments after CB entered expecting to see him, but when he walked through he was gone.

"Where is he?" he asked himself. The hostess came over, "Can I help you sir?"

"Yes, I'm looking for my friend; he just walked in a minute ago. Do you know where he is?" he asked.

"No sir. I'm sorry, you are the only person to walk through that door in twenty minutes."

"Are you sure? Maybe you missed him," Christian persisted.

"No sir, I have been standing here since my shift started an hour ago. If anyone came through that door I would have seen them. Would you like to sit?" the hostess asked as Christian pondered the mystery. "Sir, would you like to be seated?" she asked again.

His phone chimed in. It was Amy. He motioned for the hostess to wait a moment while reading the text. She rolled her eyes. "I'd love a burger, fries and Coke–Thx Hon," Amy texted.

"Sir, would you like to be seated?" she asked again, getting a little snippy.

Christian paused momentarily, reflecting before answering, "No, I'll be taking out."

The hostess looked at him with attitude, "You can do that from the counter right over there," she pointed, vaguely directing him to the cash register area, slapping the menu back on the counter.

He placed his order while surveying the diner. CB was nowhere to be seen. "Where is the lavatory?" he asked.

"Excuse me?" the waitress responded.

"The bathrooms?" he asked.

The waitress directed him to the lavatory. He opened the door, expecting he might see CB, but he was nowhere to be found. "Where could he have gone?" he wondered, going back to the counter to wait.

A waitress brought his order to the counter. "Your order's ready," she smiled, slipping him the check. "Are you ok honey?" she asked.

Christian paused, still thinking, "Yes, I'm sorry. Yes, I'm fine, thank you."

Christian drove back to campus with a lot on his mind. There were more questions than answers. What was that meeting really all about? It couldn't be as simple as a meet and greet. Van Dunne could've pulled the trigger on me anywhere. Why did he want to meet me, and where the hell did CB vanish to?

-Twenty-Two-
Happy Travels

Christian met up with Amy following her exams on Friday. She greeted him with excitement for their cross country trip. She had never travelled cross country and was excited to see New York and meet Christian's family and friends.

So how'd your tests go this morning?" he asked. "Pretty good. The extra study time really helped, but I don't want to think about it. It's over. Let's get going," she said, urging Christian to get in the car.

On their way out of town they stopped for gas and to pick up some supplies for the trip. While standing in line waiting to pay, Amy looked at the stand displaying the local newspapers. On the front cover was a big picture of RJ sitting in his hospital bed, face bruised and an ice pack on his crotch. The picture dominated the front page. Underneath the photo it said, 'Photo by Hank Fargus'.

Amy chose to laugh instead of dwell on the attack. "Oh my god," she said directing Christian's attention to the photo.

"Oh, I have to get one of these," he said enjoying the bold headline that read, 'Wellington One Ball Down!' "Look at this picture . . . my god this couldn't be more embarrassing." He studied the picture briefly. It showed RJ sitting up in his hospital bed, a total mess, and his groin wrapped up like he was wearing a diaper, holding an ice pack on it.

"Wow, he looks more stoned than the night it happened, if that's possible," Amy snickered.

"Hey, I thought CB only kicked him once in the . . . you know. How did his face get all bruised up?" Christian asked.

"I don't know," Amy said. "It's an improvement though, don't you think?" She looked at him, smiling with a victim's sense of satisfaction.

The attendant behind the counter overhearing the conversation started to laugh. He looked around the store before saying, "I heard the Little Turd fell out of bed trying to leave the hospital when the doctors told him they were going to remove his balls." He laughed continuing, "I hope they took them both off."

It was more than obvious that RJ was not well liked and most would prefer that he didn't reproduce. The attendant continued, "It's about time someone stood up to him. That bastard deserves everything he got. I got fired from my last job because of him. That's why I am stuck here. They should roast his balls in oil and feed them to the dogs," the man said seriously.

Christian and Amy jumped in the car and started the three thousand mile journey to New York. They had planned a five day crossing but Christian had added a couple of surprise stops during the trip. The trip plan had them travelling through Nevada, Utah, and Colorado where they would pick up Route 80 East and drive straight on through southern Nebraska, Illinois, Indiana, Ohio, Pennsylvania and on to New York.

The first stop . . . Las Vegas. Christian planned to surprise Amy. He told her he was making a pit stop for fuel before moving on. They had reached Vegas early, about 7:00 p.m. "Let's drive down the strip," Christian said.

"That would be great. I really had a blast here, even if you did scare the hell out of me," she said. As they got closer to 'The Rio', Christian distracted Amy by asking her to grab his wallet out of the shirt pocket that he had deliberately buried under their bags during the last gas stop.

As she dug deep to find his shirt he pulled up to the Rio All Suites Hotel and Casino. "Got it," she said, pulling the shirt from the back seat and feeling for the wallet. "There's no wallet in here," she said looking at Christian. She spun around to sit back down and noticed he was holding his wallet, "I thought you wanted me to . . . Oh my god . . . what are we doing here?" she asked with surprise. "I thought we were going to drive through to Utah tonight?" she questioned.

"I thought it would be a nice surprise," Christian smiled.

The valets opened their doors and the cool night air rushed in, "Welcome back to the Rio Mr. Asher."

"Thank you," Christian smiled, grabbing his computer carry case.

"May I take that for you sir?" the valet asked.

"No thank you . . . not this one." He popped the hatch for the valet. "Would you mind grabbing those for me?" he asked politely.

"Not at all sir," the valet grabbed the two lightly packed bags.

They were escorted to a personal check-in area managed by the concierge. "Welcome back Mr. Asher. Your room is ready and waiting. You will only be staying with us for one night this trip?" asked the concierge.

"Yes," he replied, smiling.

"I will open a line for you. Please sign here and I will get you on your way." Christian signed the registration forms and was instructed which elevators to use. Check in completed, they headed up to the room.

"What a great idea," Amy smiled as she walked over to the bank of elevators.

"Where are you going?" Christian asked smiling. "We're going over here." He pointed to the express elevator.

Entering the elevator, Christian pressed the penthouse floor. Amy's excitement grew. "How did you arrange this?" she asked. "Matt didn't do this, did he?"

"No, I called them to see if they had anything available and they remembered me," he said as the elevator prompted him to scan his room key for access to the top floors. Amy hugged him affectionately. "I asked for a nice room but I didn't think they would give us the penthouse," he said with curiosity.

The bellman was waiting for them to arrive. He had placed a welcome basket of fruits and snacks on the bar and offered his assistance with any services that they may require. Christian tipped him generously and bid him goodnight.

"Wow, this is incredible!" Amy said, admiring the two floor suite. "I never thought I'd be back here so soon. What are we going to do?"

"I don't know . . . I was thinking a shower and dinner to start," he said continuing, "What do you want to eat?"

"Not Italian!" she blurted playfully.

Christian called to make reservations. "Hello, Buzio's, this is Beverly. How may I help you?"

"I'd like a reservation for tonight please."

"I'm sorry sir, we are booked through ten-thirty tonight. Would you like to reserve a table?"

"Nothing earlier?"

"No sir, we are booked."

"Ok, I'll book for ten-thirty"

"What is your room number?" the hostess asked.

"I am in P1777."

"Hold on please." There was a pause on the phone. "Hi, Mr. Asher . . . We just had a cancellation and can get you in for eight-thirty, will that be ok?" Beverly asked.

"Yes, that would be perfect, thank you," he replied.

"I will see you at eight-thirty then. Thank you."

Christian placed the contents of his bag into the room safe while Amy filled the Jacuzzi with hot, soapy water. The two climbed into the Jacuzzi and started to unwind from the long journey. They lay there relaxing as the pulsing jet streams of hot water massaged them. Amy was picking at grapes from the gift basket when the phone rang.

They looked at each other, curiously. "They must have made a mistake with the room," Christian thought." Amy handed the phone to him, "Hello."

"Hi Mr. Asher, this is Tiffany from accounts. Madeline from the concierge desk wanted me to open a line for you."

"Okay," Christian responded slowly not really knowing what she meant.

"Did you want the entire two-hundred thousand on the line?"

"Two hundred thousand? I don't have two hundred thousand," Christian said.

"I'm sorry sir," Tiffany apologized, "Did you want the entire two hundred and twenty-two thousand added to the line?"

Christian paused a moment. Amy looked at him nervously mouthing, "What's going on?"

"Can you tell me where this money came from?" he asked.

"Yes sir, of course. My records indicate that you placed Keno bets against your line during your last visit. The winnings appear to be from that sir," Tiffany replied. "I can put all or part of it on a line of credit for you. How would you like me to proceed?" she asked politely.

"Tiffany, why didn't I know about this before I left last time I was here?" he asked.

"It seems that you had placed the bet just before you checked out. We did send notifications to your email address updating your account and sent a mailing to your home. Didn't you receive them?"

"No, I'm sure I didn't," he said thinking.

"Mr. Asher, how would you like me to proceed?" she asked again.

A stunned Christian slowly responded, "Ahh, just add a hundred to it for now."

"Okay sir, I have added one hundred thousand dollars to your line. It is attached to your card. Is there anything else I can do for you this evening?"

"No," Christian choked. "Thank you, you've been very helpful. Good night," Christian said, hanging up the phone.

"What was that about? Did they give you the wrong room?" Amy asked.

You're not going to believe this . . ." he said in disbelief. "Apparently the last time we were here, I placed a bet on something called Keno . . ."

"Yeah, and what happened?"

"I won." He said.

"Won what?" she asked, trying to drag it out of him.

"Two hundred and twenty-two thousand dollars," he said in disbelief.

Amy's jaw dropped. "No way! she yelled, splashing the Jacuzzi water in excitement. "I don't believe it!. You really won two hundred and twenty-two thousand dollars?" Christian nodded affirmatively, still in disbelief himself. "What are we going to do?" Amy asked.

He smiled, "Let's have some fun!"

The pair got dressed and headed down for dinner. They were escorted to their table and ordered. Following the meal they hit the shops. While Amy was trying on some clothes, Christian quietly arranged for another nighttime surprise.

Amy looked stunning having changed into her new outfit. He stood smitten as he watched her model her new ensemble. He smiled, "There's only one thing missing," he said, handing her a box.

Amy looked at it nervously. "Christian, you didn't have to do this," she said softly.

"I know, but I wanted to," he replied, kissing her gently. "Go ahead, open it up," he smiled with anticipation.

Amy lifted the soft velvety cover of the box and as she did, the lights reflecting off of its contents flickered on her face. She covered her open mouth with her hand as a tear rolled down her cheek. "Do you like it?" Christian asked.

Amy started to tear up. "Yes . . . Yes . . . I love it!" She hugged him tightly. "Can you put it on me?" she asked, wiping her tears.

"Gladly," he responded, removing it from the black velvet box. Amy held out her hands as Christian stepped closer to her and wiped the tears from her cheek. He slowly bent down and gently placed a herringbone two carat diamond necklace around her neck. He leaned in closer and clasped it in the back as Amy wrapped her arms around his waist and started to squeeze. "A perfect fit," Christian whispered softly.

"I know," Amy said with gentle affection and smiled endearingly.

Amy, still sniffling, admired her gift in the store mirror. It was a rounded herringbone chain that widened in the front coming to a 'V', giving the appearance of gold wings. It had two curving lines of diamonds, starting with small stones on the center of the outer edge of the 'wings' that increased in size until they met at the point formed by the wings. "I love it, but I don't deserve this," she said, looking at Christian through the reflection.

He smiled, hugging her from behind. "Yes you do . . ." he said as he squeezed her a little tighter. "Thank you," he whispered in her ear.

The romantic moment had all the ladies in the store grabbing for tissues, but it was short lived. Moments later a man inside the store yelled, "Ouch, what are you doing that for?" he asked his girlfriend who had just pinched the back of his arm.

"Why can't you be more like that?" she asked loudly, invoking an argument as she pushed him toward the exit.

Christian and Amy snickered as they heard one of the sales women say, "Good, get out. This ain't no episode of Jersey Shore."

Amy looked in the mirror. "I'm sorry, look at me. I'm a mess, my eyes are all puffy and red."

One of the workers handed her some eye drops from the counter. "Here you go honey. Don't worry about that, it's on me," she said.

"Thank you, that's so sweet of you," Amy said. "Excuse me, I'm going to go to the ladies room." She headed across the hall to the facilities.

Christian smiled as he watched her walk away. He sensed he was being watched and turned to see all four of the shop employees staring at him. Three with dreamy eyes but there's always that one. . . . She stared him in the eyes and said in a firm tone, "That's a sweet girl you have, mister. You better treat her right and don't be pulling any of this Vegas one-night-stand stuff on her and try returning that necklace tomorrow. I won't take it back!" Christian was startled by her loud tone. He smirked at the insinuation and looked at the ladies, all of who appeared to agree with her.

"I wasn't planning on it," he smiled sincerely.

Security came into the store and looked at the employees and then at Christian. Is there a problem here Mr. Asher?

"No, we were just having a conversation."

"I received a report of an argument, a woman yelling at a man."

Christian paused a moment. "Oh, you must be talking about the muscle guy who just left with his girlfriend. She was doing a lot of yelling. They went that way." He pointed toward the casino floor.

"That must be it then. Thank you Mr. Asher," the security guard said, making his way back into the casino. He glanced at the sales ladies and winked.

Christian left the store smiling as Amy came out of the ladies room. "How do I look? Better? she asked.

"Incredible!" he said. Amy gave a thankful wave to the ladies as they headed to the casino floor.

"What would you like to do now?" Amy asked.

"Let's play a little," he said. "After all, it's Vegas Baby, Vegas."

Amy smiled with a resounding, "Yahooo!" and they hit the tables. They started playing roulette for a while. Of course the eyes from above were watching their every move. It's not often a first timer hits the poker tables for 18K and then bangs out almost a quarter of a mil at Keno. This kind of activity peaks their interest.

The two of them played for an hour before Christian pulled Amy away from the table. "Where are we going?" she asked.

"I have another little surprise for you." They went outside to a waiting stretch. Christian handed the driver a card and passed him a hundred on the low side. "We'd like to go here please, it's a surprise."

"Where are we going?" Amy asked.

"You will know when we get there," he said playfully. "Here put this on," he said handing her a blindfold.

"You really want me to put this on? You're kidding, right?" she asked playfully.

"Youuuu can't be trusted. I don't want you to see where we are going," Christian said playfully.

Amy put the blindfold on and started playing the, 'I know where I am' game. "Okay, we turned left so we are heading down the strip. Ooh, I can hear the fountain at the Bellagio. Okay, we are stopped at the light . . . we didn't go too far. I can hear a roller coaster . . . Okay, I got it; we are at . . ." Before she could finish, Christian rolled up her window and turned up the music. "Hey that's not fair!" she claimed.

"Oh yes it is. My surprise, my rules," he laughed. Amy felt around for his face with both hands.

"You're gonna get it mister," she said planting a kiss on his nose.

"You missed," he snickered.

"Stop moving around," she said, planting the next kiss on his lips.

"You're pretty good at this game," he lied.

The only correct guess she had was that they turned left out of the Rio. The fountain was the sprinkler system watering the plants and trees next to a building, and the roller coaster was the tram pulling out of the Luxor.

When they arrived at the heliport the driver opened the door as Christian removed the blindfold. The pilot was there to greet them. "Mr. Asher, how are you? I am your pilot, Frank James. Are you ready to go?"

"Yes sir," Christian replied.

"What is this?" Amy asked.

"It's a little nighttime tour I arranged for us," he replied.

"Get out of here . . . I always wanted to go up in one of these," she claimed.

They hopped onto the helicopter. Frank did his pre-check and turned her over. He throttled her up and off they went, pulling up and away from the strip. "Wow . . . Vegas is amazing from up here," Amy said, snapping pictures of the nighttime skyline. Frank gave them a moonlit tour of the surrounding area, returning to circle the strip a few times before heading back. The tour was fairly quick but well worth it. The view was incredible. Christian thanked Frank for his time and said goodbye.

They went back to the hotel to play for a while longer. They hit the blackjack tables, slots and had their go at roulette one more time before heading up to the room.

Morning came quickly. They woke to room service knocking on the door. "Oh my god, who is that?" a weary Amy asked, looking over to see it was only seven-thirty in the morning.

Christian was already stirring around. "It's room service. I requested an early breakfast so we could hit the road early, remember?"

"Oh yeah, I forgot. I'm so comfortable," Amy said, stretching out across the plush bed, yawning.

Christian went to answer the door. "Good morning sir, my name is . . ."

Before he could finish Christian blurted, "Martin, how the hell are you? It's good to see you."

Martin was startled and jumped back a bit . . . "Excuse me sir. I'm sorry, you startled me," Martin said. "It is nice to see you again sir."

"Come on in . . ." Christian said. He made his request for the morning meal and excused himself.

They shared a morning feast overlooking Las Vegas and the reddish-orange glow of the mountain range beyond as the sun climbed. They bid farewell to Martin and prepped for the day's travels.

Plans in hand, they headed for the lobby. On their way to check out Christian thought, "Oh, what the hell," and headed for the Keno room to place some bets before checking out and hitting the road. The plan was to reach Keystone, Colorado, just shy of seven hundred miles.

During the first hour of the drive, Amy was quietly reflecting on the amazing events of the night before and her feelings toward Christian. She sighed with contentment, glancing at Christian as her fingers caressed the front of the necklace.

"You're awfully quiet, is everything ok?" Christian asked.

"Yeah . . . everything is great. Do you think your mom will like me?" she asked.

"Ooooooh, I don't know. She's always been very protective," he said in a serious tone. "She'll probably interrogate you. You know, put you on the rack, stretch you out and burn you with a red hot iron," he laughed.

Amy smacked his arm, "You watch way too many old movies."

"Of course she'll like you, how could she not?" he assured her.

They arrived in Keystone a quarter past seven that evening. Christian was able to arrange for a beautiful room with a mountain view. The bright lights lighting the trails yielded to a ghostly blue-grey under the moonlit sky. The sky above looked like black velvet with sparkling diamonds. After freshening up they made their way into town with recommendations for a place to eat.

Walking into the restaurant, Christian couldn't help but appreciate the structure. He looked up in awe to see the twenty foot high vaulted ceilings were supported by large diameter natural timbers harvested from the mountain. Multiple stone fireplaces were stoked, adding to the ambiance. The rough-cut, timber-lined walls accented the stone floors and wooden tables were also made with local timber. And the view . . . the view was stunning. Tall windows facing the mountainside captured the best view of Keystone.

The restaurant was filled to capacity. The bartenders and wait staff were hustling to keep the flow going as happy skiers and boarders enjoyed the nightlife. They grabbed a seat at the bar while they waited, and chatted with a few folks during the wait. One of the guys was having a real good time and started singing. Christian and Amy, having never seen spontaneous singing before outside of an old movie, joined in with the growing crowd of singers. Before they knew it, half of the restaurant was singing. The hostess came to the bar and requested that they follow her as she led them to their table.

On the way to the table a patron knocked a bottle of wine over as Christian passed. He grabbed the bottle as it fell to the floor and placed it back on the gentleman's table. He, like anyone else would, was expecting to hear a thank you, but he didn't get it. He got stunned silence. And not just from the gentleman's table the bottle fell from, but from the tables around him as well. People stopped talking and stared, some with their mouths open. He paused to look curiously at them when Amy turned back and grabbed his arm. "Are you coming?" she asked, pulling him away to the sound of the gentleman saying, "Th—Th—Thank you."

They were enjoying their appetizers when the clumsy patron walked over to his table and introduced himself. "I have to ask you. . . . How did you do that?" he asked.

Amy looked at the gentleman oddly, "Do what?" she asked.

"Oh, it was nothing, I just caught a wine bottle that was knocked over as we passed his table," Christian answered.

The gentleman interrupted, "Caught it, you never touched it."

"What do you mean he never touched it?" Amy asked.

"Just what I said . . . he never touched it. The bottle was off the table and falling to the floor and it just stopped and came back to the table," the curious man stated with conviction. "Everyone at the table wants to know how you did it."

Amy looked over to where the man was seated to see at least a dozen pair of eyes from a few tables staring toward them like kids waiting for ice cream to be served. "That's not possible . . . maybe it wasn't off the table, just close to being off the table," she said, looking at Christian. "Oh, look who we're talking about," she said to herself, smirking at him.

Christian interrupted the conversation, "A magician never revels his secrets,"

"Oh, you're a magician . . . that was incredible. That's all we could talk about since it happened. Are you sure you can't tell me?" he asked.

"Sorry, It wouldn't be a secret if I told you, now would it," Christian smiled. The gentleman, accepting the explanation, excused himself for the interruption and returned to his table.

"What was that about?" Amy asked Christian.

"I have no idea," he said, shaking his head.

"Did you knock over his wine or something?" she asked.

"No, all I remember is seeing the bottle falling and reacting to stop it. I thought I grabbed it and put it on the table. I was wondering why everyone was staring at me so strangely afterward," he said.

"But he said you didn't touch it, which is pretty cool when you think about it. Is this something else you can do, another trick?" she asked.

"I don't know," he said just as they were interrupted by a loud round of applause from the gentleman's table and the surrounding tables. Christian looked at Amy who started to laugh and clap herself as he stood up and took a bow to a standing ovation. Other tables joined in, having no idea why they were applauding as Christian stood up and took his bows. He returned the compliment by applauding the patrons and the staff.

Amy was amazed at what happened next, as was Christian. By the time the two left the restaurant, people were asking for his autograph. Some even snapped a quick pic with their phones and yet another jumped between them for a selfie. "Oh my god, who do these people think you are?" Amy asked jovially.

Morning came and Amy woke to Christian smiling as he watched the snow cats grooming the trails. "In for a couple of runs before we go?" he asked.

"Love it," Amy quickly replied, hopping out of bed.

They headed out to the slopes, rented some equipment and hit the trails. It was the best part of the day, cold and crisp with a fresh layer of snow that had fallen overnight. After a couple of warm up runs Christian asked, "How good of a skier are you?"

"I can hold my own," Amy answered confidently.

"Good, follow me," Christian said, cutting off trail into the glades, a skiable area in the trees.

He was impressed with Amy as they cut in and out of the trees following a narrow path. As they followed the path, the groomed trail dropped off steeply on the right side below the hairpin turn in front of them. Christian knew he was going to get some air.

Amy stopped and watched as Christian blew through a pile of Champagne powder, launching off the ledge and dropping thirty feet. He disappeared into the soft powder below before breaking out onto the groomed trail where he stopped to watch her.

Not to be outdone, she followed suit and blasted through the powder with an explosion as she launched herself off the ledge, also dropping thirty feet and landing in the deep powder alongside the groomed trail. She disappeared for a second or two in the deep powder before exploding out of it at velocity.

She ripped past him with a quick cut and spray yelling, "What are you waiting for," challenging him with a smile from ear to ear. She ripped down the trail. Christian pushed off left down a mogul run and found his zipper line instantly.

Amy was looking behind her for any sign of Christian when he shot out of the bug hill right in front of her. She dropped low to kick up her speed until she caught up with him. They ripped it up side by side right to the lodge.

“Wow, you are amazing! I didn’t know you could ski so well,“ he panted.

“Senior—high—ski club—champion,” Amy panted, wearing a proud smile.

Unfortunately it was time to get on the road. They headed back to their room and when they got there they saw a familiar sight. Amy noticed them first, “Oh no, not again,” she said as Christian looked up to see a couple of troopers by their room.

“Dammit, I thought they wouldn’t find us for a while,” he said under his breath. “Officers, what happened?” he asked.

“Is this your room sir?” the officer asked.

“Yes, what happened?” he asked again.

“We got a call that someone was trying to break into a car. Is that your blue Camaro outside?”

“It’s mine officer,” Amy said, running to the window to look at her car.

“Don’t worry, nothing happened to it. We pulled up while they were still trying to get in it,” the officer said.

“Did you catch them?”

“No ma’am we didn’t. That’s the problem with snow country. These guys show up on sleds and when we show up, they take off and they’re gone . . . and we can’t follow,” he explained.

“Unfortunately your room wasn’t as lucky as your car. Can you tell me if there’s anything missing?” The officer asked and continued to question them about possible motives as well as if and who they recently met that may have known their plans.

Amy picked up her clothes from the floor and put them back into her bag. Christian did the same. Christian looked at the officer, "Nothing missing. We had everything worth anything with us. All they could've taken here was laundry," Christian said.

"Well, that's probably why they tried the car," he said. The officer stayed a while longer to ask some questions. Christian explained they were on their way home from college and had just stopped for the night. The officer completed his report and headed to the front office.

They finished packing their belongings and headed to the office to check out. As Christian headed to the desk his senses heightened. The day manager came out to greet him. "Mr. Asher, I'm terribly sorry this happened. This is unheard of here. Please accept my apologies and these vouchers good for a two-night stay." Christian was preoccupied, surveying the room. He knew something wasn't right.

Christian hurried the overly apologetic manager through the checkout process telling him not to worry about it and headed out the door. As soon as he cleared the door the manager pulled out his phone and made a call only saying, "Nuevo York" and slipped out a back door, leaving the daytime manager and his assistant tied up in the back office.

Amy immediately sensed something was wrong when he got into the car. "What's going on?" she asked.

"I don't know yet, something's not right," he said, starting the car and put it into gear. "Let's get out of here." He hit the gas.

"What happened in there?" Amy asked.

"I started to get that feeling again, like before the fight, but I didn't see anything to worry about."

"Maybe it's just nerves," Amy suggested.

"Still, I think we should just drive through to New York. This is the second time in a couple of weeks this has happened. It's got to have something to do with The Cross," he expressed his concerns.

"Where is The Cross?" Amy asked.

He patted the console. "In here," he smiled.

Christian opened the console and lifted the plastic liner. Looking inside, Amy could see The Cross strapped to the carpet below. "Velcro, huh . . . Good idea," he smiled. "But what's in the box?"

"An art project," he replied, putting the liner back into the console.

"An art project?" Amy asked, a little confused.

Christian explained how he bought a cross from the Catholic charities store in town, painted it and glued fake stones on it that he had gotten at the art store and placed it in the box. "It's not an exact replica, but I'll bet it's good enough to fool anyone who isn't an expert."

"I was wondering why you didn't seem that concerned when you saw they broke into the room," she said.

"What about the weight? The Cross is heavy," she mentioned.

"Got it covered. The cross has a storage compartment in it for candles and a small vial of holy water. I replaced the candles with lead weights," he smiled confidently.

"Lead weights? Where did you get lead weights?" she asked.

"We-l-l-l-l, I wanted to get them from the lab. We use them at the base of the models, but the lab was closed up tight."

"So where did you get them?" she asked.

Christian paused a moment, "Tina's ankle weights," he said with playful apprehension.

"Good, she deserves it, that sneaky bitch!"

"The one thing we need to do now is keep our eyes open. Someone knows where we are and they're looking for something," he warned.

Amy was a bit unnerved with the thought of being chased but managed to get out a concerned "Hmmm . . . It's like Bonnie and Clyde. You know, getting chased across the country and stuff."

"Yes, it kind of is, isn't it?" Christian smiled.

"You do remember how that movie ended, don't you?" Amy kidded.

As the two rounded a curve on the narrow road to the highway Amy looked up. "Oh, I shouldn't have said that . . ." with a distraught look on her face."

"That's just what I was thinking," Christian said, looking up to see a black van pull out in front of him, blocking off the road.

Amy glanced over at him, "What are we going . . ." stopping mid-sentence to stare at him as his face began to change before her eyes.

"What?" he asked . . .

". . . To do?" she said, "What are we going to do?"

She continued to watch as his face physically changed in front of her eyes. His eyes darkened eerily as the coloring in his face changed from the reddish blush of windburn to a pale grey color. His features hardened, becoming more chiseled. It was frightening for her; she had never actually seen the change before. She had only seen him after the change and in poor lighting, but it was never as dramatic a change as she was seeing now. "Oh my god," she thought covering her open mouth in disbelief, "What the hell is happening?"

Thinking quickly, she fumbled and handed him his sunglasses. "Here, put these on," she said, more frightened of the change than the men standing in the roadway.

Christian took a quick look in the mirror, "Good thinking," as he covered his darkened eyes.

Four men had exited the van carrying assault weapons and surrounded the car, ordering them to exit the vehicle. Christian, with heightened senses, focused on their weapons and instantly noticed all but one were chambered and ready to fire. He took a deep breath and motioned for Amy to get out of the car slowly.

The men grabbed them, pushing them toward the van. A well-dressed man emerged from behind the van and walked slowly over to the pair with a cold, hard look on his face. "Mr. Asher, I believe you have something that belongs to us. Where is it?" he asked.

"Where is what?" Christian replied.

"Don't play around with me son. The Cross, where is it?" he demanded, "And take those stupid sunglasses off when I'm talking to you."

The man attempted to knock the glasses off Christian's face but Christian caught his wrist in mid swing with astounding speed and started to squeeze. Amy recognized the move from the night she met CB. The stoic man winced, surprised by Christian's speed and strength.

His men raised their guns, training their laser sites on Christian as Amy looked on nervously. "Not a good idea Mr. Asher," the man stated looking around at the hardware pointed in his direction.

Christian's senses had peaked. They were stronger than he'd ever experienced. He could hear, see and smell everything. He knew each of the men's position by listening to their footsteps as they moved to encircle him. He could hear the tendons in their fingers tighten on the triggers, activating the laser sites on their weapons.

One of the gunmen hurried to the car. Amy ran over to the car as he started rifling through their belongings. "Hey, get the hell out of there," she yelled.

Christian glanced over at her just as she was pushed back by the gunman. He released his grip on the stoic stranger, pushing his arm away. "Wise of you," he said, staring at Christian and removing his sunglasses to return a cold stare.

Amy paused her assault on the gunman momentarily as Christian removed his glasses. Relieved that his eyes had returned to their normal color, she resumed her assault on the rummaging gunman.

Christian turned his focus to Amy as she continued pulling at the gunman searching the car. "Amy let him have it," he said.

"No, you found it . . . it's not fair," she said, struggling to pull the gunman from her car.

"It's ok . . . really. Let them have it. It's not worth dying over," he said.

"Listen to your friend, Miss Kendall. It's not worth dying over," the stranger said.

Amy reluctantly stopped her assault, stepping back and pointed to the bag holding the fake cross. Christian had never seen her so angry. The gunmen tore at the bag and pulled out the foam filled box. He backed out of the car, throwing the bag at Amy's feet and stared at her for a moment before he knocked her to the ground with the butt of his gun. "Bitch," he growled, looking down at her clasping her stomach.

Christian didn't move as he glared at the gunman walking toward him to hand the box to the stoic stranger. The gunman stared back, smirking at him with sick satisfaction. The man opened the box and smiled gruffly. "Mr. Asher, this is cute. The whole acting thing and all, but you are trying my patience. Do you think I'm a fool? Where is it?" He motioned to the gunman who seconds earlier had knocked Amy down. He lifted his weapon and trained his laser site on Amy's forehead. A frightened Amy winced. "The real Cross or she dies," the man threatened.

Amy watched as Christian, tagged with laser sites, made his way to the car and opened the console. He pulled out the tray, reached down and grabbed The Cross that was strapped to the carpet and pulled it from the console. He started to make his way back to the man when he stopped, "Back him off or I toss it," he ordered. He was threatening to throw The Cross over the steep embankment. The man quickly examined the gleaming cross in Christian's hand and motioned for his gunman to lower his weapon.

Christian walked to the man and pushed The Cross into his chest. "Here, choke on it you piece of sh*t," and he turned to walk away.

The man looked carefully at The Cross and smiled confidently. "Now, now Mr. Asher . . ." Christian stopped and turned. "Don't go away mad. Here, why don't you keep this as a souvenir?" the man said, tossing the foam padded box with the phony cross at him. "It was a good try, but next time, don't put it in the box with wet paint on it," he grinned, motioning for his men to get in the van. The man admired The Cross as he turned and moved toward the van.

Christian, with his back to the van, paused and listened as all but one of the gunmen climbed into the van. The fourth gunman looked at Christian with a smug grin on his face as he passed him on his way to the van. As he passed, Christian said, "Hey," and as the gunmen stopped to look at him, Christian swung the heavy box with lightning quick speed, slamming him in the face, knocking him out cold.

The others jumped out of the van with guns pointed, waiting for orders. Christian looked down and spat on him. "Don't you ever point a gun at my girlfriend again you worthless piece of slime." He turned to look angrily at the stranger by the van.

The stranger stared at Christian with a stern expression on his face and then grinned as if he approved of his moxie. He had just taken out one of his best trained men with a box. He barked his orders to the men, "Pick him up and put him in the van," looking once again at Christian.

Christian helped Amy up from the ground as the black van sped away back toward the resort. "I'm so sorry . . . I'm so, so sorry," she said as he brushed the hair from her face.

"Are you okay?" he asked.

"Yes, I'm fine, just a little shaken . . . . It's not every day I have a gun pointed at me. But, I am getting used to the break-ins . . ." she joked nervously.

Christian smiled, giving her a quick hug. "C'mon, let's get out of here," he said, helping her into the car and closing the door.

He jumped in the driver's seat and sped down the winding road. Amy started to break down weeping when the reality of what had just transpired hit her. "Christian, I am really, really sorry that they got The Cross. But I . . ."

"Shhh, Shhh, Shhh. It's ok . . . really, it's ok," Christian calmed her. "Don't worry about it . . . they got A cross. . . . Not THE cross. But it doesn't make a difference to me which cross they got as long as you're ok. That's all that matters to me," he said, squeezing her hand.

"Thank you," she sniffled.

"It can't believe you went after that guy," he said.

"Me either. I was scared," she said.

"Me too," he added.

A few moments passed and what Christian had said finally sunk in . . . "What do you mean exactly . . . they got A cross", not THE cross? Are you telling me they don't have the real Cross?"

"Yes," he answered.

"But you said that The Cross was under the console; you showed it to me," she said.

"It was, I mean it is . . ." he said.

"So you're telling me you still have The Cross?"

"Yes," he assured her.

"How is that possible? I saw you take it from the console and hand it to him," she questioned.

"You're right, I did take a cross out from the console, but what you didn't see was that there were two crosses hidden in the console," Christian smiled. "I bought two crosses," he said. Amy smiled, relieved.

Christian continued to tell her how and why he had two imitation Ferdinand Crosses. The first didn't turn out as well as he had expected so he constructed one out of lead, matching the size, weight and feel of the original. He told her how the lead one was almost an exact match and that's the one he pulled out of the console.

"You know they're going to come after us again don't you? I don't think they'll be so friendly next time," she said with concern.

"Probably," Christian said calmly. Amy stared at him, surprised at how casual he was in his response.

"Ok, what's up? You're too way to calm about this. Those guys were ready to shoot us. They're going to come after us," she blurted.

They had just pulled up to a stop sign at the entrance to the interstate. Christian sat for a moment as a tractor trailer pulled up next to him. He smiled and put his window down. "They'll have a hard time finding us without this." He lifted his hand and showed Amy a small magnetic tracking device. He moved closer to the truck, reached out the window and slapped it up under the container's lift gate. "Let them, they can track us all they want," he smiled.

They watched the truck turn westbound, then they turned eastbound. "Whoever those guys are, they are definitely going to be pissed," Amy said.

"Who the hell were those guys anyway?" she asked.

"I don't know, but based on their accents, my guess is they are from Spain. But what's more important is, how did they know about The Cross?" Christian said thinking, "It had to be Trudeau or Balzack. One of them must have talked. They are the only ones that knew about it other than us."

"But how do you know which one talked?" Amy asked.

"Let's find out," Christian said reaching for his phone.

"Oh sh*t. I just thought of something. Our phones have GPS locators on them," Christian said, deactivating the location finder on his phone. "That should cover it. You should do yours as well," he suggested.

He dialed Balzack's house. "Hello, hello, hi, this is Christian. Is Dr. Balzack at home?"

"No, I'm sorry he's not," an elderly sounding woman responded.

"Will he be home later?"

"I'm sorry, who is this again?" the woman asked.

"My name is Christian, I spoke with Dr. Balzack a few weeks ago. Are you his wife?" he asked.

"No, I'm his sister," the woman responded.

"We were kind of working on something together. When will he be back?" Christian asked.

"I'm sorry honey, he won't be back," the woman said.

"Why, where is he?" Christian inquired.

"He died four days ago," she replied.

"Oh, I'm so sorry. May I ask what happened?" he inquired sympathetically.

"We found him slumped over sitting at his desk. We think he had a heart attack while he was working, but we won't know for sure for some time," she said.

"His desk? Are you sure he was at his desk?" he asked.

"Quite sure, that's where I found him. The poor thing was studying up on some tribe in New Guinea. I know he was excited about something that he recently came across. He was probably working on that," she replied.

Christian paused, "I'm terribly sorry for your loss ma'am. My deepest sympathies," he said, hanging up.

"What happened?" Amy asked.

"Balzack is dead," he answered thinking.

"He's dead? How?" she asked.

"His sister said they found him slumped over at his desk. She said he was studying something about a tribe in New Guinea. She also mentioned he was excited about a very big find he came across. She must have been talking about The Cross, but she didn't mention it specifically."

"He did love his work," Amy said.

"Yes, but why would he be studying about some tribe in New Guinea? It doesn't make sense. His passion was European history and South American history, and the last time I was there with him and Trudeau, he had books all over the place, and every one of them was about Europe and Spain. He was researching The Cross, not some tribe in New Guinea. Something's not right."

"The other thing that is strange is that he was found at his desk. He hated being behind a desk. He only used it as a bookshelf. Do you remember when he was looking for the wrap for The Cross?" Christian asked.

"Yes, yes I do. 'I don't have much use for desks . . . I'm a field man,'" she mimicked.

"That means somebody put him there, someone who didn't know him well enough to know he never sat at his desk," Christian concluded.

"Do you think it was . . .?" she said looking at Christian.

"All we know for sure is that he wouldn't be at his desk."

Amy and Christian talked about Balzack a while longer. Christian pushed himself driving. They drove for eighteen hours straight before pulling into an off-the-beaten-path hotel to get some rest. It was three in the morning.

They both slept restlessly during the night as every little noise drew their attention. They were back on the road again by ten a.m., pushing hard to get to New York.

-Twenty-Three-
The Last Holiday

It was one in the afternoon by the time they were approaching the New Jersey, New York border. Amy had been out cold for the past two hours, giving Christian time to think about his family situation. He wasn't quite sure how he was going to deal with everything over the holidays. His emotions were all over the place.

On one hand he felt betrayed for not being told he was adopted, not to mention the whole psychotropic meds thing. And on the other hand he had tremendous gratitude for all they had done for him and all they had done to try and protect him from exactly what was happening now.

He was sure he didn't like the idea of Matt being there to spy on him, but he believed his father was doing what was best to protect him from himself and the government. He thought long and hard, debating with himself whether or not they loved him or were just acting as his keepers. Were all those trips he went on with his father exploring remote locations actually for fun, or were they experiments to see if he would somehow accidentally show his abilities? He wasn't sure what was real anymore.

Amy started to stir by the time they approached the George Washington Bridge. By that point all he had concluded was that he was unsure of what would happen when he saw them. He was torn between his feelings for them and the feelings of betrayal he couldn't seem to shake. He considered what CB had told him about how much they cared for him from the first moment they met. If anyone outside of himself would know about that, it would be CB as he connected with him regularly as a child. He realized he had made them a family not just a couple.

CB had no doubts that they loved him, but Christian couldn't shake this feeling regarding their motives. Why was his father protecting him? What would happen if he found out about my abilities? Why did they seem so distant when he called to discuss The Cross? He realized that he couldn't be sure until he saw them face to face.

"Good morning sleepy head," he said to Amy as she was stirring in the passenger seat.

"Wow, I can't believe we are finally here," she said, yawning.

"That's the George Washington Bridge," he said pointing.

"How far do we have to go from here?" she asked sleepily.

"About two hours without traffic."

"Ok," she yawned. "I'm going to close my eyes for a b-i-t annnnd . . ." she dosed off again.

Christian smiled. He knew she was exhausted. He was very concerned about her being involved in all of this, especially since he didn't know what would happen from one minute to the next. He knew he had very strong feelings for her although he hadn't considered the "L" word up to this point.

As he affectionately gazed at her snuggled up in the passenger seat, he realized how very impressed he was with everything about her; her mannerisms, how gentle and kind she was, her playfulness and caring spirit, her sense of adventure, and of course her ability to ski. But the thing that impressed him most was that she didn't run away from him.

Even after being assaulted and having a gun pointed at her she stayed by his side. He thought how easily she could have left him on the side of the road and drove away, but she didn't. Deep inside he knew he was falling hard, but he feared for her safety. He felt happy and content when he was with her, yet deep down he had a sadness. He knew that in order to truly protect her, he may eventually have to let her go. The thought of this troubled him. If he could only find a way to protect her from the crazy things that were happening in his life. He watched as she slept for another hour before waking her.

"Amy, we're almost there," he said as he nudged her gently.

Amy started to move, sluggishly at first. "Where are we?" she asked.

"We're almost there," Christian said softly.

"Oh, oh!" she jumped up in her seat. "How much time do I have?" she asked, searching for her bag. "My bag, my bag, where's my bag?" she asked, searching frantically while still half asleep.

Christian casually reached into the backseat, grabbed her bag and handed to her. "You look great. What are you worried about?"

"I look great? Look at this! There's drool on my chin and my hair's a mess. I can't show up to meet your parents looking like this." she worried. Christian smiled, shaking his head.

They arrived at the house just after three in the afternoon. Katheryn was preparing dinner when she heard a car pull into the driveway. She looked out the window to see Christian exiting the Camaro. "Ed, Ed . . . Christian is home," she called to him, excitedly dropping the cutting board on the counter and hurrying outside to greet them.

Christian was grabbing the bags from the backseat when Katheryn emerged from the garage calling to him, "Hi honey, I can't believe you're home already. We weren't expecting you until tomorrow." She rushed toward the car with her eyes welling up as she wrapped her arms around him, giving him a welcoming hug and kissing him hard on the cheek.

"Hi Mom," he said, returning the hug and the kiss. "It's good to be home," he smiled as she nearly squeezed the breath out of him, eliminating any doubt that she loved him.

His father emerged from the house as Katheryn carried on as if she had not seen him in years, sniffling and wiping the occasional tear from her cheek. Christian's face flushed with embarrassment from the display of affection.

His father greeted him with a smile and a hug. "Hey son . . . welcome home, it's good to see you. We weren't expecting to see you so soon. How was the trip?" he asked giving him a one arm hug. He too appeared very happy to see him.

As much as Christian was happy about the warm greeting he received, he still had reservations about their original motives. He elected to withhold his concerns for the time being and enjoy the moment.

"Mom, Dad, I'd like you to meet Amy," he said, glancing to the other side of the car as Amy stepped out from the passenger side. In the hour she had to prepare, she had transformed herself from a sleepy, puffy-eyed girl with drool on her face and messy hair to the northwestern beauty she was.

She stepped out from the passenger seat and stood up slowly. The cool ocean breeze gently blew her long, light brown hair across her face. Her hazel green eyes sparkled in the afternoon sun as she cleared the hair from her face. To Christian it all seemed like it was happening in slow motion. "Hi! It's so nice to meet you both," Amy smiled, walking toward them.

Edward had just enough time to get out a "Nice to meet you," before Katheryn greeted Amy affectionately with a kiss and a hug.

"You are so beautiful . . ." she said continuing, "Come, let's go inside . . . it's cold out here. You have to tell me all about how you two met," she said, leading her by the hand into the house, still sniffling from the emotional reunion.

Amy looked at Christian stranded behind for advice on what to do. Christian smiled, shrugging his shoulders having no advice to provide. This was new territory for him. He had never seen his mother so happy to meet one of his girlfriends before.

"Wow, she is a beauty," Edward said, patting him on the back. "Can I help you bring anything in?" he asked.

Christian handed his duffel to his father. "Thanks."

Abandoned in the cold by his girlfriend and mother, Christian unloaded the car then he and Edward carried the bags into the house. They felt invisible as they passed the ladies on their way through the kitchen. Katheryn offered Amy some hot cocoa.

Amy caught Christian's eye as he passed but all he could do was smirk and shrug his shoulders as he moved quickly through the kitchen. Edward, watching Katheryn begin her inquisition, rolled his eyes in anticipation of what was to come. He handed Christian his duffel. "Sorry I can't stay for this, I've got to run to the store. Be back in a while," Edward said, sporting a smirk. He grabbed his keys and headed for the door asking, "Do you need anything else?"

"No thanks hon," Katheryn replied, resuming her conversation with Amy.

Christian picked up the pace, going up the stairs to deliver the bags to his room. When he returned to the kitchen he found it empty. He was also surprised to see that there was no hot chocolate left for him. He loved Katheryn's hot chocolate. She always added vanilla or hazelnut to it, sometimes both. He looked through the house, eventually finding Katheryn and Amy sitting in the den by the fireplace. As he walked into the den the ladies started to laugh. Amy glanced at him affectionately. It was apparent that the embarrassing story-telling had commenced.

"Oh honey, I wanted to tell you the packages you asked me to hide are in the garage. I put them in the summer storage closet," Katheryn said almost dismissively.

"Thank you," he said, retreating from the den.

An hour had passed before Katheryn and Amy emerged from the den. Katheryn requested that Christian show Amy where she could shower while she finished preparing the evening meal. He and Amy headed upstairs where he showed her where to find towels and directed her to the bathroom.

"I'm sorry about that," he said.

"Sorry about what?" she asked, smiling.

"The inquisition. Mom has a tendency to ask a lot of questions," he said, continuing. "Especially when I bring a girl home."

"She was fine. I told her how we met and we shared some stories. That's all. Exactly how many girls are we talking about?" she asked playfully.

"You're the third," he said.

"Only three?" she asked surprised, expecting to hear a much higher number.

"Yeah, after the second one ran out of the house crying I didn't think I should bring anymore home . . . not that I could. Once the other girls at school heard the story of the 'Asher Inquisition', they avoided me like the plague," he said reflecting.

"No way, I can't believe that? Your mother actually made someone cry and run out of the house?" she asked.

"Yeah, it took me almost a year to get another girlfriend. Anyone that I liked after that wouldn't come near the house unless there was a party and they could hide from her. I guess they thought my mom was crazy or something."

"Really? I didn't get that from her. She's very sweet, and she offered to take me shopping tomorrow so I can pick up some things," Amy smiled, closing the bathroom door.

Christian went down to the kitchen to catch up with his mother. He was very surprised to hear the first words out of her mouth after kissing him again were, "Amy is wonderful, I really like her." He stood quiet for a moment, stunned at her refreshingly accepting comment.

"Thank you," he said hesitantly.

"I was going to take her shopping tomorrow if that's alright with you?" she asked.

"Yes, of course. I have a few things I can catch up on while you're gone. I know she's looking forward to it," he replied. Katheryn smiled.

"What smells so good?" he asked.

"I'm making grilled chicken breast with lemon, capers and wilted spinach. Sweetheart, would you cut me eight thin slices of lemon?"

"Sure," he said, starting to slice the lemon.

"Thanks honey," Katheryn said feeling content for the first time since Thanksgiving.

She and Christian caught up as they prepared the meal. Christian helped where he could. It was apparent that Katheryn was very happy to have him home, which put him at ease.

During dinner the embarrassing story telling continued. Nothing was off the table. Christian's mother and father talked about all the trouble he used to get into with his experiments. They told Amy story after story with mutual enthusiasm. One of them was about the time when he was seven years old and someone made the mistake of telling him that cats always landed on their feet, and he set out to prove them wrong.

"We were out shopping all day. Christian was being watched by the next door neighbor. When we got home we pulled into the driveway and saw the neighbor's cat, Midnight, flying through the air," Katheryn said reflecting. "This one had constructed a catapult from the swing set, not to mention a few spare parts from the neighbor's yard," Edward said.

"Oh no . . . you didn't," Amy said, looking at Christian. He nodded affirmatively.

"He did," Edward answered, "And we came to find out later from the lady who lived behind us at the time, that he was in the yard for twenty minutes prior, flipping the cat through the air to see if it would actually land on its feet."

"Why didn't she stop him?" Amy asked.

"That's a whole other story," Christian said.

"Let's just say they didn't care for cats very much, especially Midnight. You could hear the two of them yelling at the cat every morning as they chased him from the yard," Katheryn laughed, remembering.

"Why?" Amy asked.

"We didn't know at first, we thought they just disliked cats," Edward said continuing. "Then, one day, we saw her losing it over this cat and we asked why."

"She told us the cat would sit perched on the fence, hiding behind those trees," Katheryn said pointing to the trees lining the yard, "and it would wait for the birds to come to her feeders. She complained to us, 'That cat kills one of my birds every morning and leaves the carcasses on my back porch.'" Katheryn finished.

"What happened to the cat?" Amy asked.

"If cats have nine lives, Midnight used them all," Edward said reflecting.

"That poor cat. What Christian didn't do to that poor thing," Katheryn said shaking her head feeling pity for the cat.

Christian jumped in to defend himself. "That cat lived to be twenty-four years old. I couldn't have hurt it that bad and don't forget . . . It was Mr. Brown who poisoned him, not me," he defended.

"Oh that's sick," Amy said, "Why wouldn't they just move the feeders? You can't just kill a cat for doing what comes natural to it," Amy stated.

"Who said anything about kill?" Christian said, "That cat lived another ten years after old man Brown poisoned him . . ."

Christian looked at his mother and father asking, "Do you remember when he saw Midnight up on the fence again?" He chuckled remembering, Katheryn and Edward joined in. Edward started to tell the story to Amy.

"The morning after old man Brown poisoned the cat, I think it was a Saturday morning, we were outside and we could hear him whistling and singing to himself while working in his yard. So I said good morning to him and he said, 'It's the best morning I've had in a long time,' with a smile on his face from ear to ear, which was very unusual for him. He was always so serious."

"So I said, 'Oh . . . that's good. I guess you didn't have a problem with Midnight this morning.' I remember he had a weird smile on his face, like evil glee. Then he said, 'No, I didn't and I don't think he'll be bothering us anymore.' It wasn't too hard to figure he had done something to the cat."

"We didn't see the cat all day and when Christian didn't see the cat, he went looking for it . . . and he found it. He walked up to us holding it in his arms, crying."

"Awww, that's so sad," Amy said making a pouty face.

"Midnight was a mess. He was covered in sand, wet and foaming at the mouth."

"Old man Brown had poisoned it and buried it in a shallow hole in the back corner of his yard. Sherlock here found him half out of the hole and dug him out the rest of the way with his hands," Edward said, reflecting.

Katheryn joined in, "We never expected the cat to live and told him not to expect anything, but he didn't care. He sat with that cat for three days in the garage, feeding him water with a syringe. He refused to leave its side. We had to wait until he fell asleep before we could carry him up to bed, and every morning we'd find him back sleeping with the cat." Amy looked at him empathetically with pursed lips.

"On the third night, we walked into the garage to bring him up to bed and we were shocked. He was sound asleep on the bed he made for the cat and Midnight was up, licking his face," Katheryn remembered fondly. "The next day was priceless."

"We were sitting at the breakfast nook watching the backyard with the windows open. We knew Midnight would go right back to the fence and he did. He left a big black bird on their back porch. All of a sudden we heard, 'What the hell! Son of a . . . M-A-R-Y!' Then we see him running through the yard swinging a broom, and to no surprise Midnight jumped up and over the fence and into our yard." They all started laughing.

"What happened after that?" Amy asked.

"They moved," Christian said.

"Moved because of a cat?" Amy asked.

"We'd like to think so," Edward laughed . . .

Christmas Eve day had arrived. Katheryn was preparing yet another holiday family feast with Amy's help. Katheryn had grown very fond of Amy over the days. It was nice for her to have another woman in the house. Amy equally enjoyed Katheryn's company.

Christian and Edward alike were happy to see the fondness they shared for each other. They were relieved there was no tension. As the sun set Christian took Amy outside and into the street. "Watch this," he said looking down the street as the neighborhood came alive with holiday decorations. Strings of multicolored lights turned on all over the neighborhood. Inflatable decorations came to life as their fans kicked on, filling them with air. They strolled down the street to admire the decorations, stopping in front of the Thompson's house where a small group of neighbors with their children waited to see the Thompson house come to life.

The small group of about eighteen to twenty people was only the beginning. Within minutes, hordes of people who were in-the-know were coming down the street from both directions. It started as a trickle, then a flood of people could be seen hurrying down the street. "What's going on?" Amy asked.

Christian smiled, "Wait for it," he said, watching the house.

The Thompson's house was by far the most elaborate. They were a young couple with three small children who decorated heavily for every holiday, especially around Christmas time. They had what appeared to be thousands of lights hanging from their home, starting with the candy cane fencing around the front of their home. The elaborate decorations were complete with inflatable Santas, a Santa's sleigh with all the reindeer up on the roof, a huge Frosty the Snowman, and a little version of The North Pole complete with elves, gifts and Santa's chair. There were multiple animated holiday scenes stretched out across the yard.

One of the neighborhood's favorites was an eight foot tall snow globe scene with snow swirling around inside with moving figures. There were elves climbing up the side of the house lifting packages up to one another and a small train circling the house that the neighborhood kids would line up to ride. The lights were arranged to form the shapes of beloved holiday characters, the likes of Frosty the Snowman and Rudolph, not to mention the Big Guy himself.

Amy was amazed to see hundreds of curious people rushing down the street. "Oh my god, where are they all coming from?" she asked just as the police showed up.

"Everywhere," Christian smiled.

"Why are the police here?" she asked.

"Crowd control," Christian replied, "Ever since they have been doing this, people come from all over to see it. It never used to get so crowded, maybe a couple of hundred people would come by over the holidays, but after News 12 put their house on TV, hundreds of people come by every night. This is the biggest night. It's kind of become the traditional start of the holidays in the neighborhood."

"Every year he adds something new. Two years ago he synchronized the lights to work with the music and just wait until News Year's Eve. Last year he added his own version of the ball dropping." He pointed to a sparkling silver elf on a pole.

"What does it do?" Amy asked. "You'll have to wait and see," Christian answered, smiling.

Katheryn and Edward walked up behind them all bundled up, carrying four cups of hot chocolate. "Hey guys. . . . Wait until you see what he's got up his sleeve this year," Edward said as Katheryn passed out the hot chocolate.

It was just about dark and Edward looked up to the east, "Here it comes." Amy and Christian looked up as well. He saw it coming and pointed it out to Amy. As soon as she saw what they were looking at, the sound of bells jingling started softly, playing from powerful speakers placed around the house.

The crowd began to cheer in anticipation of the lighting. Then a number spotlights turned on to the right of the house, drawing the curious crowd's attention. They cheered harder. Kids perched on their parents' shoulders were clapping with excitement as they watched the spectacle unfold. The crowd, now numbering about six or seven hundred, watched and waited.

The sound of the jingling bells faded, causing the audience to become quiet and still. Some wondered if something was wrong, but their concerns soon ended as they again heard the sound of sleigh bells jingling coming out from the speakers, low at first and then getting louder and louder. Suddenly two spotlights switched on and pointed to the sky, causing the crowd to erupt with excitement.

As the spotlights crossed the sky you could hear the faint yet familiar greeting, "Ho, Ho, Hoooo—Ho, Ho, Hoooo." The sound of bells from the speakers faded to silence as the faint "Ho, Ho, Hoooos" became louder and the sound of bells jingling were now heard coming from the darkness of the night sky.

Everyone in the crowd was looking up into darkness. As the Ho, Ho, Hoooos grew louder, so did the sound of bells jingling. A faint silhouette appeared in the darkness. The moving spotlights converged on the silhouette . . . and one small boy yelled, "Daddy, look—It's Santa . . ."

The crowd started to roar. People were cheering, the kids' faces were glowing with excitement as Santa drifted down to earth, "Ho, Ho, Hoooo! M-e-r-r-y C-h-r-i-s-t-m-a-s!"

"That is so cool," Amy said squeezing tighter to Christian.

"That is cool," Christian agreed. Amy watched with the same enthusiasm as the children's faces lit up with excitement.

Santa landed on mark just to the side of the house. As Santa's feet touched the ground, every single light on the house turned on in a flash of bright colors and the speakers started to sing. The lights appeared to come alive as they danced to the sound of Jingle Bell Rock blaring from the speakers.

Beautiful multicolored LED lights turned on and off to the music. Spotlights flashed on and off under the trees lining the property. Laser lights danced across the sky. The multiple displays flashed off and on, changing colors as if swapping colors back and forth between them. A sign on the roof made of hundreds, if not thousands, of LED lights spelled 'Merry Christmas' and flashed off and on in waves of color as it danced to the music.

The candy cane lights lining the walkways appeared to move in synchronized rhythm, giving the feeling that you were moving as the lights changed from lavender to blue to white to orange to red, moving along their length in progressive waves.

The fans underneath the inflatable decorations turned on, bringing to life a dozen or more holiday figures that appeared to wave at the crowd in the light breeze.

Mechanical figurines came to life and even the elf on top of the New Year's Eve pole was waving to the crowd. It was spectacular. Some of the cheering crowd burst into song, singing along to Jingle Bell Rock and, as if by magic, the first of the light fluffy flakes started to fall. Amy stared up at the falling flakes with rosy cheeks, sporting a smile from ear to ear. "It's like magic," she said under her breath.

Santa released his chute and moved over to his chair, waving to all that had come to see the display. The crowd was wild . . . singing and dancing. Amy pulled Christian closer and kissed him. "Thank you so much for sharing this with me, this is incredible," she said, kissing him again.

They watched as the kids hurried to line up to meet Santa and the crowd continued with the celebration. As Santa took position on his holiday throne, a bright light turned on from the side of the house and smoke started to blow across the front of the yard from behind Santa's chair. The crowd again grew silent, waiting with excitement for the next spectacle that was coming. Moments later, the mini train operated by one of Santa's elves broke through the smoke with a clanging bell and a toot toot toooooot! The crowd roared.

As the train passed, elves handed out holiday candies to the children. They had all kinds of goodies; Christmas M&M's, mini

Hershey bars, holiday Reese's Peanut Butter Cups, and more. If they made it with a holiday wrapper, it was there. One of the elves tossed Amy a large Hershey's Kiss . . . and flipped her a wink. She playfully blew him a kiss.

"What'd you think?" Edward asked, Katheryn snuggled under his arm.

"That was amazing! How did you know about this beforehand? Mr. Thompson is usually pretty secretive about what he's going to do . . . and who did the jump?" Christian asked.

"I'll tell you on the way back to the house," Edward said, trying to talk over the cheering crowd.

Minutes later they headed back to the house. Guests were expected to arrive any minute. Edward started to explain the details as they worked their way through the crowd. By the time they got there, Mac and Janice were at the door watching the spectacle. They greeted each other and introductions were made as they went inside.

Hailey and her boyfriend arrived twenty minutes after Mac and Janice. The remainder of the guests trickled in. Each commenting on the difficulty they had making it to the house with all of the pedestrian traffic in the neighborhood. It was a nice sized gathering; about eighteen people were expected and twenty-two showed up, including some of Christian's cousins who were up from Florida. They came to see the Rockettes perform in the Christmas Show and visit the world famous Rockefeller Center to try their hand, or should I say feet, at ice skating.

Hailey was very interested to meet Amy. She had heard little about her and she was as protective of Christian as Katheryn was, especially since he had shared so much about recent events with her. Her guard was up as she watched the two of them cross the room.

Christian and Amy walked over to Hailey and her boyfriend, Thomas. Hailey was in the middle of introducing Thomas to some of the other guests when she excused herself and turned to greet Christian with a big hug. "How are you?" she asked. "You know Tom, don't you?"

"Yes, hi Tom. Merry Christmas! It's good to see you again," Christian said, looking a little jealous. He too was protective of Hailey.

"Hailey, I'd like you to meet Amy. Amy, this is my . . ."

Amy cut in finishing his introduction, " . . . your cousin Hailey. It's so nice to finally meet you," she said with a gleaming smile, hugging Hailey firmly. "Christian has told me so much about you. You are so, so beautiful," she said with sincerity.

Hailey paused, searching for something she didn't like about Amy to critique. She found nothing. She immediately recognized the warmth and genuineness that she exuded. She sensed her positive energy and a strength that reminded her of Christian, and she appreciated how she looked at her cousin and how he looked at her. This was something that she had never really felt in her life. Hailey dropped her guard quickly, something that even shocked Thomas.

"It's nice to meet you too," Hailey blushed, "and look who's talking . . . You are gorgeous. I love the color of your eyes, I wish I had that color."

"Thank you," Amy said smiling.

"Excuse us, we have some getting-to-know-each-other to do," Hailey said scooting off to the kitchen with Amy. Katheryn joined them moments later.

Christian was relieved. Hailey was the only other person whose opinion he valued. He knew she would approve of her as much as Katheryn did.

"Looks like you lost her already," Tom smiled.

"Looks that way," Christian replied. "What do you say, let's get it started," Christian said.

"I'm in, you rack," Tom suggested. The guys talked as they started Round Two of the holiday pool tournament. Thomas mentioned his surprise with Hailey. He had never seen her take to anyone like she did with Amy and he had never seen her blush from a compliment.

It was her business-oriented personality; she analyzed everything and everyone, searching for a weakness or flaw to capitalize upon. Christian watched Amy talking in the kitchen with his mom, Hailey and his Aunt Janice as he racked the balls. He was happy to see they were all getting along so well. She glanced over at him often, as did he with her.

"Hey lover boy, you going to rack or stare at the girls all night?" Tom joked.

Christian threw the chalk at him playfully, "It's a lot better than looking at you all night." They laughed and started the game.

Each year everyone who played during the holiday parties would put ten dollars in the pot at the beginning of the night. The 'Holiday Tournament' as they called it, went from Thanksgiving through New Year's Day and any time there was a gathering of people playing, that was the rule. Last year they raised over seven hundred dollars which was donated to the local food pantry.

The Ashers were big on giving year round. They did this on top of donating large amounts of money to local charitable organizations. One would think it was to gain recognition, but no, they made all their donations anonymously. That's just who they were. Two very grateful and giving people.

The holiday menu weighed heavily on seafood as had been the tradition for years. It was something Katheryn was raised with, but she had also prepared a fresh ham and a roast beef as well. The feast was every bit as spectacular as the Thanksgiving gathering. The only difference this year was a suggestion made by Amy.

Amy, being familiar with large family gatherings, suggested a buffet-style dinner. She explained that it freed up your time to enjoy the party and the guests and that Katheryn deserved to enjoy herself as well, as opposed to constantly serving the guests. Katheryn took to this idea quickly, suggesting they serve the hors d'oeuvres in the same way.

They set up the hors d'oeuvres first, laying out chilled shrimp with cracked pepper and lime, Clams Casino, mussels in white wine sauce, and a homemade lobster spread, not to mention the cheeses and cheese spreads with crackers, along with the assorted olive and vegetable platters and spinach-artichoke dip.

The buffet was a success. Once the hors d'oeuvres were laid out, the ladies left the kitchen to continue socializing. The girls had made their way back to Tom and Christian playing pool. Katheryn watched as the guests formed a line around the buffet table. She glanced at Amy and smiled with approval.

The dinner was served the same way. Amy and Hailey helped set up the buffet along the large center island in the kitchen while Katheryn added some finishing touches to the table arrangements. Salads and sides were placed on the table as people walked around the variety of entrées, picking what they wanted.

Besides the ham and the roast beef, Katheryn had made roast salmon with thyme, baked halibut with julienned scallions and ginger, and a tray of split lobsters that were steaming in the center of the table. The guests sat for hours feasting and sharing stories; most were happy, others sad. Some were old and others new. Each gave thanks for the abundance they shared.

The cleanup was quick with many hands helping, then the dessert buffet was set up. Katheryn again thanked Amy for the buffet idea, explaining how funny it is that most people just follow what they have been taught to do without ever questioning if it is the best way to do things or if there was an easier way. She hugged Amy.

Amy had never seen so many desserts outside of a bakery. There were cookies piled high, cakes and pies, as well as an assortment of pastries and Danishes. There were bowls of fresh fruits and homemade whipped cream, and homemade ice creams were waiting to be scooped onto the hot apple, peach and strawberry-rhubarb pies. Christian was happy to see one of his favorite desserts that his father must have picked up; an apple cake made by a small bakery, 'Diane's', which was tucked away under a viaduct near St. Francis Hospital. Amy's eyes were on something that she had seen once or twice before, but never tasted, called 'The Lobster Tails'. "

Oh, that looks sooo good," she said to Christian, looking at the flakey pastry oozing with French cream and topped with a maraschino cherry. She wasn't disappointed.

Christmas morning had arrived and there was a four inch blanket of snow on the ground. Amy woke to the smell of fresh coffee and Christian's favorite, French toast croissants with a good sprinkling of cinnamon. She greeted the day with a stretch and a smile, squeezing the warm white comforter on the Duxianna bed. She had the look of contentment on her face.

She went downstairs and greeted Christian and Katheryn with a morning hug and kiss, wishing them a Merry Christmas. Edward emerged shortly after and joined them. Following breakfast they gathered around the tree to hand out gifts.

The Ashers weren't big on overdoing the gift giving. They celebrated the meaning of the holidays and enjoyed more the gathering with friends and family and doing things together rather than expensive gift giving. Katheryn felt she would rather spend the money on memories than expensive gifts. Most of the gifts were usually practical and useful items. Of course, over the years there were occasions, rare as they were, when they indulged in more extravagant gifts.

Christian handed Amy her gift from him and asked her to distribute the first round of gifts. She handed Katheryn hers first, then Edward's, then Christian's. On the count of three, they started tearing away at the paper.

Christian had gotten Amy a ski jacket to replace the one that was recently torn. Amy returned the favor by giving Christian a pair of Oakley wraparound sunglasses to hide, well . . . you know. Amy and Christian surprised Katheryn with a vintage metal Coca-Cola truck to add to her collection and for Edward they got the new Calloway Big Bertha driver he'd been eyeing since last summer; not that they thought it would help his game any.

Katheryn went next, passing out the next round of gifts. She handed each a card. Inside the card was an invitation, hand written in calligraphy. Her gift to all was a trip into Manhattan for dinner and ice skating at Rockefeller Center, along with a viewing of the Christmas show.

Ok, this one was a bit extravagant but it has 'Holiday Spirit' written all over it. On the bottom of Amy's card was a little note, *Plus a Day of Shopping*, with a little smiley face. Amy hugged her thankfully.

Edward went next. He handed each one a small box. On the count of three they opened the small boxes. In Christian's box was a small toy helicopter, Amy's had a toy car limousine and Katheryn's was a double. It had a Coca-Cola horse-drawn wagon. Edward started to laugh as they looked at the strange collection of gifts, then he explained.

He pointed to the toy helicopter, "This is how we are getting to Manhattan." Christian and Amy's mouths dropped open. Christian had always wanted to travel into Manhattan by helicopter. Then he pointed at Amy's toy limo, "This is how we are going to Rockefeller Center," and finally, pointing at Katheryn's horse drawn wagon, "This is how we are going to see Central Park."

Katheryn's eyes lit up. She enjoyed Central Park in the winter, especially when there was a coating of snow on the ground. It reminded her of the old holiday movies she used to watch as a child. "Now I know why I love you so much." She kissed him.

There were three large boxes and two smaller boxes remaining under the tree. Christian handed out the three large boxes. One addressed to each Katheryn, Edward and Christian. "Where did these come from?" Christian asked. "It says they're from Santa . . ." They unwrapped the boxes.

"What is this? B-L-I-Z-Z-E-R-A-T-O-R, Now You Can Oblizzerate Winter!" Amy sat quietly smiling as Christian pulled his from the box. "This is really cool, did you get these?" Christian asked.

Amy nodded affirmatively, "Yes, I thought you would be able to use them. You're always talking about snow and skiing and this is what we use. It really works well and it's quick. Here let me show you," Amy said, demonstrating The Blizz as she called it.

"Let's check 'em out," Christian suggested.

They put their coats on and went out into the driveway, Blizzerator in hand. Amy bet Christian she could clear Mom's Mercedes SUV before he could clean off her Camaro with a regular brush. "On your mark, get set . . . GO!" The two hurried to clean the cars. Christian was moving fast but Amy was way out in front. She started in the rear of the SUV and worked her way up to the front. She collapsed the brush and walked down the sides of the SUV and was done in less than 45 seconds. Amy, warm and dry, watched Christian as he hurried to finish cleaning the Camaro with his little toy brush. She was laughing at his pitiful attempt. Edward and Katheryn were watching from the window.

When Christian finally finished, he was covered in snow and soaking wet from leaning over the car. He accepted his defeat, but not before wrestling the victor to the ground for a good dousing of snow.

Back in the house Edward and Katheryn were laughing as the two warriors returned from the snowy battlefield that was the driveway. The victor was celebrated with a warming cup of tea, and to the defeated, he had to take out the trash.

Christian went upstairs to change and returned quickly. As they were seated around the table, Edward handed him the smallest of the two small packages that remained under the tree. His words were more important than the gift to Christian. "Here . . . this one is for you son," he said. Amy saw the look on Christian's face when he heard his father say 'son', and knew that meant more to him than any gift he could have received.

He opened the small box and in it was a small piece of paper. He unfolded it and just stared at it. Amy couldn't tell if he was going to scream or fall off of his chair. It was the registration to the Mustang, bearing Christian's name. "But Dad, we worked on this together . . . It's ours," he said.

"I want you to have it. You will always mean more to me and your mother than any old car," Edward said leaning in to give him a hug.

"Thank you, you don't know how much you both mean to me," Christian said, hugging him tightly.

Katheryn stood up and ran to get a tissue with Amy right behind her. The ladies returned and joined in for an emotionally charged group hug.

Christian perked up, "Oh here, this is something I want you and Mom to have," he said walking over to the tree and picking up the remaining package. "Mom, Dad . . . You've both done so much for me. I want you to have this," he smiled, handing them the heavy package.

Amy stepped to Christian's side. "It's heavy, what is it?" Katheryn asked.

"It's just a little something Amy and I picked up. We want you to have it."

Katheryn unwrapped the package and removed the lid. She and Edward looked curiously at the velvet bag contained within the box. As Edward lifted the bag out of the box, a gold chain fell from the bag. He pulled the chain, lifting their gift out of the bag. Katheryn's eyes started to well up. "Oh honey, that is beautiful," Katheryn said.

She started reading it aloud. "*Life is Family and the Love that you Share.*" "That is beautiful honey, thank you both," Edward agreed as they admired the porcelain wall placard.

"Excuse me, there's one more thing I'd like to share with you," Christian said as he went to his room, then returned with another box. Amy's hands started to sweat with nervous excitement. He returned and placed a cracked and tarnished, unwrapped box on the table.

"What is this honey?" Katheryn asked.

"It's a surprise," he answered.

Edward looked on as Katheryn removed the cover revealing another velvet bag. Edward's curiosity was peaked. Katheryn was having difficulty prying the bag from the foam filled box at first, then with one yank she pulled the heavy bag from its impression. She lay the bag on the table and pulled the drawstring collar apart, looking in. Her eyes widened.

"Oh—My—God," she said with stunned emotion, looking up at Edward.

"What do you have there?" he asked, curious to see. Katheryn reached into the bag and slid the Ferdinand VII Cross out onto the table. Edward's mouth dropped open.

"Is this real?" Katheryn asked, examining the cross and chain.

Amy looked at Christian gleaming with pride and shook her head affirmatively as Christian replied, "Yes, It's real! It looks like all of those treasure hunts I went on as a kid finally paid off."

Katheryn laughed nervously. "Where did you find this?" Edward asked, examining The Cross closely. "When you said you found a cross, your mother and I thought you were talking about a little cross, something you wear around your neck, like all the stuff you found on your treasure hunts as a kid. You always came home with something, but nothing like this."

"Oh honey, you must think we're horrible," Katheryn said remembering. "When you told us about The Cross we didn't know you actually meant . . . a cross. I'm so sorry. When you called there were so many things going on. We had just heard your father's friend Dr. Stedwell had passed away unexpectedly and we were on our way out to that cardiologist's dinner we go to every year. I'm so sorry."

"Yes, son . . . we had no idea," Edward added.

At their request, Christian retold the story minus the excitingly dangerous parts. He told them they were exploring caves along the coastline and came upon the cave, went in and found The Cross on a ledge. Of course he had to answer a multitude of questions, like how come no one else ever found it and what were you doing on the ledge in the cave?

He answered carefully so as not to alarm them as he always did growing up, but that thinking would soon be moot. He told them the cave was visible only during moon tides, a term they were well familiar with. He told them about the enormous tidal change during the moon tide and as for the ledge, he mentioned that he saw a strange shimmer on the ledge when he shone his light on it.

As un-thrilled as they were about him going into a cave alone, they were extremely excited about The Cross and enthralled with the story. "You said you brought it to someone to look at it. What did they say?" Edward asked.

Christian told them about Balzack and the details of his background. He told them about the pirate, Hipolyte Bouchard, and the story of The Cross as it was documented on the internet, being careful not to slip and mention his past life replay. He told them that he met with Balzack and Trudeau for the appraisal.

"My god, this thing must be priceless," Edward said.

"It is . . . Trudeau estimated its value in today's market for the gold and jewels alone at . . . Twenty to twenty-five million, and as far as its historic value, he said it was priceless.

"Holy sh*t," Edward slipped, letting out a rare curse word as Katheryn appeared to be almost hyperventilating. "Excuse me . . . I . . . I . . . can't believe it. This is absolutely amazing. If I thought you had found something like this, I would have sent a courier to bring it home. What do you want to do with it?" Edward asked, a bit overwhelmed.

"That's what I wanted to talk to you about. You see, after we found it the only two people who knew about it were Balzack and Trudeau. A few days after the second meeting someone broke into my room looking for something. I just assumed they were looking for The Cross.

"You didn't tell us about that," Katheryn exclaimed. "Why didn't you tell us?" she asked.

"Well to be honest, it happened right after I called you and you seemed to have a lot on your mind. And since they didn't take anything I didn't want to bother you," he answered.

"Well, what if you were home or your roommate was home?" she asked.

"Think about it mom, they waited for finals week when no one was around to see who they were."

"Did the security cameras pick anything up?" Edward asked concerned, assessing the scenario.

"No, the cameras were disabled. Whoever it was, they were professional."

"How do you know they were looking for The Cross?" Katheryn asked.

"Because they didn't take anything. Our laptops, keys and everything of value was still there, tossed around like everything else, so it must have been The Cross they were after."

"I don't like the way that sounds," Edward said. "Are you sure, no one else knew?

"Positive," Christian replied. "Are you still friends with those guys from The Museum of Natural History?" Christian asked.

"Yes."

"Do you think they would be able to take it and hold on to it for us?" he asked.

"I'm sure they would be delighted, this is an incredible find. You are aware they will want to speak to you about the details," Edward replied.

"That'll be fine, I'll tell them anything they want to know . . . 'd just really like to get it somewhere safe, if you know what I mean," Christian said anxiously.

Katheryn was a wreck having a twenty-five million dollar cross in the house. Amy stayed with Katheryn while Edward went to put The Cross in the safe. Christian followed close behind. "Hold on put this one in there," he said.

This raised Edwards's curiosity. "What? Why do you want me to put this in the safe and not the real Cross?" Edward asked.

"Dad there's more, I didn't want to upset Mom." Edward listened intently.

Christian told him about the second break in, Balzack being dead, and then about the black van in Keystone. Edward was upset with Christian for taking such a chance, but he knew Christian was right not to trust anyone. He immediately went up to his office and called his friend William Stanton from the museum. Christian returned The Cross to his bag and placed it in the closet before rejoining the ladies. They were none the wiser that the real Cross was in the hallway closet on top of some old boots.

"Hi Bill . . . Ed Asher, Merry Christmas. Thank you, your family as well. Bill, you're not going to believe this . . ." Edward was on the phone for half an hour telling Bill everything he knew about The Cross. He could hear Bill's wife in the background hounding him to get off the phone. They scheduled to meet the following day at the museum. Even though Bill was off he would never pass up an opportunity like this. He requested that Christian tag along. Ed agreed, telling him that he would be there as well and finished the call.

Edward went downstairs and rejoined everyone. Katheryn was still a little unnerved, but was handling the news much better. Edward informed the ladies that he and Christian would be busy most of the day tomorrow. "Hey, why don't you ladies go shopping tomorrow? It's supposed to be a nice day," he suggested.

Katheryn agreed that may be the best way to spend the day. "What do you think Amy? Shopping tomorrow?" Katheryn asked.

"Sounds like a great idea," she replied.

It was about noon when the doorbell rang. Christian walked over to open the door. "Oh no . . . trouble's here," he said, looking out of the window to see the Three Musketeers had arrived. Amy, curious about what he meant by trouble, walked over in line site of the door. Connor and Chris pushed their way through the front door followed by Maddy, "Merry Christmas!" they all said entering the house.

"Some show last night, huh?" Connor said walking from the entrance foyer into the living room while pulling his sweatshirt over his head.

"Hey buddy, Merry Christmas," Tweet said followed by Maddy.

Maddy gave Christian a quick hug and a peck on the cheek, "Merry Christmas."

Tweet walked into the living room to see Amy standing by the window next to the Christmas tree smiling. He stood there smiling without saying a word. Connor was still bumping around the room trying to pull his sweatshirt over his head.

Maddy walked in and smacked Tweet in the head, "What's wrong with you," she mocked. "Hi, I'm Maddy, this is Chris and that one over there is Connor. He'll be out to say hello any minute now," Maddy said.

"Hi, it's nice to meet you. I'm Amy."

Christian re-entered after hanging up Maddy's coat. "Oh great, you've already met," he said eyeing Connor still trying to pull his head out of the sweatshirt.

Not one to pass up a chance to mess with him, he started pulling on his sleeves that were flopping around in front of him and spinning him around. "Ouch, ouch, ouch . . . My nose, cut it out . . . my nose," Connor whined as the tight sweatshirt collar pulled at his nose.

The spinning caught up with him and he dropped to the floor, dizzy from the ride just as his head popped out of his sweatshirt. "You guys stink that really hurt," he said rubbing his nose and swaying back and forth from being dizzy. "I think I'm going to heave," he claimed, unaware of Amy's presence. Amy, standing behind him, snickered.

Connor forced himself up. He was still a bit wobbly when he turned to introduce himself. "Hi, I'm Connor. Excuse me," he said vurping and ran to the bathroom. Christian and Tweet started to laugh.

"That was mean," Amy said, restraining her desire to laugh. "Are they always like this?" she asked Maddy.

"No, they're worse." Connor rejoined them a minute later. He apologized to Amy and reintroduced himself. His attempts at rinsing his mouth did little to remove the smell on his breath.

Katheryn walked into the room on her way to the kitchen. "Hi, Merry Christmas," she greeted them, giving each a hug starting with Maddy, then Chris, then Connor. She noticed Connor was a little out of sorts. "Are you ok honey, you don't look so good?" she asked.

"Yeah, I'm fine." Connor replied.

"What did they do to you this time?" she asked knowingly just as the near toxic miasma from his mouth hit her. "Oh honey, don't say another word. Let me get you some mouthwash," she said, waving her hand in front of her face to clear the air. The guys cracked up.

"You guys really suck," he pouted. Amy and Maddy couldn't resist any longer and joined in laughing.

"I'm sorry buddy. I didn't think you would puke," Christian apologized, still laughing.

"Yeah, it's not like he knew you just ate a frozen breakfast burrito," Tweet laughed.

"No, did you really? You ate a frozen burrito?" Amy asked.

"Part of it was frozen," Connor replied, embarrassed.

"Ewww, I would have puked too," she said thinking about it.

Katheryn returned with a personal-sized mouthwash. "Here you go honey. Why don't you keep this. If you need more let me know," she said turning him around and gently pushing him toward the bathroom. As Connor entered the bathroom she turned to look at her son, shaking her head in disapproval.

The group caught up with each other over the next hour as they got acquainted with Amy. Katheryn returned and asked if anyone was hungry. Christmas Eve was the big night at the Asher's. Christmas Day was more relaxed. The Ashers usually attended Mass and then family and friends gathered for the afternoon. Each brought something to add to the party. It was a great way to celebrate and there was never a shortage of guests or food.

"Anyone hungry? I'm going to start setting things out if you'd like something," she asked. "Connor, would you like another frozen burrito?" she asked, her question causing a spontaneous outbreak of laughter.

"No thank you, Mrs. A., I'm good thanks," he replied adding, "You guys suck," under his breath.

"What was that Connor? Did you say something?" Katheryn asked, having a little fun.

"No, I'm good, thank you."

"Oh, that's what I thought you said," she smiled. The spontaneous laughter returned.

Christian and Amy stuck close to their friends that afternoon, catching up on all the details of each other's lives. Amy and Maddy hit it off, although one might say Maddy was a little jealous. She had always had a thing for Christian, but felt he was too good a friend to take a chance and possibly ruin a good friendship or make things weird.

Amy enjoyed getting to know them all. The group discussed their plans for New Year's Eve. They planned to hit a couple of clubs and come back to Oceanview Lane to watch the festivities at the Thompson's house.

Christian had the opportunity to speak with Hal Porter just after he arrived. They chatted up planes for a while before Hal's wife pulled him away, requesting that he stop talking about planes every once in a while.

Christian moved into the kitchen to assist Amy and his mom.

"What are you guys doing for New Year's Eve?" Katheryn asked.

"We were just going to stay local," Christian replied.

"Really, I thought you'd want to go to the city to watch the ball drop?" Katheryn asked directing her inquiry to Amy.

"I asked Amy if she wanted to go to Times Square for New Year's, but she said no."

"Really, your first time in New York on New Year's and you don't want to go to Times Square?" she asked.

"It's not that I don't want to go someday, but as much fun as that sounds, I'd much rather be here with all of you sharing the holiday," Amy said sincerely.

Katheryn hugged Amy affectionately, "Ohhh, I am so happy to hear you say that," she said pulling in Christian with her open arm.

Christian and Amy had finalized their plans for the return trip. Once they didn't have to worry about The Cross any longer their plans were to leave a couple of days past New Year's Day and drive west to Breckenridge for a few days of skiing before going back to Oregon to meet with Amy's family for a late Christmas celebration.

Edward woke early and roused Christian from bed. They decided to drive in versus taking the train with such a precious piece of cargo. The trip in went smoothly. The traffic was light because of the holiday, allowing them to make good time.

They arrived at the museum as planned a few hours before opening to see Bill Stanton standing outside of the receiving door, pacing back and forth. He was a short, stout man, slightly balding. When Edward pulled into the receiving dock, he scurried over to the car. "Is that him?" Christian asked, chuckling.

"That's him. Don't let appearances fool you. This guy's a genius and he controls the flow of antiquities throughout the world. If something is found, he knows about it."

"Hi Bill, how are you?" Edward asked.

"Fine, thanks. . . . How is Katheryn?" he inquired.

"Fine, fine. She sends her regards," he said, introducing Christian as they moved into the museum. "I'm sorry to bother you over the holiday, but I know you're going to love this," Edward said as Stanton locked the receiving door behind him.

They moved to a room off to the side of receiving. Stanton opened the room with a passcode and key. The room was temperature and humidity controlled. As they entered, there were artifacts from around the globe everywhere that were being researched for authenticity and value. Stanton explained that the room they were in was one of a half dozen or so vaults for examining artifacts, fossils and other finds.

He cleared off a spot on a table and asked to see The Cross. Christian pulled the box from his knap sack and opened it. As he removed The Cross from the bag, Stanton quietly stared, admiring it, "Oh my! This is the Ferdinand VII Cross," he said calmly, putting on a pair of white cotton gloves. "How did you come to find this?" he asked.

Christian regaled him with the story of the find. Stanton listened intently while examining The Cross. "So you found it in a cave? That sounds quite risky. You're talking about the coastline by Montaña de Oro, I'd imagine. Considering that the extremely strong currents in that area that make for dangerous surf conditions, it must have been quite treacherous, I'd imagine." Christian was amazed at the remarkable knowledge Stanton possessed, but didn't appreciate the unapproving look his father gave him after hearing that bit of information.

Stanton continued telling the history of The Cross. His knowledge went far beyond the research available on the internet. He explained that the information readily available over the 'net was censored for one reason or another.

"Have you shown this to anyone other than Dr. Balzack?" he asked.

"How did you know about Balzack?" Christian asked.

"A few weeks back he started making inquiries about The Cross. He logged into our database to do some research. He was on the database every day for over two weeks. I'm surprised that he made that mistake," Stanton said thinking. "By the way, how is he?" he inquired.

Christian paused before answering, "He died a couple of weeks ago."

"Oh, that's too bad, he was a nice chap," Stanton remembered.

"What did you mean, you are surprised he made that mistake?" Christian inquired.

"Most field men learn early on in their careers not to research one database or one topic too heavily because it can tip other interested parties off to a find. Many of the so-called archeologists today are no more that cyber thieves. They hack into data systems to find out who is doing what and where, then try to jump the claim, so to speak. Experienced field people will usually research multiple databases and topics as opposed to staying on one for long periods of time. It's odd that he would make such a simple mistake," Stanton said.

"So, did you?" Stanton asked. "Show it to anyone else?" he asked again.

"Trudeau," Christian said.

"I'm not familiar with him," Stanton said thinking.

"Balzack wanted to have Trudeau appraise it. He said they had worked together for years," Christian replied.

"Well, I can't see that as a problem. Arthur chose his people well. If he trusted this fellow Trudeau, then it's probably not him trying to get it. I'll take a look at databanks to see who has been looking into The Cross other than Balzack.

"Bill," Edward interrupted, "we were wondering if you could hold on to it for a while. At least until we figure out what to do with it. Of course, we will give the museum the first shot at it."

"Splendid," Stanton replied. "I'd be happy to secure it for you. I'd love to show it to some of my colleagues if that would be alright with you?" he asked.

"Of course, of course, feel free," Edward said.

"Any objections?" Stanton asked Christian.

"Oh no, not at all," Christian replied.

"But you should know, unfortunately, that it has already drawn the attention of others who have tried to relieve Christian of it on at least two occasions," Edward warned Stanton.

"I can understand that. Finding the Ferdinand Cross is like finding Noah's Ark. There were rumors of its existence but until now no one really knew if it did exist; especially since so little was known of it and so few had actually seen it other than the maker and King Ferdinand," he said.

Stanton continued, "I'm sure you don't need me to remind you that the problem is, once the word is out which according to you already appears to have happened, there will be a world of inquiries about it and then there are the hosts of people trying to place their claims on it. It would be best not to tell anyone where it is for now. We can deal with that later," Stanton said knowingly.

"What do you mean other people will try to place a claim on it? Isn't it, for lack of a better expression, finder's keepers?" Christian asked.

"Oh, if only it were that simple," Stanton chuckled. "It's no different than anything else today. If something has value or historical significance, any one person, group or country that came in contact with it will try to lay claim to it. It's an archeologist's nightmare. And forget about the political red tape," Stanton said pausing. "Let me see," Stanton reflected, "If memory serves me right, The Cross was shipped to Monterey in the 1800s by King Ferdinand. It was believed that Hipolyte Bouchard gained possession of it before it was lost."

"No, he didn't get possession," Christian blurted unwisely.

"How could you know that?" Stanton asked.

Dr. Asher and Stanton waited for his response. Christian, realizing his mistake quickly rebounded, "If Bouchard had taken possession of it, it wouldn't have been in the cave, or on the continent for that matter. Why would he steal it and then put it in a cave?" Christian answered wisely.

"You have a valid point," Stanton declared "but . . . common sense is rarely a defense in cases like this. Since Bouchard was a French corsair that sailed against Spain under the Argentine, Peruvian and Chilean governments, they will try to claim it as their own because Bouchard was sailing under their flags."

"And, of course, Spain will say that it's theirs because they made it and it was stolen from them. And let's not forget France and the United States," Stanton added.

"France and the United States?" Christian said inquisitively.

"Absolutely," Stanton continued, "Bouchard was a Frenchman, and even if he was sailing for Argentina, Peru and Chile, the French will say he had obtained possession of it in the midst of a war, and as a French Captain it should be considered 'Spoils of War,' so they will lay claim to it."

"And the U.S.?" Christian asked.

"Well, the U.S. will claim it is theirs because it was found on U.S. soil, so to speak."

"Do any of them have a chance?" Christian asked.

"They all do. Their lawyers will pick at it like piranhas on a carcass. It's enough to make you wish you'd never found anything sometimes," Stanton said, reflecting.

"So where were we? Ah yes, so to start you will have the United States, Spain, France, Argentina, Peru and Chile looking to claim it. And oh, I forgot, the Vatican has quite the interest in objects of a religious nature. They will try to get in on it too, among others."

The meeting at the museum lasted over two and a half hours. Christian's head was swirling with all he learned in that short time. Dr. Stanton was happy to accommodate them and take possession of The Cross for the time being. Edward wished him well and they left the museum, relieved to have The Cross in safe hands.

As they walked to the car, Christian's senses started to heighten. He reached for his sun glasses only to realize he had left them in the car. "Hold on Dad," he cautioned his father. As they turned the corner, they came face to face with a group of six young thugs looking as if they were still high from the night before going through someone's purse they had recently acquired.

"Hey man, what do we have here?" one of them said.

"It looks like lunch to me," another added and started to laugh.

"Hey fellas, we don't want any problems. . . . It looks like you're having some fun so just let us go about our business," Edward said, concerned for Christian. Christian was fighting trying to stop the heightening.

"What do you say about giving us money for lunch? Me and my friends are a little hungry," one thug smiled.

"Sure, sure no problem . . ." Edward said, reaching into his pocket for the cash he had.

"And while you're at it, that must be your Mercedes. Give me the keys for that too," he demanded, opening his jacket to reveal a gun.

Christian stepped forward in front of his father, motioning for him to stop what he was doing. "Christian, don't," Edward called, trying to stop his advance toward the gang's leader.

"What are you going to do punk?" the leader asked as the rest of his friends formed up behind him, no doubt with intent to intimidate him.

"I'm going to ask you to leave while you still can," Christian said, still fighting the heightening.

The leader laughed, "Who the hell do you think you are? I think our new friend needs some ballistic therapy," he threatened, opening his jacket.

Christian stood defiant as his father pleaded with him not to pursue this, pulling on the back of his jacket. "Don't do it," Christian warned the thug threatening to pull his gun.

The thug looked smugly at Christian and said, "F*** this, I don't have time for this sh*t," reaching for his gun. Big mistake.

Christian lost his fight to hold back the change. His eyes flashed dark as he nailed the leader with a single blow to the chest before he could pull the gun from his jacket. Edward heard the unmistakable sound of ribs cracking. The thug went limp with a long wheeze, trying to fill his lungs with air as he dropped to the ground.

Edward watched stunned as Christian advanced fearlessly toward the punks as they grabbed for their weapons. The sequence of his plan flashed through his mind in an instant. He moved faster than anyone his father had ever seen before, laying each to waste with lightning speed and agility. In mere seconds, five of them were on the ground writhing in pain. Aside from breaking the leader's ribs, he had broken two legs, a jaw, a couple of wrists and shattered one knee cap, all in a matter of seconds.

As for the sixth, he walked over to him slowly, staring at him with his glaring black eyes and chiseled features and asked, "How old are you?"

"Fif—fif—fifteen," the scared want-to-be-thug stuttered.

"Go home, go to school and forget your friends. Got it?" Christian ordered as his eyes turned back to their crystal blue color. The speechless thug nodded affirmatively as he watched Christian's eyes change back to blue and then fainted.

Edward stood in stunned silence as Christian walked over to him. "Dad, we have to talk. Want me to drive?"

"O—K . . ." Edward nodded and handed him the keys.

They got into the car and drove away as Edward stared at the six want-to-be-gangsters still lying on the ground, five of them writhing in pain. Christian realized his dad was in shock so he asked, "Are you ok?"

"Yes, I'm fine. You okay?" Edward asked out of habit. "What the hell was that?"

Christian looked at him, concerned about what he was going to tell him. "I want you to know that I love you and Mom for all you have done for me. I've never kept a secret from you and I am not going to start now. I know about everything . . ."

Christian explained it all as his father listened. He told him everything he knew about him, Stedwell, his experiments, and the case study he was working on involving the Original Fourteen. He told him he knew about the meds he was taking and everything else up to and including Matt's involvement in keeping tabs on him.

He omitted all details about his new acquaintances, CB and Van Dunne, as well as his ability to connect. He only did so to protect his father, as well as his new friends, plus it gave his father plausible deniability. When he finally finished talking they were parked in the beach parking lot ten minutes from home watching the sun drop from the sky.

Edward sighed deeply. "I'm glad you know son. I hope you don't hold it against us. Your mother and I were only trying to protect you. There was a lot of interest in Stedwell's study by our superiors and when I first laid eyes on you I knew I couldn't let you live life as an experiment. And you would have if Stedwell hadn't come up with his solution to suppress you with the meds.

They probably would have put you under lock and key. Edward explained how he bribed all involved to forget about the first night they met in the hospital with Mrs. Espinosa.

Edward continued to tell his side of the story and the reasons he and Katheryn did what they did. He told him how much he loved him and how proud he was to have a son like him. Christian listened, grateful to have such caring parents.

By the time Edward was finished it had been over five hours since they left the city. He asked Christian to text Amy to tell his mom that they would be home shortly, and he did. Christian was grateful to have all that off of his mind.

"Can I ask you something?" Edward asked.

"Sure, go ahead," Christian said.

"Can I see the scar?" he asked.

Christian started laughing. "Sure." He opened his shirt revealing the scar.

"You know if your mother sees that she's going to flip her lid," Edward laughed.

"I know," Christian said thinking. "Oh Dad, by the way . . . if Matt sends you an update on the Zeus file, don't download it to your computer."

"Why?" he asked.

"Just don't. It'll melt everything you have on your computer."

"Okay, thanks for telling me," Edward said, curious as to what Christian just said.

What Christian didn't know was that the memory stick replaced by Van Dunne, besides having a self-destruct sequence for the stick itself, also had a virus installed that was designed to wipe out any transmission regarding the Zeus file, as well as any information or communication linked to it. This was to protect Christian's computer from being hacked. Any outgoing Zeus information would be destroyed along with the computer files on the computer receiving it. Although Christian's content was safe, when Matt transferred the information onto his computer or if he forward it to anyone, the countdown began.

On the drive home Edward asked, "What did it feel like?"

"What's that?' Christian asked.

"The whole lightning bolt thing on your camping trip."

"I don't remember," Christian answered.

"Nothing?" Edward asked.

"No, not a thing. The only information I had was what Amy, Matt and Tina told me. Then I saw the video Matt took when it happened and that freaked me out a little."

"Only a little?" Edward asked.

"Yeah, at first maybe it freaked me out a lot, but then I figured that I was alive so why worry about it," Christian said.

"Hmm, you're a better man than I," Edward said proudly as they pulled into the driveway.

They walked into the house to find the ladies waiting. "What took you guys so long?" Katheryn asked.

"We were just taking care of some things," Edward answered, kissing Katheryn on the cheek.

Amy greeted Christian with a kiss. "We had the best day," she said, smiling at Katheryn. "We went shopping, had lunch and then we had a steam massage and a facial," Amy glowed.

"Don't forget the mani-pedi," Katheryn added.

"It was like being in heaven. Do you like this color for New Year's?" Amy asked showing her hands to Christian.

"Love it," Christian smiled.

"What about you guys, did anything exciting happen today?" Katheryn asked, interested.

"No, nothing exciting. We met with Bill at the museum and he took possession of The Cross for us. That was a relief. Of course we told him that someone tried to steal it already. He wasn't surprised though," Edward answered.

"He told us the history of The Cross and what to expect," Christian added. "And then he asked if he could show a few colleagues.

"We figured it was ok, it was in safe hands," Edward said and Christian agreed.

"And then?" Katheryn inquired with Amy smirking by her side.

"Nothing, we did some running around and that was it," Christian said.

"Oh, so you didn't make any new friends today?" Kathryn asked probing. "Maybe like these guys?" Katheryn added, pushing the play button on the DVR. Edward and Christian grew quiet as a replay of the five o'clock news played.

"Hi, this is Tom Caldwell back from break with headline news at five. CALL IT A CASE OF JUST DESSERTS! This morning police found these five men writhing in pain behind the Museum of Natural History. Apparently someone gave them a taste of their own medicine."

"Locals interviewed said that this gang had been harassing and robbing people at gun and knife point in this neighborhood for months and nothing had been done about it. Mark Fredrick said, 'It's about time somebody got them, they deserve everything they got and more.' AND OTHERS AGREED WITH MARK," Tom Caldwell smiled.

"We were able to pull the footage from the surveillance video behind the museum. In the video you can see the thugs rifling through someone's purse. Now watch this, and I warn you, if you have a weak stomach, this may be disturbing to you. We've slowed the video down so you can see it."

"It shows two men being approached and threatened by the six suspects. Now watch the man on the left as the suspect reaches for what looks like a gun. Bam! One shot and he's down. And if that wasn't amazing enough, he steps into the middle of the remaining suspects, all but one now holding what appear to be weapons of some kind. Look at that . . . Wow!"

"All totaled, the unknown hero left five of his would-be attackers on the ground with broken ribs, legs, and wrists. This man had his jaw broken and a shattered knee cap. Abby Layne was at the hospital and tried to interview this suspect as he was escorted from the hospital by police. 'Sir, can you tell us what happened?'"

"'Eshh ishel diablo.'"

"I don't know Tom, it must be hard to talk with your mouth wired shut but it sounds like he said, 'It was the devil,' Well it must seem so to him. Hopefully he's learned his lesson."

"I was able to interview another of the suspects, Tom, and when I asked him what happened, all he could say was 'All I wanted was money for lunch.' Well it looks like he'll be eating lunch in jail for a while. Back to you."

"THANK YOU ABBY!"

"By the time police arrived, the sixth suspect had fled the scene. Here he is shown dropping his knife and blessing himself before running off. I don't think he'll be back to play anytime soon."

"Of course the controversy will follow this story. Do we have the right to protect ourselves with force? Is this man a vigilante? Well to me, I'd like to personally thank you. To you, the unknown hero. . . . Thank you for making our streets a little safer tonight."

"This is Tom Caldwell, until tomorrow. Good Night All!"

Edward and Christian said nothing. They didn't even look at each other. They were busted.

"Isn't that a coincidence. Two men dressed like you are attacked behind a museum that you went to this morning. . . . Hmm . . ." Katheryn said, pushing the stop button on the DVR.

"Well, in their defense, you couldn't see their faces. There was so much dirt on the camera lens. Is there anything else that can place them at the scene?" Amy said, playing along.

Edward tried to offer a defense, "Well, I don't think . . . ."

"Tut, Tut, Tut, Shhh," Katheryn shushed him. "What else can be offered as evidence?" she questioned herself out loud.

"Now you wouldn't be thinking of stating the fact that the two unknown men drove away in a black Mercedes SUV oddly resembling yours, would you?" Amy asked.

"No, I don't see the need for further evidence, I move we go to judgement. What say you, Guilty or Innocent?" Katheryn asked.

Amy paused for a long moment, "Guilty. . . . Off with their heads!"

Christian stated his defense, "I think the evidence is very circumstantial. The images are blurry and thousands of black Mercedes SUV's drive around in New York every day." Edward agreed.

"Well that would be a good defense had not the jury received this intriguing evidence only minutes before you arrived," Amy pointed to Katheryn like a game show model points to a prize.

Katheryn, with a condemning smile, pushed the play button on the answering machine. "Hi Katheryn, I just wanted to call to see if Edward and Christian were alright. I saw what happened in the alley behind the museum and called the police but by the time the police came . . ."

"Hello Bill, I'm sorry I was fumbling trying to pick up my phone. . . . Now what happened exactly?" Katheryn's voice replayed loud and clear.

Christian and Edward bowed their heads in defeat. "Ok, what's our sentence?" Christian asked.

Katheryn smiled at Amy. "Dinner and Dancing at Victors Café in New York City," Katheryn said.

"Honey, do you think we should go back into the city today with our pictures all over TV? Someone might recognize the 'Unknown Hero' here . . ."

"Ok, but you are taking us there before New Year's. My associate has never been to a Cuban restaurant. Amy, will you agree to settle for Ainelli's tonight and Victor's on a date to be announced?" Katheryn asked.

"I believe those terms to be acceptable," she said playfully. "ITALIAN—WOO HOOOO!" She jumped up and down in victory.

The ruse was over and the boys licked their wounds. They didn't get off that easy and had to answer some serious questions. Kathryn and Amy were equally relieved that they were ok and uninjured, but neither was happy at the chance Christian took. The one thing they didn't mention was the speed at which Christian moved during the few seconds of the altercation. Most likely it was because of the slow motion replay which did not go unnoticed by the media. The fast version was played over and over and actually went viral overnight.

Christian was happy it was over, but knew he had one more task to complete before night's end. He knew the conversation would continue over dinner and it did, just after they were seated at Ainelli's. Micaela, the owner, greeted them as he always does and set up the drink order.

Ainelli's was a quaint little bistro that Katheryn and Edward had frequented for years. Katheryn liked the décor and they all loved the food. The design made you feel as if you were sitting in a courtyard in Tuscany. There were archways and windows with flower pots, trellises with grapevines, and beautiful water scene frescos. It was what Katheryn imagined Tuscany to be like.

Over drinks and appetizers Katheryn was let in on the fact that Christian was aware of everything. She couldn't help herself and started to cry, fearful that this would change their relationship. Christian got up from his chair and walked to her and hugged her like a son. "Mom, there is nothing in heaven or earth that could make me love you any more or less than I have in the past and I do right now."

Katheryn lost it. She hugged him like she was never going to let go. "I love you sooo much. . . . You are my life," she said sobbing.

Christian could hear the sniffles from the other side of the table and he looked up at Amy just as she said, "That's the most beautiful thing I've ever heard, but look at what you're doing to my makeup," as she held up her makeup covered napkin. Christian glanced at Amy and then looked back at Edward for suggestions on what to say. He shook his head 'No' in an attempt to warn Christian not to mention that Amy now resembled a distant cousin of the Joker from the Batman series.

Amy sat weeping from the beautiful sentiment. Her eye shadow was smeared, her eye liner was dragged down onto her cheeks from wiping, excuse me . . . blotting her tears. The napkin she was holding looked like a Picasso with multiple imprints of eye makeup and light pink lip gloss from Amy's attempts to dry her tears.

She rarely used makeup, she had no need to. She had naturally beautiful skin, hair and eyes, with long lashes and perfect coloring. That was one of the things that attracted Christian, her natural beauty. Growing up on the family farm, there was rarely a need to put makeup on.

Simultaneously, she and Katheryn looked at each other and laugh-cried. That awkward combination of laughing and crying at the same time that broke out as soon as they saw each other's faces. "Oh my god . . . look at us!" Katheryn said blotting her tears. I think we should go to the ladies room. Something tells me they didn't use waterproof makeup on you."

The ladies excused themselves and went to freshen up. "Whew!" Edward sighed, "That went better than I thought."

Christian smiled, "Thank god. I thought Mom was going to squeeze the air out of me." They chuckled.

"I'm proud of you Christian," Edward said sincerely.

There were a few moments of silence as each reflected on the moment. "What are you and Amy doing New Year's Eve?" Edward asked. Christian shared the plans he had with Amy and his friends. Edward was also happy that they would be joining them for the countdown at the Thompson house. A few minutes later the ladies returned.

Micaela brought over a bottle of champagne for the table. "I don't know what just happened, but it looked like something very special. Please accept this for your special occasion."

"Thank you Micaela, we appreciate it," Edward said as Micaela popped the cork. "Happy Holidays!" he said pouring the champagne. They raised their glasses to the Holidays and to Micaela and enjoyed the rest of their evening.

-Twenty-Four- *New Year's Gri-EVE*

New Year's Eve day had arrived and the Asher house was bustling. Maddy and Amy had returned from shopping for outfits to wear out for the evening and were trying them on to show Katheryn.

Hal Porter was over talking to Edward about his participation in the evening's events at the Thompson's home. Hal was going to fly over the Thompson home at exactly 11:59 and release confetti for the New Year. Thompson planned it so the confetti would drift down slowly like snow and appear to the viewers at the stroke of midnight, just as the elf on the New Year's Ball dropped to Father Time, starting the New Year.

"Donald put a lot of effort into this, didn't he?" Edward asked.

"You have no idea," Hal answered. "He came to the board to request a fireworks permit in September and he's been at it since. He's the one that pushed for the street decorations, and when he was told there was no money in the budget allocated for the extra decorations, he bought them. Didn't blink an eye," Hal said.

"It's good to see some holiday spirit," Ed said.

Christian and the guys were in the garage messing with the Mustang. "I can't believe he gave it to you. That's hard to top," Connor said. Christian knew what he meant. Connor's family was always trying to out give each other. At first it was a game, but as time had passed it had become a family obsession, regardless of the fact that his family has had their share of financial struggles.

"Why would I have to top that? It was a great surprise. When you think about it, nothing has really changed. The car is still going to be here, and my dad is still going to drive it. So what's to top?" Christian asked.

"I know, but he gave it to you. It's a big gift," Connor defended.

"Yes I agree, but it's not like he went out and bought me a car. We like to keep it simple on the holidays. Most of our gifts are practical things that we use every day. Not like that grill you guys got your dad last year. You know, the one that talks to you. How is that thing anyway?" Christian asked.

"The grill works great, we use it all the time," Connor replied mumbling.

"Yeah, you use it all the time to stop rain from hitting the deck," Tweet joked.

"What happened?" Christian asked.

Conner paused. "The grill stopped talking to us," he said.

"That doesn't sound too bad," Christian said.

"But when the talking grill guy stopped working so did the grill," Tweet said. The guys broke out laughing.

"Hey, it's not funny, that really sucked," Connor blurted to a laughing audience.

"When we went back to the store they said it was the computer chip or something and they wanted eight hundred bucks to fix it. We only paid a thousand for it," Connor defended.

Christian, still laughing, pointed at the grill on the side of the garage. "175 bucks, ten years old and just like yours . . . It doesn't talk," Christian and Tweet laughed.

"Hey, what's this?" Connor asked picking up the Blizzerator in an attempt to change the topic.

"Amy got them for us. Pretty cool, huh?" Christian said. "I tried it out Christmas morning, it's awesome. The guy that invented it launched it 96,000 feet on a weather balloon with a video camera. It does just about everything, but you know what it doesn't do?" he asked.

"No, what?" Connor asked gullibly.

"It doesn't talk!" Christian and Tweet cracked up.

"Hey, are you guys picking on him again?" Amy said, walking over to Connor. "C'mere," she said giving him a hug. "Poor baby . . ." she said consoling him. Connor looked over Amy's shoulder, smirking at Christian until he heard Amy ask, "Does baby want to come inside and try on clothes for tonight?" teasingly.

Connor stepped back, embarrassed. "No, baby doesn't want to try on clothes."

"Oh, what are you doing with that?" Amy asked pointing at the Blizzerator.

"I'm about to Oblizzerate my friends," Connor said.

"Hey, thanks for reminding me. Would you put that in my mother's car for me, I forgot to," Christian asked.

"Who are you guys bringing tonight?" Amy inquired.

"I'm going with Jamie," Tweet said.

"How about you, Connor?"

Connor started to answer, "I'm—"

Then Tweet interrupted, "Bringing your sister again?" he said joking.

"No, I'm bringing yours! At least I know I'll have some fun," Connor laughed.

Tweet jumped on him playfully, trying to wrestle him down to the ground in an attempt to make him take back his comment, but

Connor was wiry and quickly evaded his attempt. "No, I'm bringing Kallie," Connor said to Amy.

"Who?" Christian asked.

"Kalendra Davis," he replied.

"It's probably the name of his blow up . . ." Tweet started to say before he was pushed through the laundry room door by Connor.

"Didn't she move when we were in third grade?"
Christian asked.

"Yeah, her father got transferred back about a month ago," Connor said smiling.

"How did you know she was back?" Christian asked.

"I bumped into her at Tony's," he said.

"Ohhhh, I remember Kaleidoscope Kallie. She wore those thick glasses and always smelled like??? Eggrolls, that's it. She always smelled like egg rolls," Tweet teased.

"Yeah, that's her," Connor said. "She said she didn't have anything going on so I asked her to come along,"

"Oh, that's sweet," Amy said.

"Mom wants to know if you guys are staying for dinner," Amy inquired.

"What are we having?" Tweet asked.

"We were thinking either Tony's or Chinese takeout," Amy answered.

"Oh, let's get Chinese, this way Connor can smell like his date," Tweet laughed. Connor shoved him again. All but Connor agreed on Chinese takeout.

Amy retreated from the man cave and placed the order with Katheryn. "Wow, she called your mother, Mom," Connor said surprised.

"Yeah, why?" Christian asked.

"Don't you remember the Asher Inquisition, Crazy Katheryn or the Asher Asylum?" Tweet asked continuing, "We never thought you'd get another girl in this house, much less one that was good enough to call your mom . . . Mom," he said.

Christian smiled, "I thought about that all the way home . . ." Christian reflected. "Besides, that is not as bad as being called, "Piss Stains Padmore of the Pissing Padmores." Connor laughed.

"Hey, that's not funny. I got hit in the crotch with a football. And besides, we have small bladders, ask your dad," Tweet defended.

"I guess Kaleidoscope Kallie is looking pretty good right now," Christian said to Connor.

"Yeah, she sure is. At least I don't need to put a wee-wee pad on the car seat," Connor said laughing. Tweet jumped on him again, trying to wrestle him to the ground.

Katheryn called Christian into the kitchen. "Honey, would you mind picking up the food? The wait time for delivery is over two hours," she said.

"Not at all," Christian smiled.

"It'll be ready in a half hour. Take them with you," she said, pointing through the door at Tweet and Connor still pushing at each other.

By the time the guys had returned with the food, Tweet had received an update on the evening plans. During the meal they discussed their options with the girls. The group decided they would stop at a house party and then come back to the Thompson's house at 11:45 to bring in the New Year, after which they would hit a club or two. Connor texted Kallie telling her that he would pick her up at 7:30. Kallie's reply text said, "I'm sorry, I can't go . . ."

Everyone noticed a sudden look of disappointment in Connor's face. He was really looking forward to hanging out with her and he also knew that Tweet was never going to let him live this down. Christian, seeing the disappointed look on his face, asked, "What's wrong?"

"Nothing," Connor said, depressed, and showed Christian the text.

Tweet wanted to razz him, but he saw how upset Connor was and actually used his better judgement for a change. His phone chimed in again, it was Kallie. "Yes!" Connor said, with renewed happiness.

Connor's sadness had vanished in an instant. "Good News?" Maddy asked, seeing him smile.

"Kallie can meet us at eight-fifteen. She has to wait for her brother to get home. The text had somehow split into two messages. Whew!" he said.

Tweet got his chance. "Thank God! At least you didn't go through all that trouble to smell like an eggroll for nothing," he teased.

All but Connor had arrived at Veronica Lacey's house by eight. It was a large home built in the late eighteen hundreds and meticulously restored to its original condition. Christian had always admired the house. He loved everything about it. It had a flat roof with a fence around its perimeter and a small cupola room with enough space for a few people to look out over the horizon.

This was a popular Italianate design that was romanticized by writers early on. The romanticized version had two names; the Captain's Walk, which reportedly was used by captains to watch for ships expected to arrive in port, and the more popular, the Widow's Walk.

The Widow's Walk was romanticized by novelists who wrote stories of the reportedly many seaman's wives walking back and forth on the roof, waiting for any sign of ships on the horizon in hopes that their husbands would come home safely. The name was provided by those who waited in vain for lost ships never to return.

Christian was admiring the decorative woodwork and glass doors. The doors had all been restored, including the original wavy glass that was made in simpler times. The Laceys had devoted years to restoring each and every detail of their home.

The house was packed. From the entrance you could hear the music cranking from the back of the house where the main party room was. The Laceys had divided the house into sections. To the right of the entrance was a full bar that was already four deep. A large room to the left was reserved for the catering and, of course, the main party room in the back.

Tweet and Jamie were talking with a few friends. Madison, who had gone solo, was talking with Amy when they noticed a very attractive girl enter the room. She had long, silky black hair. The stranger made her way through the crowd over to Amy and Maddy and introduced herself. "Hi, you must be Amy and Maddy, right? Connor told me all about you. I'm Kalendra," she said.

"You're Kallie?" Madison asked, surprised.

"Yes," she smiled.

"I would have never guessed you were Kallie, you look so different," Madison said hugging her. The once awkward, pigeon-toed young girl they called 'Kaleidoscope Kallie' who wore Coke-bottle thick glasses had transformed into a stunning beauty.

Amy and Maddy welcomed her warmly, both very impressed with her appearance, especially Maddy. They started talking about how long it had been since she moved away from town and where she had lived for the last twelve plus years. Kallie was discussing the details of the years since she had been gone when Jamie took notice of her, "Wow, who is that talking with Amy and Madison?" she asked Chris.

"I don't know," he replied, catching a look at the exotic beauty. Jamie excused herself and walked over to the girls and introduced herself just as Connor walked into the room. Chris saw that he was alone.

"What's up?" Connor asked.

"What happened, no eggrolls tonight? Where's Kaleidoscope Kallie?" he asked, teasing."

"Excuse me, what did you say?" a strong and confident Kallie asked from behind him. Chris' head shrunk into his shoulders with embarrassment. He turned around and came face-to-face with Kallie.

"Eggrolls?" he squeaked out, embarrassed.

Kallie looked at him stern-faced. "Yes, it's me and I'd prefer to be called Kalendra if you don't mind . . . Piss Stains," she said confidently, putting him in his place.

Connor worked his way through the group and was greeted with a kiss. "I guess you remember Chris," he said smiling at Chris who was feeling very awkward at the moment.

"I do. I just thought he would have grown up a little, but I see he's the same little brat he was in the third grade," she said. The group snickered as she reminded him of how much of a little prick he was in school and all the nasty things he did and said to her.

Chris spent the next twenty minutes apologizing for his insensitive remarks and actions, both past and present. Connor was enjoying his groveling. Kallie smiled at him, "Is that enough?" she asked.

"Yeah, I think we can give him a break," Connor said.

Chris stood quietly listening. "Ok Piss Stains, you're good. Apologies accepted," she said, smiling.

Time flew by as they enjoyed the party and before they knew it, it was eleven-thirty. Christian and Amy gathered the troops to head over to the Thompson's house, but the news was out. By the time they arrived there were hundreds of people already gathered, including news trucks and the same reporters that had reported on the events on Christmas Eve.

Christian worked his way through the street barricades that local law enforcement had set up to close off the road to vehicles. The officer at the gate was one of Edward's patients, knew Christian, and let him and his friends through. They pulled into the driveway and made their way to the Thompson's house.

The crowd was growing in droves. By eleven-forty-five there were well over a thousand people waiting to bring in the New Year outside of the Thompson's home. The lights were flashing off and on to the music. The mechanical sets were working away. Elves perched on top of the house were waving to the crowd. The train was moving around the house and elves were tossing candy to the crowd.

The New Year was about five minutes away when Christian sensed something wasn't right. His senses started to heighten, but in the crowd of excited people singing and dancing he couldn't pick up on why. He carefully scanned his surroundings, seeing nothing that looked out of the ordinary, but still, his senses hadn't let him down before. He looked up, hearing Hal Porter's plane approaching. Maybe that was it. Maybe there was something wrong with the plane. But no, he focused on the plane and heard the door open as bags of confetti were emptied out over the crowd. Then the plane turned north for its run back to the airport.

Amy noticed his focus. "What's wrong? You have that look on your face," she asked.

"Oh, nothing. Something didn't feel right but it's okay now," he fibbed as everyone began to cheer as the countdown began... "Ten . . . nine . . . eight . . . " The waving elves started to drop the ball to Father Time. "Seven . . . six . . . five . . . four . . . three . . . two . . . one . . . HAPPY NEW YEAR!!!" The crowd roared as confetti floated down from the darkness.

Fireworks erupted from the back yard, shooting south over the Atlantic. The crowd went wild, cheering in the New Year. They roared as the American Flag appeared in pyrotechnics in the New Year sky with explosive bursts of red, white and blue. Mortar rounds were launched, exploding around the flag as sprays of color erupted above and behind it. It was spectacular.

Amy kissed Christian. "Happy New Year!" she said glowing. Christian cheerfully wished her a Happy New Year and returned the kiss. They held each other for a moment before celebrating with their friends, exchanging hugs and kisses for the New Year. It was as exciting as any New Year's celebration could be.

Christian and Amy slowly pushed their way through the crowd to Katheryn and Edward who were standing only feet away with friends and family. As they approached them, Christian could see Katheryn and Edward enjoying themselves celebrating. They were smiling at him cheerfully as he approached. Suddenly, his father's face changed from a look of joy to a look of serious concern. Katheryn yelled to him, "CHRISTIAN!" with a frightened look on her face.

"Christian, watch out!" Tweet yelled. Christian turned around and came face to face with two suits. They wasted no time squeezing the triggers on their Tasers, shooting him point blank in the chest. Some of the crowd in the immediate vicinity started to scream, inciting a small localized panic which went unnoticed by the mass of people cheering the New Year. It was so noisy that they couldn't differentiate between the screams of panic and the noise from over a thousand other people cheering.

Christian didn't flinch. He stared defiantly into their eyes as he tore the sparking Taser darts from his body. His friends stood shocked in disbelief at what they had just witnessed. "Did you see that?" Connor asked. "He just got blasted by two Tasers and it did nothing."

Edward grabbed him from behind, pulling him away from the two men. "Get out of here . . . NOW!" he said pushing him and a panicked Amy deeper into the crowd. Tweet and Connor rushed the men, knocking them to the ground as they fumbled with their uncoiled Tasers.

Only moments had passed before Katheryn, Edward and the gang were surrounded by a dozen suits. "Where is he?" Eric Channing asked the two suits.

Channing was in charge of apprehending Christian. He was less than thrilled that he had slipped away. The two suits pointed in the general direction of their escape. “Find them,” Channing said, ordering his men to search the crowd. “Not you two,” he said to the rookies who let Christian slip away. “You stay here and watch them,” he barked pointing to Katheryn and Edward then continuing, “If he gets away, Kearns is going to rip you a new one.”

Katheryn stepped forward pointing at Channing, “If you hurt my son, I’ll rip your balls off and feed them to the dogs,” she claimed angrily as Edward restrained her. Channing responded with a look of derision.

Edward pulled her back. “You don’t want to screw with these guys . . .” he warned. “We’ll get this straightened out,” he said, assuring her.

The men took off into the crowd as Christian’s family and friends were detained. Channing radioed the others, “Zeus is in the pack, keep your eyes open.”

“What’s this all about?” Connor demanded.

“None of your damn business,” Channing said as one of his underlings pushed Connor back into place. Channing radioed his men again. “Let me know when you find him,” he commanded and walked back to a waiting black car.

Katheryn was frantic wondering what was going on. Did they find him? Is he okay? And what were they going to do with him if they caught him? She wanted to get away from the group to find her son. Edward held her tightly, trying to console her. “Trust me, he’ll be fine. I know . . . I’ve seen him in action. And so have you,” he said, trying to put her mind at ease.

Connor saw how upset she was and decided to act. He looked at Tweet and motioned for him to rush the agent who was closest to him; Connor would rush the other. They both thought the Tasers were defective since they had no effect on Christian. Connor launched his assault, running toward the suit closest to him. The agent, now on alert, acted quickly and tased him in the chest, stopping him dead in his tracks. He fell to the ground convulsing.

Tweet stopped when he saw Connor hit the ground. "Get back," the other suit ordered. The shooter grinned as he looked at Connor's body twitching on the ground.

He seemed pleased that he tased the kid, so pleased in fact that he didn't see Kallie approaching. BAM! She kicked him right in the crotch. He folded over in pain, holding his groin. Kallie pushed him backward and to the ground. "Yeah!" Tweet cheered, "Yeah!" and then backed down when his eyes met the other agent's.

She bent down to attend to Connor. "Are you ok?" she asked, concerned. Connor, dazed, nodded affirmatively, still twitching a bit. Kallie tried to help him up but he fell back down. Tweet stepped in and helped a grateful Kallie lift him to his feet.

Connor's attempted attack created enough of a distraction for Edward and Katheryn to slip into the crowd. Their friends and neighbors moved close together, forming a wall that blocked the agents view as they hurried away. They were lost in the pack before the suits even knew they had slipped away.

"Son of a bitch," the agent said, noticing they had slipped away during the commotion. He started to report, "Sir, this is Davenport. The parents are gone."

There was a pause before Channing responded. "Find them . . . and bring them to me," he ordered.

"What about the rest of them?" he inquired.

"They're not important, find the parents," Channing ordered

Chris and Connor organized their friends. "We have to help them. I think I know where he's going," Chris said. He told Connor and Kallie to go along the roadway to the front of the house with the others while he and Jamie went through the back of the houses on a trail that they used as kids.

As friends and neighbors pushed through the crowd headed towards the Asher's house, they noticed more and more suits, all government agents. They were all over and had shut down the media completely. As they approached the end of the road they could see a half dozen black sedans blocking the roadway, surrounded by more agents who were scanning the crowd for any sign of Christian and Amy. When they reached the Asher's home they were turned away. They watched through the large open windows with curiosity as suits rummaged through the home, wondering what this was all about.

Christian and Amy had made it to a spot behind the house. Amy's heart was pounding. They watched as agents scoured the inside and outside of the house. A black car pulled into the driveway quickly and came to a screeching halt. The back door opened and a woman exited the car. Christian had no idea who she was, but then he saw the other door open. A familiar face exited the car. It was Matt.

"That son of a bitch!" Amy said under her breath. "How could he do this?" she asked.

"That's his job, but I thought he was helping Stedwell and my father," Christian said to himself.

Christian watched as the woman ordered the men to search the perimeter of the property. "Kearns," he whispered to himself.

"What?" Amy asked.

"That has to be Kearns. CB told me that she had taken Stedwell's place. He even suggested she was somehow responsible for his death. It's got to be her."

The men searching the perimeter were getting close. Christian and Amy backed further into the darkness of the shrubs and trees. As he was figuring out his next move, Tweet and Jamie came up the path behind them, startling Amy. "What the hell is going on?" Tweet asked just as the agent shined his light in their direction, putting the beam directly on the four of them and holding for a few seconds. Everyone froze in place. Christian readied himself to push off and run, but then the agent lowered his light. It was Matt.

"Henderson, do you have anything?" the woman called to him.

"No, nothing over here," Matt said. He started to talk softly into the bushes as he moved along slowly. "Christian, you and Amy need to get out of here now. They've got two dozen agents looking for you. Most of them are out front in the crowd right now. Get behind the cars at the head of the road and you should have a chance . . ." he said.

"Thanks," Christian said softly.

"Are you kidding, you're going to listen to him?" Amy asked. "He's one of them."

"Look . . . you don't have time for this bullshit. Kearns killed my uncle and she will do the same to anyone else to get her hands on you," he said sternly.

"Stedwell was your uncle?" Christian asked.

"Yes . . . Amy give me something personal. A watch, your phone anything," he ordered.

Amy reached in her pocket and pulled out her phone. It was the only thing she had that could be linked to them. She passed it to Matt through the trees. "I want that back," she said adamantly.

"Just wait here, and MOVE YOUR ASS when you hear the commotion. . . . Good luck."

Matt walked away, continuing to search the back perimeter of the yard as other agents were closing in on the area. They had formed a fence of agents, ten to fifteen feet apart from each other at the far end of the crowd in front, as well as behind the houses. They had moved their way through the crowd and were now getting close to the Asher home and Christian. Matt pushed his way through the trees, sea grass and shrubs, moving further away from Christian and Amy.

"Amy, I want you to stay here with Tweet and Jamie, I'll get in touch."

"No way . . . I'm coming with you," she stated tenaciously. Christian smiled, admiring her strength. He gave Tweet that particular look and Tweet knew exactly what he wanted him to do.

"What are you going to do?" Tweet asked. Christian looked at the Mustang. As he started to speak he heard Matt yell, "Stop, put your hands up," and then he fired a couple of shots into the ground.

The shots rang loud and were heard by everyone. Christian could hear his mom screaming, "Noooo, don't shoot, don't shoot him." The crowd in the street panicked and scattered through the neighborhood and away from the house and the sound of gunfire. Agents poured from the house toward Matt who was making himself visible through the brush and trees with his flashlight.

"Get Connor and keep them distracted somehow. Do whatever you need to do," Christian said. He kissed Amy quickly and pushed her back into Tweet's arms. Tweet saw a sudden glint of his black eyes and stepped back with a firm hold on Amy, not really sure of what he had just seen. Christian darted up the path behind the trees. He snuck along the neighbor's fence, watching as the excited agents pushed past Matt and through the trees and bushes to the path.

Channing walked up to Henderson. "Talk . . . what happened?" he asked. Matt gave him a description of what happened. He said he saw two people, told them to stop and fired two warning shots before they ran off. "How do you know it was them?" Channing asked.

"I found this," Matt said, handing Channing the cell phone. "I think it belongs to the girl."

Amy broke Tweet's grip and headed after Christian. "Damn it!" Tweet blurted. He fumbled for his phone and texted Connor, "Need help, back yard—Everyone."

He watched with Jamie as Christian made his way over the fence and behind the car the agents had parked in the driveway. The agents were scouring the back corner of the property as he moved unnoticed to the Mustang. Then they saw Amy hop the fence and run to the Mustang. As she reached the Mustang Pamela Kearns stepped out from behind the garage and grabbed her arm. "You're mine, don't moo . . ." and Amy blasted her in the face with a right hook before she could finish. As she fell backward, she accidently squeezed off a round, alerting the agents.

Amy jumped in the Mustang as Christian fired up the worked high performance 302. "Let's do this," she smiled nervously. "C'mon, C'mon . . . Get your ass moving Granny," she barked, referencing his normal driving style.

"Nice shot," Christian said as he hit the gas, turning into the back yard.

"Where the hell are you going?" Amy asked, looking over to see his chiseled face and dark eyes.

He smiled. “Matt said to get past those cars . . .”

“I shouldn’t have asked,” Amy said, not knowing what would come next.

The agents ran toward the Mustang as Christian spun the car around in the yard, pelting them with sand and stone, then shot through the shrubs on the side of the yard. He raced through the neighbor’s’ yards, weaving in and out of obstacles and out onto the neighboring street.

Connor and the cavalry arrived just as Chris and Jamie entered the back yard from the path. “Connor, we need to keep these guys busy. Let’s get Katheryn and Ed, then push everyone around their cars to block them in,” Tweet yelled.

He headed the charge with over twenty others following close behind him. They ran through the yard toward the agents now holding Edward and Katheryn. Edward broke free from the agent’s grip and dropped him to the ground with one punch. Katheryn was pulling and tugging, trying to break free as Edward started fighting his way out of the group in an attempt to reach his car. They broke free of their captors just as they were enveloped by the wave of Christian’s friends coming to the rescue. Tweet and Connor, along with their friends, piled on the outnumbered agents.

Katheryn and Edward jumped into the car. He saw that the crowd was pushing past the agents, and their cars had blocked the street. He started the Mercedes, slammed it into gear and drove straight through the neighbor’s fence. “Oh my god—did you see that?” Chris asked, shocked at what he just saw.

The agents started to regroup. “Let’s get out of here,” Tweet said, and they ran into the panicked crowd, mixing with them, and escaped. As they were running past the agents, Kalendra saw the suit that had tased Connor with such enjoyment. He was fighting off the stampede of panicked people, trying to hold his ground She headed directly toward him and kicked him hard in the groin on her way past. "Oh, not again," he groaned, falling to his knees, dropping his Taser.

Kallie knelt beside him and picked up his Taser. "That one's for smiling," she said in reference to his happy demeanor after tasing Connor, then smiled cutely and ran into the crowd.

Kearns was barking orders, "Get them you sons of bitches. If he gets away I'll have your asses." The agents cleared the crowd enough to pass with sirens blaring and raced down the street. Government cars were scrambling throughout the neighborhood. The panicked spectators were running for their lives as the speeding cars headed off in pursuit of Christian.

Christian and Amy hadn't made it far down the road when they were picked up by a helicopter's spotlight. The race was on. The copter reported their location. Kearns ordered all local and state law enforcement to set up roadblocks and not to pursue.

Edward saw the spotlight and raced toward that direction. Katheryn was beside herself with fear. In their wildest dreams they never would have believed that something like this would ever happen, but it had. She asked question after question about what was going to happen. Edward had no answers. He thought he and Stedwell had protected him from this.

Christian was pushing the Mustang to the max in his attempt to evade the copter, but there was no place to hide. There were only a few main roads, and most side streets ended at the water or were circles. He raced toward the parkway as agency cars pulled in front of him, trying to block his escape. He evaded them with ease. Others pulled in behind him trying to keep up with the Mustang unsuccessfully. But as he learned quickly, you can't outrun a radio.

He locked up his brakes as he approached the local shopping center. In front of them was an enormous roadblock. On the street were a dozen cars of police officers and agents with guns drawn and others pointing their glaring spotlights into the car. The agency cars rolled in behind him as the helicopter pilot hovered above the car, shining a bright spotlight onto the car, making it even more difficult to see. Amy shielded her eyes from the blinding lights with her hand. The lights had little effect on Christian.

He paused for a moment as the last of the agency cars closed in behind him. Amy looked at him anxiously just as he punched the gas pedal. The Mustang's backend lifted as the tires spun, spewing funnels of smoke into the street. He barreled toward the agents who began diving out of the path of the rapidly approaching Mustang. Just before reaching them he turned sharply into the parking lot. The back end broke loose as he powered into the lot in a controlled slide.

As they sped through the lot, a hoard of agency cars moved in to encircle him. He made the Mustang dance as he muscled his way through the maze of moving cars until he saw his opening and nailed it. The car didn't let him down. The hot tires gripped the pavement and the car shot through an opening between two agency cars with just inches on either side, causing Amy to flinch.

As they passed through the narrow opening, he could hear shots being fired. He pushed Amy down as a round came through the back window missing them both. He could see the round as if in slow motion with spiraling con trail and leading pressure wave as it passed by Amy's head, missing her narrowly.

As he approached the exit he could see there was no safe way out; it was blocked. He turned hard with agency cars still in pursuit, only to find that each of the exits had been blocked. He pulled into the middle of the parking lot and stopped, turning the engine off.

"What are you doing . . .?" Amy asked excitedly. "Let's go. Hit the gas and let's get the hell out of here," she ordered.

"No. . . . It's not worth it," Christian said, watching as the Mustang was surrounded by government cars. He took a deep breath as his eyes returned to their crystal blue color.

"What do you mean it's not worth it?" she asked excitedly.

"You have to understand. They've got everything blocked, not to mention they're shooting at us. And I couldn't live with myself if something happened to you," he said.

"Screw that, turn your eyes back on and let's go," she ordered.

Christian smiled at her. "It's just not worth it." He reached for her hand calmly.

The agents pulled up and surrounded the car just as Katheryn and Edward pulled up and exited the Mercedes SUV. Tweet, Connor and Maddy were close behind, followed by their friends.

The agents jumped out of their cars with weapons ready; some with pistols, others with assault rifles and yet others with dart guns. The chopper maintained its position, holding the spotlight on the Mustang as it hovered overhead. Kearns yanked the mic out of Channing's hands, mumbling something about incompetence. She clicked the mic, telling them to exit the vehicle slowly with hands above their heads.

As the two exited the Mustang they followed instructions given by the agent and walked to the front of the car. Christian looked to his side and could see the sad look on Matt's face, the only agent without his weapon drawn, standing only feet from Kearns. Christian gave him a thankful smile and a wink and continued to the front of the car.

Kearns ordered the men to take Christian. The agents held their laser sights on him as Davenport approached smugly. "Gotcha," he said, spinning Christian around and slamming him down hard on the hood of the car as he placed the handcuffs on him. Another agent pulled Amy to the side of the car and held her, waiting for his orders.

"Try to make me look like an asshole," Davenport said, forcefully pushing Christian's head onto the hood of the Mustang and kicking his legs apart.

"Cut it out you son of a bitch. . . . He didn't do anything," Amy yelled, struggling to break free.

Davenport looked at her smugly, telling her to shut her mouth as he slammed him down on the hood again despite her pleas. "Davenport, that's enough," Kearns said sternly. Amy broke free from the agent holding her and ran at Davenport, pushing him away from Christian.

Kearns motioned for the agent to subdue her as she continued to try and protect Christian from Davenport's abuse. While she continued her struggle with the agents, someone fired a shot. "NOOOOO . . ." Christian roared, horrified as he heard the projectile impact Amy's body. He turned quickly to see her falling to the ground with blood pumping from her head. The agent's dart had pierced her skull.

Katheryn screamed and grabbed hold of Edward as they watched in horror. He instinctively grabbed his bag from the car and started running to help her, but the agents blocked his way.

Christian roared with a sound unlike any other, a combination of pain and thunder as his eyes grew black with rage. His senses heightened instantly and he turned slowly to face the agents surrounding him. The agents stood their ground as the enraged Christian scanned them with dark, unforgiving eyes. He focused in on the agent with the smoking dart gun and pulled his arms apart, exploding the handcuffs from his wrists. Pieces of shattered metal sprayed the agents and spectators. The force was so powerful that shards of metal pierced the hood of the car.

He dropped to one knee, staring at Amy and running his fingers through her bloodied hair, a single tear dropping from his cheek onto her still face.

He stood up and roared loudly, startling a few agents who nervously squeezed off their Tasers. This served only to infuriate him more. He ripped the darts from his body and advanced toward the shooter that had moments before shot Amy. The agent lifted the rifle loaded with tranquilizing darts and fired at him twice, striking him both times. Christian pulled the darts from his body and continued to advance.

The agent was shocked he was still moving, much less advancing. He had pumped him with enough tranquilizer to drop an elephant and it had no effect. The other agents nervously aimed their weapons as he approached, ignoring Pamela Kearns' repeated orders to, "Stand down . . . Stand down."

As he fearlessly approached the agents he turned his palms up and opened his hands. Then, as if he was drawing energy from heaven and earth themselves, he threw his arms forward releasing an invisible wave of energy that sent the wall of agents flying backward.

Edward, having just reached Amy's side, watched in fear as his son released the powerful blast. He was terrified at the spectacle. He had no idea what he was capable of, but he knew he was going to do something bad as he moved closer to the shooter. "C-H-R-I-S-T-I-A-N!" he called as a small burst of pure energy shot from Christian's hand like a wispy dart and hit the car next to the shooter. The car exploded violently and flipped, sending pieces of debris into the air. The shooter was tossed back another ten or more feet.

As the car exploded and flipped, the chopper started to wobble out of control. A piece of the car had struck the tail rotor causing it to malfunction. The pilot was fighting to control the chopper and avoid the agents and spectators as it lost altitude and started to fall from the sky.

The shooter, now separated from the others, lay in pain from his injuries. Christian approached him, not hearing the calls from his father, and glared at the cowering man with his lifeless dark eyes. As the shooter stared into Christian's eyes, he saw a glint of blue iridescence. It grew brighter and brighter as Christian's focus increased on the shooter. He started to scream in agony, grasping his head as if it were going to explode. Blood started to drip from his ears and nose. The spectators, unable to see the man, winced at the sound of his horrific screams.

Edward approached cautiously, "Christian . . . Christian . . . don't do this, this isn't you." Edward pleaded, grabbing hold of his son's arm. He finally broke Christian's concentration and he stopped, shutting down his senses and looked at his father sadly. Edward could see the pain he was in. He looked crushed as he glanced over at Amy lying in front of the car.

Edward handed him his keys, "Here, take these and get out of here . . . go to Hal at the airport. His plane is warmed up. I'll let him know you're coming. Go, get out of here!"

Christian asked his father, "Take care of her . . ."

"You know I will do everything in my power . . . now get out of here."

He ran to the car, passing his mother along the way. She called to him in a soft voice, knowing he couldn't acknowledge her. "Take care of them," he ordered as he passed Tweet and Connor, jumped into the SUV and sped off to the airport.

Edward started treating Amy by the front of the car. "Get an ambulance here now," he shouted.

Katheryn ran to his side. "Oh no, oh no, is she?" she asked.

"No, not yet but if we don't get her to the hospital, she will be," Edward said concerned. "Call Hal and tell him to have his plane running," he said.

"Why?" Katheryn asked.

"Just do it," he said turning his focus back to Amy. Maddy and Jamie started to cry when they reached the front of the car and saw Amy lying in a puddle of blood. Tweet and Connor offered all the help they could, getting whatever Dr. Asher requested. The ambulance showed up moments later.

The agents jumped in their cars to pursue Christian, only to find that none of the cars lined up in front of Christian's blast would start. Anything in direct line of the pulse was fried; electrical systems, radios, batteries and phones—all fried. Kearns ran to a car in the back of the crowd. She squawked the radio, "Thank god," she said and called out her orders to all that could hear her.

Christian raced down the dark streets toward the airport with his lights off, reliving the episode in his mind. He needed to find answers but for some reason couldn't connect with CB or anyone else for that matter. As he pulled into the airport he saw Hal's plane sitting at the end of the runway waiting. He screeched to a halt and jumped out of the car. "What the hell is going on?" Hal asked.

"I can't tell you now. I need you to take me out of here. Do you still have that chute?" Christian asked.

"Yes, it's in the back ready to go," Hal replied.

"Good, let's get out of here. My father will explain everything later," Christian said, hopping into the plane.

"The radio's jumping with activity tonight. Is that what this is about?" Hal asked.

"Yes, let's just go. My father will explain it to you."

Hal jumped in the pilot's seat, "I don't know what you did but you've got a hell of a lot of people after you," he said throttling up.

As the plane started to move down the runway, a wall of choppers appeared crossing the runway. "H-O-L-Y crap," Hal blurted, staring at the line of choppers. Another chopper moved in, hovering only feet above his cockpit. He caught a glimpse of it. "A black chopper with no markings . . . I hate those sons of bitches," he said, pushing the throttles to full. The hovering chopper followed only feet overhead, forcing them to stay on the ground.

After a few attempts to get up in the air, Christian grabbed Hal's arm and shook his head no. "Thanks for trying," he said as he throttled down for Hal.

"What are you doing?" Hal asked nervously.

"Look, the choppers have us blocked in. And I don't want to see anyone else get hurt. Don't worry, I'll tell them I forced you to take me," he assured Hal.

Hal felt bad, but knew Christian was right. As the plane rolled to a stop on the side of the runway, Christian climbed out and walked to the back. He could see another helicopter had blocked the airport entrance, preventing a long line of law enforcement vehicles from entering. "This can't be good," he thought to himself.

As he reached the back of the plane he was greeted by a barrage of exploding gas canisters shot from the choppers hovering just above. As the smoke enveloped him he lost consciousness and slowly dropped to the ground.

Hal watched as the black helicopter landed and two men in black jumpsuits jumped out and ran to the front of the plane. They tagged Hal with their laser sights as two others jumped out and picked Christian's limp body off the ground and tossed him into the helicopter. They all hopped back in and the helicopter lifted off.

The pilot blocking the entrance to the small airport lifted off and joined in formation as it headed south into the darkness over the Atlantic.

Tweet entered at the backend of the airport and drove across the grass field, pulling up to the plane with a screeching halt. Katheryn burst out of the front of his car and ran up to the plane. "Where is he? she asked frantically.

"I'm sorry Katheryn, they got him," he said sadly.

"Who got him?" she asked. Hal replied by pointing to the fading lights flashing just above the waves. He told her all of what had transpired, including his thoughts on who he believed took him. She was a wreck. She was scared and nervous and wanted so badly to find out where they took her son. She realized there was nothing she could do to help him while standing at the airport.

"Where's Ed?" Hal asked.

"He's on his way to the hospital with Amy," she replied.

"That sweet little thing, what happened? Is she's ok?" he asked, concerned.

"Those sons of bitches shot her," she scowled.

"Shot her? Why did they shoot her?" he asked.

Katheryn paused, "I don't know. Ed doesn't think she's going to make it." Katheryn's strength started to fade but she forced herself to stay strong.

"Let me take you to the hospital," Hal offered.

"Okay," she said, wiping her eyes dry. Hal ran over to the Mercedes that Christian had left behind only minutes before. With a little convincing the local police allowed him to take it. Katheryn thanked the boys and told him she would be at the hospital. They offered to do anything they could and she hugged them both gratefully until Hal pulled up with her car.

Channing arrived at the same time. Katheryn made a B-line for him as he exited his car with a number of other suits. As she approached he started to say, "Mrs. Asher, we're going to need a statement from you and your hus . . ." and she smacked him right in the face.

"A STATEMENT?!" she yelled. "You son of a . . . I hold you and that murdering BITCH responsible for what happened," she launched her attack.

Hal stepped in between her and Channing who was now rubbing the stinging sensation from his face without expression as Connor and Tweet held her back. Katheryn continued her rant until Hal helped the boys put her in the car and shut the door.

He looked at Channing with disgust. "You guys are all the same. Shoot an innocent person and call it acceptable; collateral damage. Well it's not acceptable you piece of . . ." he stopped. "You're not even worth the breath. How would you feel if it was your kid in the hospital because one of your own shot him. . . . Would it be acceptable then?"

Hal's statement was received by a stone cold face, but it did get Channing thinking. It wasn't by his orders that Amy was shot; however, many times in the past, acceptable collateral damage was incurred as a result of his direct orders. This was something that haunted him on occasion, especially the ones when he pulled the trigger himself. He knew well that his actions were accepted by the government and were viewed as unfortunate circumstances. But that didn't stop the remaining little piece of soul he had that had not already turned black from tearing his insides apart when it happened. He watched Hal and Katheryn drive away as his memories softened his stone cold face.

Hal dropped Katheryn at the ER entrance. She ran through the doors and up to the admitting nurse. She inquired about Amy. "Are you family?" the nurse asked. "No . . . I'm not, she's my son's girlfriend."

"Then I am not allowed to discuss her case with you, I'm sorry," the nurse said.

"You have to tell me how she is. She's my son's girlfriend and her parents are on a cruise and can't be contacted," she pleaded.

"I'm sorry ma'am, I'm just not allowed to tell you anything unless you are a parent, guardian or family." Katheryn continued to argue her point and had just started to anger as Hal walked in.

"What's going on?" he asked.

"She can't tell me anything. I'm not a parent or guardian," she said frustrated.

Hal looked at the nurse. "Is Ed Asher in with her?" he asked.

"Yes, but I still can't tel . . ."

"What's going on here? Katheryn, are you alright?" a familiar voice asked.

It was Dr. Levy. She was called in to assist with the surgery. "Dr. Levy, this woman is looking for information on the trauma victim," the nurse said, "and she's not a legal guardian."

Dr. Levy looked at her, "Thank you for doing your job so diligently; however, this is Katheryn Asher, Dr. Asher's wife. Tell her what she wants to know," she said and hurried off to the O.R.

"Thank you," Katheryn said to the doctor as she vanished around the corner.

The nurse apologized to Katheryn and began to tell her that Amy was in surgery. From what she knew, the impact of the dart fractured her skull, sending shards of bone into her brain, causing massive tissue damage. She continued telling her that the dart had penetrated deep into her brain and snapped off sometime after impact, causing additional tissue damage and hemorrhage. Then, with a touch of insensitivity she added, "To be honest with you, I don't know how she's still alive, and even if she survives the surgery, I don't think . . ."

"Thank you," Hal interrupted the nurse abruptly, looking at her as if she were crazy. He turned Katheryn away from the nurse and brought her to the waiting room. He looked back at the nurse in disbelief, "We'll be in here if you hear anything else."

Hal tried to comfort her, but all she could do was pace and go over in her mind everything that had happened over and over again. She had cried herself out, and her emotions were turning into impatience, frustration and anger toward the people responsible.

Madison, Kalendra and Jamie arrived with the guys to wait with Mrs. Asher. She was happy to see them. Hal excused himself to go back to the airport and move his plane off the side of the runway, telling Katheryn to call if she needed anything. She handed the keys to Chris and Connor and asked that they drop him off. They obliged.

The girls sat for over three grueling hours, waiting to hear any news. At last count there were at least six surgeons in the room and, from what the nurse told them, there were more on the phone consulting through web cams.

After seeing the case, a few of the doctors in the OR contacted other surgeons who they believed to be the tops in their respective fields. Doctors all over the country were awakened and asked to assist. Finally, after hours they had stabilized her. She would live. All precautions were taken to minimize intracranial pressure and close off the smallest of hemorrhages. Her brain function, nevertheless, was questionable.

Edward thanked the team for their efforts and walked out of the OR, exhausted, her blood on his pants and shirt. Katheryn ran to him, "How is she?"

"We can't tell. She lost a lot of blood and there was extensive damage. They did everything they could. If anything changes, they'll get in touch. We have our best watching over her," he said, unsure of what lay in store for her.

"What happened with Christian?" he asked.

Katheryn looked at him with unhappy eyes as she told him what happened at the airport then added, "Christian gave himself up."

"He did what?" Ed asked.

"He gave himself up . . . Hal was trying to take off and the helicopters forced him down. He said Christian shut his plane down and thanked him before jumping out of the plane. They took him Ed. . . . They took him away!" she sobbed.

"Don't worry, we'll find him . . . I promise," Ed assured her. "Let's go home. There is nothing we can do here. It's in God's hands now."

The boys had returned from the airport. Ed walked to their car with them in silence. He said he would drive the girls home and thanked them for their support then headed for home. As they turned down the street it looked like a bomb had gone off. The remnants of panic were left behind by the thousand or so people who had earlier fled in fear for their lives. The street was lined with confetti. You could see the occasional hat or glove that was left behind in the panic. "What a mess," Katheryn said as she looked at two dark news vans parked along the roadway.

Katheryn stepped out of the car and looked down at her feet. She had stepped on a small white teddy bear that was left behind. She picked it up and reflected on Christian as a child. He had always had an attachment to teddies. She smiled weakly as she remembered.

Ed tried calling a few of his contacts with no luck so they set their plans for the next day. Priority one was to locate Christian. They planned until they both passed out from exhaustion, which wasn't long at all. By the time they had awakened, there were mobile news trucks lining the street parked outside of their house. Everyone wanted to know what had happened during the gala celebration. News of the panic was leaked out on YouTube by dozens of videos taken by spectators. Reporters, anxious to be the first to question the Ashers, were pacing back and forth on the front lawn, trying to walk off the damp, cold air and practice their questions.

The phone in the kitchen was ringing off the hook as reporters pushed redial over and over again in the hopes that someone would answer. Calls from friends and family came to their cells. Their phones chimed from dozens of text messages from curious friends offering any support they could provide.

Katheryn dragged herself out of the bedroom to go downstairs to make coffee. As she reached the top of the stairs she surveyed the room. A sadness came over her. The Christmas tree was on its side, books and papers were tossed about, and the cushions on the furniture were flipped up. She walked through the mess and into the kitchen. Ed came down minutes later and hugged her from behind, reassuring her everything was going to be fine, and then disconnected the last remaining landline phone.

Coffee in hand, a determined Dr. Asher started to call his military contacts to find out where Christian was taken. As he paced the floor, he noticed the activity outside. Photographers were peering into the house from the small openings between the blinds and window frames. As much as he wanted to do something about this invasion of privacy, he wisely chose to move up to his office. He sat at his desk for a moment and straightened up things before continuing to make some calls. He noticed a few items from his center drawer were missing, no doubt taken by the agents last night. One of the missing items was the green memory stick simply labeled 'Zeus.' He didn't give it another thought.

After hours on the phone, the general consensus was that the people that took him were with a group similar to the 'Men in Black' but a lot more secretive and a lot less funny. It was no shock to him that Pamela Kearns was somehow involved.

Edward was informed by his resources that this group was so secretive that they had no name and no one knew who they operated under. They were commonly referred to as 'ghosts'. One resource told him that the President doesn't even know of their existence, stating that they're an enigma.

As Edward finished up with one of his last calls he heard a knock on the back door. "Don't these people understand the word no? Tell them we have no comment," he said as he headed down the hallway.

It was Hal at the sliding doors leading out to the pool deck. "Hal, what are you doing here?" Katheryn asked.

"I have some information on where they may have taken Christian," he said with some enthusiasm.

"Come in, come in, it's cold out there," Katheryn said, closing the door behind him.

"That's a hell of a crowd out there," he said.

"I know, they haven't stopped all morning. You would think after we said 'No comment' the first hundred times they would stop trying," Katheryn said. "What did you find out?" she asked anxiously.

Hal started to talk as Edward reached the top of the stairs. Hearing someone other than Katheryn's voice in the kitchen he hurried down the stairs to show them the way out . . . forcefully if they preferred. As he entered the kitchen he saw it was Hal.

"Ed, Hal's here. He may have some information on Christian's whereabouts," Katheryn said enthusiastically.

"Hey Hal, how's it going? What'd you find out?" he asked.

"I called a few of my friends in the FAA. They said that they got a visit from some people who pulled the tapes from last night. They told them this was a classified op, no record of these flights were to be recorded, and as far as they were concerned, it didn't happen."

"So they got the tapes already?" Ed asked.

"Yes and no. They got the tapes, but they didn't take the back-ups," Hal smiled.

"My friend at MacArthur picked up the chopper's flight path as they approached. He's seen this before. They come in quiet. When they hit the edge of the field they spread out and rec the field before one of them touched down."

"Rec?" Katheryn questioned.

"Reconnoiter, check the field out," Hal said. "He told me there was only one other flight that arrived at the airport around that time. It was an unmarked black jet. It landed and moved to the edge of the airfield. One of the choppers set down behind the jet and lifted off a minute later. Sound familiar?" Hal asked.

"Yes . . . very," Edward replied.

"After they made their delivery the jet took off and the chopper rejoined the formation and disappeared."

Hal continued with his report. "My friends tracked them to a base in Virginia."

"Langley?" Edward asked.

"No, that's the funny part. They landed on a small strip outside of Langley. That can only mean that whoever these guys are, they're not working under government control. They want to be close enough to see what's happening but don't want the government to see any or all of what they're doing. They're spooks," Hal said, giving Edward the coordinates to the landing field. Edward thanked him.

"Hey Hal, how did you get past all the media outside?" Ed asked.

"Oh, I came through the new path you guys made last night," he said pointing to his truck parked in the backyard. Ed smiled. "I'll let you know if I get anything else," Hal said as he slipped out the back door.

Katheryn gave him a peck on the cheek. "Thank you."

Edward placed one last call to his friend, General Harold 'The Bull' Kellerman. He was as stern and tough a commander as he was a soldier. Ed had known him for years. They first met after a sniper had put two rounds through his neck and chest. Edward patched him up in the field and followed up with his treatment in the hospital. They stayed in touch afterward, becoming close friends. Kellerman was still walking around with a bullet sitting next to his heart, too close to the sinoatrial node for the surgeons of the day to remove.

"Hi Harry, it's Ed Asher. How's it going?" he asked.

"Not bad," Kellerman replied. It's still tough going through airport security though," Kellerman laughed, referring to the metal detectors at the airport. "I was wondering when I was going to hear from you. I'll assume this is regarding the events of last evening?" Kellerman inquired.

"Yes, but how do you know?" Ed asked.

Kellerman laughed, "I have my sources," he said, "Besides, it's a secret operation which means everyone knows something about it."

"What can you tell me about it?" Ed asked.

"I've got nothing . . . only rumors," he said. They talked for a few minutes. It was obvious that Kellerman couldn't talk at the time. He apologized to Edward for the lack of information and said his goodbyes, but not before setting up a meeting.

"By the way, what was the name of that restaurant you told me about, the one with the veal covered in tomatoes and onions?" he asked.

"Oh, you mean Don Peps," Edward answered.

"Yeah, I think I'll try it for lunch tomorrow, thanks. I'll check around and see if I can find out anything for you," he said.

"Thanks Harry," Edward said, hanging up.

Ed knew he was asking a big favor of his friends. None had love for these secretive agency types and how they operated, but he knew that if wind of inquiries on his behalf ever got out . . . careers could be changed, if not lost. He also knew that he would have a lot more information after lunch tomorrow in Queens.

Van Dunne was standing in his office looking out over the yard pondering as he often did when there was a knock at his door. "Excuse me sir, we have another issue," his subordinate said, passing him a large envelope. Van Dunne opened the envelope and read the communication. It was apparent he was distressed with the news he had received. "Will there be a reply sir?" the man asked.

"No . . . not at the moment," Van Dunne replied. "I will do what is necessary."

The assistant left the office as Van Dunne reflected. He had another very difficult decision to make. He walked to the book-shelf and once again removed the book, 'Awakenings' and placed it in front of the scanner on his desk. The side of the desk opened and he removed a blue crystal. It was Christian's. He gazed upon the crystal, considering Christian's fate.

-Twenty-Five-
Time Inside

Christian started to stir as he slowly came out from the effects of the gas. He found himself sitting in a chair with his wrists and ankles strapped to a chair with a metal desk in front of him. It was a cold room, lined with metal and lit by fluorescent bulbs. It had four cameras, one in each corner and one other chair beside the desk. There were two vents, one on each side of the room and four smaller circular vents, one on each wall.

His thoughts focused on Amy. He pictured her lying in a pool of blood, lifeless. He felt his insides churning at the thought of losing her.

He tried to connect with CB without success. He felt no connection to anyone or anything. That's what these people wanted. He knew they wanted him to feel separate and alone. It was psychological warfare. They wanted him to want to be out of there so badly that he would talk in order to be released. But he knew better. They weren't ever going to let him leave.

The heavy steel door opened, the hinges creaking from the weight of the door as Pamela Kearns entered. "Good Morning," she said politely as she walked to each of the four cameras in the room and disconnected them one by one. "I'm Pamela Kearns and we have an awful lot to talk about," she smiled. Christian didn't respond, not even a glance.

"It may interest you to know that you have become quite popular on the internet these days." She removed her laptop from her bag, opened it and pushed play. She watched Christian's response to the videos she was playing.

The first was the security video from the restaurant in Keystone. The video showed him stopping a bottle from falling, raising it back to the table without touching it, all with a wave of his hand. But the most interesting part was that the wine that was spilling out of the falling bottle reversed its flow and went back into the bottle. Not a drop spilled.

"This was a nice trick. Do you want to tell me about it?" she asked, watching his reaction.

"Sure, it was a magic trick," he said.

"Tell me about it?" she asked.

"A magician never reveals his secrets," he said in a way that suggested to Kearns she was barking up the wrong tree.

She pushed play to show him the second video. It was the footage taken behind the museum. It showed him taking out his attackers with lightning speed and agility. "How about this one, any comments?" she asked. Christian said nothing as Kearns continued to play the video to the point where he and his father climbed into the Mercedes and drove away. Then she pulled up a close-up side view of his face from another camera shot not released to the press that clearly showed one of his black, unforgiving eyes. "How about this," she pointed to his eyes. "This is a different look. Can you tell me how you do that little trick?" she inquired. Christian continued his silence.

"This one really got my attention," she said pushing the play button for video three. It was The Awakening. He watched as his body was raised off the ground by a bolt of lightning. The video was taken by Matt. It was hard to see details; however, you could see his body being lifted through the smoke and sand. "Still nothing?" she inquired as she opened his file and started to read from it.

"Christian Bradley Asher or should I say Williamson. You have developed some interesting talents and I am here to learn about them," she said, continuing to read the file.

Christian looked at her calmly, "There's nothing to talk about."

"Really? I've read your file, you know, the one the late Dr. Stedwell had on you. It was a very interesting read," she said.

"Why did you kill him?" Christian asked.

"What makes you think I killed him?" she asked. Christian just sat quietly. "I mean, to you it may seem as if I had some role in his death, but I assure you I didn't. His death was purely accidental," she said looking back down at his file. "I won't lie to you. I did want to get my hands on his files. His work over the years fascinated me, especially his work on the little fraternity you belong to. But he was always very protective of his work, especially your file. . . . He kept that locked away all by its lonesome. I'm sure I don't have to tell you that yours was very interesting."

"How so?" he asked.

"Let's see . . . your late father, Kurt Williamson, killed himself. It says in the report it was because of your rather unusual abilities as a child. Your mother . . . what was her name? Anita. She almost drank herself to death before being committed, and she died a few years later during a psychotic episode. All of this is reportedly a result of things you did as a child. Now I don't know about you, but I find that very interesting. These are things I would like to discuss with you openly if you're willing. You know . . . off the record," she said, lying.

"I appreciate the fact that you find me so interesting, but there is nothing that we need to discuss . . . openly or not. Katheryn and Edward Asher are my parents," Christian replied.

"Oh I see, so you choose to completely ignore your biological parents and pretend they don't even exist," she baited him. Christian chuckled. "What's so funny?" she asked.

"I know what you're interested in, and I know what you are doing. And I suggest you save your breath," he said calmly.

"Well then, if you don't want to discuss your parents, let's talk about the agent who you assaulted last night." She paused, waiting for his reply and received none. "He's in the hospital. You almost killed him. My report tells me he is suffering with cerebral edema and that both his eardrums had burst from internal pressure. Would you like to tell me how you did that?" she asked, receiving no answer.

"Or how about that little trick you used to knock down all of those agents, or that glowing dart thing that you fired to blow up the car? We couldn't find the weapon you used for that. Where did that go? Or the fact that you fried the electrical systems in a dozen cars, how about that?" she asked to closed ears. "These are the things that my superiors want to know about and until they do . . . you're stuck here," she stated with a slightly agitated tone, then paused to adjust her game plan.

"Ok then, I guess we'll start from the beginning. What really happened to your father? He yelled at you or hit you and you made his head explode? Did your mother plant a gun next to him to protect you?" she asked, attempting to draw him into her deceptive game. "Still no answer?" she asked. "I was hoping that you would be more open to discussion," she said, wholly expecting his response, or lack thereof.

"Open to discussion?" Christian said sarcastically. "Off the record? Why would I want to talk to you about anything? You raid and destroy my family's home for no reason, you surround me with your spies, you kill my girlfriend and Stedwell, and you expect me to sit here and chat like we are having tea. What part of any of that makes you think I would want to talk to you?" he asked, raising his voice.

"Your girlfriend was an unfortunate accident. Sometimes tragic things like this happen," she said, trying to appear sympathetic. "But you may like to know that she is alive. Your father saved her life." Christian perked up a little hearing the news.

Pamela only afforded him the information that Amy was alive and nothing further as to her state, intentionally omitting that she was placed in a medical coma or the fact that, for all intents and purposes, she was brain dead and on life support. She did, however, pick up on Christian's interest in the topic.

"You're lying," Christian said calmly and confidently.

"Why would you say that?" Kearns asked.

"You broke eye contact with me and looked up and to the left, suggesting you were formulating your response. You also postured yourself. Of all people I would think that a psychiatrist would know that," he stated.

"Oh, so you know I am a psychiatrist. How is it that you know that? I never mentioned it," she inquired.

"The caduceus . . . it looks just like Stedwell's," he replied.

"What caduceus?" she asked. He motioned with his head to the caduceus on the side of her bag.

"You're lying now and have been since you came into the room and disconnected the four dummy cameras."

"Dummy cameras?" she said with curiosity peaked as to how he knew about the cameras.

"Yes, dummy cameras. And I'm sure you will find the other four cameras, you know, the ones you didn't unplug, hidden behind the vents work just as well," he smiled at her knowingly.

Kearns huffed as she stood up. "Mr. Asher, we have a long time to spend together. Maybe you want to consider being friendlier and I'll think about letting you outside once in a while," she said turning to leave the room. She paused and turned back to Christian. "Here, you can have your toys back. These will be the only connection you have to the outside for a long time," she said, annoyed, and tossed a little black bag on the desk before exiting.

The contents came flying out of the bag and onto the table. Christian gazed at the contents; a bear claw on a worn piece of rawhide, a beaded armband, and a long arrowhead. He wondered what the Old One meant when he said keep them together and when the time is right you would know what to do with them.

As soon as she exited the room she heard, "Kearns . . . Kearns . . . can you hear me?" in her earpiece.

"What the hell is going on?" she asked.

"I don't know. Once you entered the room the cameras went crazy," he said.

"All of them?" she asked.

"Yes, all of them. It's the strangest thing I've ever seen," the agent said.

"What about now, do you have anything?" Kearns asked.

"No," he replied.

"Why didn't you tell me?" she asked.

"We tried, but your earpiece wasn't working either," he responded.

"Find out what happened and fix it. I want twenty-four, seven surveillance on him. NOW," she ordered, staring back at the heavy steel door.

She hurried to her office and pulled a recorder out of her bag and pushed play. There was nothing. Only the sound of static. "Son of a . . . How is this possible?" she thought, slamming the recorder down on her desk in frustration.

Christian was escorted to a holding cell under heavy guard by order of Kearns. The cell was similar to the interrogation room with the exception that it had a small viewing window through the door for the guards to check on him, a cold steel toilet and a slot where they shoved food through to him. He sat for what he thought were days, reviewing all that had happened on New Year's Eve. He determined time by the guard changes twice per day. Of course, he had no idea of what time of day it was as he had no exposure to the outside and the guards were instructed not to say or discuss anything with him.

He thought often of Amy and prayed for her wellbeing. He thought about his parents and friends, and of his Awakening and the events that followed. He spent hours trying to connect with CB, Hwei-ru, Akachi and even Van Dunne to no avail, and even more hours honing his abilities and visiting his past lives. He went inside of himself, in his mind, and trained himself with all of the knowledge and experience available to him. With each life he visited, a new door opened to another life, then another. He watched his lives as far back as he could go through his mind's eye, to a place of dark stillness.

In a short time he was in total control of his ability to heighten his senses and was able to access all the knowledge and skills afforded to him as a member of this strange fraternity of Awakened brothers and sisters.

In his cell between the guards checking on him through the window in the door, he would practice fighting skills of the ancients, mastering what took ancients a lifetime in just a matter of hours. He developed total control of his body and mind.

Pamela Kearns would visit the cell block daily. He could hear her asking the guards questions about him and what he was doing, but she never approached. It was apparent to him that Kearns was playing the waiting game. After days or weeks without human contact, people are happy to start talking again and this is what she wanted, to establish open lines of communication with him in order to start her probe and bargain for information.

Christian had been sitting and thinking for hours one day before falling asleep. Shortly after dozing off he felt someone nudging his shoulder repeatedly and thought he was dreaming. Then he heard a familiar voice, "Christian . . . Christian, c'mon get up. It's time to go."

He opened his eyes and slowly focused on CB's face but thought he was still dreaming and closed his eyes again. A moment later he got hit in the face with cold water, or at least he hoped it was water. He sprang off the bed and came face to face with CB. "CB, how did you get in here?" he asked, excited to see his friend and hugging him.

"Ok, ok, ok . . . It's great to see you too, but stop hugging me. I don't know what I pulled out of that toilet to throw at you," CB said, also happy to see his friend.

"Hey, we need to be quiet or the guards will hear us," Christian said.

CB shook his head, "Still slow to learn, huh." He showed him the needles.

They sat down on the bed and started to talk. "It's great to see you. I haven't talked to anyone in . . . how long have I been here? What day is it?" he asked.

"It's Friday, February twenty-seventh," CB replied.

"It's been that long? How are my parents?" he asked.

"They are fine."

Then Christian's mood changed to one of sadness as he asked, "And Amy? What about Amy?"

CB paused for a moment, "She's alive," CB said with a sadness in his voice. "She had massive head trauma and they placed her in a medically induced coma." Christian was crushed by the news. CB consoled him as best he could.

The two had talked for almost an hour before CB said, "Are you ready to go, or have you grown that fond of this place?"

"How am I going to do that? Do you expect me to just walk out of here?" he asked.

"Absolutely! Just like me. . . . Come on, I'll show you," CB said.

He walked over to Christian and reached out, placing his hands on both sides of his head. CB focused for a moment then a flash of images, equations, and text flashed in Christian's mind. He stepped back, quickly finding himself a little dizzy, with a look of amazement on his face. "Wow, what was that?" he asked.

CB smiled, "Just another little trick, a psychokinetic transfer of information, and something you needed to know before we get out of here," CB replied.

CB turned, moved to the door and stood motionless for a moment. Christian waited to see what was going to happen next, wondering how he was going to get through the heavy steel door. Then with one move he pushed the door open and walked through the doorway. He turned to Christian and jiggled the keys he had lifted from the guard.

"You son of a . . . How could you do that to me? You mean I've been sitting here with you for almost an hour and all that time we could have just walked out the door?" Christian asked.

"Yep . . . I thought you liked it here," CB said chuckling.

They moved out into the hallway and past the guard station. The guard was out cold, as were all of them, as they continued through the long corridors passing each of the three other check-points. CB had put them all to sleep with his little needle trick. He pulled the pins out as he walked past each guard, seven in all. "I'm going to have to remember that," Christian said as they made their way out to the cool night air.

Van Dunne's decision was made. He made his way to the book-shelf once again and pulled out 'Awakenings' and scanned it over the desk. The side panel opened, exposing the drawer full of crystals. He reached in, grabbed a crystal and sat back in his chair, contemplating the finality of his move one last time.

He lay the crystal on his desk and it started to glow. As it glowed brighter and brighter it stood up on end, projecting a blank holographic screen in front of him. Van Dunne leaned forward, sparking an exchange of telepathic information from his eyes to the crystal. The screen started to fill with images and data which flashed rapidly on the screen as the information downloaded from Van Dunne. Moments later he finished and fell back in his chair exhausted. The crystal stopped glowing and dropped to the desktop.

His associates ran in to assist him, "Sir . . . Sir . . . are you alright?" they asked, tending to him.

"Yes, yes, I'm fine," he said assuring them. "Get my car and bring it around to the front," he ordered. "We have a trip to take." The associates ordered the car be brought up as they continued to tend to a weakened Van Dunne.

Amy lay in her hospital bed motionless. The life support machines keeping her alive were beeping, pumping and hissing. The only visitors she had were Katheryn and Edward who checked on her daily, praying for a miracle, and her mother and father who had arrived the week after the cruise. They had been traveling back and forth from Oregon over the weeks to be by her side.

On her visit today, Katheryn passed a man in a suit in the hallway. She knew the look; dark suit, narrow tie and short haircut. He was government. She grew nervous as the only room he could be coming from was Amy's. She ran to the room. "Oh, thank god," she said to herself, seeing nothing was different. She noticed a card on the table and next to it was Amy's cell phone.

The card read, 'I am so sorry for deceiving you both. It was my job and something I had to do. I thought I was helping Christian and it turns out you both helped me. Had I known this would happen, I would have never allowed the charade to continue. Please know that I am eternally grateful to know you both, and you are always in my prayers, Matt P.S. As promised, I am returning your cell phone.'

Katheryn took the card and cell phone and placed it in her bag as she left the room and headed to Edward's office. She checked the waiting area and nurse's station to see if she could get another look at the man without success. She headed to Edward's office.

"Hi hon," Edward greeted Katheryn. "What's up?" he asked.

"There was an agent in Amy's room just before I got there," she said.

"Are you sure? Who was it, do you know?" he asked.

"No, but I think it was a friend of theirs; he looked familiar. Is there any way to have security placed on the room? I don't think anyone should be able to walk in anytime they like," she said.

Edward sighed deeply. "That may be a moot point now," he said sorrowfully.

"What do you mean?" Katheryn asked, concerned.

"I just learned her parents are coming in today to . . ." he paused, "I think they want us to pull her off support."

Katheryn's face dropped, "They can't do that . . . there's always a chance she'll come out of it," she argued.

"In most cases I would agree, but in this case . . . Honey, her brain function is gone. I don't see anything saving her, outside of a miracle. Even if we left support on, her systems are starting to fail. I'm afraid she's going to die one way or the other." Katheryn's eyes welled up and she ran out of the office and down to her car.

Edward ran out after her, catching up with her in the car. "When are they coming?" she asked.

"They should be here in an hour," he answered.

"I'm just going to sit here for a while, then I'll come back in. I want to be there with them," she said.

"Okay, I'm sure that'll be fine. Are you sure you're okay?" he asked. She nodded and wiped the tears from her eyes.

Edward walked back into the hospital and passed the nurses station. "Is everything alright Dr. Asher?" the nurse asked.

"Yes, everything's fine," he lied.

"It's about that girl again, isn't it?"

"Yes, it's about the girl, her name is Amy."

"Well, I thought you might like to know that she has a couple of visitors right now."

"Okay, thanks for telling me," he said, starting to walk away.

"I thought you should know they are not her mother and father and to be honest they were a bit strange," she said.

Edward looked at the nurse. "Okay, I'll look into it," he said walking away.

Edward hurried to Amy's room. When he got there, the door was shut and locked. He started banging on the door, "Open this door. Open this door now," he yelled through the door. No one answered his demand. He ran down to the nurse's station, "Do you have the key to Room 333?" he asked.

"Let me find them," the nurse responded, pulling a couple of rings of keys from her drawer.

The two of them hurried toward Amy's room, each searching a ring for the key to room 333. As they ran down the hall, the lights began to flicker off and on and they could see a bright light coming from beneath the door. "My Lord in heaven," the nurse said loudly, "What in God's good earth is going on in there?" she asked, fumbling through her keys. There was the unmistakable smell of ozone in the air.

The keys were so poorly marked it was hard to find the correct one. A couple of minutes had passed before they found the correct key. They inserted the key into the door lock, turned it, unlocking the door. Edward pushed the door and it didn't open.

He tried harder and still it would not open. The light emanating from the room was getting brighter as he continued trying to force the door open. They could hear a strange buzzing sound coming from the room, then . . . nothing. All was silent. The bright light was gone. The smell of ozone lingered for only moments more.

Edward pushed on the door and it swung open easily. He rushed inside, finding no one was there. He ran to Amy's side. The machines were all still recording, nothing had changed except one of the EKG leads had disconnected. When the nurse went to clip it back on she noticed a patch of redness under the adhesive lead tab below her left breast and to the side. She had Dr. Asher look at it. To him, it appeared to be nothing more than a minor irritation and had the nurse apply some salve to the area. "When you're done with that, I want you to tell me everything you remember about the visitors," he ordered and headed to security. "I need to check something out."

He hurried to security to review the video footage, trying to see who the visitors were. He had security pull up the footage for the past ten minutes. At first all was normal. He saw no sign of visitors in the hallway. Then all went blank. There was nothing. He had security replay the footage from the outside cameras. He saw Katheryn running out to her car, then himself as he left the building and crossed into the parking lot before all went blank. "This is strange," he thought to himself. He had security replay the footage. The only thing he noticed was the front of a car coming into the camera's view before all went blank. Every camera from the parking lot to the front entrance, up to and including the hallway monitors, had the same issue.

Edward stopped at the nurse's station for her report on the visitors before heading to his office. He opened the door reading the visitor sign-in sheet and from the corner heard someone clear his throat. His face lit up when he saw it was Christian. "Christian!" he said, running to hug him. "It's so good to see you, but how did you get in here? Where were you? Did they let you go?" Edward said, asking a rapid succession of questions. His excitement was short lived when he realized that Christian was not released.

"It's great to see you too, Dad. This is my friend Channarong."

"Hello Sir, it's a pleasure to meet you," CB said.

"Dad, we can't stay that long. They'll be looking for us. I want to see Amy. Where is she?" Christian asked.

"Of course son, I'll take you to her," he said.

Edward had them follow him through the back hallway so as not to be seen by anyone. On the way he broke the news to Christian about Amy. He explained the extent of her injuries and all that was done to try and save her. When they reached her room, Christian requested to be alone with her one last time. He slowly walked into the room, leaving them in the hallway.

As he entered the room he could see her silhouette behind the hospital curtain. He wasn't prepared to see her the way she was and broke down at her bedside, apologizing to her for not protecting her. He leaned over her bed, kissing her forehead and then whispered in her ear, "I love you" as his tears fell onto her face. He caressed her hair one last time before standing to leave.

As he walked away, he prayed for her and stepped out to the hallway. His father hugged him, "Sorry son, we did all we could. There was just too much damage," Edward said.

"Thank you, I know you did," Christian said.

"Christian, I have to tell you. The Kendalls are coming today. They're going to remove her life support." Christian was quiet.

"When are they coming?" he asked.

"They should be here any minute," Edward replied.

"I want to stay. I want to be with her when they do it," he said looking at CB. He had no objections.

"Ok, but I don't want to shock your mother. Wait in this room until they come," he said pointing to an empty room. I'll tell your mother you are here so she knows you're waiting to see her," Edward said pulling out his phone to call Katheryn.

He called Katheryn and told her to come in. When she arrived she asked what was so important. "Follow me," he said, leading her down the hallway toward Amy's room. He walked over to the vacant room and opened the door and told her to go in. As she entered the room she saw Christian standing there.

"Christian!" she cried running to him. She hugged and kissed him and rattled off the same series of rapid-fire questions Edward had asked. She was so busy with questions she hadn't even noticed CB. Introductions were made and they continued their talk. Their reunion was short but sweet. He told her where he had been, how he got out and made her understand that he wouldn't be staying, but that he would be in touch with her.

Katheryn wasn't thrilled, but was so happy to know he was alive. It wasn't more than ten minutes when Ed knocked on the door. "The Kendalls are here," he said through the door.

Katheryn and Christian exited the room with CB following. Introductions were made to the Kendalls and they entered Amy's room.

The Kendalls were not aware of the actual events of the night that Amy was shot. The government had put a gag order on any transfer of information concerning the incident. As far as they knew, she was struck by a car which resulted in the massive trauma to her head.

The group sobbed as each said their last goodbyes. Christian stood quietly with tears rolling down his cheeks. They stepped back to watch as a team of physicians removed the equipment that had supported her life for the past two months. Mrs. Kendall started to cry uncontrollably as they shut down the breathing apparatus and disconnected the hose.

The heart monitor went flat with the distinctive continuous beep telling them all . . . it was over. They stood silently for a moment looking down on her lifeless body before moving into the hallway.

Christian hugged the Kendalls and his parents. "I'll be in touch soon," he said to his mother and father. The families continued to console each other in support for their mutual loss. Minutes later Edward moved them down the hallway toward the nurse's station and waiting room. Christian and CB slipped down the back stairwell to the exit just as a team of suits reached the nurse's station.

Edward saw them and knew why they were there. They requested he follow them down the hallway as they questioned him as to the whereabouts of Christian. He excused himself from the Kendalls and a nervous Katheryn and followed them toward Room 333. He explained that he had not heard or seen from Christian since he was taken and demanded to know his whereabouts. He must have been convincing because they didn't question him further.

When they reached the room the orderly was just moving the body through the door and into the hallway when he was stopped by the suits. They pulled back the sheet to confirm it was Amy and that she was dead. One of them made a snide remark about her. "You son of a bitch," Edward said, punching the agent hard in the face and knocking him into the wall. "You and your friends did this you piece of sh*t, and you have the nerve to come here and make snide remarks," he said angrily while being restrained by two agents. He stared at the offensive agent. "I hope the day a bullet finds you that I'm the last face you see before you go under," Edward glared.

Another agent walked up the hallway and looked at the lead suit. "Same thing, all of them, inside and out."

"What are you talking about?" Edward asked.

"Nothing, are you sure you didn't see your son?" the agent inquired, suspecting.

"Yes, I'm sure."

"Okay, let's report it and take a look around," he said, motioning for the agents to search the facility.

"Dr. Asher, a peculiar thing happens to electronic equipment when your son is around, especially video and recording equipment. I was just advised that the hospital security tapes have recently had this issue. Are you sure you haven't seen him," he asked.

"Positive," Edward replied seriously. The unbelieving suit excused himself and headed down the hallway. Edward returned to the waiting room, composing himself on the way to rejoin the Kendalls and Katheryn.

Katheryn was curious as to why the suits were there. Was it to check on Amy or look for Christian? She was concerned that Christian and CB had left the building just minutes earlier and prayed silently for their safety. She noticed right off that Edward was rubbing his hand and could see blood from a cut on his knuckle, peaking her curiosity further. She smiled at him with the thought of him clocking one of the bastards responsible for Amy's death. Edward continued his conversation with the Kendalls.

"If there is anything we can do for you, please let us know. I will arrange for Amy's transportation back to Oregon for you if you would like," Edward offered.

"We would be grateful," John said.

Mrs. Kendall sobbed, "It sounds like she's coming home to visit." Edward and John led her to a seat in the waiting area by the nursing station where they continued to mourn their tragic loss. Mrs. Kendall, blaming herself for her death, "If only we hadn't taken that cruise, she would have been home for Christmas." Katheryn comforted her.

"Dr. Asher, Dr. Asher!" Edward heard a panicked voice calling. He turned to see one of the orderlies running down the hallway. "Dr. Asher, come quick . . . come quick," the frightened orderly requested. He excused himself and quickly followed the orderly down the corridor.

"What happened?" he asked. Before the orderly could answer they reached their destination, the elevator in the back of the wing used primarily to transport the deceased to the morgue.

The orderly stopped in front of the elevator, looked in and pointed with a terrified look on his face. "What's the matter?" Edward asked turning to look into the elevator. It was Amy, lying on a gurney on her way to the morgue. The gurney was only part way into the elevator and the doors were repeatedly closing and opening as they hit the sides of the gurney.

He looked back to the panic stricken orderly, "Calm down . . . calm down. Now tell me what the problem is?" he asked again as he stepped into the elevator, stopping the doors from opening and closing. The terrified orderly started explaining in broken English. He was speaking so fast Edward couldn't understand him.

As his trembling hand pointed to her body, Edward could see terror in his eyes as he cried out, "ay Dios mio. . . . Dios mio" and backed away from the elevator, blessing himself repeatedly. Edward turned his gaze back to the gurney once again and was stunned to see what had frightened the orderly. He cautiously reached out to touch it . . .

—*T*he End—

ENDING NOTE FROM THE AUTHOR

I am happy you enjoyed *Being There Awakenings*. Please be sure visit Amazon.com and give us your review, and watch for the exciting continuation of the series in . . .

Being There Discovery **. . .**

Follow Christian's continuing adventures . . . Adventures that lead him closer to the discovery of his origins and enlightenment as he develops amazing new abilities and continues to grow while the expanding search for others of his kind take him to unimaginable places.

Learn how he deals with the torment of his loss, and those responsible for his heartbreak as the fabric of his soul is torn apart by his desire for revenge. An obsessed Pamela Kearns steps up her aggressive measures in an attempt to trap Christian in her deceptive quest for glory...

Enter Your Vote **. . .**

Visit www.BeingThereAwakenings.com and cast your vote. Join with me and become part of the writing process. The most popular vote wins and will guide the opening of one of the Being There . . . series of books.

"What does Dr. Asher see when he looks in the elevator?"

Use this code to access the Fan Interactive Page, to place your vote, and submit your chapter and/or character suggestions... See you on the inside.

Access Code: 0517

ABOUT THE AUTHOR

R. C. Henningsen is the author of *Being There Awakenings,* the beginning of a series of thrilling adventures incorporating a little creative licensing on actual recorded historical events that stimulated the creation of the characters and storyline, the process of which has been millennia in the making. Adventurous since childhood, he rarely missed the opportunity to explore and test the theories of the day. This thirst for knowledge and adventure continues today and is evident in *Being There Awakenings* and the series of novels to follow. You will find some of the author's antics and escapades included throughout the series. Other than anonymously supporting numerous causes over the years, one of his passions in life is to provide education and resources to children of lesser circumstances so that they themselves can live fulfilling lives filled with passion, excitement and adventure. He currently resides in New York with his wife when they're home, otherwise you can find them exploring new destinations and searching for exciting new adventures.

www.ingramcontent.com/pod-product-compliance
Lightning Source LLC
Chambersburg PA
CBHW020825030726
47496CB00001B/102